The People Next Door

Roisin Meaney was born in Listowel, County Kerry and has lived in the US, Canada, Africa and Europe. She is the author of three previously published novels *The Daisy Picker*, *Putting Out The Stars* and the number one bestseller *The Last Week of May*, along with a children's book *Don't Even Think About It*. Roisin is currently based in Limerick where she also teaches part-time.

The People Next Door

ROISIN MEANEY

HACHETTE
BOOKS
IRELAND

First published in Ireland in 2008 by Hachette Books Ireland

An Hachette Livre UK company

Copyright © Roisin Meaney 2008

The right of Roisin Meaney to be identified as the Author of the Work
has been asserted by her in accordance with the Copyright, Designs and
Patents Act 1988.

2

A CIP catalogue record for this title is available from the British Library

ISBN 978 0 340 93287 2

Typeset in Sabon MT by Hachette Books Ireland

Printed and bound in the UK by CPI Mackays, Chatham ME5 8TD

Hachette Books Ireland policy is to use papers that are natural, renew-
able and recyclable products and made from wood grown in sustainable
forests. The logging and manufacturing processes are expected to con-
form to the environmental regulations of the country of origin.

Hachette Books Ireland
9 Castlecourt
Castleknock
Dublin 15

Hachette Livre UK Ltd
338 Euston Road
London NW1 3BH

For the coffee gang

When you leave Belford's main street and turn down Miller's Lane — the alley that runs between O'Brien's Quality Meats and Kennedy's Shoe Repairs and Key Cutting — there isn't that much to see at first. A couple of smallish, grimy windows set high up in Kennedy's graffti-covered blue side wall on your right; the steel back door of the butcher's opposite; a huddle of recycling bins futher on with the usual dishevelment of crumpled boxes propped against them; and the odd skinny cat streaking away from the tap of your shoe on the worn cobbles.

About twenty-five steps beyond the bins, the path veers to the right, around by the back of Kennedy's. No more cobbles now, only a raggedy-edged strip of tarmac, frilled with bobbing dandelions in the summer and bordered by a cement wall on one side, high enough to hide whatever's behind it (as it happens, the long since boarded-up flour mill of Miller's Lane), and tall green metal railings on the other.

Beyond the railings there's a small park. A line of unremarkable trees, clumps of variously coloured bushes, a few randomly scattered dark red wooden benches and splashes of flowers here and there, depending on the season. A scrap of a children's play area in the far corner — two swings, a slide, a seesaw, a boxed square of grainy sand. Lots of pale green, carelessly mown grass.

And then, at the end of the path, between a trio of thigh-high metal bollards, Miller's Lane opens out and becomes Miller's Avenue. And right across from the bollards stand three tall, narrow red-brick houses.

Now take the time to look a little more closely at these three joined-together houses, with their small front gardens and black wrought iron gates and railings. You might notice the brass numbers screwed into each of the three differently coloured front doors: seven on the first (deep blue), eight on the second (burgundy) and nine on the third (furze yellow).

And once you get that far, there really isn't much to stop you from pushing open the gate of number seven and walking up the short path – three or four steps, no more – and pressing the small brass bell beside the dark blue door.

24 May

NUMBER SEVEN

'You don't have to come with me.' Yvonne O'Mahony lifted the bundles of milky-yellow freesias from the white basin in the sink and wrapped a paper towel around their dripping stems. The spicy scent of them wafted up to her. 'If you're tired, I mean. You've had a long day, and I don't mind going on my own.'

Her daughter stood, brushing crumbs from the folds of her green top, pushing her dark blonde hair off her forehead. 'Of course I'll come. Don't I always come?' The heat often made Clara slightly cranky. 'Here, give me those.'

She reached for Brian's flowers and Yvonne, after a second, handed them over. Clara strode ahead of her, out the back door and down the long gravel path. Yvonne pulled the door closed behind her and glanced around the garden. No sign of Magoo – off on his travels again, sniffing around the apartment block, probably, where someone would be sure to throw him a bit of food.

In the neighbouring garden, a small grey cat sitting on the black bin in a corner of the patio lifted his head and gazed at her.

'Hello, Picasso. Don't suppose you've seen Magoo?' The cat lowered his head on to his paws again and closed his eyes, and Yvonne followed Clara down the path.

'God, the heat, still.' Clara stood by the car, flapping her skirt. 'At this hour.'

'I know.' Yvonne opened Clara's door and walked around to the driver's side. The car was like a furnace. She wound her window all the way down, turned the key in the red Micra's ignition and reversed crookedly, curving into the corner of the lane.

As she straightened up and they began to bump gently down the lane to the road, she glanced at Clara – mouth set, shoulders hunched, flowers dangling in front of her knees – before giving in, as she'd been giving in all day, to thoughts of Brian.

His face when she'd told him she was pregnant all those years ago. Both of them eighteen, Brian nearly a year with the civil service, working behind the counter in the motor tax office. Yvonne about to start college, her place in UCG waiting for her finally, after two Leaving Cert attempts.

'I'm pregnant.' Her nails digging into her palms, her teeth gritted against whatever was coming. Sitting on the hard bench outside the library.

His face, turning towards her. The horrified expression that had made her want to smash her fist into it – unfairly, because hadn't she been just as appalled when she'd found out?

'What?' The shocked look of him, the way his mouth twisted, as if she'd done something disgusting in front of him.

She couldn't answer. Her hands stayed clenched in her lap. She turned away from his face and watched his shoes instead. A half-inch of the left lace was stained with something green.

'Are you sure?'

She nodded, eyes still fixed on his shoes. They were brown nubbly suede and very round at the toes. There was a little dent in the dome of the left one. Yvonne wondered if it would spring out if she pushed it from inside. She bit into her cheek, as hard as she could bear.

'Was it the night of the results?'

She nodded again. The one night they'd forgotten the condom. The library door swished open behind them and she turned to watch an elderly man coming out.

'Fuck.'

She felt Brian's foot kicking against the leg of the bench, the thump of it up through her.

She'd been so happy, enough points at last to get into the arts course she wanted, worth the extra year in school. They'd gone with a gang to the pub at half three, staggered out of it at nine, back to his room in the house he shared with two other civil servants.

It was only the fifth time they'd had sex. She didn't remember it.

Brian reached over and pulled one of her clenched hands towards him. 'No, it's OK, really it is.' His hand was cold, it offered no comfort. 'It's OK, it was just a shock, honest to God.'

She nodded, still unable to look at him.

'Yvonne . . . love, it's OK.' He pressed her still clenched fingers. 'We'll be OK. We'll manage.'

His other hand reached under her face and pulled her chin up gently. 'I love you. We'll be fine.'

She nodded again, watching his mouth, looking at the words coming out. He was smiling now, an awful forced smile. Worse, far worse, than before.

'Yeah.' She didn't smile back. 'We'll manage.'

The ridiculous jacket he'd worn for the wedding, all lapels and unnecessary pockets, that she'd never seen before. The expression on his face as she'd walked up the aisle towards him – God, that walk had taken forever. The flash of an uncle's camera, the smiles of her friends, some child crying and being immediately shushed, her mother in the front row in her green suit, smiling, wiping her eyes with a fluff of lace Yvonne had never seen before or since.

Brian's mother in the opposite pew, looking at her son's fiancée with a very different expression.

Yvonne's second cousin Orla, standing inside the altar rails in a yellow dress and black hat, playing 'Here Comes the Bride' on a side flute, because she'd offered and they hadn't had the heart to say no.

The expression on Brian's face, when all Yvonne had wanted to do was turn and run back over the cracked maroon tiles, fly down the aisle through the thick wooden doors, and not stop until she had to.

His tears when Clara was born four months later, only the second time she'd ever seen him cry. The necklace he'd bought for Yvonne the following day, that she'd killed him for buying – ridiculous, what did she want with jewellery? What about the washing machine? How were they going to afford that now?

His awful singing, the songs he made up for Clara:

I'm a kitten from Great Britain,
I eat cabbages and carrots,
I eat mustard, I eat custard,
But my favourite food is parrots . . .

The night he drove their twelve-year-old Mini to the hospital, a raincoat over his pyjamas, going the wrong way down a street that he knew was one way, when Clara got a rash that turned out to be nothing.

The lemon cake he'd baked for Yvonne's twentieth birthday, the beige gloop that oozed out when she cut into it.

The sprinkling of his brown shavings in the bathroom sink that she eventually gave up complaining about. His hair gel that smelled of rhubarb. The black scrap of a nail on his left little finger that he'd caught in a car door as a child. The raised mole just behind his right shoulder, the coarse hairs that sprouted from it that he refused to let her pluck. The way he read the newspaper back to front.

His mother's face at the funeral, blotchy with angry grief. Yvonne holding Clara's five-year-old hand, willing herself to feel, trying to push away the unspeakable relief.

The guilt that brought tears at last, when people told her they were sorry for her troubles, that he was taken from her much too young. All those hands, all that pink and brown and white and cold and warm and smooth and calloused flesh, squeezing hers: Sorry, so sorry for your loss.

At the cemetery, Yvonne pulled up behind a filthy dark blue van and switched off the engine. She waited until Clara had got out, then wound up both windows, locked the car and followed her daughter through the rusting turnstile and along the neat rows of graves.

The gold letters on his granite headstone read Brian O'Mahony, beloved only son of Jim and Peggy, husband of Yvonne, father of Clara, and listed the first and last years of his life, twenty-four apart. No sign of moss – Peggy made sure of that.

Clara bent and laid the freesias on the rectangle of gravel in front of the headstone. Their paper towel wrapping looked too casual now – why hadn't she got some coloured tissue or a ribbon or something?

Brian had been just a year older than Clara was now, when the train he was travelling on, eighteen years ago today, had veered off the tracks and down a small embankment, killing him and an older man in the same carriage. Most of the twenty-nine other passengers had walked away; nobody else had been seriously injured. A miracle, the papers had called it.

A miracle. Yvonne's navy and white skirt was lifted by a sudden whip of wind and she pushed it back down over her knees. She should pray, but they never did, just stood there for a while and then went home.

'Here's Gran and Gramps.' Clara's hand shielded her eyes from the low, late sun as she watched Brian's parents walking towards them. Yvonne turned, forcing a smile onto her face.

Peggy walked ahead of Jim, as usual. She wore a grey coat and cradled a pot of dark yellow flowers.

Far more appropriate than a few bunches of already wilting freesias. Of course.

'How are you, Peggy?'

No handshake, certainly no embrace. Peggy nodded at a place somewhere to the left of Yvonne's ear. 'I'm as well as can be expected, I suppose.' And turning to Clara, she smiled and leaned towards her granddaughter, so Clara could bend and kiss her cheek. 'How are you, pet?'

Yvonne had long since learned to ignore the unspoken insults. After Brian's death, Peggy had distanced herself from Yvonne as much as she could and they'd met mercifully few times since then: here at the graveside every now and again, of course, and at various occasions of Clara's – communion, confirmation, twenty-first birthday – and sometimes in town, when it wasn't possible to pretend they hadn't seen each other.

And every Christmas morning – on Jim's insistence, Yvonne was sure – she spent a tortuous hour or so with Clara in Jim and Peggy's house, sipping drinks and making small talk with a scattering of their neighbours.

Brian's mother looked pretty much the same as ever, apart from the hair that seemed to get blonder each time Yvonne saw it. Same pale blue eyes, the usual powdery lilac shadow above them, same narrow, pointed nose. Same too-dark lipstick bleeding slightly into the deep lines above her top lip.

She handed the flowerpot to Clara. 'Will you put these down for me? There's a good girl.' They watched as Clara bent and placed the pot beside the freesias, and Yvonne wished again that her offering didn't look so pathetic in comparison, so washed out against the much stronger yellow in the pot.

Jim limped slowly up to them. 'Hello there, you two.' He wore a navy sleeveless top over a white shirt and pale grey trousers. 'Everything all right?'

He leaned heavily on the stick he'd been using since his knee operation. His severely cut white hair barely covered his blue-veined scalp. The round glasses perched, as usual, halfway down his nose. He had Brian's, and Clara's, brown eyes – or was it the other way around? A pale pink circle bloomed in the soft greyish folds of each cheek.

Yvonne bent to touch his cheek with her lips. 'Hello, Jim. We're grand – isn't the weather amazing?'

Was he eighty yet? He was a few years older than Peggy, and she must be well into her seventies. After Brian's funeral, back in their house, Jim had taken Clara onto his knee and read her *Green Eggs and Ham* while Peggy and Yvonne looked after the small crowd of mourners, refilling glasses, pouring tea, passing around sandwiches and trying not to be in the same room together.

And after Clara had been put to bed, when most of the callers had left, Yvonne had passed the half-open kitchen door and heard a peculiar snuffling noise. She'd peered in to see Jim hunched on a wooden chair, head bent, shoulders shaking under his charcoal jacket. She'd stood for a moment, watching him, and then she'd walked back into the sitting room, feeling completely unable to help.

Watching Jim now, standing over his only child's grave, both hands curved tightly around his stick, Yvonne wondered how much longer the dinners could go on. How many more times would Jim be able to battle across town on the second Saturday of every month, simply to make a point of having dinner with his daughter-in-law and grandchild, to show that whatever might have happened in the past was forgotten and forgiven – by him, at least?

Jim bowed his head then and blessed himself, and the four of them stood in a silent semi-circle for a few minutes. Yvonne could feel the heat of the sun on the back of her neck. Imagine – almost eight o'clock and still so hot. The best May they'd had in years. A bead of sweat ran down her back and settled into the waistband of her skirt. Under her arms, her blouse felt unpleasantly damp; she couldn't wait to peel it off when they got home. She thought longingly of a cool shower and hoped Clara wasn't planning one of her extended sessions in the bathroom.

Eventually Peggy made the sign of the cross and turned to her husband. 'Ready?' She nodded once in the general direction of Yvonne's shoulder – 'We'll be off then' – and smiled again at Clara. 'Come and see us soon, pet.'

She may as well have looked directly at Yvonne and said, 'Not you. Don't you come near my house.'

Jim blessed himself and put his free hand on Clara's arm – 'Take care, my dear' – and smiled at Yvonne. 'Bye now.'

'Mind yourself, Jim.'

Of course they didn't mention the next dinner, in just over two weeks' time. Yvonne occasionally wondered if Jim was punished for those dinners. Did he get the silent treatment when he got home? Did Peggy rant at him before he went? Or did she just ignore the fact that her husband made regular visits to the enemy? Somehow that didn't seem very likely, knowing Peggy.

Clara watched them walk away. 'She's such a cow.'

Yvonne frowned at the pot of flowers. They were the dark orangey-yellow of duck egg yolks. 'Ah, don't, love.'

'Well, she is – you know she is. I hate the way she makes a point of treating you like dirt. Does she think I don't notice?' Clara's pretty face twisted as she scowled in Peggy's direction. 'And Gramps is such a pet. I can't understand how he puts up with her.'

Yvonne smiled. 'For better or worse, I suppose.' She bent and unwrapped the freesias, pulling away the damp paper. She tried to prop the little flowers against the headstone, but as soon as she let go, they tumbled apart in a green and pale yellow spatter.

No point in saying, again, that Peggy couldn't help it, that she needed someone to blame for Brian's death – and Yvonne, who, as far as Peggy was concerned, had already ruined his life by trapping him at eighteen, was the obvious choice. No point in trotting out those awful half-truths again – Clara had been fed them often enough.

She didn't remember her father at all. She hadn't a single memory of the made-up songs she'd refused to go to bed without, correcting him sternly if he got a line wrong, or the endless games of snakes and ladders or the sock-puppet shows he put on when she had measles and, later, chicken pox. Clara had no idea what a wonderful father she'd had for the first five years of her life.

And, naturally, she hadn't a clue about how her mother had been planning to leave him, in the weeks and days before he died. And that was the problem, of course – Yvonne had no idea if Brian had said anything to his parents, if he'd confided in them about the awful little scene in the kitchen, late one night after Clara was in bed . . .

'Peace at last – she's gone off.' He'd poured his can of Bulmers into the glass Yvonne insisted on and walked towards the television.

'Hang on.' Her mouth was painfully dry. She could still taste the sardines they'd had for dinner. 'Don't turn it on a minute.'

'*Match of the Day* is—'

'I know, but just a minute.' She'd forgotten Match of the Day, the one programme he couldn't live without. No matter – she'd started now. 'I – need to talk to you.'

He perched on the arm of the sofa. 'Go on so, if you're quick. You have three minutes.'

She watched his throat move as the cider went down, heard the wet glugs of his swallows. What made a man's Adam's apple look so heartbreakingly vulnerable?

She waited until he'd lowered the drink, pushing her nails into the couch. She said, 'It's about us.' Now. No going back now.

'Us?' He looked at her. His lips were wet. 'What about us?' He started to smile. 'Is this one of those talks where you tell me I don't spend enough time with you?' He glanced towards the clock on the mantelpiece, a lightning movement she didn't miss.

'Brian . . .' There was a small, almost perfectly round bruise on the back of his left hand. It was yellow and dark blue. 'We . . . I think . . .' All her practising, and she couldn't think how to say it.

He looked more carefully at her and said, 'What's up? Tell me. Did I forget our anniversary or something?'

She'd had no idea it would be so hard. She hadn't planned on crying – that hadn't been part of it at all – yet her eyes filled suddenly with tears. 'I – I— This isn't working.' She dipped her head and brushed away the tears before they had a chance to roll down her face. 'We – us. We're not working.' There was salt at the back of her throat. She kept her eyes down, not daring to look at his face.

He laughed. The sound startled her into lifting her head. He was grinning at her. 'You're having me on, aren't you? This is April fool or something.' He slid down in to the sofa, reached for his glass again. 'Jesus, you nearly had—'

'Stop.' She put a hand on his arm. 'Brian, I mean it. I'm not joking.' His skin felt cool against her fingers. 'We've made a mistake. We should never have . . . We made a mistake, that's all. Clara was coming and – we couldn't see beyond that.'

His smile began to fade. 'What are you talking about?' He looked from her face to the hand that was still on his arm, and back to her face. He stared at her. 'What are you saying?'

She struggled for the words again. 'I'm trying – I don't want . . .' Tiny bubbles floated to the top of the cider and burst there. She imagined them hitting her skin with minuscule damp pops. 'I don't—' She couldn't say it. She waited for him.

'Do you not love me any more?'

He'd whispered it. She could hardly hear him. Do you not love me any more? Because of course she'd loved him once. Hadn't she?

She shook her head, scattering fresh tears. 'I'm sorry.' She started to reach for his hand and he pulled it away from her.

He lunged for his glass and drained it, gulping it down as if he'd die of thirst otherwise. Then he belched, deliberately loudly.

She closed her eyes, whispered 'I'm sorry' again. Her head began to ache.

'Look.' His voice was stronger. She heard the creak of the sofa as he turned towards her. She kept her eyes closed. 'Look, you're tired. You're worn out with that job – I told you not to . . .' He grabbed her hand, held onto it tightly. 'You don't know what—'

'No.' She shook her head again, forced herself to open her eyes and look at him. 'I do. Please believe me. I mean what I say. It's not tiredness, I'm not tired.' A pulse of pain thumped gently in her head.

He searched her face, still holding tightly to her hand. 'So what are you saying? What are you really saying?

'It's over.' She had to push the words out. They felt too big to get past her lips. 'We can't stay together.'

His face crumpled. 'No.' He leaned towards her and pushed his face into her neck. 'No, don't say that. No, no, please—' She felt the hot wetness of his tears, smelled the hair gel he'd refused to change, even for her. Smelled the apple tang of cider. 'I love you, you know how much I—' He slid his arms around her and pressed her against him. 'I love you.' He lowered his head until it nestled between her breasts. 'Please.' He pressed his lips to her skin, just above the V of her T-shirt. 'I love you so much.'

She wanted to push him away, but his body shuddered with sobs and she couldn't. She sat trapped in his arms, damp with his tears, until he lifted his head and ran a hand under his nose and said rapidly, 'Look, just hang on – don't rush into anything. I can take a few days off – I can do it next week, we can go someplace. I don't know, we can get a B and B, my parents will mind Clara, or yours – and we can just talk about it.' He pushed the heel of his hand into each of his eye sockets in turn. 'Will you just do that, will you just . . . please? Will you?'

Yvonne looked at his wet eyelashes and his red, swollen eyes and his stupid, hopeful face and she knew that no amount of talk would change a thing, not if they talked until they were old. But she nodded and said 'OK' because he had a bruise on the back of his hand, and because she'd made him cry, and because she didn't know how to say no.

And then, just two days later, he'd taken the train

to Dublin for a meeting, and the next time she'd seen him had been in the hospital mortuary in Athlone.

His face was unfamiliar, they'd hidden the worst of the injuries under a thick layer of some tan-coloured cream, and his brown hair was parted on the wrong side. She had reached under the sheet, lifted his icy cold hand and turned the palm over. The bruise had almost completely faded. She could barely make it out.

When they got home from the cemetery, Magoo was waiting at the back gate. As soon as the car rounded the corner of the lane he stood, stretching each leg in turn. He darted between them while they were getting out, barking happily, then trotted ahead of them up the path and stood hopefully by his empty bowl, black tail swinging in a wide arc, wet tongue lolling from his panting mouth.

Yvonne picked up the bowl and refilled it from the outside tap. Magoo ducked his head and began to slurp loudly.

The phone began to ring as Clara was turning her key in the back-door lock. 'I'll get it.'

Yvonne stood in the fading light, reluctant now to leave this glorious day behind. The air was wonderfully heavy with the scent of someone's freshly mown lawn. She listened to the *slop-slop* of Magoo's eager lapping as her gaze drifted around the garden.

Clara reappeared. 'Mum, it's Greg. I'm off for a bath.'

Greg – she should have guessed. He never forgot Brian's anniversary. Yvonne lifted the receiver, smelled

the citrus body spray Clara had taken to using lately.
'Hi.'

'Hello there.' Greg's deep, slow voice. 'Just
thought I'd give a shout, see how you're doing.'

'We're fine, Greg. You're good to ring.'

Brian's first cousin, and now one of Yvonne's
oldest friends. Like her, he'd been born in Belford and
had lived there until he'd gone to a seminary in the
midlands straight after school. He'd lasted just two
years, before leaving for a sister of one of the other
seminarians. When that relationship had ended, after
little more than a year, Greg had moved to Dublin. He
was still there, teaching music in a private – Yvonne
assumed terribly exclusive – secondary school on the
south side. As far as she knew, he'd never met anyone
else in the years since the seminarian's sister.

Greg was tall, fair and short-sighted, with
delicate, almost feminine features and a surprisingly
deep voice. He played a variety of instruments and his
knowledge of classical music was encyclopedic.
He was quiet by nature, good with children and
animals, and utterly dependable.

Three or four times a year, sometimes more often,
he made the trip back to Belford to visit his few
remaining relatives – a married sister, a few cousins on
the other side of the family, his Uncle Jim and Aunt
Peggy – and on each of these visits, he called on
Yvonne and Clara.

Greg had been Brian's best man, had stood next to
Brian watching Yvonne as she'd forced herself to walk
up the aisle, heart sinking, in the awful frilly dress her

mother had pleaded with her to wear because it would hide her figure from the busybody aunts, her father's twin sisters.

'When are you coming down again?'

'Well, we're getting holidays on Friday, and then I have a couple of weeks of summer school, but after that I was thinking of Belford for a few days.' Greg rented the small top floor of a house owned by one of the school's governors. 'I'll give you a shout.'

Yvonne smiled. 'Do that.' She was glad he'd kept in touch, glad that he hadn't been put off by what must have seemed like rudeness on her part, when he'd called around to see her a few days after the funeral. When she'd sat silently and left most of the talking to him, feeling the air thick with what wasn't being said.

Because he never once mentioned his cousin, never spoke about Brian at all. Instead, he'd told her about the other seminarians.

'Simon can speak eight languages and he's never been outside Ireland, imagine.'

'Mmm.' As if she cared about Simon or about any of them.

'And Tim left school at sixteen and went straight to the States, worked on building sites in New York for twenty-one years, and then one morning he woke up and knew he wanted to be a priest. Says he was never so sure of anything in his life.'

'Right.' She'd wondered how much longer he was going to stay.

'We have this cook called Teresa, she's been there for years. One of her sons was going for the priesthood when he got meningitis. She still talks about him now and again. He loved her tomato soup.'

Tomato soup. She was being eaten up with guilt, she felt like the lowest form of life, and he was talking about tomato soup.

She'd sat across the living room from him and picked at the skin around her nails and wondered if Clara was behaving herself for Granny O'Mahony. She tried not to look at her watch while he was talking.

He'd left, finally, and come back the following afternoon. And the one after that. He played with Clara and he drank tea and he talked to Yvonne about everything but Brian. And then one day, maybe a week later, maybe two, when she couldn't bear it any more, Yvonne had interrupted him in the middle of the kitchen, in the middle of a sentence – something about a laundry mix-up – and said loudly, 'It wasn't like it seemed, you know, with me and Brian.'

The words had resonated in the room. Greg said nothing, didn't look surprised, even. He watched her face through his thick glasses and said nothing.

'It wasn't like everyone thought.'

He waited, long legs crossed at the ankles. In the sitting room, they could hear Clara speaking to her dolls: 'No, you can't go to the shop, you're too small. I'll get you a Curly Wurly when I do the shopping, alright?'

Yvonne leant against the worktop and picked at a loose thread in the cuff of her jumper. 'I just don't want you to—' She twisted the thread around her finger and pulled. It was surprisingly resistant.

She unwrapped it and looked at the thin red line it had left on her skin. She lifted her head and glared at Greg. 'I was going to leave him. I was planning to go. I told him, just a few days before.'

It was the first time she'd said it out loud to anyone except Brian.

'We should never have got married, it was a mistake.'

She hadn't even told her parents.

'I didn't love him.'

The words fell from her mouth and left her wonderfully empty, like she felt after vomiting. Empty. Purged.

Across the room from her, Greg sat calmly. After a few seconds, when Yvonne said nothing more, he nodded. 'It happens.'

And in those two words she heard absolution. The relief was so enormous that she dropped her face into her hands and sobbed, big full tears that streamed out of her, and Greg walked over and gave her his hanky, then went into the sitting room to Clara, closing the door quietly behind him.

And even though he didn't say much afterwards, and the subject rarely came up between them again, she knew he understood and didn't blame her. And because of it, she could begin to stop blaming herself. It happens.

After she'd hung up, after Magoo was fed his supper and brought in for the night, after the kitchen was tidied, after she'd finished the paper and caught the news on the radio (a bomb in the Middle East, another politician in trouble, two more road deaths in the past twenty-four hours), Yvonne O'Mahony locked the back door and climbed the stairs.

No sign of Clara, no sound from her room. A soft murmuring from the pipes, the scent of lemons wafting damply from the empty bathroom and curling around the landing.

Yvonne left the light off in her bedroom, crossed to the window and looked out. It had begun to rain, a soft, heavy fall. The moon was up, almost full. She could see the wet, silvery outlines of the three long, narrow back gardens, separated from each other by the golden privet hedges that some long-gone residents had planted.

The knobbly shapes of the pair of apple trees next door, planted by Dan and Ali two years before. A ribbon of lawn, badly in need of a cut, running down to the trees, with a tilted rotary clothesline skewered through the middle of it. At the top of the garden a small patio, weeds pushing between the old paving slabs, shiny now in the rain. On the far side, a half-built brick barbecue topped with black plastic, a small round wrought-iron table and two matching chairs. A black wheelie bin in the corner.

Number nine's back garden, furthest away, was easily the best kept of the three. Beyond the patio decking – gas barbecue, gas heater, wrought-iron furniture – a wide bed of perfectly behaved flowers led down to a collection of neatly pruned shrubs framing an immaculate rectangle of lawn.

At the bottom, a shed built in the same red brick as the house, full of Kathryn's carefully cleaned tools, hanging in spirit-level-straight rows.

'You're so anal,' Yvonne had told her. 'Get a life.'

Kathryn had just smiled. 'You're so jealous. Your shed's like a bomb hit it. At least I can find things.'

'Exactly – if I can't find the tools, I can't weed.'

'Oh dear – jealous *and* lazy. I don't know why I hang around with you.'

Yvonne turned back to her own garden, looked out at the humped darkness of it. Just beyond the patio, her pathetic collection of herbs – a bush of woody rosemary, a little patch of struggling basil, some half-decent parsley, tilting chives, a few clumps of thyme and the mint that kept threatening to choke everything else. It was her least favourite herb – she loved the smell but hated the taste – and it was only there because Clara had insisted: 'Mum, there is no way you can have roast lamb without mint sauce.'

Beyond the herbs the same strip of lawn as next door's, only slightly less bedraggled here – and in need of a cut. She might do it tomorrow. A clothes line running down one side, strung between two poles. At the bottom, the weary-looking wooden shed, then between it and the back gate the two red gooseberry bushes that Greg had planted the week Yvonne and Clara had moved in. Hard to believe it was almost seventeen years ago now – no wonder the bushes were a bit straggly.

It had felt like a refuge, the first time she'd stepped into this red-brick house. On the far side of town from the tiny flat she and Brian had been renting. Cheap enough for the compensation money to cover most of the cost because of the state it had been in.

Walking behind the estate agent through the

musty-smelling rooms, Yvonne had hardly noticed the peeling wallpaper, the dripping taps, the cracked tiles. Before they'd even gone upstairs, she'd decided to put in a bid. Tiles could be replaced. They'd deal with the damp. And anyone could paint a few walls.

She had a job, she was earning. After Clara was born she'd taught herself to type from a book, on the typewriter Brian had brought home for next to nothing when the office was having a facelift. Between the feeds and nappy changes, she'd tapped at the keys until she felt confident enough, when Clara was eight months old, to answer an ad for a typist in the local paper. When Brian died Yvonne was on her third job, as secretary to two architects, and able to afford the repayments on the small mortgage she'd taken out to buy and refurbish number seven Miller's Avenue.

Just then, her neighbour's back door opened and two figures stepped out on the patio, bringing with them the murmur of male voices. It was too dark to see them clearly but she recognised the shape of Dan, pointing down the garden. The other man seemed to be wearing a hat of some kind. She wondered if he was a relative, come to keep Dan company for a while maybe.

Poor Dan.

After a minute, she pulled the curtains, switched on the bedside lamp, started undressing – a shower, at last – and thought again about the ridiculous thing she was definitely not planning to do.

In her bedroom, Clara gently tissued off the honey face mask she'd applied in the bath. She soaked a cotton pad in toner and wiped away the residue. She unscrewed her jar of night cream, dipped her fingers in and stroked it slowly over her face.

When she'd finished, she stood and undid the belt of her dressing gown. It slid from her body and pooled on the floor. She looked into the long mirror on the wardrobe door, took in the full breasts, the flat stomach, the puff of dark blonde hair beneath it.

Dirty girl.

She flicked off the light, crossed in the darkness to her double bed, slid between the pale blue sheets and closed her eyes.

NUMBER EIGHT

'. . . and there's parking at the end there. You drive down the lane beside number seven and it swings around the back of these three houses.' Dan O'Farrell waved in the general direction of the bottom of the garden, and as Kieran Delaney chewed his gum and pushed his hat up a bit further and pretended to see whatever was down there, a light switched on in an upstairs room next door threw a pale lemony patch onto the lawn. Something rustled in the hedge near them. Kieran wondered if it was a rat. They weren't too far from the river here.

He thought of something. 'Where's one to six?'

'Pardon?'

'This house is number eight, isn't it? And I'm assuming your neighbours are seven and nine. So where's one to six?'

'Oh.' Dan paused. 'I never really thought about it, I'm only here a couple of years myself. I suppose the apartment block down the way – maybe it replaced the original houses.'

Was there something slightly odd about this man, or

was Dan imagining it? He'd seemed normal enough on the phone that afternoon, hadn't asked too many questions, said he'd be around later to see the room. Dan hadn't realised that later meant nearly eleven o'clock.

'Oh, hello – Kieran Delaney. I rang earlier.'

Around Dan's height. Biggish nose, small, even teeth, dark eyes just visible under a mustard-coloured cowboy hat. Older than he'd sounded on the phone – Dan's first impression was fifty, at least. Wearing loose navy corduroy pants, brown shoes and a crumpled green T-shirt with 'Kilkenny Cat Laughs 2002' on the front. Hardly your average prospective tenant.

Still, beggars couldn't be choosers. Dan stuck out his hand. 'Dan O'Farrell, good to meet you. Let me show you around.' Smell of mints and something else – shoe polish maybe.

They walked through the house. Kieran didn't say very much. He didn't comment on the sitting room, didn't ask why two and a half walls were papered and the rest painted. He glanced briefly around the medium-sized bedroom on offer, nodding at the bed – bigger than a single, smaller than a double – against the far wall.

In the bathroom he walked straight to the window and pushed the net curtain aside to peer out. Only in the kitchen had he shown some curiosity, asking Dan if he did much cooking (no) and whether the oven was gas or electric (gas) and applauding the fact that Dan didn't own a microwave.

After pointing out the parking, Dan turned back towards the house. 'Will you have some tea?'

Kieran shook his head. 'Never touch the stuff, thanks.' He fished in his trouser pockets and transferred his gum into the strip of foil he pulled out. 'But I'll take a glass of water.'

In the kitchen Kieran took off his hat again and ran a hand through his still-there-but-very-white hair. He'd gone white in his early thirties. It hadn't bothered him, although he'd have preferred his eyebrows to have changed colour too. He thought it looked a bit odd, them staying so black. A bit unnatural.

Dan held a glass under the tap. 'I don't have bottled water, sorry.'

Kieran smiled. 'Never go near it. No idea how long those bottles have been sitting somewhere.' He glanced around the kitchen, noticed the floor could do with a wash, the dried-up something on top of the cooker, the scatter of crumbs on the table.

He took the glass Dan held out. Maybe he should have left the hat in the car. He'd meant to, and then he'd forgotten. 'Thanks.'

He liked the house, liked the feel of it, liked the idea of living in a place built with red bricks. And the gas cooker was a definite plus. He never fully trusted electricity to produce something he'd want to eat.

He thought he and Dan could get along, despite the age difference. Kieran generally got along with people, if it was up to him.

'Biscuit?' Dan was unscrewing the wrapper of a half-finished packet of ginger nuts that stood on the table.

'Thanks.' Kieran took a biscuit and dunked it in his glass and said, 'Well, I'm happy with the place. It's pretty much what I was looking for.'

Better just say it out, see the reaction it got. He bit into the wet ginger nut and waited.

Dan nodded, trying not to wonder why anyone would want to dunk a biscuit in cold water. No harm in it, just a bit odd.

'Right.' He stuck out his hand. 'Fair enough, that's fine with me.' May as well go for it; he could do a lot worse. Couldn't he?

So that was it. They shook hands and Kieran said, 'You haven't mentioned the rent.'

Dan stared blankly at him. He'd forgotten about the rent. It simply hadn't occurred to him to fix on a figure, even though money was the only reason he was looking for a tenant.

'Ah, right, let's see . . .' He hadn't a clue what people were paying to rent a room in a house these days, hadn't done any investigating. 'Right . . .'

He seemed so at a loss that Kieran said, 'Fifty euro a week would be about average. Including utilities.'

Dan nodded immediately. 'That sounds fine to me. Fifty a week.' He put the ginger nuts back on the table. 'So, when were you thinking of moving in?'

Amazing. No questions about what work he did, or whether he even had a job. Not a word about references, no curiosity about where Kieran had come from or why a man of his age would be wanting someplace to rent. He might be a paedophile or a terrorist. He could have just got out of jail after serving twenty years for God knew what.

He felt like warning Dan about the dangers of taking someone you didn't know into your house without vetting them properly. Maybe he could work it into a future conversation.

He considered. 'How would Saturday suit?'

'Saturday is fine.' Dan nodded, thinking, Thank God that's that. No more traipsing up and down the stairs with a succession of strangers, apologising for the state of the garden, pretending that the half-painted sitting room had only been half-painted for a couple of days, instead of six weeks. Having to keep the bathroom tolerably clean and remember to put his socks in the laundry basket.

Although, to be fair, three people was hardly a succession – two if you didn't count Kieran. One man, mid-twenties, had followed Dan around silently, tapping on walls and flicking on light switches. When they got downstairs again, he'd mumbled 'No thanks' and opened the front door and let himself out.

A student nurse, Dan's only other candidate, had been all chat until she'd looked out of an upstairs window and spotted Picasso in the garden. Then she'd said immediately, 'Oh, God, is that your cat? No way, sorry – can't bear them. They give me the creeps.'

Suddenly he thought he'd better let Kieran know about Picasso. 'How d'you feel about cats?' He should have mentioned it earlier. Hopefully he wouldn't lose another possible tenant, have to go through all this palaver again.

But Kieran's face brightened. 'Cats? I'm partial, very partial. You have one?'

'Well, it's really—' Dan stopped, then nodded. 'I have, yeah. Lives in the garden, mostly. Sleeps outside. A grey tom.'

Kieran looked even more pleased. 'Does he have a name?'

Far too happy about the cat for Dan's liking. 'Picasso.' The moment it was out, Dan realised he could have made up any name and this man would never have known. He could have said Fred or Sooty or something normal. Anything but Picasso, really – such a poncy name for a cat.

'Great name. Unusual. I look forward to meeting him.' Kieran put his glass on the draining board. 'Well, thanks a lot. I'll be off now, let you get on.'

At the front door they shook hands again, and Kieran said, 'Around two on Saturday, that be alright?'

'Fine. See you then.' Dan watched him walking down the path, settling the hat on his head and rummaging in his baggy corduroy pockets, presumably for his car keys. He closed the front door softly.

It wasn't until twenty minutes later, as he was finishing his supper of two rock-hard fried eggs and four ginger nuts, that Dan realised he had no contact number, no address for his new tenant. What if some emergency came up between now and Saturday, and Dan needed to get in touch?

On the other hand, what if Kieran didn't show up on Saturday and didn't ring to explain why? How long was Dan supposed to wait? A week? Longer? Kieran had signed nothing. They hadn't talked about a lease. Was Dan supposed to suggest a trial period in case it turned out to be a disaster?

It struck him that he hadn't asked for a deposit. He should definitely have looked for that, shouldn't he? In case Kieran broke stuff or didn't pay his rent or something.

Being a landlord had never been part of the plan. The plan was to stay married to Ali, till death them did part. The plan was to fill their house with children, not with men pretty much old enough to be Dan's father, with black eyebrows and white hair, who wore cowboy hats and dunked biscuits in cold water instead of hot tea.

Dan wondered what else there was to know about Kieran. Maybe he should have asked a few more questions. He hadn't a clue who he was letting into the house. Was Kieran Delaney even his real name? What if he played the drums all night or brought women – or men – home with him, or had a pet snake? Just because he hadn't mentioned it didn't mean he didn't have one. Look how happy he'd been when he'd heard about Picasso; a real cat lover, by the sound of him.

What if he had his own cat, just turned up with it on Saturday? Dan could barely handle one.

He took his plate to the sink. He parted the blinds

on the kitchen window and peered into the garden. Two small ovals of yellow light gazed at him from directly outside the window. He sighed heavily and opened the back door. Picasso jumped lightly down from the sill and glided in, brushing against Dan's leg. His coat was dewed with rain.

'You're going out the minute it stops.' Picasso mewed and twined around his legs. Dan poured milk into the empty plate and watched without interest as the cat lapped it daintily.

He didn't like cats in a house, didn't really like cats much at all. He especially didn't like the cat he'd inherited when Ali had walked out on him, because the man she'd left him for was allergic.

Dan knew he was allergic because his mother had told him so. Because the man Ali had left him for was his mother's younger brother, Dan's Uncle Brendan.

Dan's fifty-two-year-old Uncle Brendan, twenty years older than Ali. Dan wished it didn't all sound like some embarrassingly bad joke.

Picasso finished the milk and stretched each pair of paws in turn. Then he sat on the floor and began to wash himself calmly. Dan bent and took the empty plate away.

Ali had insisted on the cat sleeping indoors, even in the middle of summer.

'Darling, how can you even think about putting him out? Look how dark it is – and it might rain.' And of course Dan had given in and Picasso had curled up on the padded window seat in the sitting room each night, leaving a tangle of grey hair behind him in the morning.

To be fair, though, he didn't seem to hold it against Dan that he slept on the patio now, since Ali had left. He seemed happy enough in the half-built barbecue, especially since Dan had shoved an old cushion in there and put a plastic bin bag on top to keep out the rain.

And Picasso seemed to have forgotten about Dan trying to get rid of him.

Early one evening, about two weeks after Ali had gone, when the loneliness, frustration and rage had got the better of him, Dan had bundled Picasso into his cat carrier and driven several miles out of town, well past the last housing estates and petrol stations. He'd stopped by a gate into a field, lifted the carrier out onto the grass and pulled up the mesh door. 'Shoo. Go on now, shoo. Clear off.'

Picasso stood and stretched his neck forward and sniffed a few times. Then he sat down again and looked at Dan.

'Go on, shoo. Get out.' Dan tilted the carrier and Picasso half jumped, half fell from it. He padded around, tail flicking, sniffing the ground. Dan got back into the car quickly, threw the empty carrier on the back seat and drove off.

It took him less than five minutes to turn the car around and double back, appalled at himself – he couldn't take it out on the blasted cat, it wasn't his fault – but in that short space of time, Picasso had disappeared.

Dan must have searched for nearly two hours in the fading light, calling the cat's name over and over, poking into bushes, peering through hedges. At one stage, not knowing what else to do, he knocked on the door of a nearby farmhouse.

It was opened by an elderly man who poked in his mouth with a toothpick. The smell of cabbage wafted out to Dan.

'I'm sorry to bother you' – God, he felt such a fool – 'but I've lost my cat somewhere around here. I don't suppose you noticed a grey cat, did you?'

The man regarded him solemnly, taking the toothpick from his mouth. 'You lost your cat.' His brown trousers were very shiny at the knees. He wore black socks and no shoes.

'Yes – around here somewhere.' Dan was regretting his impulse. This man didn't look very sympathetic – and he might still be in the middle of his bacon and cabbage.

'Taking it for a walk, were you?'

No hint of a smile. Was he serious?

Dan decided to hang onto what little dignity he had left. 'We were in the car. I stopped to – er – take a phone call and the cat jumped out.' He turned away. 'Sorry to have—'

'Hang on.' The man disappeared, leaving the door wide open. The hall was papered with green and orange stripes. The floor was tiled in black and white. When Dan looked from the wall to the floor, the tiles danced for a second. He could hear the sound of a radio, or maybe a TV. Then the man reappeared, wearing muck-spattered wellingtons.

'We'll have a look.' He strode beyond Dan, around

the side of the house. 'What did you say his name was? That your car out there?'

'Yes.' Dan trotted after him. 'Er – his name is Picasso. But you needn't – I mean, I wouldn't want to disturb your—'

'PICASSO!' The bellow took Dan by surprise. 'HERE, PUSS! HERE, PUSS PUSS!' If Picasso was within earshot, he'd probably run a mile. The man crossed the yard behind the house and opened a wide gate that led down a dung-covered lane. 'PICASSO!' In a normal voice he added to Dan, 'Mind your shoes.'

It took Dan thirty minutes to escape. Thirty minutes of ear-splitting bellows and hopping over cowpats, stumbling through treacherously bumpy fields and trying not to be intimidated by the stares of the animals they passed (bullocks? females whose udders hadn't dropped yet?) before Dan managed to persuade the man – no human names had been exchanged – that he'd really done all he could, thanks awfully, sorry again about disturbing him.

He got back into the car and drove off, waving and smiling at the man, who stood on his doorstep observing him solemnly.

Going back into town, Dan felt like the murderer that he was. A pampered cat like Picasso wouldn't survive five minutes in the middle of the country. He might be dead already, trampled by one of those teenage bulls or whatever they were, or run over by a tractor. How could Dan have been so cruel, punishing an innocent animal like that?

And what if Ali came back and discovered what he'd done? That would be enough, surely, to send her straight off again. She'd be horrified, and rightly so.

Not that there was much chance of her coming back.

Not that he wanted her back, after what she'd done.

His black mood deepened. He could smell cow dung in the car. The empty cat carrier eyed him accusingly in the rear-view mirror. He remembered with horror that Picasso was wearing a collar with the house phone number on it – if he was found, alive or dead, Dan would be traced and shamed. He wondered if abandoning a cat was an arrestable offence.

By the time he got home, it was almost pitch dark. He parked the car and walked towards the house. And there, on the doormat, was Picasso, washing himself at his usual unhurried pace.

Dan stopped dead and stared in disbelief. Picasso took no notice of him, went on licking a paw and running it over his face.

Just as Dan was trying to decide how exactly to murder the cat – properly this time, innocent animal my foot – Kathryn came out of next door's kitchen with a bin bag and saw him.

'Oh, there you are, Dan.' She walked over to the chest-high hedge. 'I hope you don't mind but I gave Picasso a few leftovers a little while ago. He was mewing on our deck, looking a bit hungry.'

With a great effort, Dan managed not to guffaw out loud. Not only had the cat covered about eight miles in record time, he'd also managed to pick up dinner. 'No problem – I mustn't have left out enough this morning. Thanks a lot.'

As soon as he opened the back door, Picasso streaked into the kitchen and Dan forced himself not to chase him straight out again. He'd had a long walk; maybe he'd earned an hour on the window seat.

So it looked like they were stuck with each other. And now Dan had just invited a cat lover to live with them, making it two against one: great.

He ran lukewarm water over his plate and propped it against one of the glasses on the draining board. Better get in some washing-up liquid – the tenant would probably expect it. And he'd have to pick up more paint for the sitting room; he couldn't leave it half done now. He opened the back door and stuck out his hand. When it came back dry, he turned back to Picasso. 'Come on, you. Hop it.'

Going upstairs a few minutes later, he heard a car door slam. He glanced out of the landing window as he passed, and heard rather than saw next door's back gate clicking open. He turned away and went into the unnaturally tidy bathroom to brush his teeth.

Just before half past one in the morning, Kieran Delaney parked his seventeen-year-old Ford Escort outside a hardware shop in Castlebar and opened the dull green door that led to the little flat upstairs. Be nice to live in a house again, have a bit of space and a garden. Ten years was quite enough to be without one.

He'd been happy enough to move in here, after he'd sold the house. Relieved, really, to be rid of all that responsibility. Glad not to have to worry about things breaking down and needing to be replaced. Things seemed to break down a lot, in Kieran's experience. Break down or have bits fall off or just refuse to start, for no reason that he could ever see. So the apartment had suited him fine. He'd been quite happy here, really. But it was time for a change – and now that he'd made the decision, he looked forward to it.

And the cat. He smiled. The cat was a definite bonus. He hadn't lived with a cat for years.

He thought about the half-full bottle of dark orange nail varnish and single silver earring on the bathroom shelf. He considered the half-painted sitting room, the half-built barbecue. None of his business.

Be nice to have the barbecue going for the summer, though. Nothing like the smell of a chargrilled steak on a sunny day. He might tactfully suggest finishing it himself, once he was settled in. Not that he was handy that way – he'd never built anything in his life. But it couldn't be that hard, surely. Bit of cement, a few bricks. Not exactly the Pyramids.

He eased off his brown shoes – should really replace them soon – and shoved his feet into the navy slippers that someone had barely used before donating them to the charity shop. They'd been a real find, and only half a size too big. No harm for slippers to have a bit of room. Let the feet ease out after the day.

He went from the bedroom to the open-plan space that was his kitchen, dining and sitting room.

He took his violin from the case on the couch, picked up the bow, closed his eyes and began to play a Norwegian lullaby from a CD he'd bought on a long-ago holiday. He let the notes wash around him, he swam in them.

He stood in the middle of the room, oblivious to the darkness outside, unaware of the breeze that played with the scraps of litter in the street below, the car that slid past, headlights slicing through the black air. He stood in the room and played on.

New beginnings, he thought. Everything behind him now. Adam safely in the past, where he belonged.

NUMBER NINE

From the sitting room, Kathryn heard them coming up the path. She pressed the off button on the remote control and stood up, arranging her face, rehearsing her lines. Everything alright? How are you feeling, Grainne?

She opened the kitchen door as they were coming in, Justin's hand cradling his mother's elbow.

'Everything alright?' Kathryn walked over and took Grainne's handbag from Justin. 'How are you feeling? What did they say?'

Grainne's face twisted with irritation. 'Ah, what would you expect? They haven't a clue at that hospital. Sure, half of them aren't even Irish – you'd wonder are they qualified at all.'

So they hadn't pandered to her like Dr Lynch did. Probably told her she had a cold and suggested bed and two Panadols, which wouldn't have gone down well at all. Grainne never had a cold. It was flu or a chest infection or, on a good day, a touch of pneumonia.

Justin steered her around the table. 'We'll put you straight up to bed, will we?'

Grainne sighed, leaning heavily against him. 'I think so. I'm totally exhausted.'

You'd think she was ninety, the way she went on, instead of just twenty-two years older than her son's wife.

'I'll make you a cuppa, Grainne,' Kathryn said. 'And I have your blanket plugged in.' Winter or summer, Grainne had to have the electric blanket on full before she'd get in. That bed would be like a furnace tonight.

Alone in the kitchen, Kathryn filled the kettle and set a tray with the china cup and saucer Grainne preferred and a small plate with two shortbread biscuits on it, one for Grainne to eat and the other for her to leave, proving how unwell she was. Two years under the same roof had taught Kathryn a lot about her mother-in-law.

'I'll take that up.' Justin reappeared and waited while Kathryn poured water into the little teapot.

'What did they say?'

He shrugged. 'The heatwave could be causing the headaches. They told her to leave a window open in her room, drink lots of water, have cool showers, that kind of thing.'

No, that wouldn't have gone down well. Justin looked tired tonight, and older than he was. A stranger seeing them together mightn't notice the age difference. Kathryn wanted to smooth the lines from his forehead, wipe away the dark smudges under his eyes.

She poured milk into the little striped jug and held

the door open for him. He lifted the tray. 'Back in a sec.'

Kathryn filled two glasses with the end of the Burgundy they'd opened earlier at dinner – 'Just a tiny glass for me,' Grainne had said. 'I have a splitting migraine' – and brought them into the sitting room. After more than two hours sitting in the A and E department on a Saturday night, his third trip to the hospital this month, Justin could use it. She slid Brahms into the CD player and pressed play.

No point in trying to talk to him again about Grainne. What could he do anyway, when she complained regularly of stomach pains, backaches and headaches, always splitting and always migraines, and refused to take a tablet and just go to bed? She was his mother, he couldn't ignore her. Couldn't tell her to cop herself on and stop being such a bloody—

The door opened and he came in. Kathryn patted the sofa beside her. 'Sit.'

He smiled tiredly. 'God, are you a sight for sore eyes.' He sank down next to her, dropping his head onto her shoulder, resting one of his hands on her thigh, yawning. 'Jesus, that place would make anyone suicidal.'

'Poor you. Was it terrible?'

'Ah, a few drunks, quiet enough. A couple of stretchers came in, couldn't see – someone said there was an accident.' He yawned again. She felt the lift of his chest against her side.

'There was nothing on the news.' She played with his dark hair, twisting it slowly through her fingers, pulling it gently, running her nails lightly along his scalp, the way he liked it.

He groaned, turning his face into her neck. 'Have I told you lately that I love you?'

Kathryn smiled. 'You might have, once or twice.' His hair smelled of the almond shampoo they both used. He'd always been good at telling her how he felt, right from the beginning, when it was the last thing she'd expected to hear. She leaned back and closed her eyes, her fingers still moving in his hair.

He'd been with the insurance company only about three weeks, working in the same big open-plan office as Kathryn. He was in the IT department, she was a research analyst. In his first week, he'd fixed a small computer problem she had. Since then, they'd exchanged maybe half a dozen remarks, passing in the corridor, choosing the same moment to fill cups from the coffee percolator, the only two people in the lift once.

She thought he was quite attractive. She liked his high cheekbones, thought it gave him a Native American look, especially with his almost black hair. She had no idea what his second name was. When he wore suits, he reminded her of a little boy dressing up in his father's clothes. She suspected he was more at home in jeans. He didn't cross her mind after she left work in the evenings.

And then, one afternoon, she collided with him coming around a corner. Walked right into his arms practically, and spilled a just-filled paper cup of water all over the jacket of his little-boy's suit.

'Oh!' She jerked back, too late to avoid the splash.

'Oh, I'm so sorry.' He smelled of nutmeg, something spicy. The front of his jacket was splotched a darker blue than the rest. The stain was in the shape of an upside-down Italy. 'It's just water, though.'

He inspected the damage, opening the jacket and pulling the wet side up towards his face. 'Damn.'

Kathryn fished a tissue from her pocket and held it out to him. 'Here, you can blot it – I'm sure it'll be fine when it dries.' He wasn't going to make a fuss, was he? The suit was hardly expensive.

He ignored the tissue. 'No – I mean damn, why couldn't you have thrown coffee over me, or tomato soup or something?'

'What?' She stared at him. He wasn't smiling.

'So I'd have to get the suit cleaned and you'd feel you had to offer to pay and of course I'd refuse.' His eyelashes were unfairly long and very dark. He was about the same height as her, maybe an inch taller. 'And then you'd be feeling so guilty you'd say yes right away when I asked you out to dinner.'

Kathryn laughed. 'You're daft.'

'Quite possibly.' He stood, hands in his pockets, watching her. Still no hint of a smile. 'So, tell me, was it coffee or soup?'

'What?'

'Did you just spill coffee or soup over me?'

And Kathryn McElhinney, thirty-four years old and tired of sitting in watching The Late Late Show every Friday night, stopped laughing and said, 'It was beetroot soup, actually. I'm terribly sorry – it'll leave an awful stain, I'm afraid.' She hoped to God nobody was near enough to hear them.

He looked down at his jacket again. 'Beetroot – damn, my good suit's ruined.' His teeth were slightly too big and very white. 'It'll have to be dry cleaned, I'm afraid.'

Kathryn tried her best to look apologetic. 'Well, I insist on paying.' What was she saying? This wasn't a bit like her. She wasn't the kind of person who flirted with someone she barely knew – least of all someone who was clearly quite a bit younger than her. 'It's the least I can do.' What the hell? She hadn't been out on a date in more than two years.

'Absolutely not, I won't hear of it.' He paused. 'But maybe you'd like to come out to dinner with me sometime?' It was like the notion had just occurred to him.

Kathryn smiled. 'You're not really serious about that, are you?' And then, all of a sudden, she hoped he was. Now that he'd planted the idea in her head, she realised how pathetically in need of being taken out to dinner she was, by anyone.

'Of course I'm serious – going out to dinner is not a joking matter. In fact, I won't take no for an answer.' He considered. 'Will we say Friday? That'll give me time to get the suit cleaned.'

Kathryn nodded solemnly. 'Friday is fine, thank you.' She turned and walked back to the water cooler, hoping he was watching her. Glad she'd decided on the black skirt that morning. Showed off her legs nicely.

And it had been on Friday evening, on the way home from the restaurant, after mussels and rack of lamb and strawberries, that twenty-five-year-old Justin O'Connor – wearing not the awful blue suit but grey denims and a black shirt – had told her for the first time how he felt about her.

'I've wanted to ask you out since we met, since that time I fixed your computer, but I was sure someone like you would be attached.'

She didn't know whether to be embarrassed or amused. 'How do you know I'm not?'

He took his eyes off the road and glanced at her. 'I made a few enquiries.'

She tried not to look too pleased. 'I suppose I should be flattered.'

He didn't respond. He drove carefully, indicating well in advance, slowing as he approached traffic lights, whatever colour they were. She'd found it touching. There was a small frayed rectangle just below the left knee of his jeans. He wore dark grey canvas shoes and no socks. His hair ended in tiny curls at the nape of his neck. He'd cut himself shaving, a short red line just under his chin.

They turned at the shopping centre where she'd spent far too much on tonight's green top. They passed a young couple, his arm around her shoulders, her hand in the back pocket of his jeans, leaning in against him. Further on, a small dog sniffed at the base of a lamppost, then hop-trotted on.

After a while Justin had said, 'Don't laugh at this. There's something about you that I find . . . completely fascinating.' He turned into Miller's Avenue and pulled up outside number nine. 'Also, you're beautiful.'

He switched off the engine and leaned back in his seat, lifting her hand from her lap and holding it. 'And you smell gorgeous.'

His hand was warm and dry. It had felt safe to her.

How could someone so young be so confident? It wasn't Dutch courage – he'd drunk water at dinner. She looked at his hand, holding hers lightly. Also, you're beautiful. It should have sounded corny and contrived – she wasn't beautiful, far from it, mousy hair, pale grey eyes and extremely ordinary – but it didn't.

I'm years older than you was on the tip of her tongue, but she didn't say it. She wondered if he'd enjoyed the evening half as much as she had. She'd forgotten how lovely it was to be made to feel attractive.

She wished he was older. No, she wished she was younger.

'Well . . .' She eased her hand from his and reached for the door handle. They'd had a good time – better just to leave it at that. 'Thanks for dinner, I really enjoyed it.'

He didn't seem to mind not being asked in. 'You're very welcome. Feel free to splash water over me anytime.' Before she had a chance to react, as she was pushing down the handle, he leaned across and put a hand to the side of her head and turned her face back towards him and kissed her goodnight, a warm quick kiss that caused something to flicker pleasantly inside her. He tasted of strawberries.

'See you on Monday.'

She watched him drive off, back to his mother's

house across town, in the black Honda Civic he'd bought when he'd got his first job three years earlier. At least it didn't have L plates. At the age of thirty-four, Kathryn McElhinney had just been out to dinner with a man who was still on his first car, who still lived at home with his mother.

She suddenly wondered who she was closer in age to – him or his mother. Not that it mattered in the slightest. The evening had been a pleasant blip, but that was all. A one-off, something to laugh about with her friends – as, no doubt, he'd be doing too, first chance he got.

But that wasn't what had happened.

The music stopped just then. Justin sat up and stretched. 'Come on, let's go to bed – I'm half asleep already.' He turned to her. 'What are you smiling about?'

'I was just thinking about when we started going out.'

He grinned. 'I remember. You ran a mile any time I tried to get close. I had to practically drag you out a second time.'

He'd waited until she'd run out of excuses – meeting friends, headache, evening class, because what was the point? – and then, one afternoon, he'd made his way over to her desk and peered at her computer screen. 'Pretend you're showing me a problem.'

Kathryn glanced around. Nobody was taking any notice of him. 'My computer's working perfectly, thanks.' His hand, planted on the desk beside her, was lightly tanned. His fingers were slim for a man's.

The small button on his pale blue shirt cuff was sewn on with black thread. She remembered his hand on the side of her head, turning her face towards him, and felt the same lightning shiver in her abdomen.

He raised his voice slightly. 'I'm not sure why it's doing that.' In the next cubicle Fiona turned briefly towards them, then went back to her screen.

Without changing his stance, his eyes still on Kathryn's computer, Justin reached into the breast pocket of his jacket, pulled something out and set it on her desk. 'I'm going anyway – are you going to make me seem totally pathetic with an empty seat beside me?'

Kathryn looked at the theatre tickets. The show was nothing special – an amateur production of some play she'd never heard of – but he'd bought two tickets and he was asking her to go with him. She leaned back in her chair and smiled. Her face was towards the screen but her eyes were on him. 'You don't give up, do you?'

'Not when I want something, no.' His dimple was fatally attractive. 'Not when I think I have the slightest chance of getting it.' In a louder voice, he said, 'I think I see the problem.'

What if he managed to charm her into bed eventually, then boasted to everyone else about the older woman he'd pulled? She'd spend her time avoiding him after that, trying to ignore the sniggers behind her back. She'd feel like a right fool. She might even have to look for another job.

But what if he really was interested in her?

It wasn't completely outside the bounds of possibility, was it? How would she know if she didn't take a chance with him? Was she brave enough to risk it?

She had a lot to lose. But she had a lot to gain too. She said, 'Actually, I'm free on Thursday.'

'Good.' He put the tickets back into his pocket and straightened up. 'Pick you up at seven – we can grab a bite beforehand.' She couldn't read his face. The half-smile could have meant anything. 'OK?'

She nodded, unsure all over again. And then he said loudly, 'Oh, there's just one more thing you should remember.' He leaned towards the screen again. 'Look, this icon here . . .' Kathryn sat forward in her chair and he whispered, 'Thanks, I look forward to it.' His face was inches from hers. She could feel his breath on her cheek. She smelled coffee. And then he was gone.

She took his hand now and curled it in hers. 'You know very well why I resisted you – or tried to.' She loved his hands, the slim fingers so familiar now. The bump near the tip of his little finger, the narrow ovals of his nails. 'You know why I was so hard to get.'

He stood up and pulled her after him. 'Because you thought you were old enough to be my grandmother or something.'

Kathryn laughed, loving the lack of importance he'd always placed on their age difference. 'Something like that. You go ahead, I'll be up in a minute.'

In the kitchen she poured what was left of the wine down the sink, rinsed the glasses and put the empty bottle outside the back door, halfway to the recycling bag in the shed. No need to give Grainne anything to comment on in the morning – she never missed an opportunity.

And, of course, it would sound terribly harmless. 'Don't tell me the wine is all gone from last night, Kathryn – a bottle lasts no time at all, does it?' Or another time, 'That top is quite snug on you, isn't it, Kathryn? No harm – a bit of weight never hurt anyone.' Or 'Would you look at her? Mutton dressed as lamb. At least you dress for your age, Kathryn.'

Not that Grainne needed an excuse these days, not with Kathryn's forty-fifth birthday coming up in a couple of months. That was enough to keep her going.

'Aren't women having babies older now? There's no reason why you still couldn't have one. Granted, I'd had my two by the time I was thirty-three, but that doesn't mean everyone has to. Did you see that woman in the paper the other day who had a baby in her fifties? I know that's a bit extreme, but still. You shouldn't let the little . . . setbacks in the past put you off. Think how happy Justin would be if you had a baby. I'm sure he's dying to be a father.'

And Kathryn would nod and agree, wincing silently at the little setbacks, and push her nails into her palms to keep from shouting at Grainne to stop, to just shut up. A stillborn baby and two miscarriages weren't 'little setbacks', they were agonies that never went away, they were ghosts that Kathryn couldn't, or wouldn't, let go. And with each birthday, with each higher number, with each treacherous tick of her biological clock came the stronger possibility that they were all that she and Justin might ever have.

Two years after they were married, a perfect baby boy with Justin's long eyelashes had died in her womb a few days before he was due to be born and nobody could explain why.

A year later, when Kathryn was thirty-nine, one miscarriage followed another, both within two months of conception. Again, there seemed to be no reason and no one could tell them what they were doing wrong.

Since then nothing had happened. Now she was almost forty-five, and terribly afraid.

To be fair to Grainne, she might not realise how hurtful her remarks were. She'd never had a miscarriage or a stillbirth, just two healthy children – even if she'd disowned one of them twelve years ago for having the audacity to be gay. Which meant that Kathryn, old as she was, unsuitable as Grainne clearly considered her to be, was her only hope for a grandchild.

Maybe she meant well.

Or maybe she knew exactly what she was doing. Maybe she took pleasure in hurting Kathryn, in punishing her for ruining Justin's chances of being a father.

Kathryn sighed as she climbed the stairs. She mustn't think like that. Justin loved her – he was always telling her how much he loved her. He didn't care about the age difference and he certainly didn't blame her for the absence of children. Her mother-in-law was just a sad old hypochondriac with too much time on her hands, not worth getting upset about.

She stopped at the landing window, caught a quick movement in the hedge between them and number eight. Picasso probably, out wandering in the night like he'd been since Ali had left.

It was beginning to look like she wasn't coming back. Kathryn had bumped into Dan a few times lately, but he hadn't made any reference to Ali's disappearance and it wasn't something you could bring up casually.

Yvonne thought she'd probably run off with someone: 'What other explanation is there? Dan is hardly the type to wallop her over the head and bury her under the apple tree.'

Kathryn argued that there didn't have to be a third party. 'Maybe she just decided they weren't suited. Maybe she went off him.'

They hadn't seen that much of Ali when she was there – a real career woman by the look of her. Always very smartly dressed, usually rushing off someplace with a businesslike black bag slung across her chest. Dan had told Yvonne once that Ali was a lawyer, a solicitor or something. They seemed polar opposites to Kathryn – Dan, so laid back and down to earth, could hardly have been described as a career man.

Yvonne had to agree. 'I'd never have put them together.'

But then, who'd have put Kathryn McElhinney and Justin Taylor together? Who'd have thought she could possibly make him happy?

Who'd be surprised if he left her for a younger woman, someone who could give him babies who survived?

Cut that out. She turned from the window and opened their bedroom door.

Justin was unbuttoning his shirt. She crossed the room, finished off the last few buttons and placed her palms on his bare chest. He smelled of toothpaste.

Justin pushed away the always-there thoughts of his lost son – Joey, they were going to call him Joey – and smiled at Kathryn. 'You know, I'm not sure I've got the energy tonight.'

She propped her chin on his shoulder, slid her hands around his back. 'That's alright – I can wait till the morning.'

Kathryn had taken him by surprise. He hadn't expected her, hadn't been looking for her. He hadn't planned to get married until well into his thirties, foolishly assuming that the right woman would oblige by not putting in an appearance until then.

His mother had done her best to change his mind. 'Women age faster than men – you'll be tied to an old woman while you still have plenty of energy.'

'I've made up my mind. I love her. She loves me. What does age matter?'

'You can forget about having a family.'

'She's got lots of time – she's only in her thirties.'

But then the heartbreak of Joey had happened,

and while he was still reeling, still trying to make sense of it, Kathryn had begged him to try again. And one after another, two more babies had slipped away.

And now time was running out. Hope was running out. *You can forget about having a family.*

Kathryn walked towards their little en suite bathroom and Justin peeled off his shirt and began to unbutton his jeans.

Three weeks later: 16 June

NUMBER SEVEN

'You'll never guess what Chloë did yesterday.'

Yvonne bit into her cheese and pickle sandwich and looked up at the perfectly blue sky and tried hard to sound interested. 'What?'

Dolores leaned back on the park bench. 'Guess.'

'Won a medal?' That was usually a safe bet: it was a rare weekend when Dolores's daughter didn't arrive home with some prize or other from one of her many after-school activities. Chloë had cups and medals and trophies for everything from horse riding to ballet to swimming.

But Dolores shook her head. 'Remember, it was Mother's Day.'

'Oh, yes, of course.' Clara hadn't done anything for Mother's Day; they didn't go in for that. 'Er, did she make you breakfast in bed?'

'Even better. She cooked dinner for the whole family from scratch – she even did all the shopping. Shepherd's pie and apple crumble with custard.' Dolores bit into her pear and waited for Yvonne's reaction.

'Wow, that's great.' Yvonne pulled off a bit of crust

and threw it onto the ground and watched a thrush hop quickly towards it. So Chloë was a master chef, along with everything else. 'And she's only . . . ' God, how old was Chloë again? It wasn't as if Yvonne hadn't been told often enough '. . . ten, is it?'

'Just gone eleven. Fionn and Hugo washed up afterwards. I was a lady of leisure.' The thrush ducked his head and grabbed the bread and flew off. 'Martin and I didn't know ourselves.'

'Very nice.' Yvonne sneaked a glance at her watch. Ten more minutes and they'd be able to go back. 'You'll have to let Chloë into the kitchen more often.' She wondered if she was the only worker who looked forward to the end of her lunch hour.

She and Dolores didn't eat together every day. Some days Dolores went into town to meet her husband, Martin, for lunch. Other times, when she really couldn't face another sixty minutes of her colleague boasting about the three most perfect children in the universe, Yvonne would invent some reason why she had to go home – the plumber was due or she was expecting a phone call. Or she'd have an errand to run in town, once she was sure Dolores wasn't heading the same way.

They worked in the Miller's Avenue health clinic, diagonally across from the three red-brick houses, just beside the park. Dolores was based upstairs as secretary to the two doctors there while Yvonne manned the main reception desk downstairs and handled the administration for Pawel Tylak, whose surgery was also downstairs.

Pawel was a forty-year-old Polish-born dentist who'd arrived in Ireland from the UK two years before and set up his practice shortly afterwards in the recently opened clinic, creating the need for a second secretary.

Yvonne, fed up with her job as PA to two estate agents who never stopped arguing, had read the advertisement in the local paper and applied.

Pawel had cropped blond hair, very blue eyes and even white teeth, and his English was usually more grammatically correct than Yvonne's. He was perfectly polite to her, but revealed virtually nothing about himself. After almost two years with him, all she knew about Pawel, mostly by accident, was that he'd been educated in England, that he'd never been married and that his father had been some kind of diplomat in London.

She guessed that he was around her own age. He didn't appear to have much of a sense of humour, but she was willing to give him the benefit of the doubt and put it down to shyness.

He was always at work before her in the mornings and he was usually there when she left at five. She had no idea where he lived or whether he had any friends or family in Ireland, and he knew as little about her. Theirs was a purely professional relationship, which suited both of them perfectly.

At five to two, Yvonne and Dolores walked the short distance back to the clinic.

'So what did you get up to at the weekend, then?' Dolores slid a look at Yvonne. 'Bet you had a lot more excitement than boring old married me.'

Another recurring theme: Yvonne's eventful social life. Dolores was somehow convinced that her colleague spent every weekend painting Belford, and possibly the surrounding towns, bright red. She refused to believe that Yvonne ever sat in on a Saturday night eating mashed bananas on toast and watching whatever film was on offer. No, Yvonne was free and single so she had to be living it up with every available male for miles around.

'I'm afraid Clara's the one who has all the excitement in our house. She went to a concert in Galway with her boyfriend yesterday.' Yvonne rummaged in her bag for the clinic keys, wishing she had more to report. Who wanted to admit that her weekends were that uneventful? 'I cooked dinner for my father-in-law on Saturday night – I told you he comes once a month.' Which, on an excitement scale of one to ten, would probably fall somewhere between two and three. Then she thought of something else. 'Oh, and I'm going out to dinner this evening with a friend.' There, that should keep Dolores happy for a while.

'What – a man friend?'

'Yes.' Yvonne felt a tiny bit mean, making it sound like a date.

'Who is he? Where did you meet him?'

She had to come clean. 'Well, he's a kind of a relation, really. I've known him for years.'

'A cousin?'

'Well, no . . . at least, he's not my cousin – he was my husband's.' She was sorry she'd mentioned Greg.

Dolores frowned. 'So he's not related to you.'

'No, but—'

'Where's he taking you? Or is that a surprise?'

'Oh, nowhere fancy, probably the little Italian place on Curtin Street.'

Dolores walked up the clinic steps behind Yvonne. 'You must tell me about it tomorrow. Boring old married women need all the juicy gossip they can get. I'll try not to be too jealous.'

Yvonne had never met Dolores's husband or any of her three children. They lived on the outskirts of a small village about ten miles outside Belford, in the house where Martin had grown up. Dolores had told Yvonne that he worked as an accountant in Charleton, a town another twenty or so miles beyond that, where the children attended various schools.

Yvonne turned her key in the door and slipped the snib to keep it open. They walked through the lobby together. No sign of Pawel – probably eating lunch in his surgery, as usual. Yvonne dropped her bag by her desk and opened the appointments book, running her finger down the list of names. Looking busy, hoping that the hint would be taken.

Dolores glanced at the closed surgery door. 'Pity he wouldn't ask you out.' She made no attempt to lower her voice. 'He'd be a good catch.'

Yvonne stared at her, appalled. What if Pawel heard her? 'Ssh – don't be ridiculous.' Why did married women always feel the compulsion to marry off their single friends? She picked a file from the bundle on the shelf behind her and leafed through it, willing Dolores to go.

'I wouldn't rule it out if I were you. That's all I'm saying.' Dolores finally turned towards the stairs. 'Well, enjoy your evening, if I don't see you later.'

Yvonne watched her walking upstairs. That pleated skirt did nothing for her – if anything, it emphasised Dolores's wide hips. If she even wore shoes with a bit of a heel sometimes, to give her some height, instead of those flat courts she always slopped around in. And her hair, like a bush around her face, just crying out for a good cut. She'd obviously let herself go since she'd pulled Martin.

Not that Yvonne was any great authority on style. Unremarkable brownish-reddish hair cut into the same short bob for the past twenty years. A collection of reliable, but she suspected terribly boring, skirts and trouser suits hanging in her wardrobe since the year dot. No variation for ages in her shade of pink lipstick, despite the samples Clara kept bringing home from the make-up department at work.

She hadn't a clue how to apply eye make-up – anytime she tried, she ended up looking like some kind of demented banshee. Clara had attempted to teach her once or twice, but had quickly lost patience: 'You're useless, Mum, you don't even try to do it properly.' And she was right. Yvonne couldn't summon up enough interest in eye shadow and mascara to make a real effort.

Not that Greg ever minded what she looked like. There was never any pressure with him to be remotely attractive. He was just Greg, her late husband's first cousin, whom she'd known for more than twenty years.

He was like the brother she'd never had. Despite Dolores's wishful thinking, this evening's dinner with Greg couldn't be further from a date.

But at some stage, she was going to have to learn how to use make-up properly, like it or not. Because the next time she sat opposite a man in a restaurant, hopefully not too far into the future, she was determined to look as good as she could. First impressions counted for a lot, she knew that.

She wondered how long it would take Peter to suggest a meeting. Of course they'd only been emailing for two weeks, it was early days. But he seemed nice, if a little serious, and Yvonne was curious to see if he lived up to his own description: blond hair, blue eyes, six feet tall, slim build. He sounded very interesting indeed. Pity he hadn't posted his photo on the site – some members did – but then, Yvonne hadn't put hers up either. Imagine if someone she knew saw it.

She tried to picture Dolores's face if she ever found out that Yvonne had joined an internet dating site. That would be worth seeing. Not that Yvonne had the remotest notion of telling her.

Mind you, if someone had told Yvonne herself just three weeks ago that she'd be considering a date with a man who'd made contact with her over the internet, she'd have been just as surprised. But recently, after vowing for years that she'd never dream of going near those websites, she'd wondered if they'd be worth a try. What had she to lose? She could be totally anonymous, put up no photo, use a made-up name until she felt confident enough to reveal her real one.

So she'd taken the plunge one evening when Clara was out with Barry. She'd entered her details, called herself Deirdre (her second name, so not completely made up), paid her three-month subscription (much cheaper than she'd been expecting) and sat back nervously to see what would happen.

Nothing had, for the first few days. She felt a bit put out when she logged on, entered her password and saw 'no new messages' coming up on the screen. Was she expected to make the first move? No, that was definitely beyond her – she'd die rather than send an email to a complete stranger and risk him ignoring it. If anyone was expecting her to take the initiative, he'd have a long wait.

And then, four days after she'd joined, she got her first message. It was from Easyrider, and it came right to the point.

'I like doing older women.'

She checked his profile and discovered he was twenty-two – a year younger than Clara. She deleted his message and wondered if she'd get her money back if she contacted the site management.

But the next night there was a message from Peter39.

'Hello there. I read your profile and I was wondering if you'd like to chat.'

According to his information, he was a year younger than her. He put 'professional' as his occupation. He enjoyed good wine and old films. He had no children, had never been married. He lived in the country. For his ideal first date, he had written:

I would like the lady to choose so that she would be relaxed.

Yvonne's reply took her twenty minutes.

'Hello, Peter. Nice to hear from you. Yes, I'd enjoy a chat. Tell me a little more about yourself.'

Not too eager. Friendly and casual. Giving him the opportunity to talk about himself – weren't men supposed to like that?

He replied the following night. He told her he was from abroad and that he'd come to Ireland a few years ago to pursue a personal relationship that hadn't worked out, but had stayed on afterwards because he liked the Irish way of life.

Yvonne told him she was widowed with one daughter. She said she was sorry his relationship had failed and felt slightly guilty for the lie.

He sympathised with her about her husband's death. He told her he regretted not having children. He said he enjoyed being with his nieces and nephew whenever he got a chance to see them, which wasn't often. He added that he was interested in hill walking and sailing.

She told him she'd done some hill walking a few years ago, but hadn't found it very enjoyable because of the bad weather. She didn't add that she'd joined the hill walking club in the hope of meeting new men and had left when it became clear that all the remotely interesting ones were married.

He told her he was a Capricorn.

She told him she was a Pisces.

He told her he couldn't cook, but that he liked spicy food.

She sent him a very simple recipe for stir-fried beef with ginger.

He said—

'Yvonne?'

She whirled around, feeling like a guilty schoolgirl. Pawel stood in his doorway. 'Just to let you know that Mr Doherty called while you were out to cancel his Thursday appointment. He'll ring again to reschedule.'

'Right – I'll make a note.' Yvonne pulled the appointments book towards her. The surgery door closed behind her with a soft click. Pawel didn't believe in making unnecessary noise. Just as well he didn't believe in reading minds either.

The front door of the clinic was pushed open as she was rubbing out Mr Doherty's name and Yvonne looked up with a bright smile on her face for Mrs Nugent.

NUMBER EIGHT

The hat was home. It hung, as usual, on the left handlebar of Kieran's dark blue bicycle, which leaned against the wall in the hall. Dan pulled his front door key out of the lock and listened. From the kitchen he heard the soft murmur of music – Lyric FM, when Kieran had any say – and the subdued little rustling that meant someone was moving around. He smelled fish and frying onions. Was there ever a more appetising smell than frying onions?

His mouth watered as he draped his jacket over the bicycle's saddle and rested his umbrella on the carrier. Handy, having someplace to put everything.

He'd meant, ever since he and Ali had moved in, to attach a row of hooks to the wall, something to take the jackets and keys, but typically he'd never got around to it, had been happy to drape his jacket over the banisters, to drop his keys on the bottom stair, much to Ali's annoyance. But now there was the bicycle, which Kieran used much more than his car, and it did the job perfectly. Dan tried to imagine Ali's face if she saw a slightly battered (but still perfectly serviceable) bike propped against the wall in her hall.

Not her hall now, of course. He opened the kitchen door.

'Ah, there you are.' Kieran's face was lightly flushed. He wore a yellow and blue striped apron over his usual corduroys and rumpled T-shirt. His hair was rumpled too – he got considerably more dishevelled when he cooked. Picasso lifted his head and eyed Dan from the kitchen chair. Dan eyed him back. A truce, he supposed you'd call it, what he and Picasso had now. Dan turned a blind eye to the cat in the kitchen and Picasso didn't venture any further into the house – at least, not while Dan was around.

'It'll be fifteen minutes.' Kieran adjusted the oven temperature. The kitchen was filled with the most appetising aromas and the sink was piled high with saucepans, wooden spoons of various sizes, and bowls.

'Grand.' Dan considered tackling the saucepans, then decided they could wait. 'I'll have a shower so.'

Nothing had been agreed between them. No official arrangement had been made or even suggested, but almost three weeks into his tenancy, Kieran was most definitely the cook, and Dan had no objection.

He'd never eaten so well. He couldn't cook to save his life and Ali hadn't been much better. Between them, they'd lived off a combination of frozen meals and takeaways, with the occasional leathery chicken or charred steak if one of them had taken a notion to attempt a meal.

Since Ali's disappearance, Dan had avoided the takeaways where they were both so well known, and had lost his appetite for the frozen pizzas and chicken kormas. His evening meals had settled into a pattern, usually involving something out of a tin and either eggs or sausages. Nothing that had to be peeled or chopped, nothing that took more than five minutes to cook. A small saucepan and a frying pan were all he needed.

On his first evening in the house, Kieran had poached a salmon steak, boiled new potatoes and steamed spinach; he had whisked flour, milk and dill into melted butter to make a creamy sauce that he drizzled over his fish. In fifteen minutes he had produced a meal that would have taken Dan forever and probably still would not have been edible.

Dan had wrapped a slice of white bread around two sausages. 'That looks good.' He tried not to stare at the plate opposite him. He loved salmon, hadn't had it in ages.

Kieran cut into the pale orange flesh. 'I like to cook, always have.' He loaded his fork with spinach. 'Just taught myself as I went along, really.' He dipped the fork into a puddle of sauce.

Dan's sausage sandwich could have done with some of that sauce. 'I don't go in much for cooking.'

'No?' Kieran speared a little potato. 'It's not for everyone, I suppose.'

Dan unrolled his bread, slathered ketchup in and took another bite. It tasted slightly better. 'Good skill to have, though.'

'It is.' Kieran cut another chunk of fish. 'It's handy alright.'

Dan chewed and swallowed. Against such competition, his sausages had completely lost their appeal. Maybe they should eat dinner at different times. Maybe they could set up a rota for the kitchen so Dan wouldn't be tormented.

The following evening, Kieran grilled a pork chop, boiled some baby sweetcorn and sugarsnap peas and gently stewed a chopped Bramley apple.

Dan fried two eggs, opened a tin of beans and made a mug of tea. Kieran drank water.

The tantalising smell of perfectly cooked pork wafted around the kitchen. Dan needed a distraction. 'Are your parents still alive?' Might as well find out a bit about the man he'd taken into his house.

'Both gone.' Kieran cut into his chop and added a helping of apple sauce. 'Father died of TB when he was young, I don't remember him at all, and Mother got a stroke that killed her eventually. I looked after her as long as I could, but I had to put her in a home at the end.'

'You were an only child?'

'I was. Father died before they had a chance to have any more, and Mother never remarried.'

The night after that, Kieran told Dan he'd sold the family home to finance the nursing home fees for his mother. 'I didn't need a big house to myself. Took a lease on a little flat above a hardware shop. It hardly felt like a move – I was less than a mile from the house. Mother only lasted two years in the home, though.'

Dan tried hard to keep his eyes off the plump chicken breast on Kieran's plate. The golden wedges of potato, the carrot batons shiny with butter. 'You never bought another house after she died?' He lifted his tuna and onion sandwich. A blob of salad cream slid out and plopped onto the table.

Kieran shook his head. 'I could have, but . . . I don't know, I'd got used to the flat by then, it suited me fine. Although I did miss a garden – it's nice to have it here.' He took a sip of water. 'I find something appealing about not being tied to a property. I like having my options open.'

He cut into the chicken. Dan's eyes flicked down to the succulent flesh.

'Also, I figured that since I've got no dependants, what was the point of leaving anything behind me? I'd have no one to leave it to.'

While that made perfect sense to Dan, he found the notion unsettling. Would he be thinking like that in twenty years' time? Would he decide to sell this house at some stage, find a little flat to rent and live off the money because there was no one to leave anything to when he died? He scooped up the salad cream blob and transferred it to his plate.

Kieran eyed the half-eaten sandwich. 'I'm thinking of doing a fish pie tomorrow night, but it's as easy to do it for two as for one. Would you be bothered at all?'

Dan did his best to look only mildly interested. 'That sounds good, as long as you let me get the ingredients. What would you need?'

From then on, Kieran had produced most of the evening meals and Dan kept the fridge stocked. Dan didn't offer to cook and Kieran didn't suggest it.

After dinner Dan did the washing up and Kieran went out to the patio to smoke his one cigar of the day. It was the perfect arrangement.

Over the course of a few more dinner conversations – the only time, really, that they were together – it emerged that Kieran had worked as a reporter for years in various parts of the country. 'I wrote for a number of different provincial papers, everything from obits to sports results. I moved around a fair bit.'

'But you grew up in Castlebar.'

'That's right, and Mother still lived there, so I used to go home as often as I could to keep her company. And when she got the stroke, I gave up the job I had then, which was in Athlone, and moved back to Castlebar.' Kieran shook a wok of chopped vegetables, sprinkled soy sauce in, and everything sizzled loudly.

'Back to the home place.' Dan was sitting at the table, a can of beer in his hand. Picasso was sprawled on the floor in a square of sunlight.

'That's right. Mother needed someone with her and I didn't like the idea of paying a stranger to do it.'

'So you got another job.'

'Well, I did and I didn't. As long as I was making a move, I decided to try my hand at being my own boss. I made contact with the publications I'd worked for in the past and offered my services as a freelance contributor. I told them I'd do anything as long as I could work from home – review books, write a cookery or gardening slot, make up crosswords, that kind of thing.' He added strips of beef to the wok and splashed in more soy.

The salty, savoury smell wafted around the kitchen. Dan's stomach rumbled loudly in response. He drained what was left in the can.

Kieran shook the wok again. 'So that's what I'm still doing. I write a cookery column for one and review books for a few others, and in the summer I do the occasional gardening feature.'

Book reviewer – that would explain the scatter of paperbacks in the sitting room, the bundle perched on the side of the bath, the collection on top of the fridge.

Another evening, Dan took cutlery from a drawer, filled a jug with water. 'You said your mother died eight years ago.'

Kieran was whisking a sauce for their roast lamb. 'Right. Eight years in August.'

'So . . . you were ten years in the flat altogether?'

'That's right.'

'What made you move?' Dan took two glasses from a shelf. 'And why did you choose this place?'

Kieran's story intrigued him, as much for what wasn't being said as for what was. There had been no mention of his ever being married or attached to anyone. And what had prompted his move to Belford, eighty miles from Castlebar? His work hadn't changed. He hadn't mentioned friends or family here.

Kieran shrugged and stirred the sauce. His back was to Dan. 'Ah, it was just time for a change, I don't know. And why Belford . . . no idea, it could have been anywhere.' He lowered the heat under the broccoli and bent to take the lamb from the oven.

And that was it. Not very informative, but Dan could hardly demand a fuller explanation.

Perhaps inevitably, Dan was becoming more interested in food. In the supermarket he picked up a loaf of bread called 'garlic and rosemary foccaccia' and brought it home. The crust was hard, but inside it was the colour of avocado, soft and holey as a sponge, and it tasted interesting. He explored the salad section and came home with radicchio and Chinese leaves, leaving the butterhead lettuce alone. For the first time in his life he bought potted mussels and goat's cheese.

And then, one night, it was Kieran's turn to ask the questions. He sprinkled salt on a baked potato and said, 'I'm guessing you haven't always lived on your own.'

Dan had assumed it would come up eventually. 'No. My marriage broke up a couple of months ago.'

Kieran nodded. 'Sorry to hear that. Must have been tough.'

'Yeah.' Dan dug his fork into the floury potato. 'We were married two years.'

'Right.'

'Picasso is really her cat. She left him here.'

'I see.' Kieran looked at the cat, perched in his usual chair. 'I gathered you're not big on cats.'

Dan had to smile at that. 'Not really.' After a while, he said, 'It was my wife who persuaded me to go freelance. Up until we met I was working for a publisher, earning about two-thirds of what I do now.' He'd already told Kieran about the proofreading and copy-editing.

'And you have the office in town.'

'Yeah – gets me out of the house.' Although calling it an office was pushing it. 'Cubicle' would have been more apt, or even 'broom cupboard'.

Every weekday morning, Dan left the house around nine and walked the short distance through Miller's Lane to the main street. He turned left at Kennedy's Shoe Repairs and Key Cutting, passed Clery's newsagents, the Daisy Belle boutique, Sullivan's pub and the Lotus Blossom restaurant. Then, less than seven minutes after leaving his house, he opened a green door and climbed two and a half flights of stairs, past the homeopath and the beauty therapist on the first floor, past the little toilet on the next half-landing, past the accountant on the second floor, past the point where the serviceable brown stair carpet ended, till all that lay ahead of him was an unpainted plywood door.

His office was a lot smaller than his bathroom at home, with one small window that barely allowed enough daylight in, a fan heater that turned the room from freezing to tropical in under ten minutes, a table that just about held his laptop, a single chair and a phone line. It suited Dan perfectly.

In theory, he could have worked at home – all he really needed was a computer and internet access – but when a friend had mentioned the little room that was going for next to nothing above his girlfriend's cousin's homeopathy business, just about the time Dan was thinking of going freelance, the idea had appealed to him.

He liked the notion of going to the office like everyone else, and he was under no illusions about his lack of focus. So easy at home to wander into the kitchen for coffee, to while away half an hour over the hedge with a neighbour. The more he thought about it, the more he realised how much he needed an office.

Ali thought the idea was ridiculous. 'You're paying good money for this' – she stretched out an arm and almost made contact with the opposite wall – 'when you can work at home for nothing?'

Uncharacteristically, Dan had stood his ground. 'It's plenty big enough for what I need, and the weekly rent is less than I can earn in half a day.'

Ali was unimpressed. 'That's not the point.'

He put a hand to the back of her neck and squeezed gently. 'I want to get out of the house, just like you.'

'So go for a walk at lunchtime.' But she didn't pull away.

'And I'll get a lot more work done than if I was at home.' He tapped the pads of his fingers along the top of her spine. 'I'll make sure I'm home before you in the evening. I'll pretend I was there all day.'

Ali shared rooms with two other solicitors in Charleton, about thirty-five miles from Belford. Her commute, on a good day, was forty minutes each way. Considering that she rarely left work before six in the evening, Dan felt quite safe in making this promise.

'It's still money down the drain.' She wasn't happy. 'I suppose you've got to sign some kind of a lease so you'll be stuck with paying for this, even when you discover I'm right.'

Dan kneaded the flesh of her neck quite hard. 'There's no lease – I didn't have to sign anything.'

No need to mention the three months' rent he'd paid upfront. She hadn't asked about that.

'Well . . .' Her head dropped forward, yielding to his hands. 'I suppose if you must . . .'

He put his mouth to the side of her neck and bit. She tasted of peanuts. He spoke against her skin. 'C'mon, I'll buy you dinner. Chinese or Indian?'

After Ali had walked out on him, the office was even more of a haven for Dan. It was where he went to escape the reminders – the overmantel mirror she'd found at a car boot sale that only needed a touch-up to the gilt frame. The picture she'd given him for his last birthday. The rug they'd brought back from their honeymoon in Turkey. Her cat, Picasso.

Everywhere he looked in the house, there was something to bring her into his head.

In his office, which Ali had avoided after that first visit, there was nothing to torture him. No pictures, no mirrors, no rugs on the worn wooden boards. He'd bought the heater when the air had sharpened last autumn.

The beauty therapist downstairs was about fifty, with severely cut pale brown hair and clothes that floated after her when she walked. She nodded solemnly whenever she and Dan came face to face on the stairs. She smelled of baby powder.

The homeopath, Thomas, was less aloof. He and Dan had gone for a pint a few times when they happened to be leaving together. Thomas was in his late fifties, divorced a number of years ago and sharing a house with his older, widowed brother.

'We have our own habits, we don't always see eye to eye,' he told Dan, 'but, by and large, I have to say it's a lot less hassle than living with a woman.'

And so far, after nearly three weeks of sharing his house with another man, Dan had to agree. Kieran didn't complain if Dan left a damp towel on the bathroom floor, if Dan's socks didn't always make it to the laundry basket. He never objected to feet on the coffee table. A few crumbs on the worktop didn't bother him, or a scrap of marmalade in the butter dish or a kitchen floor left unswept for more than a day.

It wasn't perfect, of course. Kieran was an insomniac, up and down the stairs at all hours, sometimes turning on the telly in the middle of the night so the muffled sound floated up to Dan, directly overhead.

And Kieran broke things. In the few weeks he'd been there, he'd exploded the kettle by plugging it in empty. He'd dropped one of the six crystal tumblers that Dan's parents had given him and Ali last Christmas. He'd snapped off one of the washing machine knobs so now they had to use a screwdriver to change the settings. He'd somehow managed to crack the wooden toilet seat (Dan didn't ask), forcing them to sit sideways or risk the excruciating sting of a trapped thigh. He'd broken his key twice in the front door lock and wrenched a socket from the wall when he was pulling out his electric toothbrush charger.

He was always most apologetic when any of these

incidents occurred, always made every attempt to repair or replace any casualties. To tell the truth, none of them really bothered Dan. What did a broken kettle matter when water boiled just as easily in a saucepan? So what if you had to position yourself a little more cautiously on the toilet seat? What was the loss of one glass when they had five left between two of them? Who cared about a broken washing machine knob? It wasn't as if either of them used it that often.

On balance, Kieran's arrival had been a good thing – particularly his arrival into the kitchen. And he was always pleasant company. He didn't try to talk during the news or sulk when *Match of the Day* came on, and he replaced toilet rolls and bleach, often before Dan realised they'd been running low.

And every so often he played the most beautiful music, standing between the two apple trees at the bottom of Dan's garden.

The first time Dan heard it, the evening after Kieran had moved in, he assumed his new tenant had the radio on upstairs or was playing a CD. He lowered his book and listened. The music wafted in through the open sitting room window behind him; Kieran must have his bedroom window open too.

Dan didn't know much about classical music – he and Ali had shared a devotion to Pink Floyd, the Kinks and early David Bowie – but he was taken with this piece. It dipped slowly, the notes coiling themselves into a wonderfully haunting melody, then soared up again dramatically, each phrase more poignant than the one that had gone before.

Dan was entertained for twenty minutes or so as one piece followed another, with a slight pause between each. They seemed to be played with the same instrument – it sounded like a violin to Dan, or something else with a bow. Very pleasant.

After a while it stopped and Dan got up and went into the kitchen to make tea. As he plugged in the newly replaced kettle (Kieran had insisted, although Dan was perfectly happy with the saucepan), the back door opened and his new tenant walked in carrying a violin. 'Hello there.'

Dan stared. 'Was that you? Were you playing the music?'

'You heard me?' Kieran laid the violin on the table. 'I went right to the bottom of the garden.'

'I thought you were the radio. You're very good. You don't have to go outside.'

Kieran smiled. 'Actually, I like to play in the open – it gives the music room to breathe. I was stuck inside when I lived in the flat and the sound always felt too big. It's much better here.'

Dan put a teabag into his mug. 'Have you been playing long?'

Kieran took a glass from the draining board and filled it with water. 'All my life, just about. Mother sent me for lessons kicking and screaming when I was eight. It was a good few months before I could admit that I actually liked it. Now I think I'd die if I couldn't play.'

'What was that piece you played first, the one that kept going up and down?'

Kieran thought. 'I'd say it was 'The Swan', from

Carnival of the Animals. It's really a piece for piano and violin. Do you play anything yourself?'

Dan laughed. 'No, apart from air guitar at the discos about twenty years ago – I was good at that.' He ran his hand along the curves of the violin. 'I was afraid you might turn up with a drum kit.'

Kieran laughed, unwrapping a strip of chewing gum from its foil cover. 'No danger of that.'

The funny thing was, Kieran hadn't a note in his head. Dan would hear him humming sometimes in the bathroom, horribly off key. His whistling, equally toneless, set Dan's teeth on edge. How could he play so well and be utterly tone deaf?

But, all things considered, Kieran's arrival had been a good thing. Not the ideal scenario, of course – in Dan's perfect world, Ali would still be there and Brendan would have emigrated to Australia ten years ago – but for someone Dan had been forced to take in, Kieran was perfectly OK.

When Dan came downstairs, showered and changed, the fish pie was out of the oven and Kieran was ladling bubbling, creamy chunks onto two plates.

'That looks good.' Dan's fried egg and sausage dinners seemed so pathetic now. He wondered suddenly how he'd go back to them if Kieran decided to move on – he might have to learn how to cook. The thought, surprisingly, didn't terrify him.

'Oh, almost forgot. This arrived for you today.' Kieran took a blue envelope from the worktop and held it out to Dan.

Ali's slanting, spiky handwriting jumped out at him.

His stomach somersaulted. 'Thanks.' He folded it and stuffed it into his jeans pocket. The first letter she'd written since she'd left, just over two months ago now. The first contact since she'd driven off, crying, in her navy Golf . . . He took an open bottle of wine from the fridge, splashed some into a glass and shut her out of his head. Or tried to.

He tasted his fish pie. The sauce was buttery and rich with onions. The cod flaked in his mouth, just firm enough. 'This is great, really.'

They'd met on holidays in Ballybunion, Dan and Ali. He was twenty-eight, Ali was two years younger. She'd been with her sister, he'd been with two friends he'd known since secondary school.

They'd gone swimming at the same time and she'd saved his life – or so she always insisted.

'I was just fooling around.'

'You were going down for the third time. I'd hardly call that fooling around.'

'I was only doing it to get your attention.'

'Well, you certainly managed that – I could hardly miss you, spluttering and waving like a mad thing.'

He'd been trying to impress her, of course, showing off out of his depth, pretending to be a much better swimmer than he was. The wave had caught him off guard, had swept him up and thrown him down. His mouth had filled with rushing, salty water. His ears thundered with the sound of the sea. He could see nothing, felt himself being dragged by the current, broke the surface briefly, gasping for air, flapping his arms frantically, and sank back under—

And then he was being pulled upwards, someone was grabbing his hair, a hand came around his neck and cupped his chin. He broke the surface again and thrashed his arms, trying to get his balance back.

'Hold still, would you? Just relax, for fuck's sake.'

She was competent, Ali. One of those people who got things done instead of just talking about doing them. She'd sailed through law school, had her pick of companies when she'd flashed her first-class honours degree at them.

He took another determined bite of pie. 'What's the flavouring in this again?' If Ali'd heard him, asking about flavouring.

'Dill, mostly, but a little parsley too.'

She was Dan's third girlfriend and he was the fourteenth man she'd slept with. They married in Ali's home town and all of Dan's family were there.

Including Brendan Fitzpatrick, his mother's youngest brother.

Well, whatever she had to say now could wait. Dan was in no hurry.

He reached for his wineglass. 'And the sauce?'

'Just flour, butter, milk, black pepper, salt – and a bit of wholegrain mustard to give it some bite.'

The corner of the envelope pushed against his hip.

'I'm copyediting a book on fishing at the moment. It lists the best places to fish around the country, how to contact the licensing authorities, that kind of thing. Might try my hand at it some time – fishing, I mean.'

'Yes, I've done a bit, in Loch Corrib mostly.'

It wasn't as if she could have anything to say that he wanted to hear. She was hardly writing to tell him she'd made a mistake. Hardly begging him to let her come home.

He pushed back his chair, picked up his plate. 'Sorry, I just remembered an email I need to send – better do it while I think of it. I'll put this in the oven. It won't take long.'

In his room he tore open the envelope, still telling himself he didn't care. Whatever she had to say didn't matter now.

Dear Dan, she wrote.

Yeah, right.

I hope this finds you well—

Oh, very well. Extremely well. Never been weller, in fact. He raced ahead.

—and I'm sorry again that things went the way they did.

Like she'd had no choice. Like Brendan had been holding a gun to her head, forcing her to leave him.

I'm writing now because there are things we need to sort out.

Things we need to sort out?

I'll give you a ring in the next few days and we can arrange a mutually convenient time to meet, if you're agreeable.

A mutually convenient time. If you're agreeable. Like she was writing to one of her clients instead of to the man she'd slept beside every night for more than two years.

Naked, she always slept naked, winter and summer.

He pushed the image out of his head.

Take care,

Ali.

Not *love Ali*, obviously. Never *love Ali* again.

He screwed up the single blue page and flung it at the wastepaper basket beside the wardrobe. Then he went over, picked it up from the floor. He opened it, smoothed it as best he could and read it through again.

. . . there are things we need to sort out. What did she mean by that? Did she want to collect the CDs and books she'd left behind? Was she going to say they'd have to sell the house they'd bought together because 'they' no longer existed?

He read it through a third time, searching for the tiniest hint that she was unhappy, the most minute suggestion that her letter was really a cry for help. *I'm sorry again that things went the way they did.* Would she say that if she was perfectly happy now? And *take care* at the end – didn't that sound almost like an endearment?

And *Dear Dan*. She could have just said Dan, couldn't she?

He dropped the crumpled page onto the bed and went downstairs to finish the dinner he suddenly didn't want. He'd have to wash it down with a whole lot of wine.

Kieran tried to let it go. He pushed Adam away a hundred times a day. He did his best to keep his mind from going over and over that night in his head, inventing a dozen different endings except the one that had actually happened.

The one that maybe he could have prevented if he'd tried. And it was that thought, the terrible, unforgivable fact, that he couldn't shake out of his head – that maybe he could have made a difference, if he'd tried. But he hadn't. He'd just stood there and let it happen. He'd done nothing, nothing.

It kept him awake in Dan's red-brick house. Kept him pacing his room, and when that became too small, kept him wandering through the house, too tired to read, flicking through the TV channels for anything to shorten the night.

If he'd been alone he would have played the violin, like he used to in the flat. That had worked sometimes. But he couldn't play music with Dan upstairs, so night after night, he switched off his bedroom light and closed his eyes and waited for sleep.

And night after night, Adam kept him awake.

NUMBER NINE

'Only a month to go.' Grainne cut a carrot disc in half and smiled across the table at her daughter-in-law. 'You must be getting excited.'

'Not really.' Kathryn reached for the dish of potatoes. 'I don't take much notice of birthdays any more.' She touched her chin. 'You've got some gravy there.'

'Thank you, dear.' Grainne lifted her pale blue linen napkin, one of a set she'd given Kathryn and Justin at Christmas, and dabbed lightly around her mouth.

Listen to them, you'd think they were the best of friends. You'd swear they never had a cross word between them – and, of course, they didn't. Grainne was much more subtle than that.

'Pass the butter, love.' Justin, as ever, trying to keep the peace. Sensing the atmosphere, feeling the tension, as he always did. The two women closest to him, walking on eggshells around each other.

'I suppose you'll have a bit of a do.' Grainne looked enquiringly at Kathryn. 'Don't worry, I'll make myself scarce.'

Oh, she was so clever. Waiting for Justin to say, as of course he did, instantly, 'Now why on earth—'

And Kathryn butted in hastily: 'But we're not planning anything.' The last thing she wanted was a big fuss, another opportunity for everyone to be reminded of how much older than Justin she was. Because that was exactly what Grainne wanted, to keep twisting that particular knife in Kathryn's side. To keep punishing her.

'Oh, but you'll have to mark it in some way. Your forty-fifth – that's quite a milestone.' Grainne beamed across the table. 'Even just a small crowd. You could invite your friend from number seven—'

'Yvonne.' Grainne had met her several times. She knew very well her name was Yvonne. Why pretend she didn't?

'Yes, and maybe a few people from work – they'd know both of you, after all.' Grainne turned to Justin. 'What do you think, dear? Shouldn't we do a little something to celebrate?'

We. So much for making herself scarce.

Justin was saying, 'Whatever Kathryn wants . . .' Ever the diplomat.

'We'll think about it. There's plenty of time.' She'd wait till they were alone, convince him that she'd rather spend money on something more worthwhile than a few hours' partying – a weekend away, maybe, just the two of them.

Not, she realised, with a familiar dart of anger, that there was much chance of them getting away on their own anytime soon. Justin would worry about how his precious mother would cope without them, when in reality Grainne was as well able as Kathryn to look after herself. Perfectly able to cook, perfectly capable of walking after a Hoover or making a bed.

But when she'd broken her hip two years ago, Grainne had needed someplace to convalesce when the hospital released her, so of course they'd taken her in, just until she became fully mobile again. And in the few weeks it took for that to happen, Grainne managed to drop enough subtle hints to Justin to convince him that it would be cruel to send her back to her own home.

'She hates the thought of living alone again – she's got used to the company.'

She'd got used to being looked after, more like it. Got used to having her washing done and her meals cooked and her doting son around to ferry her to hospital every time she felt a little twinge.

At first, Kathryn tried to be tactful – Grainne was his mother, after all. 'Of course she's welcome here, but darling, I think it would do her good to be independent. She might begin to feel useless if she stayed here with us doing everything for her. She's still very capable of being on her own.'

And when that didn't work, when Justin kept trying to convince her that Grainne just needed company – 'I'm sure she doesn't expect us to wait on her hand and foot, I'm sure she'll make herself useful' – Kathryn, dreading the thought of living full-time with Grainne, changed tack.

'But it's our house. It's not fair of her just to land in on top of us when she doesn't need to. We'll have no privacy – she'll be here all the time.' It sounded childish and selfish, but she didn't care.

Justin's face had hardened. 'Not fair? It's not fair for her to feel lonely, to want a bit of company? That's a bit mean, don't you think? We've plenty of space here.'

'We haven't got that much. This house isn't exactly—'

'So are you saying you don't want her because we haven't enough room? I thought you were worried about her losing her independence. Make up your mind.'

She let out her anger then. 'Your mother is well able to live on her own. You can visit her as often as you like – I'll visit her. She can have all the company she needs.'

'And she'll still go to bed on her own every night, and wake up on her own.'

'She did that no problem before she broke her hip. What's changed now?'

He looked at her then, a look that shocked her with its coldness. 'Right then, since it's clear you don't want her, I'll tell her we can't keep her.'

And he'd turned to go, and of course Kathryn, never able to bear his anger, had grabbed his arm to stop him. 'Look, if it means that much to you . . .'

He'd promised they'd still have time to themselves and they'd hardly know Grainne was there, and it wouldn't make much difference at all, having her living with them.

And Kathryn had nodded, as if she believed every word.

In the two years since then she'd held her tongue. What good would it have done? Grainne was with them now – forever, it looked like. Oh, her house was still there, lying empty at the other end of town, but she showed not the slightest inclination to go back to it.

And there wasn't anyone who could help them out with her, who could take her for a couple of weeks now and again to give them time to themselves. Justin's father William certainly wasn't a candidate, having quietly departed the marriage twenty-nine years before to move in with his business partner's fiancée.

Justin's only sister, Ann, lived in Spain – not that she would have been much use to them even if she'd been around the corner. According to Justin, his mother had hit the roof when Ann announced, at the age of twenty-one, that she was gay.

'Told her never to darken her door again – I think she actually used that phrase. They haven't laid eyes on each other since.'

'How many years ago was that?'

'Let's see, it must be twelve now.'

Twelve years without seeing your only daughter. Twelve Christmases. Twelve birthdays.

'Did Ann ever try to make contact?'

Justin shrugged. 'She phoned a few times at the start, but Mother just hung up on her.'

'Does Grainne ever ask you about her?'

He shook his head. 'She's a stubborn woman, my mother.'

Kathryn could think of several less charitable words than 'stubborn' to describe her mother-in-law. Now thirty-three, Ann Taylor lived in Seville with her partner Suzannah, an American artist she'd met one summer when they'd both taught English in Galicia. They'd opened a small restaurant and an even smaller adjoining craft shop, and they lived upstairs in a surprisingly spacious loft apartment full of Suze's paintings and ceramics.

Justin and Kathryn had spent a week there in the spring, two years before, and had sat every evening under the stars on the roof garden, wrapped in rough cream blankets and drinking red wine. Grainne's name hadn't come up once in the week.

Suze had painted Kathryn lying in a hammock one afternoon, wearing a short red dress, one hand resting on her stomach and the other trailing over the side. She was dappled with sunshine, her cheeks were flushed and she looked perfectly happy. They'd brought the painting home, had it framed and hung it over their bed.

Three weeks after that, Grainne had tripped over the flex of her iron and broken her hip.

Now Kathryn took another sip of wine, conscious of her mother-in-law's eyes on her, and cast around for a safe topic of conversation. Something that would move them away from her birthday.

She turned to Justin. 'Con's retirement do is on Friday, isn't it? Remind me to make a hair appointment tomorrow.'

'Oh, yes, I need my roots doing too.' Grainne placed her knife and fork neatly side by side on her empty plate – nothing wrong with that appetite – and smiled at Kathryn. 'Would you be a dear and make an appointment for me some afternoon?'

'Of course.' Kathryn began to gather plates. 'I'll try for Wednesday, will I? Might as well get the bargain.'

Grainne's smile slipped a little. 'Any afternoon will do – it doesn't have to be Wednesday.'

'Right.' Because Wednesday is half-price day for senior citizens and you don't like being reminded that you're one of them, even though you never lose an opportunity to remind me of my age. 'I'll just take the first free slot, then.'

As Justin began to talk about the old mill up the lane finally being demolished – 'I heard there's going to be an arts centre there' – Kathryn loaded the plates into the dishwasher and glanced out the window.

There was Dan in next door's garden, pushing that old hand mower of his through the grass. See how he was struggling – his lawn must be full of lumps and bumps. No wonder it was always such a fright. Kathryn kept meaning to offer him the loan of their petrol mower and kept forgetting to mention it when they met.

He must be uncomfortable. Even from this distance, she could see his T-shirt clinging to his back. How long was this heatwave going to go on? Must be nearly a month already and no sign of a break in the weather. Not that she was complaining – Grainne did enough of that for all of them put together. The heat gave her migraines, it kept her awake at night, look how it was ruining the garden . . .

As Kathryn was about to turn away from the window, an older man came out of the house next door and immediately Dan's little grey cat hopped down from the bin he'd been sitting on. The man shouted something to Dan, who waved a hand and went on mowing. The man bent, vanishing from Kathryn's view, and reappeared a second later holding the grey cat in his arms. Dan's father, maybe, calling around to see how his son was coping with the break-up of his marriage.

'Kath? Finish it?' She turned to see Justin holding the almost empty wine bottle over her glass.

Kathryn nodded. 'Please.' Let Grainne pinch her mouth together as much as she wanted, Kathryn would drink what she liked in her own house. She walked back to the table and picked up the potato dish.

'Everyone ready for dessert? Raspberries and cream – I thought we might have them out on the patio.'

And immediately Grainne said, as Kathryn had suspected she would, 'Oh, in this heat? I'm sorry, dear, I don't think I could stick it. And that lawnmower next door is making a terrible racket. You two go out and I'll stay in here.'

Kathryn gritted her teeth as she put the dish on the draining board. 'Not at all – we'll have it in here. It really doesn't matter.'

'Would you mind awfully?'

'No, of course not.' She turned to Justin. 'Would you dish them out, love? They're in the fridge. I'll be back in a minute – just remembered a call I have to make.'

Clara answered the phone. 'Hang on, I think she's out of the shower.'

Kathryn heard her calling for Yvonne. She took deep breaths as she waited, sitting on the edge of her bed. Safely out of earshot.

'Hi, what's up?'

'Look, I know it's still miles away, but I wanted to invite you to my birthday party.'

'What? You've certainly changed your tune – I thought you were dead against having anything. What's brought this on?'

'You mean who.'

'Don't tell me she's worn you down?'

Kathryn shook her head. 'No – in a way, it's the opposite. It's my new strategy.'

'Your what?'

'Well, you know how she keeps on at me to do something for my birthday?'

'Yeah, so you tell me.'

'And it's because she wants to draw as much attention to the age difference as she can, right?'

'If you say so.'

'I do say so. I could throttle her sometimes. God, it's such a relief to say that out loud. Anyway, I've decided that the best way to deal with her is to show her I don't care, that it doesn't bother me in the slightest. I'm going to have a party and make sure everyone knows it's because I'm forty-five.'

'Good for you – take away her ammo. So, is it going to be a big bash?'

Kathryn hesitated. 'Well, maybe not that big. Just a few from work, and yourself, and Clara if she feels like it, a few bottles of champagne and nibbles probably. We'll see. Hopefully she'll take to her bed with a headache – sorry, a migraine – and we'll be able to enjoy it.'

Yvonne laughed. 'By the way, I have to ask, have you met Dan's new tenant yet?'

'Tenant? I didn't know there was one.'

'There is. I met Dan the other day and he mentioned someone had moved in.'

Kathryn remembered the man on the patio. 'Oh, I did see someone just now. I thought he was Dan's father.'

'Oh, great – he's that old? I was hoping he'd be eligible.'

Kathryn laughed. 'Actually no, he's not that old, more . . . mellow. Quite pleasant looking, from what I could see. And speaking of pleasant looking men, how's the internet hunt going?'

Yvonne lowered her voice. 'You do remember you're sworn to secrecy, don't you? Not even Justin – you promised.'

'My lips are sealed. How many dates have you lined up?'

'No dates yet, but one promising contact. We'll have coffee at the weekend and I'll fill you in. Now, I'd love to stay chatting, but I have to dash – Greg's taking me out to dinner and I'm only half dressed.'

As she hung up, Kathryn hoped again that Yvonne understood how careful she had to be – God only knew who she might meet through one of those sites.

But maybe it was worth a try.

Yvonne had made several attempts to meet men in the past – evening classes in everything from car maintenance to French, hill walking and amateur dramatics – and each of them had been a pretty impressive failure. She deserved to find someone nice this time.

Kathryn walked downstairs and into the kitchen in time to hear Grainne complaining loudly about the raspberry seeds getting stuck in her teeth.

Two days later, she phoned the hairdresser's from work.

'What are you having done?' the girl asked her.

Kathryn watched Justin across the open-plan room, bent over a computer in the accounts department. 'I'm getting my roots touched up so my husband won't leave me for a younger woman.'

She heard the girl's laugh. 'Good for you.'

'Oh, and I need to make an appointment for my mother-in-law too. Could you make that one for Wednesday afternoon, please? She's a pensioner and she likes to get the half-price deal.'

She hoped Justin wouldn't look over at her. He'd wonder why she was smiling.

Five days later: 21 June

Number Eight

Dan waited for his pint to settle.

Monday evening, this early, the only other people in the pub were two men playing cards in a corner. The younger one shuffled, splitting the deck cleanly, splicing the two stacks together with a quick rattle, gathering up the full deck and thumping it on the table once, twice, then repeating the sequence. A single crutch leaned against a nearby chair.

The air in the small pub was heavy. A late afternoon sunbeam, glimmering with dust motes, slanted in through the front window and threw a yellow pool onto the wooden floor. A fly darted around the room, landing briefly on tabletops and chair backs. The older card player slapped his open palm onto the table and said something that made his companion laugh.

The barman leaned on the counter reading the paper and picking absently at a scab on one of his knuckles. Dan didn't know him, had never been in this pub before, on the far side of Belford. He supposed that was why Ali had suggested it – no danger of bumping into anyone they knew.

He was early. She wasn't due for another twenty minutes, but he'd got sick of trying to proofread the same few paragraphs over and over. His mind couldn't settle on the frozen food market in Holland, kept jumping about, pulling up images he'd spent the last few weeks trying to forget.

The first time they'd gone out, a few days after she'd allegedly saved his life, it was to a play in what used to be a church in Listowel's main square. Her choice – he'd asked her if she'd like to go for a drink and she'd said, 'Actually, I'd rather see a play, if it's all the same to you.'

He kept glancing sideways at her, safe in the dimness of the theatre. She wore glasses, little purple-rimmed oval ones that should have clashed with her coppery hair. At the interval she drank rum and Coke with two slices of lemon and no ice and laughed at Dan's Homer Simpson socks. During the second half, she reached across and took his hand and held it lightly on her thigh. He felt the heat of her, remembered her body in the yellow bikini she'd worn on the beach, and promptly got an erection.

In John B Keane's pub afterwards she told him about Picasso. 'He's adorable – completely grey with these huge dark blue eyes. He's tiny – he still falls over when he tries to wash himself. D'you like cats?'

'Er, yeah, I suppose so.' It wasn't a complete lie. He might like cats if he ever lived with one. He might feel differently about them if he owned one.

They got pizza slices at a takeaway afterwards – dried up pepperoni, past-their-best mushrooms – that they fed, in the end, to a stray dog they met on the main street. Outside her B and B she had said, 'Well, I'd ask you in, but . . .'

Her perfume was warm and heady. She had half leaned, half sat against the stone wall outside the house and hooked her index fingers through his belt loops. His three pints gave him the courage to take her face in his hands and brush his lips against hers. As he was about to draw back, she put a hand behind his head, opened her mouth and bit his bottom lip, just hard enough to bring his erection hurrying back. He pressed his hips against her and she laughed softly into his mouth.

'Down, boy.'

The first bed they shared was in a little hotel in Lisdoonvarna, three weeks later. The sheets were decidedly nubbly. Neither of them noticed until the morning.

He'd forgotten her birthday last year and she'd thrown a shoe – one of his – at him.

She'd cried when Picasso arrived home after a two-day absence, minus the tip of his tail.

She couldn't eat strawberries without black pepper. Honey brought her out in a rash. She had strong political views. She slept on her stomach.

She'd stood in front of him two months ago and said, 'Look, I'm in love with Brendan.'

With Brendan – so of course Dan had known she was joking. Uncle Brendan, who'd given them a cheque for two hundred euro as a wedding present. Who'd danced with the bride like all the other men, who'd kissed her cheek when she and Dan were leaving for the hotel at Dublin Airport.

Brendan, who'd helped them move into the red-brick house they'd bought just before the wedding, then stayed to share their first takeaway dinner there.

Brendan, the only one of his mother's brothers who'd never got married.

'Yeah, right,' Dan had said, smiling. 'You and Brendan, love's young dream. Stop messing around and come and eat this before it gets cold.'

But of course she hadn't. They'd already eaten their last meal together, and he'd had no idea.

And this afternoon, all afternoon, the thought that he was about to come face to face with her again – the first time since that horrendous night – had kept him from giving a tuppenny damn about the frozen food market in Holland.

Finally he'd clicked his laptop shut and come away early. Might as well be sitting over a pint as over a job he couldn't concentrate on.

His stomach rumbled and he was tempted to ask the barman if he did sandwiches – he'd been too keyed up to eat lunch – but then he thought of the steak that was waiting for him when he got home, with Kieran's spicy pepper sauce that took the roof off your mouth. He'd keep his appetite for that. Better go easy on the pints though.

He wondered what Ali would say if she knew he was buying fillet steaks on a regular basis these days. In the two years they'd been together, they'd probably eaten steak half a dozen times – and most of those times would have been in a restaurant. He wondered if she still hated cooking or if she and— His mind refused to go any further with that thought. He couldn't bear to imagine them doing anything together, even something as innocent as cooking a meal.

Or not so innocent. He remembered trying to make pancakes one Shrove Tuesday, remembered Ali dipping a spoon into the jug of batter and pasting it solemnly into his hair, then running from him, shrieking, when he'd tried to get even.

He remembered how that night had ended up. How she'd washed his hair, poured jugfuls of hot water over his head, sitting opposite him in the bath.

He picked up his pint and took a deep, savage swallow.

In the corner, one of the card players laughed loudly, swooping on the small bunch of coins on the table and sweeping them towards him.

The phone in the hall had rung two nights ago. He'd been upstairs, had heard Kieran coming out from the kitchen to take it. Had listened for the shout that he knew would come.

'Dan? For you.'

He'd waited until the second hand of his watch had crawled jerkily from three to seven, then got up and walked downstairs, taking his time. Straightening a picture that didn't need to be straightened. Tapping with his middle finger on the banisters as he walked.

'Yes.'

'Dan, it's me.' She sounded hesitant.

He said nothing. He could hear her breathing as she waited.

'Who was that who answered the phone?'

'A friend.' What right had she to know how she'd changed his life? How she'd forced him to change his life?

'Right . . . you got my letter.' It wasn't a question.

'I did.' Not an inch would he give her. He turned his hand over and studied his nails. They needed clipping. There was a fresh slit in the wood of the banister, about three inches long and quite deep. He wondered how Kieran had managed it.

'There's, em, there's something we need to talk about – something important. Can we meet somewhere?'

He thought about meeting her, about sitting beside her and watching her talk, watching her wave her hands around, tucking her hair behind an ear and pushing her glasses up on her nose. And then he thought about watching her getting up afterwards, leaving him to go back to—

'Can't you talk on the phone?'

'No.' She spoke quickly. 'No, I can't. This isn't something I can – Dan, please, just for half an hour, that's all. Please. I really need to see you.'

Why was she so desperate to meet him? He'd wondered suddenly if Brendan knew. 'Can't you at least tell me what it's about?'

'Dan, I can't, not over the phone. But it's really important for both of us.'

Both of us. He pressed a finger hard on the slit in

the banister, felt the rough edges of the splintered wood. Both of us. 'OK. Where do you want to meet?'

The fly buzzed past his ear and his hand flew up, too late. The tabletop was pocked with small black circles – had people stubbed their cigarettes out on it when they could still smoke inside?

One of the card players got up and crossed the room to a door that said 'Toilets'. His companion cleared his throat and spat into the empty fireplace nearby. The barman licked his thumb and turned a page.

Dan lifted his glass and took another deep swallow. His stomach rumbled again and he checked his watch – half six exactly. He tapped his glass on the table and then lifted it. The barman nodded and reached for a pint glass and slanted it under the Guinness tap.

By the time it was poured, she'd be there. Ali was always punctual.

At that minute, as the thin stream of pale, creamy liquid was running down the side of the tilted glass, the door was pushed open. He turned his head slowly, fingers tightening on the empty glass.

She looked the same. No, she looked different. Her coppery hair wasn't hanging loose, it was caught up on one side with a long sparkly clip thing he hadn't seen before. She was wearing a red top and a narrow grey skirt with tiny red dots in it. She carried a small black bag.

She looked younger, and softer. She was pale and her face had fleshed out slightly. Dan stood up quickly as she walked towards him. His chair grated against the floor. A toilet flushed somewhere.

'Dan.' She smiled quickly, glanced around the pub.

He felt the tingle of sweat on the back of his neck. 'What'll you have?'

She dropped into a chair. 'Pineapple juice, no ice, a slice of lemon, please.' He caught a whiff of her perfume as she sat – the same, still the same – and he turned towards the bar. The toilet door opened and the card player came back in, glancing briefly at Ali as he crossed to his table.

Standing at the counter, Dan felt her gaze on him. Taking in the stonewashed jeans she'd always liked, the dark blue T-shirt with the small red pony on the breast pocket that she'd bought him for his last birthday. He'd pulled it out of a drawer two days ago, thrown it into the washing machine, and everything else in there – boxers, shirts, towels, socks – had come out a faded, streaky blue-grey. Kieran hadn't seemed to mind about the hankies.

Pineapple juice. He'd never known her to drink juice – it was always rum and Coke or, once in a blue moon, gin and tonic. She'd never worn her hair like that. Never, as far as he remembered, owned any red clothes – hadn't she always said she hated red? Was she systematically changing everything? Had her life with him been so awful that she'd had to redo every aspect of it?

As he walked back to the table with their drinks, the door opened again and a group of people walked in, talking noisily. Dan heard '. . . but he didn't even realise, you know?' and '. . . every time she does it, I mean every single time . . .' and '. . . they never arrived. She sent them six weeks ago.'

'Well.' Ali held her glass, twirled it between her fingers. 'How've you been?'

He shrugged. 'OK.'

Her hair ornament flashed when she moved her head. Her nails were painted white at the tips – another first. She was wearing a thin gold bracelet he hadn't seen before. She had new glasses, with blue and green frames.

Her wedding ring was gone. Her fingers were bare.

A sudden lurch of rage shot through Dan – she was the one who'd fucking proposed to him, it had been her idea to get married. Two fucking years, that was all she'd lasted. His fingers tightened on his glass as he shifted in his chair, looked past her to the group who had come in, now standing at the counter. Fuck her.

The men wore dark suit trousers and white shirts, with the sleeves rolled to their elbows. Two of the women wore black skirts and cream shirts and the third was in a red trouser suit. The barman shovelled noisily into the container of ice, held glasses under oversized upside-down bottles, tonged in slices of lemon.

'How's Picasso?'

Dan let his eyes wander back to her. A tentative smile tilted the sides of her mouth. Seeing his anger, trying to mollify him. Probably realising that he'd noticed the ring gone. Ali missed nothing.

Dan wasn't mollified. 'Picasso? He's OK, I think.' He drank and wiped the foam from his mouth. 'I don't see much of him. He sleeps outside now.'

Her smile faded abruptly and immediately he was ashamed. That was cruel, that was beneath him. What had been the point of it?

'I took in a tenant.' He tried to make amends. 'That was him on the phone the other night. He loves Picasso, feeds him fish heads. Sneaks him into the house when I'm not looking.'

Her smile didn't come back. 'Look, Dan.' She put her untouched glass down and laced her fingers together. 'There's no point in beating around the bush. I may as well tell you why I'm here.'

She raised her grey eyes and looked at him properly for the first time, and Dan knew, all at once, what she was going to say. She wanted to come back, it had been a terrible mistake. It was Dan she loved, not Brendan.

The card players stood up, one slipping the deck into his jacket pocket, the other one limping on his crutch to the counter with their two empty glasses clamped between the fingers of his free hand.

He wondered if she'd cry. He'd put his arms around her, tell her he loved her too. They wouldn't give a damn that the office workers could see them.

She could move back in tonight – he'd go with her to pack her stuff. Maybe she had it already packed. Maybe it was out in the car.

Kieran would have to move out, of course. Dan hoped he wouldn't be awkward. Just as well now he hadn't signed a lease. Picasso would miss him, but he'd get over it, with Ali back.

She was coming back, he knew it. He was positive.

'The thing is—' She pushed her glasses further up on her nose. 'God, I don't quite know . . .' She took a deep breath, still looking directly into his eyes. He felt a trickle of sweat trailing down the side of his face. He opened his mouth to help her out, and closed it again. This had to come from her. The fly buzzed past his face and this time his hand didn't move.

'The thing is, Dan, I've just found out that I'm pregnant, and it's yours.'

And for the life of him, as a burst of laughter erupted from two of the women at the bar, as one of the men said, 'Ah, come *on* now', as the door thumped shut after the card players, Dan O'Farrell couldn't think of a single thing to say to that.

Two weeks later: 4 July

NUMBER SEVEN

'Now close.'

Yvonne felt the little brush sweep across one eyelid, then the other.

'Open.' Caroline stood back and studied Yvonne's face. 'OK.' She picked up a little pot of something that looked alarmingly green. 'Close again.'

More sweeping, then a little skittering around with the brush. She was going to look a right clown. What on earth had possessed her to pay good money for someone to paint her up like a trollop? She could have done that herself for nothing, and in a lot less time. She'd have to find a loo and scrub it off.

'Now open and look down.' Caroline held a mascara wand in her hand.

Yvonne eyed it doubtfully. 'I wonder if we could leave that out?' It mightn't come off so easily. She might end up worse than ever.

Caroline raised her perfectly shaped eyebrows. 'No mascara? Absolutely not. No woman should leave the house without it. It opens up the eyes and adds drama – and you definitely need it, with your eyelashes.'

Yvonne held her ground. 'But it always makes me look like a panda.'

'You'll only look like a panda if you rub your eyes, so don't rub them. Now, hold still.' Caroline's free hand tilted Yvonne's chin upwards. 'Look down.'

Yvonne wished she had the courage to stalk out. What had happened to the customer always being right? She thought of what else she could have done with thirty-five euro. Bought herself a new swimsuit – her old one was practically indecent, it was so worn. Had a night out with Kathryn, a few drinks and a pizza. Treated Clara to that citrus body lotion she loved. Had her legs waxed – they were badly in need.

She blinked instinctively as the wand pulled at her lashes.

'Don't blink.'

Thirty-five euro to be ordered around by Hitler in a white coat.

'Now close your mouth.' Caroline held what looked like a colouring pencil. Yvonne clamped her mouth shut – what else could she do?

'Not so tight – close it gently.'

Dinner with Greg a few weeks ago had been pleasant, as always. Seafood platter, a bottle of straw-coloured wine and a brandy each afterwards. He'd told her he was flying to Tuscany for a fortnight in August, staying at a friend's villa in the countryside.

'Sounds great. Why don't I have friends like that?'

He'd smiled. 'Why don't you come with me? I know they wouldn't mind.'

'God, don't tempt me.' She imagined two weeks

lying in the sun by a pool or wandering through the galleries of Florence or sitting under the shade of an olive tree with a book and a glass of something cold. Wonderful.

And completely out of the question. 'I'd never get two weeks off in August at such short notice – and anyway, I really don't have the cash after that roof job.'

'You could come for a week. All you'd have to pay for would be your flights – and the odd plate of spaghetti.'

She'd laughed. 'You make it sound as easy as going to the corner shop.'

'It is – and I'd love to have your company.'

But she'd shaken her head. 'Thanks, Greg, it's a lovely thought, and I'm tempted, really I am, but there's no way. Bring me back something local.'

'Don't smile – relax your mouth.'

Caroline was brushing colour onto her lips. Why had Yvonne let herself be talked into this foolishness? Kathryn was fairly sensible most of the time, but she didn't always get it right.

'Go on – it'll really boost your confidence, knowing you look terrific. And I've heard good reports of that woman – Mary at work, her daughter had her make-up done there when she got married, and Mary said she looked fantastic. Go on, you've nothing to lose.'

Nothing except thirty-five euro and twenty-five minutes.

'Right, I think that's it.' Caroline stood back again and examined Yvonne's face. 'Here.' She handed Yvonne a mirror and waited. 'See what you think.'

How on earth was she going to pretend she liked it? Full of dread, Yvonne took a deep breath, lifted the mirror to her face – and said softly, after a few seconds, 'Good God.'

Her eyes were dramatic, all dark-edged and green-lidded, framed with eyelashes that she could have sworn were longer and thicker than they had been twenty minutes ago. Her cheekbones – she had cheekbones! – were defined with subtle colour, a healthy glow, and her skin was clearer than she ever remembered it, not a single broken vein to be seen. Her lips seemed fuller, in a much paler colour than the one she usually wore, a kind of pinky-beige with a slight gloss to it. Much more flattering, she had to admit.

She really did look better, but in a beautifully natural way. She looked as if she'd been born with that face.

'Wow – it's great. I love it.' Yvonne tilted her chin, turned her head. From every angle she had improved.

'You should love it. You look ten years younger than when you came in.'

Yvonne laughed into the mirror. 'Really? Well, that can't be bad.' Caroline might be lacking in the niceties of conversation, but she more than made up for it with her talent. 'Thanks a lot.'

'Enjoy your evening.' The barest hint of a smile crossed Caroline's face and vanished as quickly as it had appeared. Probably avoiding crow's feet.

Driving the thirty-five miles or so to Charleton – thank goodness she'd thought to tell Peter she lived there, where there was little chance of bumping into anyone she knew – Yvonne wondered if Kathryn's turquoise top was a little too low cut; she wasn't used to having such an impressive cleavage.

'I don't want him to think I'm sluttish.'

But Kathryn had insisted. 'You don't want to come across all prim and proper either. No harm to tease him a little, let him know what may be on offer – eventually.'

A truck roared past, surely much too fast. What time was it? She checked the dashboard clock: ten to eight. Another fifteen minutes' driving ahead of her – just enough to be slightly late. She turned on the radio and Sean Keane was singing 'Blackbird' by the Beatles.

Brian had been a big Beatles fan; his favourite song was 'Something'. They'd chosen it as their first dance after they were married.

What had their first date been like? She tried to remember. They were both seventeen when they'd met at the tennis-club disco. She still wore the awful brace on her teeth that her mother had insisted on getting her at twelve. Brian had been standing nearby with a few of his friends and there was the usual pushing and jostling and sniggering. Eventually he'd come over and asked the girl standing beside Yvonne if she'd like to dance.

The girl took one look at Brian. 'No, thanks.'

His face flooded with colour. Yvonne was mortified for him. Without thinking, she grabbed his arm and pulled him onto the dance floor. 'C'mon – I'm dying for a dance.'

She'd rescued him, and he'd fallen in love with her.

He was her first real boyfriend. When they'd finally slept together a few months later, in his narrow rented bed, it was the first time for both of them. Yvonne found it terribly disappointing. Why had nobody told her it would hurt so much and be so messy and be over so quickly? Where was the magic? Where was the ecstasy she was supposed to be feeling?

And why hadn't she had an orgasm? Shouldn't that have been part of it, making up for the pain? She'd given herself orgasms plenty of times – why hadn't it happened with Brian? She thought of the beautiful women in the films, moaning with pleasure, arching into their partners' bodies. No mess there – not even smudged lipstick.

She had to brace herself when they tried again, a few nights later, and it wasn't much better. And just as they were beginning to get the hang of it, they'd got drunk on the night of her Leaving Cert results, forgotten about the condom, and she'd got pregnant.

She hoped Clara's first time had been better. She wondered which of the boyfriends it had happened with – because, of course, at twenty-three, Clara was bound to have had sex with at least some of them. Not that Yvonne was ever likely to find out. On the one occasion she'd attempted, clumsily, to talk about contraception, fifteen-year-old Clara had cut her off. 'It's OK, Mum, we learned about that at school, years ago. I know all that stuff.'

'Oh . . .' How times had changed. At fifteen, Yvonne hadn't had a clue. The closest her school had come to explaining about sex was their religious education teacher, Sister Montgomery, telling them that their bodies were temples of the Lord and should be treated accordingly, that boys had no willpower so it was up to the girls not to be tempting them because once boys were tempted that was it – they had no control over their vile urges.

The subject of sex or contraception had never come up again between Clara and Yvonne. Maybe most daughters felt embarrassed to be having those kinds of conversations with their mothers. Yvonne would just have to hope that Clara was behaving responsibly, particularly as she herself hadn't exactly been the ideal role model.

But so far, so good. Apart from changing boy-friends with alarming regularity, Clara seemed to be coping with that part of her life. She'd never, as far as Yvonne knew, been broken-hearted when a boyfriend had disappeared – if Yvonne commented on the absence of the latest, Clara usually shrugged and said, 'Oh, that's finished. It didn't work out.'

But actually, was her apparent lack of regret such a good thing? Shouldn't Clara be investing a bit more emotion in relationships? Maybe she just hadn't found the right man yet. No harm in that, she had plenty of time.

Yvonne sighed. So much guesswork, so many questions to which only Clara knew the answers. And they'd been so close, once upon a time. For several years after Brian's death, Clara had clung to Yvonne, reluctant, at the start, to let her mother out of her sight. They'd done so much together – from the minute Yvonne picked Clara up from her parents' house after work, they were hardly apart until Clara's bedtime. They went shopping or to the pictures, they cooked dinner together or they curled up on the couch and watched television. Of course, Clara had her own friends too, but more often than not she seemed just as happy to spend time with her mother.

And then, somewhere along the way, Clara had changed. She couldn't say exactly when, but Yvonne had become aware of a withdrawal, of Clara pulling away from her. Perfectly natural, of course, when she was growing up, to want her independence; to be honest, they'd probably been a little too close before that. But still, Yvonne had found this new distance difficult to take.

'She'll get over it,' Yvonne's mother assured her. 'In a few years she'll be your pal again. Every girl goes through it.' So Yvonne had waited, had held her tongue when Clara made another excuse not to go shopping, disappeared to a friend's house or up to her room for the evening, leaving Yvonne alone. It'll pass, she told herself. I can wait.

But it hadn't passed. Clara had never come back, or not in the same way. Of course they got on fine. Nobody seeing them together would have said there was a problem, but Yvonne sensed a lack of closeness, an invisible boundary between them, that try as she might, she couldn't penetrate.

Kathryn told her to count her blessings. 'She could have broken your heart – look at all the girls who go totally off the rails after they hit their teens.

She could have gone on drugs, got pregnant, anything. I'd say keeping things to herself is a very minor offence. And I know she doesn't tell you about the boyfriends, but eventually they put in an appearance, don't they?'

Working in the hardware section of Belford's only department store, Clara had plenty of opportunities to meet men – and with her looks, she was rarely without a willing escort on a night out. But if it weren't for her opening the door to them now and again, Yvonne would never have known they existed.

She sighed again. Clara was who she was, just not given to confidences – or not with her mother at any rate – and Yvonne would have to live with it. She turned up the radio and switched her mind to the evening ahead.

She'd been to the restaurant twice before – once for dinner with Clara for her nineteenth birthday, shortly after it opened and everyone was talking about it, and last year for lunch with Bernie, an old friend, between trawling through the end of the summer sales in Charleton's various boutiques.

The menu was nicely imaginative, using local ingredients wherever possible. Yvonne hoped they still served the goat's cheese and berry roulade that she and Bernie had discovered there last time.

Thinking about food made her realise how starving she was. Normally she and Clara ate around half six. Hopefully Peter wouldn't object to a woman with a healthy appetite.

She passed the sign that told her she'd reached

Charleton and drove slowly through the narrow streets to the restaurant. She pulled into a parking space and turned off the engine.

What time was it? She pushed up the sleeve of Kathryn's top and checked her watch. Ten past eight. She felt a skitter of nervousness. What if he wasn't there yet? She'd have to sit and wait for him without even a gin and tonic to give her a bit of courage – she daren't, not on an empty stomach, not with that drive home.

She hoped he wouldn't mind that she hadn't used her real name. She'd meant to tell him before they met, but hadn't been able to figure out how to put it without sounding ridiculously paranoid. She'd just have to come clean tonight. Hopefully Peter wasn't his proper name either.

She studied her reflection in the rear-view mirror – no lipstick on her teeth, face still looking good. She should buy that shade of lipstick and maybe that green eyeshadow and the mascara too, it made such a difference. Clara would show her how to put them on properly, and she'd pay attention this time.

She checked her neckline – show him what's on offer – and ran her fingers through her hair. Had that last cut been a bit short? She smiled at the woman in the mirror.

You look ten years younger. You're a confident, sexy woman. He's lucky to have your company for the evening.

She wondered if she had a flirtatious smile. She practised batting her eyelashes, then stopped in case she messed the mascara.

She slung her bag over her shoulder and opened the car door. Nobody on the street – hopefully he was sitting inside, feeling just as nervous. She locked the car and started walking towards the restaurant door.

The evening was cooler than recent ones. She should have brought a shawl or a jacket. But it would be warm inside and she'd probably be going straight home afterwards.

Unless they hit it off. Unless, right from the start, they clicked and they went for a drink afterwards and sat in some cosy bar for hours because neither of them wanted the date to end. Unless they ended up booking a room in one of Charleton's hotels. She pushed open the door of the restaurant, tingling with anticipation.

And there, at a little corner table, looking every bit as nervous as Yvonne felt, wearing a navy suit she'd never seen on him and the yellow buttonhole rose they'd agreed on in their last email, sat Pawel Tylak. Her boss.

When Yvonne's daughter Clara was ten, she had gone on a school tour with her twenty-six classmates, their teacher, the special needs assistant for Mark, who had ADHD, and three parents. They got the bus to a smallish city, fifty-three miles from Belford.

Part of the tour involved a visit to a museum, which was full of skeletons of animals, ancient weapons and dummies dressed in musty-smelling clothes from years ago. When they went in, they were met by a man with no hair, a red face and a wide bottom that made the girls elbow each other.

He wore grey trousers and a navy blazer with gold buttons, and led them around the main room, telling them about the exhibits. Clara was soon bored.

She edged away from the main group, pretending to be fascinated with whatever was under the glass cases she was passing – dirty arrowheads, rows of dusty medals, yellowing pictures of old people in black clothes, tattered pages covered with scratchy, blotched writing that she couldn't read.

She reached an open doorway. Nobody called her name, nobody put a hand on her sleeve and told her she had to come back. There was no one else in the main room with them, apart from one man in a dark green coat and a brown hat, who was studying one of the dummies and didn't seem to notice her.

She slipped through the doorway and found herself in another room with no glass cases, just lots of paintings on the walls and wooden benches in front of them. She snorted at the thought of sitting on a bench staring at a painting. How dumb was that? Like pausing a DVD and watching the still screen.

She moved on, through a second doorway that led out into a corridor. She passed a door with 'Toilets' written on it, thought about whether she needed to go and decided she didn't. Just past the toilets was another doorway to her left. She turned in.

It was smaller and more dimly lit than the previous rooms, with a big screen on the far wall. She stood behind the benches – more benches, three rows of them – and watched what was happening on the screen.

A head-and-shoulders picture of a man appeared

with floppy black hair, a pale face and round glasses. That was replaced, a few seconds later, with another. Same glasses, more black hair and a small, tidy moustache. Both men were vaguely familiar to Clara. Everything was in black and white. A woman appeared on the screen then, in an old-fashioned dress with a wide lace collar and hair that looked as if it had been folded up, like an accordion, then released. A string of pearls hung around her neck, resting on the lace collar.

Just as Clara was about to turn away – this was almost as boring as watching a painting – a bit of moving film came on, a man carrying a briefcase, walking down a street in quick motion. It reminded Clara of the old Charlie Chaplin films they sometimes showed on TV on Sunday mornings and she giggled.

'It's funny, isn't it?'

Clara swung around. The man with the brown hat was standing behind her. She hadn't heard him come in. She couldn't see his face properly because of the shadow the brim made and because of the dimness of the room. She thought he might be a bit like Graham, who worked in the newsagent's at the corner of their road. She liked Graham – he let her take whichever sweet she wanted from the Pick 'n' Mix when she went to get milk.

'It reminds me of Charlie Chaplin,' she told the man, and he nodded.

'Yes, you're right – I'd never have thought of that.' He stepped closer to her. His voice was soft. 'You're with the group in the other room, aren't you?

On a school tour, is it?'

There wasn't much point in denying it, with her uniform on. While Clara was wondering if he was going to tell the teacher and get her into trouble, he said, 'Don't worry, I won't tell them you escaped. It'll be our secret.'

Clara smiled, relieved. She wondered if he was Graham's brother. 'Do you know Graham?' she asked him. 'In Belford?'

He nodded. 'He's a great friend of mine.' Then he pointed to the screen. 'I bet a smart girl like you can recognise some of those people. They're all famous Irish writers – but I'm sure you knew that.' He pointed to a small box on the wall beside the screen. 'You can get headphones to listen to a commentary. Next time you're here you can do that.'

Clara watched the black-and-white people hurrying around. She didn't know what a commentary was, but she liked that he thought she did.

It was mostly men on the screen. One was quite fat, his nose was bumpy and his hair looked like he never washed it. Clara didn't think he could be a writer with dirty hair like that. Another wore a tweed coat and had a face like a school inspector's.

'That's Flann O'Brien.' The soft voice was right behind her now. 'He wrote funny books, about policemen and bicycles. I bet you'd like them.'

His hand came to rest lightly on Clara's shoulder. He was pointing to the screen with the other hand. 'And that man, he's James Joyce. He wrote a very famous book called Ulysses. I'm sure you've heard of it.

Maybe when you're older, you'll read it. Only very clever people can understand it.'

She nodded, even though she hadn't heard of *Ulysses*. She felt grown up – he was talking to her like a grown-up. James Joyce's moustache was a little bit like Hitler's. Maybe she should say that, so the man would know how good at history she was.

A man with a shock of upright white hair came on the screen.

'Now that one—' he bent towards her '—is Samuel Beckett.' His mouth was practically touching her ear. It felt ticklish, his breath was hot, but not unpleasant. His fingers smelled of soap. He squeezed her shoulder, just a small squeeze.

Samuel Beckett had the same hair as Grandpa Gavin.

'What did he write?' Clara's shoulder gave a tiny twitch. The man didn't seem to notice.

'Oh, lots of things, stories and plays.' His hand slipped from her shoulder and trailed lightly down her back. She felt the tiny weight of it running along the length of her school jumper, down to the place where her skirt began. She took a tiny step forward, and her knee bumped into the nearest bench.

'The most famous play he wrote was *Waiting for Godot*.' Such a soft voice he had. His breath kept tickling her ear. She could feel a giggle somewhere inside her, but for some reason it didn't come out.

'Waiting for what?'

'Godot.' His hand rested on the curve of her bottom now. Clara felt a stirring of unease low in her tummy – he wasn't hurting her, but all the same it was making her feel a bit funny. He wasn't supposed to touch her bottom. She tried to edge sideways, but his foot was suddenly blocking hers.

'G-o-d-o-t.' He began to stroke her bottom softly, making circles with his hand. 'He died in Paris.'

Clara could feel her skirt riding up. Every circle was lifting it higher. She wondered if he was trying to see her knickers. She couldn't remember which ones she was wearing. She was trapped now between him and the bench. Her heart thumped against her chest. She pressed her knees against the bench.

'*Waiting for Godot.*' His voice was different now, faster and softer. He was almost whispering. 'A very famous play.' Then his hand ducked suddenly under her skirt, and she felt him scrabbling around, pulling her vest out of her knickers. His breath was loud in her ear – 'It's about two men' – hot breath now on the back of her neck, hot fast breath—

Clara found her voice: 'Stop—' She tried to pull away, but his other hand, the one not under her skirt, slid around her waist. 'No, stop—' She squirmed and he held her tighter.

'Two men who are waiting for someone to come along, but he never comes.' He hooked his fingers into the waistband of her knickers.

'No, stop—'

Suddenly he yanked her knickers down over the cheeks of her bottom, making her gasp, and in the same soft voice, he said, 'I won't hurt you unless you scream. If you scream I'll hurt you.'

'Please, I won't—' She was shaking now, with terror and humiliation.

'Aaah.' He pushed her knickers down further, then slid his hand right underneath her, forcing it between her legs, pushing her thighs apart. 'Ah, there now. There we are now.'

'Please stop, don't—' She tried to wriggle away again, but she couldn't escape his fingers, going where nobody went, not even her mother. Her face was burning hot, her heart almost bursting out of her. 'Please—'

'Oh, you're a dirty girl,' he breathed. 'Oh, there's a dirty girl now.' He used a knee to slide her knickers further down her legs and she felt them dropping to her ankles. 'Ah, now. There we go.'

Clara's eyes flooded with tears, blurring the faces on the screen. She couldn't turn, she couldn't move. Somebody waddled quickly down the road again with his briefcase.

'Dirty . . . dirty . . .' The man kept breathing out the word, as his fingers went back and forth underneath her, as he pushed himself against her back, thumping steadily against her, half grunting now, 'Dirty . . . dirty . . . dirty—'

Clara squeezed her eyes shut. She tried to squeeze everything shut. She wanted to go to the toilet, badly. He was forcing his fingers upwards now, burning her, hurting her. She tried to push her legs together, but his hand was in the way. The tears spurted from between her tightly closed eyes and rolled down her face. She could smell herself and she burned with shame and fear.

She tried again to wriggle from his grasp, but his free arm was clamped around her waist. She was completely trapped.

Then he gave a sort of jerky shudder and slumped against her, leaning heavily, almost toppling her over the bench. His fingers stopped moving.

Was he dead? No, she could still hear him – feel him – breathing harshly against her. Clara struggled to turn her head, but she was still pinned too tightly to move. Then, abruptly, the man shoved her away from him. Clara stumbled forwards, half toppling over the bench, her hands flying out to break her fall, her knickers still around her ankles, her heart still hammering inside her.

And then, as she lay sprawled there, shaking all over, she heard him walking out of the room. When she couldn't hear his footsteps any more, she pushed herself away from the bench, jerked her knickers up with trembling fingers and smoothed down her skirt. Then her legs gave way and she collapsed onto the bench.

She smarted, she stung down there. It felt horrible. She felt dirty. She wiped her wet face with the back of her hand. The urge to go to the toilet was almost overpowering, but she was afraid to leave the room. What if he was still outside? She squeezed her thighs tightly together, and that helped a bit.

She could still feel his hand. The echo of it was still down there, doing what it had done.

She wondered suddenly if she'd been raped. They'd learned about good touches and bad touches in class, but nobody had mentioned the word 'rape' – that was something she'd picked up somewhere along the way. She wasn't sure what it meant exactly, but she knew it was something bad to do with sex that men did to women.

It hadn't worked the way her teacher said. She was supposed to say no, to get away, to tell someone she trusted, but none of that had happened. She'd said no, but he hadn't listened. She couldn't get away because he had been too strong, because he'd said he'd hurt her if she screamed. There was no way she could tell anyone what the man had done – she'd be killed for leaving the group if she said anything. They'd probably tell her it was her own fault for leaving the class and going off by herself.

Anyway, she wasn't hurt, not really. Just scared and a bit sore, but that would go away, wouldn't it? It was her own fault. She tried to steady her breathing, tried to take deep breaths.

Her knickers felt damp. She must have wet them a bit. She squeezed her thighs closer together. She'd have to move soon, go back to the group before they missed her.

Suddenly her teacher's face appeared in the doorway. 'Oh, Clara, there you are. You know you were supposed to stay with the class – you can't just wander off on your own like that, you gave me an awful fright. Anything could have happened.' She looked crossly at Clara. 'Come on, quickly. We're going to go for lunch.'

Clara stood up, glad of the dimness in the room.

'I need to go to the toilet,' she said.

The blood on her knickers terrified her. Had he cut her? Had he had something in his hand? She flushed the toilet, took off the knickers, dipped them into the toilet bowl and scrubbed hard until the red was almost gone.

Then she squeezed them out as much as she could and put them back on. They felt pleasantly cool against her still burning skin. She left the toilet cubicle and washed her face and hands. Then she walked out carefully to join her classmates for chicken and chips.

NUMBER NINE

Kathryn unrolled the navy socks and added them to the pile in the washing machine. What else could go in with darks? She rummaged through the laundry basket and found Justin's jeans at the bottom. Turning them inside out, her hand brushed against a bundled-up something in one of the front pockets. Money, probably. He was so careless with money. She put her hand in and pulled it out.

It wasn't money, it was some kind of receipt. She unscrewed it and read 'fragrance €65.00'. It was dated last Wednesday. He'd paid in cash and got five euro change.

Kathryn smiled. A bit predictable, but he'd know he was on safe ground with perfume. She hoped he'd got her usual Yves St Laurent and not taken a chance on anything new. She remembered him coming home from Dublin once with a Jo Malone one she really hadn't liked – hopefully he'd learned from that.

A week to her birthday, and she was actually looking forward to a bit of a fuss, now that she'd decided to go for it. They weren't inviting a big crowd, just seven including Yvonne, who was coming on her own as Clara wasn't free. Dan wouldn't be there either – he'd told Kathryn he had plans, which she doubted.

Justin's cousin, who worked as a barman in town, was going to wear a dinner jacket and pour champagne, and they'd ordered a selection of canapés from the local deli and a cake from a little bakery off the main street. If the evening was fine, they'd be out on the patio.

Kathryn had spent far too much on a silk top and skirt that the sales assistant assured her looked wonderful and that she was hiding from Justin until the night. She was taking the afternoon off and getting her roots done and then she was having her face made up by the lady Yvonne had been so impressed with.

Everything sorted, a nice, no-fuss affair – yes, she was definitely looking forward to it now. Best of all, Grainne wasn't happy.

'Don't you think a sit-down dinner would be more appropriate, rather than this' – she made a face – 'bits of food on trays? That's more suitable for young people, surely?'

Oh, she was so predictable, bringing up age wherever she could. It was laughable, really.

Kathryn had shaken her head, careful not to smile. 'Oh, no, buffets are the in thing now with every age group. And the canapés won't be on trays, they'll be properly spread out on a table and everyone can help themselves. It's less formal than a dinner. People prefer it, really.' She'd be charming and reasonable if it killed her.

Grainne wasn't finished. 'But you can't serve food outside: it'll be overrun with flies and it'll go bad in the heat.' She turned to Justin. 'Tell her, dear.'

Much to Kathryn's relief, Justin had had the sense not to get involved. He lifted his hands and said, 'Nothing to do with me, Mother. This is Kathryn's night, she's in charge.'

No, Grainne wasn't a bit happy now that it looked as if Kathryn had decided to embrace becoming forty-five. It had been that easy after all to get the better of her. Now maybe she'd begin to accept that her son had chosen an older woman, and learn to live with it.

She might even decide to move back to her own house, now that she couldn't annoy her daughter-in-law any more. Kathryn smiled – talk about wishful thinking. It would take more than one setback to shift Grainne.

She threw the perfume receipt into the kitchen bin, added Justin's jeans to the washing machine and closed the door. She poured detergent into the drawer and started the cycle. As she straightened, something caught her eye outside, some movement on next door's patio.

She glanced across, but all she could see from that angle were a shoulder and an arm. She heard the clank of metal, someone whistling. Funny, she hadn't taken Dan for a handyman.

She walked upstairs with the laundry basket, put it back in the bathroom. Then she crossed the landing to her bedroom and peered out the window.

There was Dan's tenant, standing by a higgledy-piggledy heap of bricks. As she watched, he slathered something from a white bucket onto Dan's barbecue with a trowel – something grey and gloopy; was that some in his hair? – and positioned a brick carefully on top. Of course – he was finishing it. About time; must be at least a year since Dan built the first half.

Kathryn looked carefully at the growing barbecue. Were the new bricks a little lopsided? Did it lean slightly to the left? Maybe she was imagining it. What did she know about building anything?

Then she heard a faint 'Is that you, Kathryn?' from her mother-in-law's bedroom. She groaned quietly before settling a smile on her face and turning away from the window.

'Coming.'

NUMBER EIGHT

From his bedroom window, Dan watched Kieran set down another brick and tap it into place with the handle of his trowel. The barbecue was certainly taking shape, even if that shape was slightly peculiar, with a few bricks sticking out at odd angles. It looked to Dan a bit like something a couple of ten-year-olds might have cobbled together on an idle afternoon.

Who cared, though? A wobbly barbecue was the least of his worries right now. Who cared about a couple of unevenly cooked steaks, a few half-burnt sausages?

'I could finish off the barbecue, if you like,' Kieran had said a few evenings ago, and Dan had agreed. These days, Dan was agreeing to anything. If Kieran had suggested sinking a pond in the garden and stocking it with piranhas and maybe the odd crocodile, Dan would have told him to go right ahead.

For the past couple of weeks Picasso had been sleeping in the shed, in the basket that Kieran had brought home one day. 'Fifty cents,' he told Dan. 'That's all they wanted for it.'

Dan wondered how Belford's charity shops had stayed in business before Kieran's arrival. He rarely came home from town without some trophy, usually kitchen related – an apple corer, a garlic press, a hand whisk, a much newer steamer than the one Dan's mother had donated (along with several lidless saucepans) when he and Ali had bought the house.

'I'm a great believer in charity shops,' Kieran told Dan. 'People donate things they've hardly used. I hate to see stuff wasted.'

Once he came home with what he claimed was a cat toy, a bright pink feather tied with a bit of elastic to a length of bamboo. Kieran would shake the stick, making the feather dance, and Picasso would leap around after it like a kitten.

They were definitely a team now, Kieran and the cat. Picasso adored Kieran, nuzzled against his leg while he was cooking, bounded onto his lap any opportunity he got. In turn, Kieran kept Picasso supplied with the fish heads Dan assumed were scrounged from the shops in town. He fervently hoped Kieran wasn't going through dustbins after dark – there was a limit to recycling.

He supposed he should be grateful to Kieran for looking after Picasso. Dan could cope with the cat in small doses, but there was definitely no bond between them. At the end of the day, Dan was more of a dog man – and even if he hadn't been, Picasso would always be Ali's cat.

Ali. His insides lurched, as they always did when he thought of her. He turned from the window and leaned against the sill. He closed his eyes and, right on cue, Ali walked into the bar again and told him she was pregnant.

'It's mine?' He could hardly believe it, didn't dare believe it. 'You're sure?'

Ali shot him a look that was gone before he could decide what it said. 'I'm sure. I'm eleven weeks gone.' She sipped the pineapple juice.

Not rum and Coke because she was pregnant. Eleven weeks pregnant. She'd left him just under ten weeks ago. It must have happened the very last time they'd had sex.

The thoughts slipped quietly into his head, one after another. And then an unspeakable one followed that made him blurt out: 'You are going to keep it, aren't you?'

Ali nodded quickly, frowning. 'Of course I'm going to keep it. You know how I feel about that, for Christ's sake.'

'OK, sorry.' He tried to clear his head, tried to sort his thoughts. 'Well . . . that's—' he stopped. What was it? Just after your wife leaves you for someone else, she finds out she's pregnant with your child. What in God's name would you call that? 'Wonderful' hardly covered it. 'An unfortunate turn of events' didn't come close. 'Incredibly weird timing' might be going in the right direction.

But whatever they called it, he and Ali had made a child together. She'd have to come back now, wouldn't she? Even if it was only for the sake of the baby. Dan could live with that. He'd learn to live with it.

She might even fall in love with him again eventually. It had happened once, hadn't it?

He searched for a way to put it to her. He'd have to try to be tactful. She'd probably be a bit embarrassed about the whole thing. Walking out on him one minute, telling him he was going to be a father the next.

He was going to be a father. Someone was going to call him Dad. Daddy. Someone who might even look a bit like him. He could talk about 'my child'. 'My son.' 'My little girl.' He struggled to keep the smile off his face.

'So . . .' He searched for the right words. 'What happens now?' Watching the foamy rings clinging to the sides of his glass. Not watching her. Afraid, suddenly, to watch her.

Out of the corner of his eye, he saw her shrug. 'Well, I suppose nothing for the—'

No, not nothing, don't say nothing. He interrupted. 'I mean – this changes things. It has to change things, doesn't it?' She must see that. She had to. 'You're pregnant, and it's mine. You have to – we have to . . . make arrangements. It's our child.' Terribly lame, but he couldn't say it. He couldn't beg her to come home. It had to be her idea.

Ali twirled the glass slowly between her hands. She hated her short fingers, wore only narrow rings because she thought they made them look longer. Kept her nails long for the same reason. He knew so much about her.

The fly landed on the table beside his beer mat.

He slapped his palm down loudly, making Ali jump. 'Sorry.' A few heads swivelled at the bar, then turned back.

'God, don't *do* that.'

'Sorry.' The fly buzzed around his ear. He ignored it.

Ali put down her glass, rubbed her hands along her thighs. 'Well, of course we'll make arrangements when the time comes.' She met his eye and the briefest of smiles skittered across her face, then was gone. 'We'll sort things out. Plenty of time. We have months yet. I just thought you should know now, that's all. '

She wasn't coming home. He kept his eyes on her face and after a few seconds she looked away. She wasn't coming home because she didn't want to. Being pregnant didn't change that – why would it? She was with Brendan now, where she wanted to be. What an idiot Dan was.

He drank, deep swallows, conscious again of how hungry he was. Ali glanced at her watch as he lowered his glass.

The watch he'd bought her on their honeymoon.

'Don't let me keep you.' Resentment flooded through him again. 'Lover-boy will be waiting – or should I say lover-man. Long time since he was a boy.'

'Don't do that, Dan.' She reached across the table for his hand and he snatched it out of her way, almost knocking over his glass. 'Look, this child will be as much yours as if we were still together, I promise.'

'But we're not still together. You're with Brendan, and you're not coming back.' He threw it across the table.

Her eyes widened. 'Coming back? Oh, is that what you thought? Oh God, Dan, I'm so sorry, I'm really—'

'You can't – you can't just sit there and tell me you're pregnant with my baby, then walk away. You can't do that.' His voice shook and he didn't care. He gripped the edge of his chair.

Ali stood up quickly. Dan stayed where he was. 'I have to go. I'll be in touch, OK? We'll sort everything out, I promise.'

'Yeah – like you promised to stay married to me.' The bitterness flooded his mouth, he spat the words out. 'Is Brendan looking forward to being a daddy?'

Her voice was maddeningly calm. 'It's natural that you're upset.'

He raised his voice. 'Don't you tell me—' Heads turned again. He glared back them and clamped his mouth shut.

Ali picked up her bag. 'I'll call you soon. We'll talk when you've had time to digest this.' She turned and walked out.

He didn't answer, didn't watch her as she left. She'd hardly touched her drink. He saw the faint pink stain on the rim. He grabbed his glass and strode to the counter. The group shifted slightly to let him order another pint.

When he woke up he didn't remember getting home. He had a hazy memory of telling Kieran the wonderful news he'd just got from his wife and, to his utter mortification, he remembered crying, sobbing into his hands at the kitchen table. He remembered wolfing down the steak that Kieran eventually fried for him with onions.

The following morning he plodded to his office, full of extra strength Disprin, sat in front of the computer and struggled through the day's quota of work.

Since then, in the two weeks since Ali's announcement, he'd been completely unable to get his head around the fact that he was going to become a father to a child who would grow up in another house, raised by another man. Whatever way you looked at it.

Oh, he'd have contact. He knew Ali would be scrupulously fair about him seeing the child. Once a week, maybe. Every other weekend, possibly. The odd holiday, two weeks in Ballybunion. She'd dot the 'i's and cross the 't's on that one – it would be terribly above board and civilised.

But Dan's son – or daughter – would be raised by Dan's Uncle Brendan, to all intents and purposes. And try as he might, Dan could not get his head around that.

God knows what Kieran must think. God knows what Dan had said to him that night – all he could remember for sure was warning Kieran, between mouthfuls of steak, to stay away from women. But he must have said a lot more – not that Kieran had mentioned it since then. Dan had probably told him the whole sorry story, whether Kieran wanted to hear it or not.

He turned to look out of the window again. The barbecue was almost a foot higher than it had been, and so far as it was managing to just stay upright. Kieran was still bent over it, tapping another brick into place.

Picasso was watching from his usual position on the bin.

Dan should help. He couldn't mope around forever. And, useless at DIY as he was, he didn't think he'd make things any worse out there.

As he pulled his shirt over his head, he heard a car out at the back. Justin got out of his maroon Zafira and shouted something to Kieran as he walked quickly up the path. Kieran laughed and waved.

Life went on. Dan rummaged in the bottom of the wardrobe and found the ancient orange T-shirt he'd worn to start painting the sitting room, so long ago now it seemed. Something else he needed to tackle sometime – couldn't leave it the way it was, half paper and half paint.

'White paint,' Ali had insisted. 'Plain white paint. If I have to look at those roses for much longer I'll throw up.'

So white paint it had been. And Dan had been halfway around the room, half the roses had disappeared, when Ali had told him about her and Brendan.

Life went on. In a few months Dan's child would be born. Barring misfortune, nothing could change that. He pulled on his oldest pair of jeans and went downstairs.

Six days later: 10 July

Number Seven

Pawel's head appeared around the door. 'Could you bring in Mr Ryan's file please?'

'Of course.' Yvonne riffled through the pastel-coloured files on the shelves behind her, pulled out Sean Ryan's and walked into Pawel's surgery with it.

'Thank you.' His smile was perfectly polite, just as it had always been. He took the file from her, opened it and Yvonne left the surgery, closing the door quietly.

Thank God they'd got past the embarrassment, survived the awfulness of that evening in the restaurant – although it would be a long time before Yvonne could think about walking in and seeing him sitting at the table, waiting for her, without blushing to her roots and wanting to crawl under something big. God, that was up there with trying to rub off someone's birthmark or opening your parents' bedroom door to find them having sex.

'You said your name was Peter.' She'd blurted out the first thing that came into her head. 'I had no idea—'

'My father's name is Peter, in English.' He looked as dismayed as she felt. She imagined him buying the yellow rose and sticking it in his buttonhole, full of expectation. 'You said your name was Deirdre.'

'Deirdre's my second name. I didn't want to—'

It was awful. A man at a nearby table was watching them over his menu. Yvonne pulled out the chair opposite Pawel and sat down. What else could she do?

'Pawel, I'm sorry about this. I wasn't trying to deceive you.'

He frowned. 'Well, I don't—'

'But I never imagined you'd be on the internet—'

'Well, I haven't ever—'

'Not that it's any of my—'

'No, that's—'

It was horrible. Each of them breaking into the other's protests, both equally mortified. Finally their stuttered explanations faded into silence. Yvonne studied the tablecloth – white, some embossed material, a line where the iron had folded it running from her place setting to his. She could see her reflection in the knife that lay in front of her.

Her made-up face, when all he'd ever seen at work was a slick of lipstick. A wave of heat washed over her, which she hoped fervently was hidden from him by the foundation.

Pawel spoke again. 'You see, I had no idea you were a widow, and you never mentioned what work you did in your emails.' He paused. 'And I never thought you would be . . . on the internet, like me.'

'No, I never did anything like that . . . not until recently.'

She supposed it was the kind of thing you should just laugh at – turning up for a blind date and finding your boss waiting for you. If someone had told her that story over coffee – 'You'll never guess what happened to my friend lately' – she'd think it was hilarious.

Not right now, though. Right now she and Pawel were sitting opposite each other in a restaurant and a waiter was heading in their direction, and as far as Yvonne was concerned, there was nothing funny about their situation.

'Good evening.' The waiter's nails were bitten, but his black jacket was beautifully cut. 'Would you like to order some drinks?'

Yvonne had never felt more like a stiff gin in her life, but of course that was out of the question; they weren't staying. She was preparing herself for their undignified exit when Pawel said, 'Yvonne? What would you like?'

She stared at him. 'Er, I'll have a gin and tonic, please.' What else could she say? Any argument would only add to the general embarrassment.

When the waiter had left, Pawel picked up the menu. 'Well, now that we're here, we may as well eat.' He didn't seem thrilled at the prospect, but under the circumstances that was hardly surprising.

Yvonne toyed with refusing, with having the drink and going home – what on earth would they find to talk about for at least an hour, given the disastrous start to the evening? – but then she decided again on the path of least resistance. It was certainly a less embarrassing scenario than walking out after the gin and tonic – nobody went to a restaurant for a drink – and besides, she was starving. She took a deep breath, picked up her menu and said, 'Fine.'

So they stayed for dinner. Yvonne ate vegetable and prawn kebabs and Pawel had pork with marsala and juniper. Neither of them ordered a starter or a dessert and the wine list stayed closed. Pawel had coffee afterwards, Yvonne had mint tea.

They talked about hill walking: he enjoyed it, she didn't, much, because of the weather. Sailing: he was thinking of buying a boat, but they were so expensive in Ireland. Cooking: he'd never learned, she'd always enjoyed it. (He didn't mention the recipe she'd sent him, and neither did she.) Music: he liked classical, she preferred country. Books: he only opened them for work, she always had at least three novels on the go.

They agreed that the food was good in the restaurant. He hadn't been there before. She told him about Clara's birthday meal.

They got by, but there was a trickle of embarrassment running through the conversation that made every mouthful a trial. They rushed to fill any little pause. They laughed too loudly at each other's weak jokes. Every so often Pawel would start drumming on the table lightly with his fingers, then catch himself and stop.

She had to admit he looked good. His white shirt was dazzling against the navy of his suit, the pure white of a brand new shirt. She wondered if he'd bought it specially for the date. His tie was dark orange with a thread-thin navy diagonal stripe. He wore oval silver cufflinks. He was clean shaven and his nails, as usual, were immaculately manicured.

Why hadn't she recognised him from his description? Tall, blond, blue eyed – it was Pawel to a T. And he'd told her he was foreign – it seemed so obvious now. If either of them had posted a photo on the site, this could have been avoided. Yvonne certainly wouldn't have responded to an email from Pawel, and she was quite sure he would have ignored one from her. They were work colleagues, no more.

Wait till she told Kathryn, who was dying to hear about Yvonne's first internet date. She'd laugh, of course. Who wouldn't?

When the bill came, Pawel insisted on paying, and Yvonne, anxious again to minimise the awkwardness, didn't try to dissuade him. They walked out together and stood on the path. Yvonne pointed towards her car, just a few feet away.

'Well, there's me.' She put out her hand, arranged a polite smile on her face. 'Thank you very much for a lovely meal.' She searched for a way to lighten the atmosphere. 'Sorry again about the mix-up – but at least we ate well.'

Pawel managed a half-smile that was just as polite as her own. He shook her hand. 'I'm glad you enjoyed it, Yvonne. Good night.'

Neither said, 'See you on Monday.' Pawel waited while Yvonne got into her car. She put her key into the ignition, conscious of him standing on the path. Such a gentleman. She wished he'd forget his manners and leave her to it. She pulled away, waving out the window at him. He waved back solemnly.

All the way to Belford, she played Patsy Cline loudly and drove slightly too fast. When she got home it was twenty past ten and Clara was watching television in the sitting room.

She couldn't not go in. As far as Clara knew, Yvonne had been meeting up with a friend she hadn't seen in a while who'd recently moved to Charleton. At least now Yvonne would only have to put up with Kathryn's amusement.

'You're early.' Clara had a bare foot propped up on the couch, four of the five toenails painted purple. Her head was wrapped in a cream towel. 'Wow, I like your make-up.'

Yvonne leaned against the door jamb. She'd forgotten about the make-up. It seemed like six months since she'd walked out of Caroline's little salon, all excited at the prospect of meeting Peter. 'I decided to treat myself, for the laugh.'

'Nice. So, how did it go?' Clara bent towards her foot and dabbed at her little toenail with the brush. 'Did you find enough to keep the conversation going?'

Just about. Yvonne smiled. 'It was fine, we had a good chat.'

'Think you'll meet up again?'

First thing Monday morning. 'Possibly – we didn't make any arrangement, but she has my email address.' Talk about one lie begetting another.

One thing was for sure: she wasn't going near that site again. If it wasn't sex-mad youngsters emailing her, it was her boss fooling her into thinking he was someone else. She'd forfeit the membership – no money was worth the evening she'd just had.

She stayed away for three days. On the fourth, when she and Pawel were finally able to look at each other properly, when the agony of embarrassment she felt whenever she had to talk to him began, finally, to lessen, she typed in her password and pressed enter.

Just for curiosity. Not that she had the slightest intention of responding to anyone who might have contacted her. Absolutely not. She was just curious, that was all.

There were four messages in her inbox, none from Peter. Naturally. One was from manofsteel, who'd emailed a couple of times before. Yvonne had responded to him without much enthusiasm; Peter had sounded more interesting. This time, manofsteel was telling her about his voluntary engineering work in Somalia the previous year.

The other three messages were from strangers: one was from Benwallace in Cincinnati, who asked if Yvonne lived anywhere near Cork, where his grandmother, Martha Cleary, came from. Another was from Goodlookingguy, asking if she liked adult movies. The last was from Dirtyoldman and simply read 'How about it?'

She still had the guts of two months' membership left – be a bit of a shame to waste that. She deleted the other three messages and answered manofsteel.

Hello again. Nice to hear from you. Somalia sounds very exciting, and very different from here. Was it hard to come back to Ireland after nearly a year abroad? I've never gone away for longer than two weeks, and France is the furthest I've been.

What else? Emailing strangers was harder than it sounded. Did he care that she'd never lived abroad? Would she tell him about going to meet an internet contact and finding her boss waiting for her? No, of course she wouldn't.

What kind of music do you like? I'm a country music fan, mostly American – Johnny Cash, Patsy Cline, Dolly Parton, Billy Ray Cyrus. Did I mention that I'm widowed, with one grown-up daughter? My husband died in an accident, nearly twenty years ago now. I work as a receptionist in a health clinic just across the road from where I live.

That would have to do, she was out of inspiration. She shut down her computer and got ready for bed.

The following night – last night – manofsteel replied.

It wasn't hard to come back from Somalia. I missed the pint of Guinness and the rain, and the home comforts in general. I've never been to France, would you believe? Must go there sometime, drink the wine, eat the snails. I'm sorry

*your husband died so young – that must have
been tough, bringing up a child on your own. I
got divorced last year, after five years of living
apart from my ex-wife. Relief all round.*

*Our musical tastes couldn't be more different.
Country music brings me out in a rash. I'm an old
rocker, the Stones, Clapton, Pink Floyd, Joe
Cocker. We'll have to agree to differ, and get
headphones.*

He signed himself Joe. He was ten years older than
her. He sounded nice, and fairly normal. Maybe she'd
keep emailing him for a while, see how it went. What
had she to lose? She'd already been totally humiliated
– surely the law of averages meant it couldn't possibly
happen again.

'Come on, Yvonne, you're doing overtime.'

She looked up from her desk and there was
Dolores, lunchbox in hand. 'Oh, is it that time
already? Hang on a sec.'

She and Dolores hadn't had lunch together all
week. Dolores had been off work with a sore throat on
Monday and Tuesday, and when she'd come back,
Yvonne had found enough reasons – a trip to the
hardware shop for wood stain for the shed, shopping
for an outfit for Kathryn's birthday, a visit to the
library with overdue books – to avoid her on
Wednesday and Thursday.

Silly as it sounded, Yvonne was convinced that
Dolores would sense that something had happened
between herself and Pawel and wouldn't rest until

she'd got the whole story out of her. She was already so eager to pair Yvonne and Pawel off – the thought of her discovering that they'd had dinner together was too awful to contemplate.

But today, Friday, the excuses had run out. They walked down the street, turned into the park and made their way to the usual bench. The sky was mottled with clouds, but so far there was no sign of rain.

Dolores opened her lunchbox and took out a tub of cottage cheese. 'Fionn is entering a painting competition. His teacher has high hopes.'

'That's great.' For once, Yvonne was grateful for Dolores's children – they'd keep the conversation away from her social life. 'So he's artistic, then?'

'Oh, yes – gets it from Martin's side of the family. I can't draw to save my life.'

Yvonne unwrapped her cheese and tomato sandwich. 'And the others? Are they arty too?'

Dolores considered. 'Well, Chloë's very good – you should see the cat she drew the other day. I must bring it in to show you. Hugo is more into the academics, though. He came top in his class at biology in the Easter exams. Did I tell you?'

Several times. 'I think you might have mentioned it. They're all doing very well, aren't they?'

And just as Yvonne was beginning to relax, Dolores dipped her spoon into the cottage cheese and said, 'So, what have you been up to lately? Any more dinner dates you're not telling me about?'

To her horror, Yvonne felt a blush flooding her face. She bent over her sandwich, pretended to be picking something out of it. 'Dinner dates? No, not since the one with my . . . cousin. And I told you that wasn't a date.'

Dolores stared. 'You're going as red as a beetroot. Come on, what are you hiding?'

'Nothing – there's nothing to hide, believe me.' But the evidence was there – Yvonne could still feel the heat in her cheeks. Forty-two, and still blushing like a sixteen-year-old.

Dolores was studying her. 'Is there a little romance starting up, then, with you and your cousin?'

It was a straw, and Yvonne clutched at it gratefully. 'Well, maybe just a harmless flirtation, nothing serious.' She apologised silently to Greg. 'But he has invited me to Tuscany next month – he's going to stay in a friend's villa for two weeks.' That should keep her well away from Pawel.

Dolores's eyes widened. 'You're joking.'

'No, I'm serious. Don't worry though, I'm not going. Can't leave you in the lurch, and anyway I've no money.'

Thank God Greg had rescued her, even if it meant that Dolores now believed that he and Yvonne were an item. It was safer than having her find out about Pawel, much safer. And she could dispose of poor Greg in a few weeks, no harm done.

'Oh, that's a shame.' Dolores put the lid back into her empty cottage cheese container. 'Martin and I went to Tuscany on our honeymoon.'

Yvonne stared at her. 'I thought you went to Canada – didn't you tell me you visited his sister?'

Dolores looked blank for a second, then shook her head. 'No, that was for our first anniversary. Tuscany was the honeymoon. I should know.'

'Right.' It wasn't surprising that Yvonne had got it wrong. She hardly paid much attention to Dolores's chatter. She finished her sandwich and checked her watch – half an hour to go. 'I'm cooking dinner for my father-in-law tomorrow tonight. He usually comes on the second Saturday of the month, but I was out last Saturday, meeting an old schoolfriend, so I had to switch him. And I'm off to a birthday party tonight, in a neighbour's house.'

Thankfully, Dolores was quite happy to hear about Kathryn's party, and Yvonne's budding romance with Greg was temporarily forgotten.

NUMBER NINE

'You look lovely. That colour is so good on you.'

Kathryn smiled. 'The tag said raspberry sorbet, so of course I had to buy it.'

'And the necklace is perfect with it.'

'A happy accident.' Kathryn sipped from her glass and added, 'I love what you're wearing.'

Yvonne looked down at her lilac blouse and wide-legged, cream trousers. 'Thanks. About time I splashed out on some decent clothes. Clara had taken to walking ten paces behind me when we were out together.'

Kathryn laughed. 'She's a hard act to follow, that daughter of yours. Always so up to the minute.'

'Yes. Being twenty-three is half the battle, of course. I think she might be single again, by the way. Haven't seen poor Barry around lately.'

'Really? Did she tell you?'

'Oh, she tells me nothing – I won't know for sure until the next boyfriend shows up.'

'Mmm.' Kathryn paused. 'And speaking of boyfriends—'

Yvonne groaned. 'Oh, don't – you've had your laugh.'

'No, I'm not laughing, honest. Just wondering if you and Peter have got over your mutual mortification?'

Yvonne grimaced. 'Just about. It took a while, but I think it's safely in the past now.'

Justin appeared holding a bottle. 'You ladies ready for a refill?' The bartender cousin had had to leave for work half an hour earlier.

'Yes, please.' Kathryn smiled at him. 'Are you having fun between serving drinks?'

He topped up their glasses. 'Absolutely. And the birthday girl?' He leaned and brushed Kathryn's cheek with his lips. 'Doesn't she look marvellous, Yvonne?'

'She certainly does.' Yvonne watched him threading his way through the people on the patio. 'Now there's a man in love with his wife. Have I mentioned how jealous I am of you with your handsome husband?'

Kathryn sipped. 'Every time you see me. We're going to have to find you a nice young man of your own.' She ran a finger around the rim of her glass. 'I still say Greg would be perfect.'

Yvonne groaned. 'Yes, and you've said it often enough – and now I have Dolores at work convinced that Greg and I are about to ride off into the sunset.'

'How come? I didn't think she even knew Greg.'

'She doesn't. But I sort of pretended we're an item.

I was terrified she might find out about Pawel somehow. I figured it was the lesser of two evils.'

Kathryn giggled. 'Poor Greg, the lesser of two evils. Well, if you're not interested in him, it looks like it's back to the Internet for you.'

'Actually—' Yvonne stopped and glanced around. Another couple were dangerously close, but they seemed to be deep in conversation.

'Actually what?' Kathryn was staring at her. 'Are you telling me you've got someone else lined up?'

'Ssh – not quite.' Yvonne sipped the cold champagne, enjoying the gentle buzz in her head. The evening was just warm enough to linger a little longer on the patio. Justin was lighting the candles in the glass lanterns that sat on top of the fence bordering the decking. 'I was going to tell you in a while, if anything happened.'

'Go on.'

'Ah, it's nothing, really – just this fellow called Joe sounds nice. We've emailed a few times. I'll let you know if there's any development.'

'You certainly will, you trollop.'

Yvonne looked around the little patio, glowing softly now with candlelight. 'Shame your mother-in-law's missing all this.'

'Very funny.' Kathryn made a face. 'That woman's the biggest hypochondriac you could meet. Migraine, my foot. D'you know what she gave me for my birthday?'

Yvonne smiled. 'Not yet.'

'A pair of anti-ageing creams, one for night time, one for day. Talk about subliminal messages.

She never misses a trick.'

Yvonne laughed. 'Oh, very tactful. I thought you said you were going to invite Dan, by the way.'

'I did, but he made an excuse I didn't believe for a minute. Poor thing probably doesn't feel very sociable.'

Yvonne reached for a smoked salmon roll from the nearby table. 'Have you met the cowboy yet?'

'Cowboy? Oh, the tenant. No, but I've seen the hat. Priceless.'

Yvonne had glimpsed him a few times in the garden, talking to Dan or feeding the grey cat. Once or twice he'd cycled past her in the street, whistling. You couldn't miss the hat. 'Poor Dan – imagine having to share your home with a stranger just to pay the mortgage.' She tried to keep a straight face. 'I notice they've finished off the barbecue.'

'God, did you see it? Not a clue, either of them – and they'll never get that cement off the patio. They're well matched.'

The light faded, striping the sky with purple and pink. In their glass casings, the candles glimmered softly. Vivaldi's 'Summer' wafted from the stereo.

From her bedroom window, Grainne watched her daughter-in-law's birthday party. Forty-five years old. Look at her, smiling and laughing as if she had something to celebrate. Wearing a suit that was much too young for her. Drinking champagne that had probably cost Justin the earth.

In the dimness of her room, Grainne smoothed the end of the linen curtain between her fingers.

Much later, Kathryn studied her husband's face in the mirror as he opened the clasp of the beautiful necklace he'd given her for her birthday, and she wondered again who he'd bought the perfume for.

NUMBER EIGHT

He could eat a horse; nothing like a few pints to put the edge on your appetite. Dan belched comfortably as he walked past number nine. Some kind of music was playing – he could barely hear it. Something civilised, no doubt.

Maybe he should have gone, it had been nice of Kathryn to invite him. There'd be decent grub there too. But the chicken korma in the white bag under his arm smelled damn good.

He checked his watch, peering in the almost-dark: nearly ten. He wondered if Kathryn had believed his excuse – a night out with friends – and then he decided that he really didn't care. She'd probably only asked him because she felt sorry for the deserted husband. Dan got on fine with Kathryn and Justin, but he'd hardly call them his bosom buddies.

And who would he have known there anyway, apart from Yvonne? He'd never been any good at small talk, had hated trying to make conversation with Ali's solicitor colleagues at their Christmas parties. At least he wouldn't have to endure that any more.

He hadn't intended going out tonight, was planning to park himself in front of the telly as usual. Kieran was away for the weekend, visiting a cousin in Donegal, and Dan had bought a six-pack and a frozen pizza. But somehow the empty house had got to him. It felt like it had just after Ali had left and he couldn't bear it, he'd had to get out, had to be somewhere busy enough that it would stop him thinking his same bitter thoughts.

So he'd walked the three blocks to a pub he and Ali had often been to. He could have gone further, made sure he wouldn't bump into anyone they knew, anyone who might ask him why Ali wasn't out with him. But he had to meet people eventually, they'd have to learn what had happened. Might as well get it over with.

As it turned out, the pub was pretty quiet. Not surprising, really, when he thought about it. Middle of summer, most people were probably away, lying on a beach somewhere or strolling through a gallery or doing whatever normal people did on holidays.

He and Ali had talked about going to Italy this summer.

He nodded at the barman – Jim? John? Dan could never remember – and pointed to the Guinness tap. 'One of those.'

'Haven't seen you in a while.' Jim/John held the pint glass under the stream of stout. 'Where's herself?' There it was.

'We've split up.' The first time he'd said it out loud. 'She ran out on me.'

The barman shot him a sympathetic look. 'Ah, hard luck, mate. Sorry about that.' He put the half-full glass on the counter to settle and turned to take a bottle of Scotch from the shelf behind him. 'Here.' He poured a measure and put it in front of Dan. 'Chaser on the house.'

'Thanks.' A free drink for the abandoned husband. Dan never drank whiskey, apart from an occasional hot one on a bitterly cold winter's night. He sipped, and it hit the back of his throat and he felt the warmth as it slipped down. 'That's good.'

'Twenty years in the making. You won't get much better.'

Three pints and two chasers later, the pub had filled up a bit and Dan had met a few regulars who asked him about Ali. The more he said it, the easier it got. His wife had left him – so what? It happened every day. Two other couples they used to socialise with had split up too, one after just eight months of marriage.

He didn't mention the pregnancy. He wasn't ready to share that item yet.

In the end, hunger got the better of him – that, and the knowledge that one more pint would have him out for the rest of the night, and he didn't fancy holding his head all day Sunday.

He got a takeaway from the Indian restaurant two doors down from the pub – another regular haunt of his and Ali's, but the man behind the counter was unfamiliar and Dan didn't have to tell him why his wife wasn't with him.

As he reached Miller's Avenue, nicely mellow, and turned in at his gate, the door of number seven opened and Yvonne's daughter walked out.

'Hi, Dan.' She wore a deep green mini-dress. Her legs were very long. Dan tried not to stare at them. What was her name again? Heidi? Johanna? Ali had called her the Bombshell.

'Hello. Off out for the night?' Great, very intelligent. It's ten o'clock on Saturday, she's walking out of her house done up to the nines, and you ask her if she's going out. Brilliant. No wonder you're going home with a chicken korma.

She smiled. 'Just the cinema with a few pals. We're going to see the new James Bond.' She raised her beautifully arched eyebrows. 'Want to come?'

Oh, he was tempted. For a few seconds, Dan almost said yes. To be surrounded by sweet-smelling young women who'd help him forget about Ali for a few hours – it was almost irresistible.

But then she said, 'Oh, you have a takeaway.' She sniffed. 'Mmm, smells like Indian.'

Dan nodded. 'Chicken korma.' He wished he could remember her name. 'My dinner.' In the street-light, her hair was extremely shiny. Her lips were shiny too, and dark. He wondered what she'd do if he grabbed her and stuck his tongue between those shiny lips. Probably slap his face. He grinned at the thought.

Clara laughed. 'I'd say you've had a few drinks, Dan.'

'Just a few.' He must look pathetic, rolling home half sloshed on a Saturday night with his dinner in a paper bag. Just his luck to be spotted by the best-looking woman in the neighbourhood.

'Well, I won't keep you – wouldn't want your

chicken korma getting cold.' She touched his arm briefly. 'Maybe I'll drag you to the cinema another night.' And then she was gone, leaving a sharp, fruity scent after her. Much lighter than Ali's heady perfume, which he'd sometimes felt he was drowning in.

He watched her walk towards the alley that led to the main street. What was she? Nineteen? Twenty? When she'd rounded the corner, he turned back towards his front door, rummaging in his pocket for the keys. Food, before he dropped with the hunger.

As he was tipping the chicken onto a plate, her name leapt into his head.

Clara.

One week later: 18 July

NUMBER NINE

Kathryn pushed her little fork further into the softened earth and slowly teased up the dandelion root. Amazing how long those roots were, even the young dandelions. Nosing down deep into the ground, determined not to be disturbed without a struggle.

She threw the weed into her trug and shifted the green foam kneeler a bit further along the flowerbed. She loved gardening, loved trying to get the better of the dandelions and the bindweed that kept coming back, no matter how often she pulled them up. She had to admire their stubbornness, even as she battled with it.

The only trouble with gardening was that it gave you time to think. What else could you do in the soft, twittering late-afternoon atmosphere, with little to distract you, your hands working automatically, no need to concentrate on what you were doing? Was it any wonder, when it had nothing else to do, that your mind began to play with the thoughts you kept bundled away the rest of the time? Began to unfold them and shake them out, allowing them to fill every space in your head and torment you all over again?

She eased up another budding dandelion, pushing her fork into the earth, rocking it slightly. The perfume was a mystery, no doubt about that. But there could be an explanation. Justin might have bought it for somebody's birthday, some relation maybe or someone at work, and forgotten to mention it. A bit unusual, certainly – he was normally very anxious for Kathryn to help him out with any presents that had to be bought – but it could have happened.

The perfume wouldn't have been for Grainne – her birthday was in October, and anyway she never wore perfume: she said it gave her a headache. And Justin's sister Ann's birthday wasn't until January – and Kathryn always bought her present.

Maybe it was for Suzannah's birthday. But would Justin even know when his sister's partner's birthday was? And why would he buy her a present out of the blue when they never had before?

No, it made no sense, whichever way you looked at it.

But maybe it wasn't perfume he'd bought at all. 'Fragrance' could as easily mean aftershave or cologne he'd bought for himself. But he wasn't out of aftershave – the half-full bottle was on the bathroom shelf. And she'd checked the presses in the bathroom and in their bedroom and found nothing else. No new bottles or jars, nothing that would explain the receipt.

Round and round, filling your head, tormenting you.

If it was just the perfume, she could have lived with it – she'd have given him the benefit of the doubt, assumed there was an innocent explanation and forgotten about it in time. She trusted him, after all. He loved her. Wasn't he always telling her he loved her? Hadn't Yvonne said, at her party, *there's a man in love with his wife*?

But then, two days ago, Kathryn had been polishing in the hall and had seen something white, a piece of paper, under the phone table and she'd stooped to pick it up. She'd read 'goods €35' and 'delivery €5'. She'd looked at the top of the receipt and seen the local florist's name.

Flowers, bought and delivered somewhere, a few days before. Someone in the house had bought flowers in Blooms Day and asked for them to be delivered. Not Kathryn, and surely not Grainne – she'd said often enough that bouquets were a shocking waste of money.

So it must have been Justin. He must have gone to the florist's and ordered a bouquet and had it delivered.

But Kathryn hadn't had any flowers recently, apart from the potted orchid one of their work friends had brought to the birthday party. So whose house had this bouquet been delivered to?

Perfume, and now flowers. Oh, there could still be an innocent explanation, and Kathryn prayed that there was. But what was she to think, kneeling there beside the dandelions?

She was nine years and seven months older than him. Since their marriage she'd had a stillbirth and two miscarriages. Chances were, she wouldn't give him children. He was still in his thirties, still a young man. She was facing her fifties.

And yesterday she'd looked out of the sitting room window and seen him chatting to Yvonne's daughter on the path in front of the three red-brick houses. Clara, in her early twenties. Attractive, vivacious, laughing at something Justin had said. Wearing a pink gingham top and denim shorts that stopped six inches above her perfect knees.

Clara could give him babies, lots of them. Clara had years of having babies ahead of her.

Kathryn threw her fork into the trug and got awkwardly to her feet. Time to put the dinner on; she and Justin were going to the cinema later. She wasn't a big James Bond fan, but Justin loved him.

She walked towards the house, pulling off her pale yellow gardening gloves and stamping her feet once or twice to get rid of the pins and needles.

NUMBER EIGHT

'Hello?'

'Dan, it's me.'

'Yeah?' His heart jumped. He ignored it.

'Well, I just thought I'd give a ring to see . . . how you are.'

How thoughtful of you. 'I'm fine. Did you want anything else?'

He heard her sigh. 'I wish you weren't like this, Dan. I'm sorry, I'm really sorry how things turned out.'

'Yeah, me too. I'm sorry you're having our child. I'm really sorry that happened.' He didn't know where it was coming from, this rage. It was pouring out of him. He could do nothing to stop it. 'I'm sorry I made you pregnant just before you decided you preferred my uncle.' Stop it, shut up. He leaned against the wall, phone pressed to his ear, heart rattling against his ribs.

Silence for a few seconds, and then her voice, thick with tears. 'I've got to go.' A click, and a soft buzzing.

He stayed leaning against the wall, kept the phone to his ear. After a while the buzz changed to a thin beep.

He hung up and walked into the kitchen.

Kieran turned from the cooker, saw Dan's face and turned back. Something sizzled in the pan. The room smelled of garlic.

Dan sat at the table and put his face in his hands. 'I've made a right mess of things.'

Kieran shook the frying pan and lowered the heat under one of the saucepans. 'It's a shame things didn't work out.' This was the first time they'd mentioned it since the night Dan had come home drunk.

Dan kept his eyes on the table. 'I told you she's pregnant, didn't I?'

'You did, yes.'

'It's mine. I told you that, didn't I?'

'Yes.'

Dan lifted his head. 'What a fucking awful state of affairs.'

'It is. It's awful.' Kieran sprinkled something from a bottle onto the pan and stirred. 'Have you talked about – you know, after it's born?'

'No. I can't. I can't face it.' Dan put his head back into his hands. 'He'll be raising it, I suppose. I'll see it at weekends and stuff.'

'Mmm.' Kieran poured milk into a saucepan. 'I was left at the altar – I never told you that, did I?'

It was so unexpected that Dan lifted his head out of his hands. 'No, you didn't.'

Kieran stirred. 'I was thirty-eight. She was a waitress in a little café where I'd go sometimes for breakfast on a Saturday. Geraldine, that was her name.'

Dan watched him, stirring steadily.

'I finally plucked up the courage and asked her out. She could have been married for all I knew, but she wasn't. She was a few years older than me.'

He turned off the ring and poured the sauce into a jug.

'She had a son, about fifteen. I don't think he took to me, really. Not that I'd blame him – I wasn't good with that age group, didn't know how to talk to them.'

He opened the oven door and lifted out the dish with the salmon steaks.

'We went out for a few months and then I proposed, three times in the space of a week. The third time she accepted.'

Dan got up and took cutlery out of a drawer and began to set the table. Kieran turned off the gas under the frying pan. Dan put salt and pepper on the table. Kieran took two plates from the oven and lifted a salmon steak onto each one.

Dan looked at him. 'What then?'

Kieran shrugged, added stir-fried vegetables to the plates. 'Nothing. On the day, she didn't show, and after a while everyone went home.'

'Did you ever see her again?'

Kieran nodded. 'Oh, yes. I went back to the café after a few weeks and she was still there.' He brought the plates to the table.

'But . . .' Dan searched for the words. 'What did she say? Did she explain? Did you ever find out . . . ?'

'Oh yes. It was because of Adam, the son. She didn't feel she could go ahead with it, you see, when he was so against the idea.'

'But he was only—'

'I know, yes, but obviously he was old enough to influence her.' Kieran handed Dan the little jug. 'Sauce?'

And that was that. Nothing more to be said, it seemed.

'Thanks.' Dan took the jug and poured the creamy sauce over his fish. 'By the way, there's a James Bond film on at the cinema. Fancy going tonight?'

'James Bond?' Kieran considered, a forkful of salmon halfway to his mouth. 'Yes, why not?'

'I'm sorry,' she said. 'I really am.'

He'd known she'd be sorry. She was a good woman. He'd seen her face when he'd walked in, the way her hand had flown to her flushing cheek. The way she'd come straight over when he'd sat at his usual table, the way she'd said 'Kieran.'

'It's OK,' he told her, picking up the menu.

'It's nothing to do with you.' She lowered the coffee pot and rested it on the table. 'At least, it's not that I didn't want to.' She bit her bottom lip. 'It's . . . well, it's because of Adam – he . . . he just couldn't get used to the idea . . .' She trailed off.

Kieran watched her fingers smoothing the front of her apron. Red from washing up. 'It's OK.' He would have liked to reach out and take her hand, fold her red fingers in his. 'Really, it's OK. I'm OK.'

'I'm sorry. I really am.' Her yellow pencil stuck out of her pocket. There was a pink rubbery bit on the end of it.

Kieran nodded. He looked at the menu and said, 'I think I'll have poached eggs this morning, for a change. And no sausages, just rashers and white pudding. And some brown bread.'

She looked at him for a second with an expression he couldn't read, then pulled out her pencil and notebook and scribbled. He could see the other waitresses watching them. One of them, the red headed one – Carmel, was it? – had been at the church.

Geraldine slipped the notebook back into her pocket. Kieran wondered what she'd done with the engagement ring he'd given her.

He remembered his mother's angry tears at the church, after they'd finally had to admit that Geraldine wasn't coming.

'What did she have to say she'd marry you for?' she kept demanding. 'Why did she have to do that to you?'

He remembered the embarrassed faces of their guests, the twenty or so people they'd mustered between them, how some had avoided his eye as they'd shuffled out.

It wasn't until the church was almost empty that he'd realised her parents hadn't been there. Or Adam, her son.

He watched her lift the coffee pot and walk back behind the counter. Carmel said something to her that he couldn't make out. Geraldine shook her head, tore his order from her notebook and handed it through the hatch to someone.

He'd forgotten to say soft poached eggs. He hoped they wouldn't be too hard when they arrived. He hated them hard. He opened his paper and began to read about the latest peace deal in the Middle East.

NUMBER SEVEN

Greg,

Thanks so much for the offer, but I couldn't possibly let you pay my flight to Italy. It's much too generous, and I'm much too proud! Seriously, I'm very touched, but I just can't. You'll have to soldier on in Tuscany without me, but thanks again for the offer – I really do appreciate it. Have a great time, and see you when you get back.

Love Yvonne xx

Barry –

Look, you have got to stop this. I'm not going to change my mind. I've explained that it's nothing you've done, we're just not right for each other. You're a nice guy, I'm sure you'll meet someone *else soon. You need to move on now and forget about me. Please stop texting me all the time, and stop sending flowers. There's no point.*

Clara

Hi Joe,

Well, I'm relieved to see we do have a bit in common after all. I love long walks too, especially if they come complete with sunshine and coastal views! And no, I don't play a musical instrument, but I do like the sound of the cello – so mellow and full-bodied. I have to confess, though, that I'm not a big fan of the cinema. I'd much rather see a good play than a film. Unfortunately, Charleton has just the one small theatre, but occasionally it attracts a decent offering. There's also a new arts centre planned for Belford, less than an hour away. Otherwise, I get my fix any time I go to Galway or Dublin.

It's interesting that both your sons ended up living in Rathfarnham. You didn't mention if either of them has children. I'm dreading the day Clara makes me a grandmother – hopefully not for a few years yet!

Well, I've rattled on long enough now, so I'd better stop.

All the best,

Deirdre

Siofra –

Hurry up back from France. Matty's just isn't the same without you on a Friday night! You must be fluent by now, especially with that sexy builder to help you out – although I presume you're not too interested in his vocabulary!

Well, Barry's being a major pain, texting me all the time, begging me to take him back. I just emailed him to say bugger off. I feel like telling him exactly why I dumped him, but it's still top secret – you're the only one who knows. We had a chat the other night and I flirted like mad, but he's playing a bit hard to get. Not that that'll stop me!

OK, gotta go – Mum just shouted up that dinner is ready. See you on Friday, we'll hit Matty's with a bang!!!

Clara xxx

'I forgot to ask what Kathryn thought of your birthday present.'

Yvonne dried the last plate and hung the tea towel on its hook. 'She was delighted. She said she'd never had a proper massage.'

Clara peeled off her rubber gloves. 'Oh, I'd say that good-looking husband of hers obliges every now and again.'

Yvonne smiled. 'Possibly.'

Clara brushed the crumbs from the table into her hand. 'He's years younger than her, isn't he?'

'Well, eight or nine. But they're obviously mad about each other.'

'You think?' Clara emptied the crumbs into the bin and got the brush. 'I can't understand what he sees in her, to be honest.'

'What?' Yvonne frowned. 'Why not? I think they're perfectly suited.'

'Well, he obviously didn't pick her for her looks – I mean, she's OK, but nothing to write home about. And she's probably too old now for kids. I just thought he'd go for someone younger, that's all.'

Yvonne took off her apron and hung it on a hook by the sink. 'Well, all I know is that they're mad about each other – it's obvious when you see them together.'

There was silence in the kitchen while Clara swept the floor and Yvonne wiped the draining board and squeezed out the cloth. Then Clara said, 'I meant to tell you, I met Dan coming home, the night of Kathryn's party. It was early, I was just going out, and he was a bit drunk.'

'Was he? Poor Dan.' Yvonne draped the cloth over the edge of the sink. 'I was sorry he didn't come to the party – it might have done him good. He probably couldn't face trying to be sociable.'

'Looks like his wife is gone for good, doesn't it? And who's that man staying with him, with the funny hat?'

'He's a tenant. Dan probably needed some help with the mortgage after Ali left.'

'Was there another man?' Clara took the dustpan and brush from their hook.

Yvonne looked at her, amused. 'Why the sudden interest in the neighbours?'

Clara collected what she'd swept and emptied the dustpan into the bin. 'No reason.'

'Well, I haven't a clue why Ali left – you'd have to ask Dan that. And speaking of break-ups, what about poor Barry? I'm assuming he's gone.'

Clara's face took on the closed look so familiar to Yvonne. She'd strayed into personal territory again. 'Yes, we've broken up, and I'd rather not discuss it, if you don't mind.' She lifted the plate of scraps from the worktop and turned to the back door. 'I'll give these to Magoo.'

And that was that. Shutters down again. Yvonne checked that the cooker knobs were turned off – a habit she'd picked up years ago after she'd gone to bed one night and left the oven on. Then she glanced around the tidy kitchen, took the newspaper from a chair and brought it into the sitting room.

One day later: 19 July

NUMBER EIGHT

He dialled her number and waited, counting the rings. Three, four—

'Hi, Dan.'

So his number was still in her phone's address book. He still existed there. He closed his eyes. 'Hi.'

A pause, and then she said, 'I'm glad you rang.'

'I just wanted to say sorry. There was no call for the stuff I said last night.'

'That's OK.' She spoke quickly. 'I can understand—'

'Yeah, well,' he didn't want her understanding, 'I just wanted to say that.'

He hung up quickly. That was all he could handle for now. He pictured her slipping her phone back into her pocket. He wondered if she was in Brendan's old farmhouse. Maybe she was walking into another room right now and saying, 'You won't believe who just phoned.'

He'd often been in that house. Brendan had bought it when Dan was in his mid-teens, and he remembered calling over with his parents shortly afterwards, with the dark blue lamp they'd bought as a housewarming gift.

Brendan had given them tea in blue mugs and thick slices of Battenburg cake, and they'd walked through the house together. He remembered Brendan telling him he was welcome to stay the night anytime he wanted. Winking at him behind his parents' backs and Dan smiling at him. Man to man.

In the car on the way home, his mother had got cross with his father for saying that Brendan had bought a pig in a poke, that he could smell the damp as soon as they'd walked in.

The last time Dan and Ali had visited Brendan was about two months before Ali walked out, when they'd called around to see Brendan's two new lambs. They'd eaten wedges of the shop-bought apple tart they'd brought with them and Brendan had joked with Ali about giving him the recipe, and she'd said it was a family secret, that she'd have to kill him if she told him.

And now, looking back, he remembered how quiet Ali had been in the car on the way home. 'You OK?' he'd asked her, and she'd said yes, she was just a bit tired, her period was on the way. They'd bought a Chinese takeaway and opened a bottle of wine when they'd got home, but she'd gone to bed with a headache soon after the meal, leaving him to finish the wine on his own.

Funny, the things you remembered.

Brendan hadn't appeared when Ali was moving out. From the dining room window Dan had watched her loading her bags into the boot of her Golf.

He'd seen her struggling through the front door with them, tears running silently down her face, and he'd made no effort to help her.

She'd been pregnant then. About a week, a little over a week pregnant, and neither of them had known.

He went out to the back garden. After a week of broken weather the sun had decided to reappear and Kieran was turning lamb chops on the barbecue. Underneath the wire grid, potatoes wrapped in tinfoil lay among the red coals. There was a jug of water and a glass on the little wrought-iron table. Beneath it, Picasso sat washing himself.

A dog barked. Dan followed the sound over the hedge and found himself looking at Clara O'Mahony lying on her stomach on a cream blanket, almost at the bottom of number seven's garden. Her little dog snuffled in the grass nearby.

Clara wore yellow and blue bikini bottoms and she'd unfastened the matching top, so her back was bare. Her skin was pale golden and glistened slightly. She was reading, propped up on her elbows, and Dan could see the curve of the breast nearest to him, the nipple just hidden by her arm.

He turned abruptly to Kieran. 'Anything I can do?'

'You could get the salad – it's in the fridge – and the dressing.'

Lifting out the bowl of mixed leaves, cubed feta cheese and olives, Dan thought back again to his days of spaghetti out of a tin, sausages wrapped in sliced bread, dried-up poached eggs on toast.

He really must learn to cook, Kieran wouldn't be here forever. Next time he was in the library, he'd enquire about classes – give him something to do in the evenings. Take his mind off any other distractions in the neighbourhood.

He pulled a can of cider out of the fridge and popped the top and poured the pumpkin-coloured liquid into a pint glass. He found the little bottle of dressing that Kieran had mixed earlier. He took the pair of salad tongs Kieran had found in a charity shop and stuck them under his arm. Then he brought everything out to the patio, doing his best to ignore the view over the hedge.

Her body was perfect. He bet her skin was like velvet. She must have men crawling out of the woodwork to get at her.

Two weeks later: 2 August

NUMBER NINE

Kathryn stirred her coffee. 'Pity the good weather didn't last.'

'Mmm.' Yvonne picked up a triangle of shortbread. 'We had a good run of it though.'

It had been raining steadily for three days now, the soft summer rain that Kathryn usually loved, knowing that her flowers were drinking it gratefully. Now, it irritated her.

She reached for some shortbread, then changed her mind. A pound up last week. 'So tell me about this Joe fellow. What's the latest? Any sign of him wanting to meet you?'

'Not yet. It's only been a few weeks though. Early days.'

'So what else have you found out about him? Didn't you say he lives not too far away?'

'Well, depends what you'd call far. He's in Ashfield.'

'Seventy miles. Well, it's not the other end of Ireland. And what else?'

Yvonne thought. 'He plays the electric guitar – badly, he says. He has two grown-up sons, both married in Dublin. They have kids, or one has. And he can't understand why I like country music.'

'Well, there I have to agree with Joe. Anyone else of interest floating into your inbox?'

'No – a few others have made contact, but nobody sounded that exciting so I didn't bother responding.'

Kathryn sipped her coffee. 'No sign of Clara and Barry getting back together then?'

'Barry? No, doesn't look like it.'

'And is there anyone else on the scene?'

'Not that I know of.' Yvonne paused. 'Although she seems a bit distracted lately, so maybe she has her eye on someone. No doubt I'll find out in due course.'

'Mmm.' Kathryn turned her head towards the window again. 'God, will this rain never stop? I feel like I'm getting cabin fever.'

Yvonne looked at her. 'Are you alright? You seem a bit – tense.'

Kathryn shook her head. 'Sorry, no, I'm fine. Just the time of the month – and Grainne being her usual painful self. Don't take any notice.'

After Yvonne had left, Kathryn took the cups to the dishwasher and stood gazing out at the drizzle. She was so tempted to confide in Yvonne – God, she really needed to pour out her fears to someone, to have them laugh and say 'Don't be silly, you're imagining things' – but for once, Yvonne was the last person she could talk to.

In case it was Clara.

Because by now Kathryn knew there was someone else. The perfume, the flowers – and yesterday the phone call. It was the phone call that had convinced her, the phone call Grainne had told her about.

The two women had been in the sitting room, watching the six o'clock news. Justin had gone to the garage on the corner for petrol for the mower. A mushroom and bacon quiche was cooking in the kitchen.

Grainne had waited until the ad break and then she'd turned to Kathryn. 'Don't let on I asked, but is Justin planning a surprise for my birthday?'

Kathryn stared at her. Justin hadn't mentioned Grainne's birthday. Wasn't it still weeks away, the beginning of October? 'What makes you think that?'

'Well.' Grainne darted a look out of the window, 'when I came in here earlier, he was in the middle of a phone call and he just hung up, really suddenly, and he looked quite guilty, I thought.'

Kathryn's heart plummeted.

'So I thought it had to be something secret – and with my birthday the next big occasion . . .' Grainne looked eagerly at Kathryn. 'And if anyone would know, you would.'

For the life of her, Kathryn couldn't think how to respond. 'Well, I don't—'

Then Grainne laughed. 'Oh, there you go, being loyal to him. I suppose he's sworn you to secrecy.'

Kathryn nodded, trying desperately to keep her expression neutral. Trying not to let her dismay show.

'I'll just have to wait so.' Grainne settled back into her armchair, a satisfied smile on her face.

Kathryn kept her eyes on the TV screen. The

garage was three minutes away – what was taking him so long? He must have been gone at least a quarter of an hour.

Plenty long enough for a phone call, well out of earshot of anyone at home.

She should talk to him of course. Just come out with it, and ask him if there was someone else, if he was having an affair. Even though at this stage the evidence seemed overwhelming, wasn't there still the tiniest chance that Kathryn had got the wrong end of the stick?

Maybe there was a completely innocent explanation for all this. Maybe Justin would laugh and say, 'What? Perfume? Oh, that was just—'

Just what? What could it possibly be? What possible reason could your husband have for buying flowers and perfume for someone else and not telling you? And of course that phone call had had nothing to do with Grainne's birthday – of course he'd have told her if he'd been planning anything for that. So he must have been talking to someone he didn't want his mother – or his wife – to know about.

She couldn't bear it, simply wouldn't be able to cope, if Justin admitted there was someone else, that he loved someone else. So she couldn't ask him.

What was she to do? She stood at the window and watched the drizzle falling onto her flowers and she felt terribly afraid.

Three weeks later: 23 August

NUMBER EIGHT

Dan took the plastic sheet out of the big brown envelope and held it up to the light. Someone could have told him it was a fish or a dinosaur and he'd have believed them. No matter how he looked at it, it made little sense. But then, all of a sudden, he picked out the curved shape of the body, the minuscule fingers, the roundness of the head – and yes, there it was, the tiny shadow of his son's penis.

His son. His and Ali's son. His heart melted. He could feel his whole chest softening, oozing. Ridiculously, his eyes filled with tears and he put up a hand and swiped them away. They'd made a baby together. He breathed in deeply, twice, three times. Gazed again at his freshly made son. My boy.

He thought about a little boy who looked like him. Maybe they'd have the same colour hair, the same eyes. He'd take him fishing, teach him how to cast a line, do all the clichéd things fathers and sons did. He'd read *James and the Giant Peach* to him, the first book he remembered his own father reading to him at night. He'd buy him his first football. People would know, when they saw them, that they were father and son.

He wondered if Ali appeared pregnant yet. At what stage would it start to show? She was four and a half months gone now, halfway there. Was she craving any unusual food? Did Brendan have to get up at night to make her a sausage and marmalade sandwich? Was she eating properly? Getting enough vitamins or whatever pregnant women were supposed to get?

He studied the sheet again. He took it into the sitting room, where Kieran sat reading the paper. 'Here, have a look at this.'

Kieran took the sheet and peered at it for a few seconds. Dan waited. Kieran raised his head. 'What is it?'

'My son.' Dan had no control over the beam that suddenly spread across his face. 'That's the first ultrasound.'

Kieran peered down again. 'Is that the head?'

Dan crouched beside him. 'No, there it is. And they're the arms, see the fingers.'

'Oh, yeah – and these are the legs here?'

'Yes, and the knees. And the toes.'

'When is it due?'

'Beginning of January.'

'Have you thought about names yet?'

'Not really'. Dan had wondered about that, wondered how he and Ali would sort it out. They'd have to choose together, however they managed it.

He'd cast around among the names in his family – his father Sebastian, his grandfathers Seamus and Jack, his uncles Tom, Tony, Gerard . . . and Brendan.

Nothing leapt out at him. He liked some of the old Irish names – Fiachra, Oisin, Eilbhear. He liked Daniel too, although that might be a bit self-indulgent.

He'd told his parents about the baby. His mother had answered the phone, as she always did. If she was out of the house, Dan's father ignored it.

'Hello, love. How are you?' The same worried note in her voice, the note that had been there ever since her brother had stolen her son's wife. 'Everything alright?'

She'd had no contact with Brendan since it had happened. She'd told Dan that Brendan had rung the house a few times and she'd hung up on him. And Ali certainly wouldn't have phoned. So they wouldn't know about the baby.

'Nothing wrong, I hope?'

'No. Nothing wrong.' Dan took a deep breath and said, 'There is some news though.'

She cried when he told her. Passed the phone onto his father, who kept saying, 'God above, I don't believe it.'

He remembered taking Ali to meet his parents for the first time, the week before she'd asked him to marry her. She'd brought them a box of expensive Belgian chocolates that Dan knew neither of them would eat. His mother had worn lipstick and the shoes she kept for funerals. His father had put on a tie.

Dan would invite himself home to Sunday lunch this week, he'd bring the plastic sheet and they could see the first photo of their grandchild. They'd eat roast beef probably, then apple tart and custard, and they would try not to mention Brendan's name.

They were probably getting excited at the thought of their first grandchild, but they might be reluctant to admit it, even to each other, under the circumstances. They'd ask about Kieran, and Dan would tell them how he was planning to start going to cookery classes in September, how he'd seen an ad in the local paper. He'd tell them work was going fine, he was getting plenty of books to proofread and copyedit.

They'd feel a bit happier after he'd left, reassured that he was coping.

He was coping. Ali had left him and he hadn't fallen apart. He was going to work every day, he was looking after the house. He'd finished painting the sitting room last weekend, only a few months after he'd started. The barbecue was up and running – OK, it was no masterpiece, but it worked. He was coping.

But January . . . That was another story altogether. He couldn't wait for January. He dreaded January. He didn't want to think about what would happen when January came. He went upstairs to put the ultrasound somewhere safe.

Castlebar, the previous April

About twenty feet ahead of Kieran, the pub door was pushed open and a man came out, lurching heavily against the jamb. At the sound of Kieran's footsteps, he swung his head to look at him, one hand out to steady himself against the pub wall.

Kieran approached the swaying figure, a pinprick of unease darting through his abdomen. Although it was just past eight, the night was darkening; the narrow street was deserted. From the pub came the cacophonous buzz of several voices talking together. Someone gave a high-pitched laugh – or was it a scream?

Kieran moved to the outer edge of the path as he drew nearer to the drunk man – and then, with a lurch of recognition, he realised who it was. Kieran had seen him around town, of course, over the years, but they'd always managed to avoid a face-to-face meeting.

Too late to turn around now, too late to do anything but keep going. Kieran ducked his head slightly, put up a hand to grab the collar of his jacket and pull it tightly around his neck. Kept his eyes on the road ahead, quickened his step.

'Hey.'

Kieran didn't react, kept walking. They were almost abreast. Kieran's grip tightened on his collar.

'Hey.'

Louder. Reluctantly Kieran lifted his head. The scowl was the same, eyes slitted. 'Look who it is.'

He shoved himself off from the wall and swayed in front of Kieran, blocking his way, breathing hot, beery gusts into Kieran's face. He wore a thin black denim jacket missing the bottom button and baggy, well-worn jeans. Dark shoes underneath. His thinning brown hair was plastered to his head. Thinning already at – what? He must be about thirty.

Kieran gave a nod and stepped off the path, but Adam reached out and caught his arm and peered closely into his face. Kieran stood and waited – what else could he do? To free his arm would involve some kind of tussle, and he shied away from that. Better to wait it out. No sense in antagonising a drunk man.

Adam's hair smelled of smoke. A pocket of small white-headed spots curved around the base of one nostril. The edges of his mouth were brown-rimmed. His chin was studded with black stubble. There was a tiny, high-pitched wheeze at the end of each exhalation – asthma? Cigarettes?

He was taller than Kieran by about three inches now, but much thinner. The knuckles on the hand that clutched Kieran's arm were bony. His grip was tight.

'How're you doing?' As he slurred out the words, a fleck of spittle landed on Kieran's chin. He tried to pull away, but Adam's grip tightened. 'Hey, no hard feelings, mate?' He grinned loosely, showing narrow, yellow teeth. 'Right?'

He poked Kieran painfully in the sternum with two braced fingers. 'No hard feelings man, right?' He dropped Kieran's arm, but stayed planted in front of him. Swaying on the path, putting up a hand again to steady himself against the wall. 'How're you doing anyway?'

Kieran walked quickly past him, heart thudding, the after-feel of Adam's fingers still on his chest. The last time they'd met properly had been about a week before the wedding that had never happened. Adam looking daggers at Kieran when he'd called to take Geraldine to the pictures.

'Hey—hang on!' Kieran realised, with a fresh lurch of dismay, that Adam was stumbling after him. 'Hang on – hey, wait, I want to talk to you.'

Making surprisingly good progress despite his drunkenness. Stumbling against the wall every so often, but managing somehow to maintain the short distance between them. 'Hang on, will you? Hey, I just want to talk, for fuck's sake—'

Kieran crossed the street, quickening his step. Heading towards the river, almost running now.

'Hey!' How was Adam managing to keep up? 'Fucking *wait*, will you? I just want to fucking well *talk* to you.'

Kieran reached the path that ran along by the river. The shopping centre car park was five hundred yards ahead – tonight was late opening so it would be busy. He'd cut in there and lose him, surely.

Beside him, barely three feet away, the river flowed, black and immense. Kieran could hear its soft splashing. Squares of yellow from the buildings on its opposite bank threw dancing blobs of light onto its surface. From somewhere a car horn, a burst of music.

'Jesus—' Adam was wheezing loudly now. Kieran could hear the high whistle clearly. 'What the fuck is wrong with you? I just—'

Then a shout and, abruptly, silence.

Kieran risked a glance over his shoulder and, seeing nothing, stopped and stood breathing heavily.

The path was clear. Nobody was there, nobody yelling at him to slow down. And then he heard it – from the water, maybe a dozen feet behind him, a gurgled cut-off shout, a splash of frantic movement.

Adam was in the river. He must have fallen in.

An arm burst up, thrashing the water, scattering

the surface into a million dancing lights, causing an arc of drops to fly up, glittering beautifully. Another shout, very clear this time – 'Help!' More furious splashing.

Kieran stayed where he was, horrified, every limb frozen. Another eruption from the water again, another cut-off yell. He couldn't move, couldn't make a sound. Could only stand transfixed, listening to Adam drowning, straining to hear as the shouts died away, as the splashing stopped, as the soft *lap lap* of the water became audible again.

And then, from the direction he and Adam had come, he heard running footsteps, saw the dark shapes of two figures racing towards the place where Adam had fallen in. Heard a splash, heard shouts—

'Any sign?'

'Can't see a thing.'

They hadn't spotted him. Kieran forced his legs to move then, began to back away quietly until he could barely hear their voices. When he was sure he was out of sight, he turned and walked rapidly along the path.

As he reached the gateway that led into the shopping centre car park, a siren sounded in the distance, getting closer. Only then did he allow himself to sink onto the bonnet of a blue Ford Sierra, legs suddenly turned to rubber.

NUMBER SEVEN

'You'll never guess where Martin's taking me for our anniversary.'

They were in the room to the left of Yvonne's reception desk. It was officially a staffroom, but it doubled as a store room, so anytime they ate lunch there, on the days it was too wet or cold to go to the park, they had to thread their way through boxes of medical supplies to the steel-legged table at the far side of the room.

On the table there was a kettle and a small fridge. A tiny sink was wedged into the corner. Nobody except Yvonne and Dolores ever used the room for lunch.

Yvonne filled the kettle and plugged it in. Dolores and her guessing games. 'Somewhere in Ireland?'

'Oh no – we're flying there.'

'Paris? Rome?'

'Venice. He told me last night. We're staying in a hotel right on a canal.'

Yvonne smiled. 'That'll be lovely. The highlight of my weekend will be picking gooseberries and making a tart. Who'll look after your kids?'

'His mother. She's a real pet.'

Yvonne listened to how wonderful Dolores's mother-in-law was and how fabulous Dolores and Martin's weekend was going to be. She thought about Grainne in number nine, the bane of Kathryn's life. She thought of her own mother-in-law – or rather, thankfully, ex-mother-in-law, who hadn't crossed her threshold for more than sixteen years.

Jim and Peggy were in Lisdoonvarna for their usual two weeks, doing whatever people did in Lisdoonvarna – could you still drink the sulphur water? They were staying in the bed and breakfast they always stayed in – it must be pretty impressive for Peggy to go back every summer. Yvonne bet she kept the owners on their toes.

Dolores tapped the shell of her hard-boiled egg with a spoon. 'How's your glamorous daughter?' She'd met Clara once or twice, when Clara had called around to the clinic to talk to Yvonne.

Yvonne peeled the clingfilm from her sandwich. 'Oh, fine. Between boyfriends at the moment, but that doesn't usually last long.'

'But nobody special so far?'

'Nobody special, no.'

Lately, though, Clara had definitely been preoccupied. Maybe there was someone else whom Yvonne didn't know about yet. Well, he'd show up sooner or later.

'Kettle's boiling. You're miles away.' Dolores dropped bit of eggshell into her lunchbox. 'Bet I know who you're thinking of.'

Yvonne poured water over her teabag. 'Actually, I was wondering what I'd have for dinner tonight.'

Dolores snorted. 'Like fun you were. So is he back from Tuscany?'

'He got back a few days ago. I haven't met him yet – he's in Dublin.'

'But he'll be down soon?'

'He will – in a week or two, he said.' Yvonne squeezed her teabag against the side of her cup and dropped it onto the crumpled clingfilm that had held her sandwich. 'So tell me more about Venice. Have you seen any pictures of the hotel?'

Imagine what Dolores would say if she knew Yvonne was keeping a much juicier piece of information from her. Imagine her face if Yvonne said, 'Actually, around the time that you and Martin will be taking off for Venice, I'll be going out to dinner with a man I've never met. I've been internet dating, you see. This is the second man I've agreed to meet – the first was Pawel, although we didn't know we were emailing each other because we'd both changed our names.'

Dolores would probably keel over, or at least be totally speechless. Yvonne was almost tempted – just to see her face.

Joe had finally suggested meeting up, almost six weeks after he'd first made contact. I'll be in your neck of the woods on business on Friday, he'd written. Maybe we could grab a bite to eat?

He'd asked her to suggest a restaurant in Charleton, and Yvonne had picked one she hadn't been to before, at the far end of the town from where she'd met Pawel.

They'd arranged to meet in the restaurant at half past seven. Joe would book himself into a hotel in Charleton for the night.

He'd put his photo on the site. He had thinning dark hair, cut short, and a small, neat moustache. In the photo he wore a pale blue polo shirt and he was smiling. He didn't look psychotic and he wasn't anyone she knew. Hopefully her second attempt at finding love on the internet would be a little more successful than the first.

She sipped her tea and listened to Dolores telling her why it wasn't a bit fair that her Fionn hadn't won the painting competition after all.

NUMBER NINE

Grainne looked up from her book as Justin walked into the sitting room. 'Is she back yet?'

'No.'

Kathryn had gone into town to use Yvonne's birthday massage voucher.

'I feel like a treat,' she'd said the night before. She was applying cream to her throat, using long, upward strokes with the backs of her fingers. Justin was lying on the bed, watching her. 'I need a treat.'

He got up and stood behind her, put his hands on her shoulders. 'You've been working too hard.' He tried to meet her eyes in the mirror. 'Kath?'

'Yes?' She looked up then, screwing the lid back onto the jar.

'You OK?'

She stood up quickly and shook off her slippers. 'I wish you'd stop asking me that.' She turned back the duvet and got into bed. 'I'm tired, that's all. Can we have the light off, or are you going to read?'

And when he'd slipped in beside her, she'd turned away from him, like she'd been doing for weeks.

Grainne folded down the corner of her page and closed the book. 'Sit down. I want to talk to you about something.'

'What?'

'Sit down – I can't talk to you when you're standing over me.'

He sat in an armchair across from her and waited.

'I'm concerned about Kathryn.'

Exactly what he'd been expecting. 'Are you? Why?'

'She's not been herself. You must have noticed it.'

Justin nodded slowly, reluctantly, not wanting to say anything to his mother that might sound negative towards Kathryn. 'She seems a bit out of sorts, I suppose.'

'I think I know what's wrong.' Grainne stopped. 'Although I'm not sure I should be telling you.'

Justin waited. Of course she'd tell him.

'You see, I think . . .' Grainne ran a finger up and down the spine of her book. 'I think she may be going through the menopause.'

'What?'

Grainne put up a hand. 'Well, we can't rule it out, you know. She is heading into her late forties, it's not unheard of. And remember, I can recognise the signs.'

Justin tried to stifle his annoyance. 'No. It can't possibly be the menopause, she's much too young.' He wanted to slap her hand down. 'It can't be that.'

'She's almost ten years older than you.' His mother's voice took on a new edge. 'You seem to forget that quite a lot.'

He let his anger out then. 'Why do I need to remember it? You never miss an opportunity to remind me – or Kathryn. You make sure she never forgets how old she is.' He stopped, appalled. They never spoke to each other like this. 'I'm sorry, it's just – you do go on about it a bit.'

Grainne sounded offended. 'I'm only looking out for you. I know how much you always wanted children—'

He opened his mouth, but she put up a hand again to stop him.

'No, hear me out. You have to accept that in all probability Kathryn is not going to give you a child. Whether this is the menopause or not – and I'm pretty sure it is – she can't carry a baby to full term. We both know that.'

'I don't care about children.' But he avoided her eye.

Grainne said nothing. After a minute, Justin stood up and left the room.

He was sitting on the patio with a glass of beer when Kathryn got back. She came out carrying a paper bag. 'I bought you this.'

It was the autobiography they'd seen reviewed a few days earlier in the paper that Justin had said he must get. He smiled up at her, touched. 'Hey, thanks, love. How was your massage?'

'Good. I enjoyed it.'

He stood. 'Will you have a glass of wine?'

'Ah no, I think I'll have a lie-down.'

'Want me to come up?'

She smiled faintly. 'No, I think I need to sleep. See you later.'

Justin watched her walk indoors. It couldn't possibly be the menopause. Wasn't forty-five much too young?

But something was wrong, that much was obvious. Something she couldn't, or wouldn't, talk to him about.

Which made two of them. Some couple they were, these days. He drank his beer and listened to the music coming faintly from two gardens away.

Upstairs, Kathryn looked out of their bedroom window and saw Clara O'Mahony lying, half naked, on a cream blanket in the garden. She took in the gleaming, butterscotch skin, the firm curve of Clara's buttocks, barely covered by a pair of bikini bottoms. The feet, twitching in time to whatever music was playing on the little radio beside her.

From this distance, it was impossible to say whether there was any cellulite on the slim thighs, but Kathryn was willing to bet that the skin there was perfectly silky and undimpled.

She wondered how much Justin could see from where he sat. Was that what had brought him out the back? Had he seen Clara through the window, maybe, going out to lie down?

She imagined him stroking Clara's thighs. She imagined him kissing his way down her smooth, golden back, cupping her breasts, slipping off her briefs—

No. She turned quickly from the window and began to unbutton her top with angry, trembling fingers.

Three days later: 26 August

NUMBER SEVEN

Yvonne drove slowly through the streets of Charleton till she saw the restaurant's latticed windows ahead and, luckily, a parking space not far from the door. She turned off the engine, checked her reflection, ran a hand through her hair.

No make-up session today – no time – but she'd invested in the lipstick and eye shadow Caroline had used, and she'd swiped Clara's mascara from her room and done her best with it. Joe would have to be happy with that.

She pushed open the restaurant door. A couple sat at one table, another couple just behind them. Three women to her left, glancing over at her. And at a table half hidden by a pillar, a man sat alone, studying the menu.

Yvonne walked across; it had to be him. 'Joe?'

The hair was lighter than it had seemed in his photo, the little moustache had gone, but the face was pretty much the same. He got quickly to his feet. 'Yvonne, sorry, I never heard you come in.' He reached for the dove grey pashmina she'd borrowed from Clara

– 'Here, let me take that for you' – and draped it over the back of her chair. Then he put out his hand. 'I'm delighted to meet you finally.'

Thank God, he seemed perfectly normal and presentable. Yvonne shook his hand. 'Me too.' No yellow rose this time – neither of them had suggested anything like that. He wore a white shirt and a checked sports coat – she couldn't see his bottom half. He was quite tanned. His hands were broad, the nails a little long for her liking, but clean enough. A hotel key sat by his side plate. He was staying in room fifteen.

He handed her a menu. 'Now, I'll give you a chance to see what you want to order – and what kind of wine do you fancy?'

'Oh, no wine for me, thanks. I'm driving.'

'I thought you lived in Charleton?'

'Well, I'm a few miles outside the town.' She hated lying, but there was no way she could risk meeting someone in Belford.

'Oh, I see.' He picked up the wine menu. 'Well, I'll have a look anyway, you can always have the one glass – or we could put you in a taxi and you could collect the car in the morning.'

'Well, maybe . . .' She'd have to get out of that one when the time came. She scanned the dishes – fairly unadventurous, loin of pork, spare ribs, chicken curry, salmon steak, vegetarian pizza – and watched him out of the corner of her eye as he studied the wine list.

Hopefully they'd have plenty to talk about. He didn't seem like the kind of person you'd have to drag a conversation out of. She could tell him about Clara, and her job at the clinic. Maybe they could talk about music – although their tastes were so different, she doubted that that topic would get them very far.

Books – they hadn't mentioned books in the emails.

She ordered melon and salmon. He asked for soup of the day and pork and, without asking Yvonne, a bottle of Sancerre. She would have preferred a gin and tonic beforehand and no wine, but he didn't suggest it. She asked the waitress for a jug of water.

'So.' He smiled, leaning back in his chair. 'Here we are. The first meeting. You know,' he was staring at Yvonne, 'you can tell a lot about a person in the first five minutes.'

Yvonne laughed. 'Well, you've had about four so far – how am I doing?'

Joe grinned. 'Ah, no, obviously I have no complaints. I was more worried about what you thought of me.'

She pretended to consider. 'Well, I'd prefer a bit longer than five minutes to judge anyone – but so far I'm happy enough.' She paused. 'Why don't you tell me a bit more about yourself?'

The time passed. The food was perfectly fine, if not the best she'd ever tasted. Joe did most of the talking. No, he wasn't much of a reader, apart from a few papers on Sunday. He watched far too much TV, he'd taken up the electric guitar in his early twenties, he'd been a member of a terrible rock group for a few brief years and he enjoyed a game of cards now and again. He was a mechanical engineer and he was currently working on contract for an American company based in Ashfield.

He drank quickly, leaving his water glass practically untouched. Yvonne let the waitress pour her a glass of wine, but she mostly drank water. Joe noticed and remarked on it a few times. 'You can't leave all that wine to me – I could make a fool of myself.'

But he seemed to have no trouble drinking what she didn't. He ordered cognac afterwards and Yvonne asked for coffee.

'So' – he sat back, hands behind his head – 'how has such an attractive woman ended up on her own?'

Yvonne smiled. 'I've no idea, really.' She was wearing the lilac blouse and cream trousers she'd bought for Kathryn's birthday party and she felt good in them. They'd been worth the pretty hefty price tags.

'You're not telling me you haven't had offers?' Joe was studying her, gazing intently at her.

'Well, a few, I suppose.' Yvonne felt slightly uncomfortable. She wished he wouldn't stare like that. Maybe the wine was going to his head a bit. 'Tell me about your grandchildren,' she said. 'You told me you had – two, is that right?'

He picked up his almost empty brandy glass. 'My son Patrick's children. A boy and a girl. She's seven, he's ten.' Was there a tiny note of impatience in his voice? He drained the glass and lifted it in the air. 'Think I might have one more of these – why don't you join me?'

Yvonne's heart sank. 'No, really, thanks.'

'Go on – you've hardly had anything.'

'No, honestly. Brandy isn't my thing anyway.'

'Have something else then – a liqueur.' He was lifting his hand for the waitress. 'A crème de menthe, how about that?'

Yvonne began to feel irritated. 'Joe, I really don't want anything to drink. In fact, I'd rather get going now, if you don't mind.' She'd had enough, more than enough, of small talk for one evening. It wasn't as if he was all that interesting.

He raised his eyebrows. 'I didn't know I was having dinner with Cinderella.' His words were beginning to run into each other.

Yvonne forced a laugh. 'Well, I like to get my beauty sleep.'

He smiled thinly. 'OK, OK, I'll get the bill.'

He paid with a credit card, brushing aside Yvonne's offer to go halves. 'Not at all. I insist.' The coolness she could handle – what did she care, since they weren't likely to meet again? She'd certainly had enough of him, and she imagined he felt the same.

'Right, thanks very much. That was very nice.' She took her pashmina, wrapped it around her shoulders and they walked through the by now fairly crowded restaurant. Yvonne hoped he wouldn't stumble against any of the other diners on the way out.

When they were standing on the path, she held out her hand. 'Well, thanks again, Joe, it's been a lovely evening.' Pity they'd ended up on a bit of a sour note – it hadn't started off too badly.

He looked at her hand but made no attempt to take it. 'That's it? A handshake?' Definitely slurring now – the fresh air must have affected him.

The nerve of him – as if she owed him anything. She did her best to keep the smile on her face. 'I'm afraid so. I hardly know you, after all.'

He didn't laugh. No trace of a smile. Yvonne slung her bag over her shoulder. Enough of this nonsense. 'Well, I'll be—'

'You could come back to the hotel for a nightcap, no strings attached. It's just' – he turned, stumbling slightly – 'up there a bit.'

God, a nightcap, with him getting steadily drunker – the last thing she wanted. 'Ah no, thanks all the same, Joe. I really should be getting home—' She took a step away.

His hand shot out and grabbed her arm. 'C'mon, one little drink won't kill you. It's still early.'

His grip was strong. Yvonne glanced around, but the dusky street was deserted. A prickle of fear darted through her. 'Look, sorry, but I really—'

'C'mon – one drink, that's all I'm asking.' He leaned towards her and put his free hand at the back of her neck. 'Come on, half an hour.' She could feel the heat of his breath, she could smell the brandy.

She tried to wriggle out of his grasp, but his grip tightened on her neck. Still nobody around. She pushed against his chest with the flat of her hand, angry now. 'Look, I told you—'

The change was abrupt, startling. He snarled, 'You needn't think I'm shelling out over a hundred euro for nothing, you bitch.' He pushed her up against the railings outside the restaurant and lunged for her mouth, forcing his tongue between her lips.

His fingers dug painfully into her neck.

Her bag dropped with a thud, the pashmina slid off her shoulders but was held halfway to the ground by their pressed-together bodies. With her free hand, Yvonne thumped against his side, but she was too close to him for her blows to have any effect. She was trapped between him and the railings – she could feel the hardness of the iron poles against her back.

Suddenly he released her wrist and lunged under her top, forcing his hand upwards. She heard a ripping sound as he pushed his way under her bra and began to knead one of her breasts roughly. Yvonne twisted, trying to work her elbow between them, but there was no room, he was too close. Her top was half open – she could feel the night air on her skin. She grabbed his hair and pulled hard. He grunted and rammed his tongue further into her mouth, forcing her head backwards.

He reached for her buttocks and pulled her into his groin. She felt his erection. He ground it against her and again she tried to wrestle free, straining to shout, but all she could manage, with his mouth on hers, were muffled groans. He groaned too and pressed himself harder against her.

And then, finally, she heard – at last, at last – the door of the restaurant opening.

Joe dropped his arms abruptly, stepped away from her and walked rapidly up the street without a backward glance. The couple who'd come out looked curiously at her.

'Are you alright?' the woman asked.

Yvonne pulled her top together – at least two

buttons gone – and wrapped the pashmina shakily around her. 'I am now.' She watched Joe's retreating, stumbling figure. 'He got a bit . . . carried away.' She tried to smile and failed. She wiped her mouth with the back of her trembling hand. She could still taste him.

The man bent and picked up her bag, and the woman said, 'Do you want to go back in and sit down . . . or phone someone?'

'No.' All she wanted to do was go home. 'Thanks, I'm fine now, really.' Her heart still pounded. She still felt his grip on her neck – would she have bruises in the morning? She took a deep breath and chanced a smile. 'I'm grand now, thanks to you two.'

'How are you getting home?' The woman was still concerned.

Yvonne pointed down the street. 'My car's just there.'

They insisted on walking the few steps with her and watched while she unlocked the car and got in. 'Lock the doors,' the man ordered, 'and take your time. Don't drive till you feel ready. We can wait a bit with you if you like.'

Yvonne thanked them again, told them again she'd be fine. She took a few more deep breaths and watched them walk away and felt her heart slow down a little. Then she forced herself to count to a hundred before she started the engine and eased the car slowly away from the path. She kept her eyes firmly on the road, didn't glance at the small, ivy-covered hotel as she passed it.

With any luck he'd empty the mini-bar, then fall downstairs and break his neck.

Once she'd driven past the town limits she pulled in again and rested her head on the steering wheel. She was never going near that website again. She thought of his tongue in her mouth, like some kind of horrible, wriggling snake, and her stomach lurched with the memory.

Fifty minutes later, she pulled into the lane behind the three red-brick houses and switched off the engine. Then she stayed sitting in the car. Clara hadn't gone out – she was nursing a head cold – and Yvonne wasn't ready to face her yet.

She felt the back of her neck gingerly. A tiny bit tender still. She'd wear her black jumper in the morning in case there was a mark. She wound down the window – nice calm night, a little bite to it, lots of stars. She reclined her seat a little and sat back, breathing slowly and steadily, with Clara's pashmina draped over her.

In all the years since Brian she'd slept with a handful of men, none of whom she'd loved. There'd been the hill walker – George, was it? He'd told her he was separated, had nice grey eyes and a pleasant smile. They'd gone on a hill-walking weekend in Mayo and on the second night they'd both had a little too much to drink and he'd come back to her single room. The sex had been unexciting and over too fast. He'd called her the wrong name as he came. Neither of them had suggested repeating the experience.

There was the man she'd got chatting to once in the dentist's waiting room, they'd gone out a few times. There was Kathryn's divorced cousin who was visiting one summer from the States.

A substitute teacher of Clara's who'd invited her for a drink after the parent-teacher meeting.

And once, shamefully, a good-looking plumber she'd found in the Golden Pages when her bathroom sink needed replacing. He'd been quite sweet and she'd enjoyed him.

But none had lasted. None had hung around long enough to see if they could come to mean more than a passing fling. At forty-two, all she had to look back on was one disastrous marriage, pathetically few brief encounters – and, thankfully, only one real moron, this evening.

At least Pawel had behaved like a gentleman. At least he hadn't attempted to rape her. His only crime had been causing her acute embarrassment. She smiled in the darkness. A blind date with her boss; she could see the funny side now.

She wondered suddenly if she'd have been attracted to Pawel if he hadn't turned out to be her boss, if it had been a real first meeting. He was certainly good looking and intelligent – maybe they'd have hit it off. She smiled again. She'd never know now.

She breathed deeply, feeling calm at last. The air smelled pleasant, cool and fresh, lightly scented with someone's flowers. Apart from Jim, the only proper male friend she had now was Greg. Thank goodness for Greg, restoring her faith in men anytime she needed it restored. He was such a rock, so steady, so dependable.

Pity he'd never settled down himself, he'd have made some woman a great husband. There must surely have been other women over the years, after that first failed relationship, but he'd never mentioned them to Yvonne.

She remembered thinking for a while, when she'd met him first, that Greg might be gay. She remembered asking Brian, who'd scoffed at the notion, even though he'd had to admit that Greg had never had a girlfriend he'd known of. But then they heard he'd left the seminary, and soon after that, he'd told them the reason. Greg wasn't gay, he'd just never met the right woman. Such—

She tensed – was somebody coming? Yes, footsteps approaching from one of the garden paths. She wound up her window as quietly as she could. Maybe if she ducked she wouldn't be seen.

But then the sound stopped and for a few seconds there was silence. Then she heard the first few notes of a bow being drawn across a violin's strings. She looked towards Dan's garden, astonished, but an apple tree hid whoever was playing. Not Dan, surely?

And after a minute, she eased the window down an inch, leaned back again, closed her eyes and let the music wash over her.

A week or so later: beginning of September

CONVERSATIONS

Morning, in the supermarket

'Hello, Dan.'

He turned and saw his neighbour pushing a trolley in the queue behind him. 'Hey, how are you?' He noticed the dark shadows under her eyes.

'Grand, thanks. The weather's holding out, isn't it?'

'Mmm.' Dan put his basket at the end of the checkout. 'How's Justin?'

'He's fine – but his mother's in hospital having tests so he's a bit worried about that.'

'That's too bad – hope it's nothing serious.' He began to transfer his groceries onto the conveyor belt. Natural yoghurt, onions, a fillet of lamb, beef tomatoes, milk, goat's cheese slid slowly away from him. A very different basket to the one he'd have been checking out a few months ago. 'Any idea what's wrong?'

'Not really. She's been complaining of headaches lately, so they're checking it out.' Kathryn pushed her trolley a little closer to the checkout. Dan saw free-range eggs, a jar of olives, butter, a box of Weetabix, a packet of funny tea – chamomile or something. 'How are you getting on these days, Dan?'

If he'd had a cent for every time someone had asked him that lately, he could have retired in the morning.

'Fine, never better. Lots of work, keeping busy, you know yourself.' Getting on fine without Ali. Saying it without saying it.

Kathryn was definitely less perky than normal. Probably worried about her mother-in-law.

Dan hadn't heard a word from his since Ali had left, surprise, surprise. He and Siobhan hadn't exactly taken to each other; he'd got the distinct impression that she hadn't considered him good enough for her daughter. Dan wondered what she thought of a fifty-two-year-old farmer.

Midday, over the hedge

'Working hard.'

Yvonne smiled at him. 'Hi Dan – haven't seen you in ages.' She stood and walked towards him, brushing her hands on her jeans.

'Yeah, I've been keeping busy.' He liked Yvonne. 'How's things?'

'Fine, apart from my disaster of a herb garden.' She made a face. 'I'm trying to tame them, but they're a mess – I'm wondering if I shouldn't just dig the whole thing up.'

'That's funny.' Dan pointed to a row of little wooden tubs on the far side of his patio, each sprinkled with greenery in various stages of growth.

'Kieran's just started a herb garden here. He likes to use them in cooking.'

'Oh, look at that – so nice and tidy.' Yvonne smiled. 'We're all dying to meet him.'

Dan laughed. 'I'll let him know – he'll be flattered, I'm sure.'

'So he likes to cook.'

'Yeah, he's very good. I'm signing up for classes, actually – I'm crap in the kitchen, compared to him.'

'You're going to cookery classes?'

'Yeah, in the Tech. I'm registering this week.'

'Well, good luck. Kathryn and I will expect an invitation to dinner when you're trained up.'

He laughed again. 'We'll see.'

'Well, better get back to this awful job.' Yvonne half turned away, then said, 'Oh by the way, I'm assuming Kieran's the one who plays the violin?'

'That's right. You've heard him?'

'Yes – lots of times actually, but I thought it was the radio or something, until just the other evening. He's good, isn't he?'

Afternoon, in number eight

'Dan? It's me.'

The same heart flutter whenever he heard her voice. He wondered if it would ever go away. 'Hi. How are you?'

'OK. Well, a bit tired, but otherwise . . .'

'Still working?'

'Oh, yes – I'm not giving up till Christmas.'

'That late? Shouldn't you go sooner?'

He heard her laugh softly. 'I'll be fine.' A short silence, then she said, 'I was wondering – well, we were wondering . . .'

We. Dan stiffened.

'. . . if you'd be willing to meet us and talk about, you know, the arrangements for afterwards. How we're going to—'

'No.' His hand was clenched on the phone. 'I don't want to meet him, I never want to – God, how can you even think—' The rage stopped him

'OK, sorry.' She spoke quickly. 'Really, I'm sorry, I didn't think. Well, maybe we could meet then, just the two of us?'

'Or maybe we could do it through solicitors. How about that?' He pressed disconnect and stood there, fuming.

One step forward, ten steps back.

Late afternoon, number seven's kitchen

'You're home early.'

'We closed for stocktaking – I told you this morning.' Clara opened the fridge. 'Are we out of water?'

'It's on the list. Can you make do with the tap?' Yvonne arranged potato slices on top of the meat in the casserole dish and bent to put it into the oven. 'By the way, I was talking to Dan a while ago. Guess what – he's taking cookery classes.'

Clara turned off the tap. 'What? Dan?'

'Well, he says his tenant's a great cook and has kind of shamed him into it, but I think it's more to do with Ali being gone – he's just trying to fill in the time, I'd say.'

Clara sipped water. 'I wouldn't even know where to find evening classes.'

Yvonne thought. 'I think Dan mentioned the Tech.'

'Right . . .' Clara leaned against the sink. 'Maybe I'll sign up too – might be a laugh.'

Yvonne stared at her. 'You? You're better able to cook than I am.'

Clara smiled. 'Like I said, it'd be just for the laugh – and there's always something to learn, I'm sure.'

Yvonne emptied a bag of cooking apples onto the table. 'It's kind of sad, though, isn't it? This is like finally admitting Ali's not coming back.' She rummaged in the cutlery drawer.

'Mmm.' Clara cradled her glass, one foot kicking absently at the press behind it. 'Still, if a marriage is over, it's over. Best to face up to it and move on.'

'I suppose.' Yvonne began to peel. 'Oh, and you know that violin music we keep hearing? It's not the radio, it's Dan's tenant.'

Clara nodded. 'Yeah, I knew it was him, I forgot to tell you I saw him the other night. He looked a bit weird, standing down there between the trees.' She sipped from her glass again. 'Any news on Justin's mother?'

Yvonne shook her head. 'No – they haven't got any results yet. It must be a worry though.'

'Mmm.'

After dinner, number eight's kitchen

'You've been spotted.'

'I have?'

Dan poured boiling water onto his teabag. 'One of our neighbours – Yvonne, in number seven. She saw you playing the other night. Thought you were the radio up to that.'

Kieran looked interested. 'Is that the blonde young one?'

Dan laughed. 'No, it's her mother. She was very impressed.'

Kieran thought. 'Don't think I've seen the mother.'

'Brown hair, nice looking. She has a herb garden out there that could do with your help. I was showing her your tubs . . .'

Late evening, number nine's sitting room

'You look tired. Any news yet?'

Kathryn shook her head. 'No but I have to admit I'm not inclined to be too worried. What's the betting they find nothing? You know what Grainne's like.'

Yvonne sipped her gin and tonic. 'But still, if they're giving her tests, they must be taking the headaches seriously.'

'Maybe.' Kathryn shrugged. 'Or maybe they're doing it to keep her quiet. She must be the most regular visitor to A & E.' She tapped a finger against her glass. 'Might be a good thing, though – I mean, if they do all the tests and find nothing, there's her credibility gone. But of course Justin's worried.'

'Naturally. What time are you expecting him back?'

Kathryn sighed. 'Anytime now, visiting ends at nine.' She sipped her wine. 'So how's the beautiful Clara? I haven't seen her in a while.'

Yvonne smiled. 'She's fine, thinking of going out to one of the Aran Islands with a few friends next weekend if the weather's OK. There's some kind of music festival on.'

'Sounds good. And no new man on the scene yet?'

Yvonne hesitated. 'I'm not sure. I thought for a while there might be, but there's no sign. She's rarely gone this long without a boyfriend.'

After another pause, Kathryn said, 'But there might be someone new and she just hasn't mentioned it.'

'Could well be, knowing Clara.' Yvonne sighed. 'I know I'm always saying it, but I really wish she'd confide in me more, Kath.'

Kathryn said slowly, 'Maybe you're as well off. Ignorance is bliss, isn't it?'

Same room, an hour later

'There's something I need to talk to you about.'

Kathryn's heart skittered. Here it was, what she'd been dreading for weeks now. In a way, it was a relief. 'What is it?'

Justin sat on the arm of the sofa. He rubbed his eyes. Was he as tired as she felt? 'I've been wanting to tell you for ages, but I wasn't sure how to.'

Kathryn said nothing. Her hands felt cold. She kept her eyes on his mouth.

'Look, may as well come out with it.' He lifted his

head. 'I want to quit work. I'm not happy there – it's not for me. I hate being on a computer all day, can't stand the monotony. I want to leave and do something else.'

Kathryn stared at him. It was so unexpected that she was genuinely lost for words. She didn't know what to say, hadn't a clue.

'You're shocked.'

'No, no.' She found her voice. 'Surprised – I had no idea, that's all. I thought you enjoyed your work.' He'd never mentioned being unhappy there before.

His mouth twisted. 'I didn't mind it so much, up to a few months ago, although I was never that mad about it. And then, I don't know . . . I'd suddenly had enough of staring at a screen all day.'

'You'd had enough.' She was still struggling to adjust. Steeling herself for her husband to announce that he was leaving her, and then to hear this.

Justin nodded. 'Yeah. I know it must sound a bit weird, out of the blue like this, but I've been thinking about it for ages and I can't not say it any more.'

'No, you had to. ' She studied his face, searched it for something else, found nothing.

He held her gaze. 'So what do you think? Am I crazy, at this stage, to be considering a total change of career?'

Kathryn tried to focus on what he was saying. A total change of career? What did his career matter, compared to their marriage? 'Well, have you any alternative in mind?'

Justin hesitated. 'Actually, I have. I always fancied teaching, and now there's a degree you can get online, I wouldn't even have to go back to college. I could keep working, study at weekends and maybe in the evenings.' He was watching her closely. He cared what she thought.

Kathryn spoke slowly. 'If that's what you want, then go for it. You have to be happy in your work.'

'Thank you.' He reached for her hand and squeezed it. 'You're cold.'

'Just my hands.'

He moved closer. 'I love you.'

When she didn't answer, he said, 'Kath.'

She couldn't speak.

He put an arm around her. 'What's wrong? I know something's wrong. Tell me.'

She opened her mouth. Why did you buy perfume for someone else? Who were the flowers for? Who were you phoning? This was her chance. He was asking her to tell him. Maybe he wanted her to bring it out into the open.

She couldn't say it. Saying it was much too terrifying.

'Nothing, I'm sorry. I'm just a bit fed up lately.' She tried to smile. 'I think it's . . . turning forty-five.' Coward, coward.

He drew her into him. 'You crazy woman. Is that all? You've been so miserable lately. It's just a number. You know I don't give a damn about that.'

'I know.' Her voice was muffled against his chest. Her eyes filled and she blinked away the tears.

'And you're really and truly OK about my daft notion?'

'I am.' She breathed in the smell of him. 'If it's really and truly what you want.'

Maybe it was over. Maybe it had been a mad summer fling and now it was over.

Maybe he really and truly loved her again.

Two weeks later: 19 September

NUMBER SEVEN

Yvonne fingered the knobbly turquoise stones set in the silver bracelet. 'You really shouldn't have.'

'Well, I did, so let's have no more of that.' Greg peered at her over his glasses. 'Have you decided? Because I have.'

Yvonne scanned the list of dishes. 'Sorry – too busy admiring my present. What are you getting? I bet it's the crab claws and the stir-fry.'

He laughed. 'We've definitely been friends for too long.'

'No, you're just so predictable. I'm going to have the crispy duck and then the plaice.' She closed the menu. 'Now, tell me everything.'

He was tanned and rested looking. Really, he was quite handsome. She knew him too well to appreciate that most of the time. His dark grey shirt was well cut, with a thin blue stripe running through it. She assumed he had plenty of money – what would he spend it on?

'Well, the villa was quite small, just two bedrooms, and very basically furnished, the bare necessities.

But the area was spectacular. I did some great walking – and of course I visited Florence and Pisa.'

She groaned. 'I'm sorry I asked. Were they wonderful?'

'Of course they were. Look at this.'

They went through the photos. He described the food – 'The basil, the olive oil, the pasta sauces.'

'And the ice cream – I've heard about the ice cream.'

'The ice cream is out of this world.' He described the churches and galleries. 'You don't know where to look, there's so much to see. Even if you're not big into art, you have to be impressed.' And the Italians: 'Very friendly, very dramatic. Good sense of humour.'

'I really wish I could have gone.'

'So do I.' He smiled as he cracked a claw and scooped out the meat.

Yvonne told him about Dolores going to Venice for her anniversary. 'They took loads of photos but their camera fell into a canal on the last day. She brought me a bottle of wine, which made me feel quite guilty.'

He told her about his landlord's decision to sell the house in Dublin. 'I'm not too upset really – it's high time I invested in one of my own.'

'But they're so expensive now, especially in Dublin.'

'Mmm. I might have to move out a bit, start commuting.'

They had plenty to talk about, plenty to keep them chatting over his beef stir-fry with baby sweetcorn, onions and pepper strips on a bed of basmati rice and her fillets of plaice with pumpkin wedges and creamed leeks. Lots to say as he sipped dessert wine afterwards – he loved dessert wine, she detested its syrupy sweetness – and took a forkful of her lemon cheesecake.

So it wasn't until their coffee had been poured and Yvonne was dipping her mint chocolate straw into the steaming liquid that Greg said, 'There's something I want to tell you – and ask you.'

She bit off the melting dark chocolate tip. 'What?'

Greg stirred his coffee. 'I'm not quite sure how to say this, really.'

'Sounds serious.' Yvonne crunched the rest of the straw, watching him. 'You look serious.'

'Well, it is fairly serious.' Greg put down his spoon and laced his fingers together. They were very brown against the white tablecloth. He took a deep breath, then let it out again and said nothing.

Yvonne swallowed her chocolate and stared at him. 'Greg, what is it? You're making me nervous. There's nothing wrong, is there?' Please God don't let him have a terminal disease.

He smiled quickly. 'No, nothing at all, nothing wrong. I'm just not sure how to put it, that's all.' And before she had a chance to respond to that, he said, all in a rush, 'The thing is, Yvonne, I'm in love with you – I have been for ages, for years, really – and it would make me extremely happy if you would consider marrying me.'

NUMBER EIGHT

The teacher was from Australia. He was tall, gangling and young – mid to late twenties, Dan guessed. His name was Douglas. He told them he'd worked as a junior chef on a cruise ship for four years. 'Then I got sense.' Some polite laughter. 'I got a job in a hotel in Melbourne, worked my way up to head chef – and then I met an Irish girl. She dragged me back here.'

Dan glanced around. Three other men, the rest female, as far as he could make out. Maybe a dozen altogether. He couldn't see everyone – the room was too long and narrow. People stood in pairs, two to a table. The woman beside him was in her sixties or thereabouts. They'd introduced themselves a few minutes earlier, just before the class began.

'I'm Judy.'

'Dan.' He'd nearly said 'Punch'. Ali would have appreciated that.

Douglas showed them how to measure a level teaspoon, how to rub margarine into flour – 'Lift it, let the air in' – how to mix liquid into dry ingredients, how to knead – 'Keep it light, don't hammer it, use the heel of your hand.'

By the end of the first session they'd all produced a dozen scones. Dan had heard about Judy's husband, who had multiple sclerosis, and her two cats, Tigger and Tux. 'Short for tuxedo – he's black and white.'

He told her about Picasso and about his job. He didn't mention his wife running off with his uncle, then discovering she was pregnant with Dan's baby. He figured he might save that for the second night.

Judy's scones were slightly overdone. Dan's had turned out pretty well, according to Douglas. 'Well done, mate, nice and light.'

It wasn't until they were leaving that he saw her near the back of the room, gathering up her things.

He waited at the door. 'Small world.'

Clara smiled. 'Hi Dan. Spotted you earlier. Mum mentioned you were doing classes, but I'd no idea they were these ones. What did you think of tonight?'

They walked along the corridor together. 'I enjoyed it.' He held up his bag. 'Douglas said my scones were nice and light.'

Clara laughed. 'Well done – mine weren't too bad either.'

They reached the door. Clara scanned the cars. 'Did you drive?'

'Nope, it was such a nice evening I walked.'

'Me too.'

On the way home, they talked about Grainne's news and agreed that it was terrible. Clara told him about her friend Siofra's month in France.

'She was on a volunteer project. They were helping to build a youth centre in a village in the south.'

He told her about a week in Ennis with friends. 'We went fishing and I caught a wellington and half a suitcase.'

She talked about her weekend on Inis Meán. 'We didn't get a wink of sleep. It was wild.'

When she flicked her hair or lifted a hand to push it off her face, he smelled lemons.

As they turned into Miller's Avenue, Clara said, out of the blue, 'I'm sorry about your wife, by the way.'

Dan was touched. 'Thanks.'

There was a short silence and then Clara said, 'I broke up with a boyfriend not so long ago.' Then she added quickly, 'But of course that's nothing like your situation.'

They reached his gate. Dan pushed it open. 'Well, see you next week.'

''Bye, Dan.' She lifted a hand. 'Hope the scones go down well.'

They had two each for supper, with gooseberry jam that Dan had bought in the market. Kieran was impressed. 'Very light, very tasty, well done. I'll soon be out of a job.'

She was too young for him. Not that he was looking for anyone – far from it. But even if he had been, she was much too young.

Pretty, though, and she'd smelled great. And she'd just split up with her boyfriend.

But much too young.

NUMBER NINE

There was a tumour in Grainne's head. It had been there for quite some time, growing quietly, and now it was too big to cut out. There was nothing to be done. Grainne was going to die, probably in the next six months.

Dr Lynch had put it much more tactfully, of course, in his surgery, where he'd summoned them to give them the news from the hospital. But that had been the gist of it.

Justin had phoned his sister Ann in Spain and his father William, living in Limerick now. Ann was going to come over as soon as Justin thought he could broach the subject with Grainne.

William, on the other hand, had told Justin he'd feel uncomfortable visiting – and he guessed Grainne wouldn't appreciate it either – but he asked Justin to keep him informed of her progress.

Grainne had taken the news very badly. She'd hardly left her room in the ten days since Dr Lynch's gentle announcement, even though she was still perfectly mobile. She lay in bed, stared at the opposite wall and hardly responded when they talked to her.

She ate very little, would probably have eaten nothing if she hadn't had to take some food with the tablets she'd been prescribed. A slice of the quiche she loved came downstairs barely touched. A little dish of ice cream was left to melt, ignored, until Justin took it away. She hardly looked at the bowl of black grapes – her favourite fruit – that sat on her bedside locker for days, until they started to shrivel and Kathryn took them away.

The tablets were mostly painkillers. 'That's really all we can do for her,' Dr Lynch had told them. 'Just keep her as comfortable as you can, and in a few months, if need be, we can see about getting her into a hospice.'

But Justin was having none of it. 'We'd rather have her at home,' he told the doctor. 'We can manage.'

'We can manage, can't we?' he asked Kathryn later that evening. 'We can talk to those daffodil nurse people – we can get someone in to help if we have to. And Ann will come over to stay for a while if we need her later, I know she will.'

And Kathryn had said yes, of course they'd manage. She wouldn't have wished this on her mother-in-law for the world, no matter how strained things had been between them. What a horrible thing to happen to anyone. Hard to believe that this time next year, barring some kind of miracle, Grainne wouldn't be with them.

Justin had told his superiors the news at work and he'd been given compassionate leave for the next couple of weeks, and part-time hours after that for as long as he needed them. His plans for a career change had, of course, been put on hold.

Funny how things worked out.

Kathryn sipped her peppermint tea. Grainne wasn't the only one who'd lost her appetite lately: none of them was eating right. When had she and Justin last sat down to a proper meal together? Kathryn found the peppermint tea soothing when she couldn't face cooking or eating.

She was looking forward to seeing her sister-in-law again. They hadn't met since Justin and Kathryn's trip to Spain two years before. She wondered how Grainne would react to the prospect of seeing the daughter she'd disowned so long ago. Maybe the knowledge that you were dying softened you, let you put aside old quarrels. They'd have to wait and see when Justin found the right time to broach the subject of Ann's plans to visit her mother.

Kathryn lifted her cup, inhaled the minty steam. The one good thing about all of this was how it put everything else into perspective. It made her realise that whatever had gone on with Justin over the last few months wasn't the huge thing she'd made it out to be, not compared to this.

From now on, Kathryn was going to look to the future, forget what may or may not have happened in the past and move on. Accept that she'd never know what Justin had done and live with it. She loved him, and she knew he loved her too.

The oven pinged and she went to take out the tray of almond cookies that Grainne used to love.

Three weeks later: 7 October

NUMBER SEVEN

She yanked out a clump of mint and added it to the small pile at her feet. The smell was heavenly – pity about the taste. And pity the plant didn't behave itself. Crowding out the rest like that till they could hardly breathe.

'Disgraceful,' she told Magoo, and he wagged his tail at her.

She sniffed the air. Was there a hint of autumn about the place? She enjoyed its tang, the smell of bonfires and the crackle of leaves, the frosty morning air.

Magoo snuffled around her, sniffing at the grass. Pawing at the freshly turned earth.

'What do you think?' Yvonne asked him. 'Will my herbs survive, or are they doomed?'

His tail wagged again. He liked being spoken to.

'So anyway, remember I told you about Greg?' Yvonne said. Magoo sat, his tail thumping the ground. 'You know Greg – he throws your ball.'

Magoo barked.

'Yes, you remember him. Nice man, comes and

takes me out to dinner sometimes.' She pulled out another clump of mint. 'Well, he's asked me to marry him. What do you think of that?'

She put her head to one side, looking at Magoo.

'What's that? What did I tell him? Well, I said I needed time to think.' She dug some more, then looked at him again. 'That was OK, wasn't it?'

He barked again, pushed his head into her hand.

She ruffled his hair. 'So now I'm thinking about it.' She pulled his ear gently. 'But you know what, Magoo?'

She stopped. The air was very still. Somewhere a bird was singing the same little tune over and over.

'I'm thinking I might say yes.' She put a hand around his long jaw. 'But don't tell anyone.'

She hadn't mentioned the proposal to Clara or to Kathryn – well, poor Kathryn had her hands full with Grainne right now. She didn't want to say anything to anyone until she'd made up her mind, until she'd decided whether she wanted to spend the rest of her life with Greg.

Was he her closest friend? He was certainly her closest male friend. She loved him, didn't she? She looked forward to seeing him. He was good to her, very generous and dependable – oh, you could depend your life on Greg. He'd be good to Clara too, they'd always got on.

So there was every reason for saying yes. It made perfect sense. She put down her fork and sat on the grass with an arm around Magoo's neck.

Greg's wife. Going on holidays together. Sitting down to dinner every night, telling each other about the kind of day they'd had. Getting into the same bed a few hours later.

She wondered what kind of lover he'd be.

She heard a door sliding open on next door's patio. Footsteps, then clattering. The tenant – what was his name? She'd forgotten – cleaning the barbecue. He was a great man for a barbecue. She heard out-of-tune whistling. Was he wearing that awful hat? The hedge was too high for her to see. Imagine, they hadn't met yet – he'd moved in months ago.

And Dan with his cookery classes, Clara doing them too, as if she needed them. She'd come home from the first class with a bag of lighter-than-air scones. She'd been baking scones since she was twelve. Yvonne asked her if she'd seen Dan and Clara said, 'Yeah, he was there. We walked home together.'

Yvonne heard the tenant's footsteps going into the house again. She stood up gingerly, easing the pins and needles out of her calves. Then she picked up her fork and turned to Magoo. 'I suppose you want feeding.'

He barked again, happily.

NUMBER EIGHT

In the second class, they diced onions and carrots, crushed garlic, stirred cream into stock and made soup, then toasted cubes of day-old bread for croutons. In the third, they made dough, cut tomatoes, sliced mozzarella, chopped mushrooms, scattered herbs and went home with pizza.

In the fourth, they beat eggs and sugar together, squeezed lemons and lined tins with pastry, then poured in the filling and baked tarts. And it was raining.

People tended to keep to the places they'd taken up at the first class, so Dan and Judy had become a couple. Judy told him about her mother's Christmas cakes. 'She was famous for them, kept half the neighbourhood supplied. She baked them in August, two at a time. Took about a week. She put dark rum into them. The kitchen smelled like a brewery.'

She told him about her husband's potato allergy – 'He can't even take a tiny bit before he starts sneezing. I wouldn't mind, but he loves them, the creature' – and their trip to Lourdes two years ago, in the hope of curing his multiple sclerosis. 'We said all the prayers, did all the treatments, and he was no better coming home. I suppose they have to ration the miracles.'

He told her about Kieran. 'He's a great cook – he inspired me to come here, actually.' Pity Judy was married. She might have suited Kieran fine, even if she was a good bit older than him. He wondered if her husband was going to last much longer. He asked her if she liked violin music and she told him she never listened to music, didn't see the point of it, really, she'd much rather watch *Fair City* or *Eastenders* on telly, or a nice film.

He thought maybe she and Kieran might not be so well suited after all.

After every class Dan walked home with Clara. She told him she liked to hear Kieran playing the violin: 'The first time, I thought I was dreaming.'

He told her about the baby, his baby. He didn't know he was going to tell her, it just dropped into their conversation.

'God, that's a bit weird, isn't it?' And he agreed that it was, definitely, a bit weird.

After a few minutes, she said, 'So – are you going to share the upbringing or what?'

He shrugged. 'We're trying to figure that out now.'

Ali had written to him after he'd hung up on her that last time. After she'd called him back three times over the following few days and he'd hung up again, three times. The letter was short. He knew it by heart.

Dan,

Since you would prefer to go through solicitors, I'm sending you the name of mine. If you change your mind, please be in touch.

Best regards,

Ali

And underneath, a woman's name he didn't recognise, an address and a phone number. Reading it, he'd felt bereft.

On the evening of the fourth class, he'd come out of the house and realised it had begun to rain lightly since he'd got home from work. He decided to drive – might be pouring later. It hadn't rained for a good while, except at night. He'd hear it pattering on the roof before he fell asleep, trickling into his dreams.

Clara always went straight from her job to the classes – the department store stayed open late on Thursdays, like a lot of Belford's shops. There was no sign of her when Dan walked into the long, narrow room. He crossed to his and Judy's table. 'Hello. Lovely weather.'

Judy smiled. 'There you are, Dan. Ah, I don't mind the rain. I'd rather that than live in a desert.'

'How's your husband?' He felt obliged to ask each time.

And Judy's answer hardly varied: 'Ah sure, as well as can be expected, the creature.'

She'd told him they had two children, both living abroad. The son worked on an offshore oil rig somewhere in the North Sea; the daughter lived in Paris, married to a photographer. Judy's husband had been diagnosed sixteen years ago, but had been in remission for twelve.

As they whisked egg yolks for their lemon tarts, Dan told her about Grainne. 'She's been given six months, her daughter-in-law says.'

'Tch, the poor woman, that's terrible. How old is she?'

Dan thought. 'Around seventy, I'd say.' He knew Judy wasn't far off that herself. 'Not old.'

Clara arrived, shaking the drops off a grey scarf as she walked in. Her hair was tousled. She smiled and waved at Dan as she went down the room to her usual table.

While the lemon tarts were baking, they learnt how to blanch and sauté, how to make a roux and how to keep sauces from getting lumpy.

Dan was surprised at how much he was enjoying the classes. Cooking had never interested him before and he'd never put much thought into creating a meal. Now he was discovering a fascination with it, the idea that you could combine various ingredients, stir, blend and mix, until something new came out. You could experiment, change the flavours, try new combinations. He was hooked.

At the end of the class, the room smelled wonderful. The lemon tarts emerged, marigold yellow speckled with a darker caramel, firm to the touch.

Douglas went around doling out tinfoil. 'You're all doing very well. Now, when you get home you take a bowl of single cream and whip it until it stays in peaks for a couple of seconds after you pull the beater out. You have a slice of tart and cream, then do ten laps around the block. Next week we'll be healthier, I promise.'

'I'm driving,' Dan told Clara as they walked down the corridor.

'I had to wait for the bus,' she said. 'That's why I was late.'

He opened the passenger door first. 'Hop in.'

He was acutely aware of her, sitting less than a foot away from him in the car. 'You've changed your perfume.'

She laughed. 'How observant of you. I've switched to my winter one now.' It was warmer and flowery, and it still didn't remind him of Ali's.

He'd gone back to the solicitors who'd handled the purchase of the house. He was told they didn't operate in the area of family law, but that they could recommend someone who did.

Family law – that was ironic. What would you call the kind of family his son was going to be born into? A mother who was living with his great-uncle, a father he might see only now and again. Some family.

He rang the number they'd given him and arranged to meet the new solicitor.

'David Burton.' The handshake was firm. He was about Dan's age. He listened while Dan spoke, scribbling on a pad in front of him.

When Dan lapsed into silence, he tapped the page with the end of his biro. 'It's an unusual situation.'

'Yes.' Dan hoped he wasn't being charged God knew what to be told what he already knew. 'I'm wondering if I can apply for full custody once the baby's born.' He was sorry he hadn't said 'my baby'. Because hadn't he as much a right as Ali to bring up their son, if not more? Wasn't she the one at fault here, having deserted the marriage to shack up with her husband's relative? If that didn't show she was an unfit parent, nothing did.

But David Burton wasn't encouraging. 'It simply doesn't work that way, I'm afraid. You can take a case, certainly – nothing to stop you applying for custody – but I wouldn't be doing my job properly if I pretended you had a hope of getting it.' He saw Dan's expression and said, more gently, 'You have to understand that both you and your wife have equal ownership, to put it very crudely, of the child—'

'But she deserted the marriage. She's gone off with my uncle, for Christ's sake. How can that be a stable home for any child?'

The solicitor dropped his biro and rested his hands on the desk. 'Dan, you need to let go of the fact that it's your uncle. Believe it or not, that has no bearing on the case—'

'No bearing? How can—'

Dan's interruption was ignored. '—and it won't further your cause one iota if you become fixated on it. Your wife walked out on the marriage, end of story. Who she left you for is immaterial.'

Dan glowered at the polished dark wood of the table that separated him from this man who was saying all the wrong things. What did he know anyway? He hardly looked as if he'd had a lot of experience. He might even be younger than Dan.

'I can't believe that he'd be allowed to raise my son just like that.'

David Burton picked up his pen again, ran a finger along its barrel. 'Dan, you must remember that the child is the innocent party in all of this. He's had nothing to do with any of it. If you start a war with his mother, you've got no way of knowing what that's going to do to him, or to your relationship with him in the future.'

Dan glared at him. 'So that's it. I let her keep him. I get no say.'

The solicitor spoke gently. 'It's not a question of her keeping him – as I said, you've got joint ownership. Ideally, it's up to the two of you to work out a sensible arrangement whereby you share responsibility for his upbringing.' He hesitated. 'You need to understand, though, that from a legal point of view, the mother is commonly regarded as the primary carer and her place of residence will be seen as the most likely one for him to live in.'

'So you're pretty sure that's what would be decided if I went ahead and took a case? That the child would live most of the time with . . . them?'

'In all likelihood, yes, with you getting alternate weekend custody, say, and some holidays, possibly midweek access too.' Again the solicitor paused, studying Dan. 'Do you think there's any possibility of you and your wife working something out between you?'

Dan lifted his shoulders. 'That's what she wants.'

'I'd strongly advise you to think about it. It'll mean swallowing your anger and being prepared to compromise, but in the long run it'll make things a lot easier. I can draw up a draft agreement, if you like, that you can run by her.'

And that was it. All Dan was being offered was exactly the same as Ali had wanted. It took all he had to shake hands with the man and tell him he'd think about it. What was there to think about, except how much the idea of Brendan raising his son appalled him?

'You're miles away.'

Dan changed gear, gave Clara a brief smile. 'Sorry – a lot on my mind.'

They got to Miller's Avenue. Dan drove up the lane beside Clara's house and stopped at her back gate. It was still raining, the drops splattering against the windscreen before the wipers swept them away.

Clara reached into the back seat for her lemon tart and wrapped the grey scarf around her head. 'Well, thanks very much – I'd have got drenched if I'd had to wait for another bus.' And before Dan could react, as he was about to say 'Not at all', she leaned across and touched the corner of his mouth briefly with her lips.

'Goodnight, Dan.' The softest of kisses, barely there at all.

And she was gone, slamming the door, leaving her flowery scent behind. He drove the few extra feet until he was beside his gate. Then he switched off the engine, took his tart from the back seat and got out. The rain pelted against his face and made little metallic pings as it bounced off the tinfoil.

He walked up the path. There was a light on in the kitchen. Kieran looked up from the newspaper as Dan opened the door. 'Terrible night.'

Dan ignored Picasso, who eyed him calmly from a kitchen chair. They ate two slices of warm lemon tart each, with a scoop of ice cream instead of cream. Dan told Kieran about the class. He told him about Judy's cat having kittens in the drum of the washing machine, and Douglas's confession that he could only drink Guinness with a dash of blackcurrant, and Judy preferring *Eastenders* to music.

He didn't mention Clara. He didn't tell Kieran about her lips against his mouth for an instant, or his almost overwhelming urge, as she opened the car door, to pull her back, turn her face towards his and kiss her properly.

NUMBER NINE

'What?' Kathryn's hands flew to her face.

Dr Lynch smiled. 'You weren't expecting it.'

'No, it was the last thing I . . .' She stopped. 'The last thing.' She lowered her hands slowly. 'Are you sure? I mean, could you be wrong?'

'No, you're definitely pregnant. About seven weeks. You haven't had a period in that time, have you?'

'No, but I thought maybe it was my age – I thought it might be . . .'

She had thought it might be the menopause, and the idea had been terrifying. The notion that she might be pregnant hadn't occurred to her as the cause of her queasiness in the mornings, her sudden aversion to coffee, her general loss of appetite – because she'd never been sick before, had sailed through each of her doomed pregnancies, feeling exactly as she always did.

She had to ask: 'What are my chances of keeping it? You know my history – and I'm forty-five now.'

Dr Lynch wrote on his pad. 'I don't blame you for being nervous, but there's no reason why you shouldn't carry this baby to full term. Your earlier miscarriages, and the stillbirth, are no indication that you'll have any problem now. All the same, we'll take every precaution, even if it means keeping you flat on your back for a lot of the next few months.'

She thought of her mother-in-law. 'I'll be needed at home – with Grainne.'

Justin's compassionate leave had run out and he was back at work part-time, twenty hours a week, ten of which he could do from home. After making a few enquiries they'd found Marzena, a Latvian who'd trained as a nurses' aide in her home country and who cleaned houses in Ireland. Marzena came when Justin was out at work, just so somebody would be in the house with Grainne.

Dr Lynch considered. 'The timing could have been better, certainly, and Justin's going to have his hands full with both of you. But you need to look after yourself now, Kathryn – and your baby. You must do what's best for him or her, and for you.'

She passed Yvonne's desk on the way out. Yvonne was putting on her jacket.

'Oh good, I was hoping you'd be back down before I left. Everything alright?'

'Fine – just a tummy bug, he said.' She hated lying, but what else could she say? It was far too early to tell anyone, even Yvonne. 'I'll live.'

'Oh, poor you – why don't you come home with me and I'll make a pot of tea?' Yvonne lowered her voice. 'I'm trying to avoid having lunch with Dolores – I've had a bellyful of her this week.'

Kathryn smiled and shook her head. 'I won't, if

you don't mind. Justin is at home and I promised I'd be straight back.'

'Oh, sorry, I didn't think. How're you coping?'

'OK – she's very down all the time, of course, but at least Justin's persuaded her to get up for an hour or two in the afternoons. And she's not in any pain. They've given her loads of pills. She sleeps a lot. And Ann's coming at the weekend. Grainne actually agreed to it.'

'Good. And you?' Yvonne searched her pale face. 'Are you really alright?'

Kathryn almost told her – she was bursting to – but she couldn't. 'I'm fine, really. This thing just has to take its course.'

Too much uncertainty. Too much at stake to say it out loud, even to Justin. How could she tell him this news now, give him fresh worry with all that was happening to Grainne? She'd have to wait until the first three months were over, when they could begin to hope.

'Can you keep a secret?'

It was so unexpected, so the wrong way around, that Kathryn almost laughed. 'What?'

They were walking down the clinic steps. The sun was out, mopping up the earlier puddles. Yvonne linked her arm in Kathryn's. 'Greg asked me to marry him last month.'

'Oh my God.' Kathryn stopped, amazed. 'What did you say?'

'I told him I'd think about it.' Yvonne smiled.

Kathryn stared. 'And have you?'

'I have, and I'm going to say yes. He's coming

down at the weekend and I'm cooking dinner for him on Friday night. I'll tell him then.'

'Oh, wonderful.' Kathryn hugged her. 'I'm thrilled. He's lovely.'

'He is.'

She'd often wondered if it would happen, with Greg and Yvonne. Greg had been around all the time she'd known Yvonne. Almost eleven years now, since Kathryn had bought number nine Miller's Avenue and Yvonne had called around a few days later with a sponge cake to welcome her to the neighbourhood. They'd taken to each other right away.

And every so often, over cups of coffee or glasses of whatever in each other's houses, Yvonne would say 'Greg's coming down for a few days' or 'I'm going up to Dublin. Greg's taking me to a play.'

Kathryn had met Greg a few times over the years, the last time at Clara's twenty-first party. Yvonne had rented a small marquee, invited Kathryn and Justin around, and Greg had been there, and a crowd of Clara's friends and even her grandparents – even her grandmother, who had no time for Yvonne – had put in a brief appearance.

Greg was very pleasant, and undoubtedly he and Yvonne were close. It was about time, more than time, for them to move on. As far as Kathryn could see, they stood a good chance of making it work. Wasn't friendship just about the best basis for marriage you could get? And they'd been friends for so long, Yvonne and Greg.

'Can I tell Justin?'

'Yes, but wait till after the weekend, till I've given Greg my answer – just in case.'

'Right.' Kathryn squeezed her arm as they approached her house. 'I'm absolutely delighted. Congratulations. We'll have to arrange a little celebration when it's official.'

'Definitely.' Yvonne did seem happy. She deserved a bit of happiness after so long on her own. And she was certainly owed a bit of good luck, with her recent internet disasters.

The house was quiet. Justin wasn't in any of the downstairs rooms. He must be up with Grainne. Kathryn made a cup of peppermint tea – she hadn't even recognised her first craving – and brought it out to the patio. She stood there, trying to take it in.

Pregnant. She was pregnant. For seven weeks she'd had a baby growing inside her. Now, finally, she could put the past behind her and face this wonderful, terrifying future.

She prayed to her baby: Stay with me. Be born. Live.

One day later: 8 October

NUMBER SEVEN

Her father-in-law spooned buttered spinach from the white dish. 'I'm like Popeye – I love this stuff.'

For all his thin frame, Jim could eat. Yvonne pushed the bowl of potatoes closer to him. 'Here, have more of those.'

'Thanks dear.' He turned to Greg beside him. 'I'm a lucky man to have two lovely cooks looking after me every time I come here.'

Clara laughed. 'You're such a charmer. Isn't he, Mum?'

'He certainly is.' Yvonne wondered how he'd take their news. They'd decided they might as well tell him tonight.

The previous night she'd given Greg her answer. She'd roasted a chicken and served it with baked onions and potato croquettes. Clara had gone upstairs afterwards, so Yvonne and Greg had taken their coffee into the sitting room. Yvonne had put a match to four little tea-lights that sat on the low table, and switched on the lamps that were dotted around the room. The fire she'd lit earlier flickered gently.

Greg had stretched out his long legs, cradling his coffee cup. 'So . . . how've you been?'

Yvonne smiled. 'Is that really what you want to know?'

He looked at her for a minute. 'No.'

She put down her cup and reached for one of his hands. 'I've thought about it, and I've decided to accept your proposal.'

A smile bloomed in his face. He brought her hand to his lips and kissed it. 'You've made me very happy, Yvonne. Thank you.'

She grinned. 'Thank you for asking. Now' – she moved from her chair and sat in his lap – 'how about giving your new fiancée a proper kiss?'

It was different. Their kiss was tentative, almost passionless. But she shouldn't have been surprised – it took quite a leap, didn't it, to move from friendship to a physical relationship? And they'd been friends for so long . . . they'd need time to be comfortable with this new situation. It would happen, she was sure.

So they were officially engaged. As soon as Greg had left, Yvonne went upstairs and tapped on Clara's bedroom door, half anxious, half excited.

'Come in.' Clara was brushing her hair in front of the mirror. She wore a pale pink dressing-gown.

Yvonne sat on the bed. 'I've got something to tell you.'

Clara met her mother's eyes in the mirror. 'You and Greg are getting married.' She laughed at Yvonne's surprised expression. 'Oh, come on, Mum, you don't need to be a rocket scientist. He was mooning at you all through dinner and you've been a million miles away lately.' She put down her hairbrush, turned from the mirror and held out her arms. 'Congratulations. It's high time.'

Yvonne hugged her. 'Are you sure you approve?' Maybe this would bring the two of them closer at last. 'I didn't know how you'd feel about it.'

Clara dropped her arms and turned back to the mirror. 'Oh, Mum, what's not to approve? As long as Greg doesn't decide to come over all fatherly and start bossing me around.'

Yvonne laughed. 'Hardly – you're a bit old for that. And I think he knows he'd never get away with it.' She watched Clara pulling the brush through her blonde hair. 'He's always been very fond of you.'

Greg had wanted to take the three of them out to dinner the following evening to celebrate, but it was Jim's night to visit.

'I'd hate to cancel him – he likes his routine. And it'll give us a chance to tell him.'

Now she waited until the plates had been cleared away, until she'd filled the percolator with the decaffeinated coffee Jim preferred and the cups were passed around the table.

'Jim, Greg and I have a bit of news.' May as well say it out. She took Greg's hand and said, 'Greg has asked me to marry him, and I've accepted.'

For a moment there was silence. In the corner, the fridge shuddered. Then Jim said, 'Well, that's . . . ' He looked from one to the other. 'Well, that's just . . . that's good news.'

Yvonne watched his face. 'You don't disapprove?'

'Of course not.' But Jim still seemed to be searching for words. 'Not at all – you just took me by surprise, that's all.' He turned to Greg and held out his hand. 'Congratulations.'

Maybe she shouldn't have blurted it out like that. Greg was Brian's cousin, after all. She'd married Jim's son and now she was about to marry his nephew. Maybe that was a bit much to expect him to handle.

Just then Clara's phone rang and she went into the hall to answer it.

There was another short silence in the kitchen. Then Jim said, 'Have you a date set at all?'

Since her announcement, the atmosphere had altered. There was a tension that hadn't been there before.

'We're thinking about next summer.'

Jim smiled. 'Good.'

She braced herself. 'You'll tell Peggy?' God only knew what Peggy would say.

Jim nodded. 'I will, certainly.'

And Yvonne was quite sure that if she asked him next month how Peggy had received the news, his account would be carefully censored.

Clara stood at her bedroom window in the dark. Next door's garden, in the faint moonlight, was pretty much like their own.

She wondered if Dan was in bed. She wondered which bedroom was his. Maybe he was lying asleep on the other side of her wall. Maybe he was awake, thinking about his wife.

Or maybe he was thinking about her.

Had the kiss been a mistake? He would have been surprised – he wouldn't have been expecting it. But would it have been welcome, or would he have been dismayed by it?

Of course it was crazy – the whole thing was crazy. He was still getting over his wife running off. It was much too soon for him to get involved with anyone else. Didn't every magazine warn about rebound relationships?

No matter. She was willing to take the risk; they couldn't all fail.

But would he try to avoid her now after the cookery classes? Would he try to find some excuse so he didn't have to drive her home any more? Or – her heart sank – would he stop coming to the classes altogether? Had her impulse driven him away?

Well, she'd soon find out. And the awful thing was, she didn't know which outcome would be worse. She'd be devastated, of course, if Dan wasn't interested, if nothing ever followed the kiss.

But if he was interested, if by some miracle it turned out that he felt the same way she did, well, that would open up a whole new scenario that completely terrified her.

Dirty girl.

She turned from the window and got into bed, knowing that sleep would be a long time coming.

Six days later: 14 October

NUMBER NINE

Kathryn had forgotten how like Justin his sister was. Ann had his chin and his mouth, and their hair was exactly the same dark brown. But Ann was smaller than her brother by a good six inches, and Justin, unfairly, had the long eyelashes.

She arrived by taxi from the station – she'd forbidden Justin or Kathryn to collect her – and she brought wine and delicately scented soaps and a rug that Suze had woven in burnt, sunny colours, and she went straight upstairs to see her mother.

Kathryn and Justin waited in the kitchen. The minutes ticked by. Grainne had taken some time to be persuaded to allow her daughter to visit. After half an hour, they heard the bedroom door opening and a minute later, Ann appeared.

She sat on a kitchen chair and smiled at them shakily. 'I need a drink.'

'Was it bad?' Justin took the corkscrew from its hook.

'Ah – I wasn't expecting it to be easy, so I wasn't surprised.' Ann sighed. 'I'm still not forgiven, of course, for blackening the Taylor name, but at least she's talking to me – even if she's saying nothing, really.' She watched Justin pouring the deep red Spanish wine.

Kathryn said quickly, 'Just a half-glass for me, love.' Dr Lynch had told her a little wouldn't hurt. She turned to Ann. 'Did you ask her about dinner?'

'She said she's not hungry – she's thin, isn't she?' Ann looked at her sister-in-law. 'I'd say you've lost a bit of weight too, since I saw you last.'

Kathryn smiled. 'Oh, I'm sure I'll put it on again soon enough.'

Over the following few days, Ann went into town and brought home pink iced buns and blueberry sorbet and greengage jelly, and mandarin oranges and cartons of cranberry juice, and she put together colourful little meals and brought them upstairs on trays. Nobody commented when the trays came down virtually untouched.

On her fourth day, Ann brought Grainne into the bathroom and touched up her roots.

On her fifth day, she came downstairs and said to Kathryn, 'Do you know anything about this?'

Kathryn looked at the small white box. 'What is it?'

'It's perfume, not even opened.'

Kathryn took it from her and read Coco Chanel. The price sticker was still on it: sixty-five euro. 'Where did you find it?'

'In her wardrobe, right at the back. I was sorting through boxes of photos and I saw it. She never wore perfume – someone must have given it to her as a present.'

Kathryn shook her head slowly. 'I've never seen it before.'

Sixty-five euro. Had Justin bought the perfume for his mother after all? But he hadn't said a word – he would surely have mentioned it. And why would he buy her perfume, knowing she never wore it?

Yet here it was, still in its packaging, months later.

Because it had to be the same perfume, didn't it? The price was the same, everything fit. And Justin must have bought it because the receipt had been in his pocket.

Unless . . . unless someone else had put it there. The thought came from nowhere.

Someone could have put the receipt into Justin's pocket, knowing that Kathryn, who always did the laundry, who was so careful about checking pockets, would be sure to find it.

And, of course, she'd be bound to find the second receipt too, the one for the flowers, sticking out from under the phone table, where she'd couldn't miss it when she was cleaning the hall.

The more she thought about it, the more perfect, awful sense it made. Kathryn remembered the phone call and realised that it had been Grainne who'd told her about it. She only had Grainne's word that it had ever taken place.

That had been a clever move, to tell Kathryn she thought it was a surprise for her birthday. She must have been pleased to come up with that little touch.

She'd made up the whole phone call – and naturally, Kathryn had believed her, because why would Grainne lie?

Because she wanted to split us up. Because she was infuriated that her son had married an older woman. Because I couldn't give him children.

But none of that mattered now. The only thing that mattered was the realisation that Justin hadn't been having an affair. It made her want to weep with happiness and relief.

She handed the box back to Ann. 'Seems a shame to let it go to waste. Why don't you take it?'

Later that night, when Justin and Ann were sitting by the fire, Kathryn went up to Grainne's bedroom. She opened the door, walked inside and sat on the chair by the bed. The room was dimly lit with one small lamp.

A collection of little bottles sat on the bedside locker with various pastel-coloured pills inside them. Grainne lay on her back, eyes closed, lids fluttering.

She wore a peach nightdress with cream scalloped lace at the neck. Her skin was tinged with yellow. Her cheeks had begun to sink; it was easy to imagine the shape of the skull beneath. With each breath, she made a tiny popping sound. She looked small and harmless, lying asleep in bed. A small, harmless old woman.

'Grainne,' Kathryn said softly, 'are you awake?'

No response. No movement, apart from the fluttering eyelids and the tiny, shallow breaths.

'I just wanted you to know that I'm pregnant,'

Kathryn whispered. 'I'm almost two months pregnant, and I'm not going to lose this baby. It's going to survive. It'll be born, in April or May.'

Grainne lay still.

'I'm sorry – it would have been nice for you to see your grandchild.'

The air was heavy in the room. Grainne's eyelids fluttered.

'Justin loves me. Your son loves me. He doesn't care about my age. We'll be together until one of us dies.'

After a minute, Kathryn stood up and left the room, her heart singing with happiness.

NUMBER EIGHT

It was ridiculous. It was all wrong. The timing couldn't have been worse. It was only six months since Ali had left. Dan was going to be a father, Ali was having his baby. It was all impossibly complicated, and it would probably get a lot worse.

Clara was twenty-three. He was thirty-two.

She was very pretty. Her smile lit him up. She made his heart beat faster. She gave him butterflies, made him feel like some gormless, lovestruck teenager. She smelled wonderful. It was all he could do to keep his hands off her. He wanted to bite her, to lick her, to suck her up.

She lived next door, a dozen feet from him. He wished she was a million miles away. He wished she was in his bed, wrapped around him. He lay awake, thinking about her. He fell asleep and she was there too. She slid out of his dreams and followed him to his office. She pestered him while he tried to work. He was driven mad with her. He pushed her away, he pulled her closer.

What if Ali hadn't left? Would he be obsessed with Clara now? No, because without Kieran he'd never have gone to the cookery classes. He'd never have met her every Thursday night, they'd never have walked or driven home together. Up to when the classes started, he hadn't exchanged more than a dozen words with Clara O'Mahony, hadn't given her a second thought.

Imagine if Ali knew he couldn't stop thinking about the Bombshell.

Tonight was their fifth class, halfway through the course. The evening was cold, with a stiff breeze. Dan drove.

Clara was there already. He waved down the room at her. She smiled and waved back. He hadn't laid eyes on her all week, since she'd kissed him – how many times had he relived that brief touch? – and got out of the car.

Judy was waiting for him at their table.

'There you are, Dan. Wonder what delights Douglas has in store for us tonight.'

He pulled off his jacket, threw it under the table. 'He said it'd be something healthy anyway.' He was acutely aware of Clara behind him. Was she watching him?

They cooked a vegetarian flan. They made pastry, rolled it out and lined a flan tin, pricked it all over and baked it blind. They crushed garlic and chopped peppers and onions. They peeled carrots and sliced them wafer thin, and grated cheese and beat eggs. They sprinkled salt and pepper and they chopped parsley and sage.

And all the time Dan thought about Clara. He answered Judy's questions and even asked some of his own. He watched as Douglas showed them how to gather the pastry into a ball, and he thought about Clara.

It was ridiculous. It was all wrong. He longed for the class to end so they could be alone. He couldn't wait for the journey home, with her sitting so close to him in the car. He wished they lived on the other side of the country, a good four hours' drive away.

His flan came out a little flat. There was a definite, if not very deep, dip in the middle. 'Not to worry, mate,' Douglas told him. 'Oven temperature might have been a bit low. I'm sure it'll taste OK.'

He waited for Clara by the door, as usual. He watched her walking towards him. 'Hi. How's your flan?'

She made a face. 'Well, it turned out fine, but it's not my kind of food. I hate vegetarian.'

'Mine's flat,' Dan told her. 'My first failure.'

She laughed. 'Poor you.' Outside, she looked around. 'Are we driving home tonight?'

We. His heart flipped. 'We are.' He pointed. 'I'm over there.'

In the car she told him her mother was getting married. 'We've known Greg forever. He was actually a cousin of my dad's. You've probably seen him – tall, thin, glasses.'

'Wow, Yvonne getting married.' Dan turned a corner. 'How do you feel about that?'

'OK, I suppose. I mean, he wouldn't be my choice – a bit safe – but I'm not marrying him, and I don't suppose I'll be living at home for much longer, so it won't affect me a whole lot.'

'When are they getting married?'

'Sometime next year, in the summer.'

'I suppose you'll be a bridesmaid.' He smiled, imagining her in something long and flowing.

She made a face. 'I'm hoping she won't ask. I'd probably have to wear a horrible shiny dress.'

Dan laughed. 'You'd look good whatever you put on.'

Silence. He glanced over and she was smiling.

When he stopped the car, she turned to take her flan from the back seat. 'Well, thanks again.' Her face was inches from his. He was powerless. He reached across and ran the back of his hand along her cheek.

She whirled towards him, almost dropping the flan. 'Hey.'

'Sorry, I couldn't help—' He was mortified. She'd storm out and avoid him forevermore.

'Hang on.' She put the flan on the floor in front of her and slid it under her seat. Then she turned back to Dan and leaned across.

Her mouth was soft. She tasted faintly of mint. She'd had plenty of practice. When the kiss was over, she whispered his name. He felt sixteen again, hot with wanting her.

And there was nothing ridiculous about it at all.

Kieran went to the funeral because that was what you did. An accident was what they'd called it in the paper. A tragic accident. A young man, only twenty-nine. Survived by his mother, Geraldine.

The two men who'd heard him fall in, two passers-

by who'd come running to help, were there. Kieran
recognised them from their pictures in the paper.

The coffin was covered with a white cloth. A small
basket holding a few envelopes sat on the end. A single
bouquet of yellow and orange carnations was draped
across the top. A head-and-shoulders photo of Adam
in a gold-coloured frame stood on a small folding table
beside it. He was wearing a suit and tie and smiling.
That picture had been in the paper too.

Kieran hadn't seen Geraldine properly in years.
She'd left the café abruptly, a few months after their
relationship had ended, and since then he'd glimpsed
her across a shop floor a few times, ahead of him in a
supermarket queue, sitting beside another woman in a
red car once, parked outside a library. He'd never
approached her on those occasions, never tried to
speak to her.

She sat hunched in the top pew beside her mother,
her navy coat pulled tightly around her. (He'd sat in
exactly the same place once, in a new grey suit.) Her
pale brown hair was sprinkled with white and thinner
than he remembered, her scalp clearly visible
underneath it. She rocked gently, head bowed.

She hardly registered the people who paraded past
to shake her hand, with their mumbled offerings of
sympathy. When Kieran approached, she looked
blankly at him. Her face was a mottled pink and red,
her eyes almost closed with the swollen flesh that
surrounded them.

'It's Kieran,' he heard her mother say quietly
beside her. He took Geraldine's hand and pressed it.

She was cold. Her skin felt rough and dry. Her hand shook slightly.

'I'm sorry,' he told her. She nodded and dropped her head again, her hand slipping out of his. He shook hands with her mother and with a man he didn't recognise in a brown suit and black tie who sat beside them.

He walked back down the aisle, past the straggling line of bundled-up mourners, past a child with fat red plaits who stood at the back holding an elderly woman's hand, and who stuck out her tongue at him. Past the concrete bowl of stagnant water in the vestibule, past the stand of curling-paged magazines and the pockmarked noticeboard announcing pregnancy counselling and pilgrimages to Lourdes and Knock and Medjugorje.

He hadn't killed Adam. He wasn't responsible for the body lying in the dark coffin under the white cloth. Even if he'd jumped in, chances were he wouldn't have saved Adam. He couldn't swim, he might have drowned too.

He had nothing to blame himself for, nothing. He turned out of the churchyard and walked away quickly, undoing his tie as he went.

One month later: 17 November

Number Nine

She waited until he'd switched off the television. Then she said, 'I have some news.'

Justin dropped the remote control onto the coffee table. 'You have?'

'Yes.' Her eyes filled with tears. She waited for him to notice them.

For a minute he said nothing. Then he said softly, 'Oh, God.'

Kathryn put out her hands and he held them tightly. 'Say it.'

'I'm pregnant.' The tears spilled over.

'Oh, God.' He pulled her against him. She felt the thump of his heart. 'Oh my God.'

After a while, he lifted his head. 'How long?'

'Thirteen weeks, almost.' She'd lost the other two at eight and nine weeks.

'Why didn't you tell me sooner?'

'You had enough on your plate without the worry.' She smiled at him, wiped a sleeve across her face. 'I wanted to wait until . . .'

He pulled her towards him again. 'Come here to me.'

She leaned into him and he put a palm against her stomach. 'Hello there.'

She laughed. 'I hope you're not expecting an answer.'

'Kathryn.'

'Mmm?'

'Look at me.'

She sat up.

'Even if anything happens with this baby—' She drew in her breath and he said, 'No, listen, even if anything happens, I'll never stop loving you. Never, never.' He put a hand under her chin. 'Do you hear me?'

'Yes.' The tears came again, rolled down her cheeks.

'So,' he said, wiping them away with his thumbs, 'I fancy Anastasia for a girl, and . . . Fauntleroy for a boy. Are you happy with that?'

She laughed. 'Whatever you say.'

NUMBER EIGHT

Dear Dan,

I can't believe you're serious about looking for full custody. Surely we can sort this out amicably – don't you trust me to be above board and fair to you? You've really hurt me. If you persist, we'll be forced to contest – you leave me no choice. Please, please reconsider.

Ali

You've really hurt me – so they were even now. The thought gave Dan no pleasure, no satisfaction.

David Burton had tried again to talk him out of it. 'You haven't a hope, Dan, I've told you that. All you'll do is make things worse.'

'What? Worse than they are now, with me maybe seeing my son once a fortnight, if I'm lucky? Tell me how exactly they could get worse.' He could hear how childish he sounded, and he didn't care.

'You'll create bad feeling. You'll subject your child to the misery of having parents at loggerheads with one another.' David shook his head. 'But, of course, it's your decision, and if you're convinced there's no other way, I'll go ahead and prepare a case.'

Brendan had phoned about a week after Ali's letter. Kieran had answered and handed the phone to Dan. 'For you.'

'Hello?'

'Dan, it's Brendan.'

And he'd probably said more, but Dan had slammed the phone down before anything else reached him. He'd left it off the hook for the rest of the evening and Brendan hadn't tried again on any subsequent day.

And in the middle of all that anger and bitterness, when the thought of what Brendan had done made him want to put his hands around his uncle's throat and throttle the life out of him, when not being near his unborn son felt like a physical pain – in the middle of all that, there was Clara.

They told nobody. They waved hello across the tables in the long, high-ceilinged room every Thursday and Dan took his place beside Judy, and after class they said hello to each other as they always had and they walked down the corridor together, for all the world like next-door neighbours.

And then they stole away in Dan's car.

They went to a quiet little pub out the road, where a turf fire flickered in the blackened fireplace and a row of elderly men perched on high wooden stools and had brief conversations with each other along the length of the counter. They sat at a table in the corner nearest the fire and held hands and whispered to each other, even though nobody was close enough to hear.

Or they went to the cinema and hid in the back row and didn't watch whatever was happening on the screen.

'I'm too old for you,' Dan told her.

'Cop yourself on,' Clara answered.

'I'm in the middle of this mess with Ali,' he said.

'I'll risk it,' she promised.

'What do you see in me?' he asked her.

'A lovely man,' she told him. 'A lovely, kind man. And you're not bad-looking for an old fella.'

So far they hadn't gone beyond kisses. They hadn't gone beyond kisses because Clara told Dan, the third time they visited the little pub, that she was a virgin.

'You're joking.' It was the last thing he'd expected to hear.

'No.' She said nothing more for a few minutes, turned to gaze into the fire. Dan waited.

Finally, she turned back to him and said, 'The thing is . . .' another long pause, 'the thing is, something happened to me when I was young.' She bit her lip. Her fingers gripped his. 'I've never told anyone this before, not even my mother.'

Dan stared at her. 'What?'

Clara took a deep breath and said quickly, 'A man abused me – sexually, I mean. I was on a school tour.' Her face was pale.

'Christ.' Dan pulled his chair nearer to hers, put an arm around her shoulders. 'How old were you?'

'Ten.'

'Did he . . . rape you?'

'Well, he . . .' She stopped again and Dan could feel the trembling in her shoulders. He held on, tight.

'He . . . put his fingers . . . in me.' Suddenly she gave a shaky laugh. 'So I suppose, technically, I'm probably not a virgin.' She paused. 'I was bleeding – I thought I was dying.'

'Jesus.' Dan was horrified. 'You never told anyone?'

'No. I was afraid, and embarrassed. I'd left the group, gone off by myself. We were in a museum. I figured it was my own fault.' She turned back to the fire. 'So anyway, I can't seem to bring myself to . . . go there again.'

'To . . . ?'

'Sleep with someone, have sex – whatever you want to call it.' She chewed her lip. 'I suppose I'm afraid – I don't know. It's all mixed up with what he did.'

Dan said, 'Listen, that's OK. You don't have to—'

'But I do want to.' She turned back to him and watched his mouth. 'That's why I'm telling you . . . I really want to, with you.' She gave him a shaky smile. 'That's if you still want . . . I mean, after what I've just told you, I wouldn't blame—'

'Ssh.' He stroked her hair. So silky. 'Of course I do. I'd be mad not to. But only when you're sure you're ready. You'll be safe with me, you know that.'

She squeezed his hand. 'I know.'

Sometimes, usually in the middle of the night, when the arguments were circling in his head, Dan told himself this thing between them was doomed. Clara deserved someone better, especially after what she'd been through. She deserved a man who could devote himself to her wholeheartedly, not someone still tied to a failed marriage.

He'd finish it next time he saw her – he was being selfish, he wasn't being fair to her. But then he'd think of her with someone else, imagine some other man undoing the damage that had been done to her, and his noble intentions would shrivel.

Douglas announced, on their second last evening, that the tradition was to go for drinks after the last class. 'I'll buy the first round,' he promised, 'as long as you're not all on double brandies – and on condition that you lot keep my glass filled for the rest of the night.'

'Do you want to go?' Dan asked Clara in the car on the way home. Her hand rested loosely on his thigh, just above his knee. Underneath it, through the denim of his jeans, his skin flamed.

'Why not? It might be a laugh.' After a second, she added, 'And it doesn't really matter if the cookery people suspect we're a little more than friends, does it?'

'No, I suppose not.' They'd probably never meet any of them again – and he liked the idea of other people seeing them together, treating them as a couple. 'Let's make it clear we're a little more than friends.'

Clara laughed. 'Give them something to talk about.' She squeezed his thigh gently.

He'd mentioned to Kieran, casually, that the girl next door was doing the cookery classes too.

'The little blonde one?'

'Yeah. I give her a lift home sometimes, when it's raining.'

He'd have liked to tell Kieran. He liked the idea of saying it out loud. 'Clara and I are . . .' What were they, though? Seeing each other? He always thought that expression was a bit silly. In a relationship? Going out? Dating? Together?

Together – that was good. 'Clara and I are together.' He said it out loud in his bedroom with nobody to hear him. He watched her hanging clothes on the line in next door's garden – a lemon top, a pair of green tights, two navy towels, a blue and yellow cardigan. He saw her bending to ruffle the dog's hair on her way back to the house, swinging the empty laundry basket. He waved, but she didn't look up.

He wished he knew how it was all going to work out.

NUMBER SEVEN

Yvonne knocked on Pawel's door. His last patient had left a few minutes before.

'Come in.'

He was standing at the table in the corner, a green file open in front of him.

'Sorry to disturb you.'

'Not at all.' He screwed the cap onto his fountain pen. 'What is it?'

They were fine again, back to how they'd been before the dinner. Receptionist and dentist, nothing more. He probably never even thought about it now. She wondered sometimes if he'd met anyone else, or if their experience had scared him off the website. Hopefully not.

'I just wanted to let you know that I've recently become engaged. I'll be getting married next summer.'

'Ah.' He looked surprised, as she'd known he would. How could she be getting engaged when she'd been out meeting men from the internet so recently?

'It's someone I've known for a long time.' She felt he deserved an explanation. 'We've been friends for years.'

'I see.' He put out his hand. 'I should congratulate you. I hope you'll be very happy.'

'Thank you.' His hand was cool, his grip loose. The last time they'd shaken hands they'd been saying goodnight outside the restaurant, just before she'd scuttled home, mortified.

'And . . .' She paused. 'Pawel, I'm afraid I'll have to give up this job.'

'Ah,' he said. 'I see.'

'I'll be moving to Dublin after the wedding. My, er, fiancé' – how strange that still sounded – 'works there.'

They were going to find a place to rent in Dublin, stay there until Greg took early retirement in about ten years. Then they planned to move back to Belford, to number seven Miller's Avenue.

And Yvonne had assumed that Clara would continue to live in the red-brick house, until the subject had come up between them a few nights before.

'Mmm, we'll see, summer's a long way off. Anyway, no big deal if I'm not here, you can always rent out the house, make a bit of money on it.'

Yvonne had stared at her. 'If you're not here? Are you going somewhere?'

Clara shrugged. 'Well, not right away. I mean, not that I know of right now. I'm just saying, summer's ages away, anything could happen.' Then she smiled. 'Who knows? I could fall madly in love and be whisked off.'

Yvonne studied her. This was the perfect opportunity, wasn't it, to ask, 'So, have you anyone in mind?' But she knew from experience that Clara would laugh it off, so she held her tongue. When Greg phoned the following day, Yvonne told him what Clara had said.

He didn't sound surprised. 'She's being practical – she's bound to meet someone sooner or later. It wouldn't be a problem, would it, letting the house?'

'Well, I suppose not, but—'

Handing over her house to people she didn't know? Giving the keys to strangers, watching them bring their things in, letting them use her dishes, sleep in her beds . . .

She said nothing. What could she say?

She told Dolores she was getting married. Amazingly, Dolores didn't seem all that pleased. 'Well! You're a dark horse. When did this happen?'

'He asked me a few weeks ago and I had to think about it for a while.'

'Were you not sure or something?' Dolores stared at her.

'Well, it's a big decision.' It was almost as if Dolores was annoyed with her. 'I thought you'd be happy I was getting married. You were always asking me if I'd met anyone nice.'

'I know. I am happy for you – congratulations.' Dolores didn't look happy. Her rhubarb and custard yoghurt sat untouched in its white plastic tub. 'So when's the big day?' Very strange.

The other evening, for a laugh, Yvonne had logged on to the internet dating site. Her membership had lapsed so now, as a basic member, she still had access to her inbox but couldn't exchange contact details with anyone who sent her a message.

There were twelve, all from unfamiliar names. As she was deleting them, unread, one by one, she heard the faint sound of a violin outside. Wasn't he cold, out in this weather? She crossed to the window and peered out, but the shadow at the bottom of Dan's garden could have been anything or anyone. She leaned against the window for a minute, listening.

She hoped he was well wrapped up. At least his head would be warm, in that hat.

One week later: 24 November

Number Seven

'She's been a bit weaker in the last while, and her sight's failing – the specialist said that would probably happen. We'll have to see about getting her stronger glasses. She's very down all the time too.'

'Poor thing.' Yvonne unplugged the kettle. 'I wonder if it would have been better not to tell her – I mean, do you think that psychologically it makes someone give up if they know they're dying?'

Kathryn thought. 'Well, I think I'd rather know, if it was me. But maybe it would be better if I didn't. We're very lucky to have found Marzena, she's so patient with Grainne. And she probably doesn't understand half of what Grainne says to her, which is no harm.'

'Mmm.' Yvonne poured water into their cups. 'I don't know how you can drink that stuff.'

Kathryn smiled. 'Well, for some strange reason, I've totally lost my taste for coffee.'

'Have you? The only time that happened to me was—' Yvonne stopped abruptly.

Kathryn watched her face, still smiling.

Yvonne's mouth dropped open. 'Oh my God – you're pregnant.'

Kathryn's beam widened. 'I'm due in May.'

Yvonne flew around the table and hugged her. 'Oh, that's fantastic – that's just great. I'm so pleased for you.'

'Thanks.' Kathryn stirred her peppermint tea. 'That was my tummy bug, remember?'

Yvonne stared at her. 'What? The time you went to see Gerry Lynch?'

'Yes.'

'But that was weeks ago – you met me right after you came out of his surgery and said nothing, you rat.'

Kathryn laughed. 'I know, sorry – it was too early. I was scared.'

'Of course you were.' Yvonne paused. 'So you're over the three months?'

'Almost fourteen weeks. I didn't even tell Justin till last week.'

'He must be over the moon.'

'Delighted.''

'And how did Grainne take the news?'

Kathryn hesitated. 'We haven't told her yet. We thought we'd wait another while.' She lifted her cup. 'Now, enough about me – tell me how everyone took your news.'

'Well, my parents are delighted – they've always liked Greg.'

'And Peggy?'

'Would you believe she phoned, about a week after I'd told Jim. Very civilised and polite, wished me all the best.

Jim was probably standing behind her holding a gun to her head.'

'Oh dear.' Kathryn smiled. 'Shame herself and Grainne never met. They'd probably have got on like a house on fire.'

The door opened and Clara appeared. She wore her pale pink dressing gown and her hair was wrapped in a blue towel. 'Hi, Kathryn. What's so funny, you two?'

'Oh, nothing.' Yvonne got up and plugged in the kettle. 'Just a bit of nonsense. Want coffee?'

'No, thanks.' Clara opened the fridge and took out a bottle of water. 'How're you keeping, Kathryn?'

'I'm fine.' She watched Clara's face. 'Actually, I'm pregnant.' She'd never get tired of saying it.

'Wow, that's great – congratulations.' Clara twisted off the lid. 'Must be catching – so's Dan's wife.'

They stared at her.

Kathryn said, 'Is she?'

Yvonne said, at the same time, 'How d'you know that?'

'He told me. She's due sometime in January, I think.' After a second, she added, 'And it's Dan's.'

'What?' Yvonne's jaw dropped further. 'Dan told you all this?'

Clara smiled. 'Well, I certainly didn't make it up.'

'And due in January . . . when did she leave him?'

Kathryn thought. 'Around April, wasn't it, or May?'

'So she must have got pregnant right before that.'

'Yeah, probably.' Clara turned towards the door. 'Well, I'd better go and finish getting ready. See you, Kathryn.'

They listened to her light footsteps on the stairs.

Yvonne looked at Kathryn. 'What about that?'

'I know – can you believe it? What a mess. Wonder what'll happen now.'

They were silent for a minute. Then Kathryn said, 'Where's Clara off to anyway?'

'She's going to the last cookery class tonight. They're making pancakes and having a bit of a party, then going out for a drink. She got off work an hour early so she could come home and get ready.'

Kathryn smiled. 'Sounds to me like there's someone she wants to impress.'

'Actually, I was wondering that myself. I was going to ask Dan to fill me in since he goes to the classes too, but maybe I should leave him alone – sounds like he has his hands full.'

'Mmm – he's got more to worry about than Clara's latest romance.'

And the possibility never crossed their minds, not even for an instant, that Dan might have anything to do with it.

Clara stroked on eyeliner with a steady hand. She wore new underwear, a pale green bra and matching girl boxers, both edged with cream lace.

She sprayed perfume on her wrists, between her breasts, behind her ears. She began to dress – a rusty orange top he'd admired on her before, her favourite grey hipster jeans. As she did up the buttons on the fly, she thought about opening them again later. Maybe he'd open them. Her heart thumped steadily in her chest. Her stomach flipped every time she summoned his face into her head.

She imagined them in bed together. In Dan's bed, next door, tonight. The thought made her dizzy with longing and fear.

It was going to happen. 'Whenever you feel ready, let me know,' he'd said, and tonight she was ready. Oh, she was afraid – she was more than afraid, she was terrified. But Dan would look after her. She trusted him completely.

You'll be safe with me.

She'd wait till they were on the way home from the pub, when they were both relaxed and happy. She'd tell him it was time, she was ready. He'd bring her home and take her upstairs and—

She shivered, hugging herself. She checked her handbag – clean knickers, perfume, money, lipstick, toothbrush, and the packet of condoms she'd thrown casually into her shopping basket earlier in the week, like normal people did.

She left the room, closed the door and walked downstairs, full of anxious hope.

NUMBER NINE

Kathryn gave Grainne a bath once a week. She filled it with water and shook in a handful of the mineral salts her mother-in-law liked. She undressed Grainne, helped her over the edge and held onto her while Grainne lowered herself slowly into the lightly scented, steaming (but not too hot) water.

She washed Grainne's hair – just one shampoo. She was careful not to let any of the lather trickle into Grainne's eyes. She poured shower gel onto a soft sponge and massaged it onto Grainne's body in gentle circles.

She helped Grainne out of the bath, wrapped her in a warm towel and dried her feet carefully, between each toe, before putting them into slippers that had been sitting face down on the radiator. Then she towelled the rest of Grainne dry – gently, gently – and helped her into her clean nightdress. She dried Grainne's hair, using the warm setting on the drier, and parting it to the left, as Grainne preferred.

She read to Grainne every evening after dinner when Justin had gone for a walk to get some air.

She read short stories from the magazines Grainne liked, and the problem pages and the letters and the gardening notes.

She played CDs for Grainne. She played Debussy and Chopin and Bach, and she played Mary Black and Maura O'Connell and Dolores Keane. All Grainne's favourites. She cooked egg-white omelettes and steamed fish and made mushroom soup from scratch.

She cut Grainne's nails. She laundered her sheets, her underwear and her nightdresses. She bought her a new bed jacket in powder blue. She polished the top of Grainne's bedside locker, the window sill and the dressing-table.

And sometimes, late at night, she sat in Grainne's room while Justin was downstairs watching television or on the internet. The bedroom was stuffy and slightly too warm, but Kathryn didn't mind. In the faint light from the lamp on the locker, she sat and watched her mother-in-law dying.

She thought about the wonderful irony of herself and Justin preparing to welcome a new life into the house while Grainne had already begun to leave it. She thought about all the times Grainne had humiliated her, all the times she had reminded Kathryn of her age, of how much older than Justin she was. All the little digs, the slights.

She imagined Grainne going in to buy the perfume. Getting a lift into town with Justin, as she used to do, telling him she needed a few things, that she'd meet him in half an hour. Browsing through the bottles on the shelf, picking out the Chanel.

Maybe telling the sales assistant that it was a little present for her daughter-in-law.

She pictured Grainne taking the receipt and stowing it carefully in a pocket of the jeans Justin had left in the laundry basket.

She saw her going into the florist's another day, choosing a bouquet and arranging to have it delivered to a fictitious address, throwing the receipt under the hall table when the coast was clear.

And all the time, while Grainne was systematically attempting to destroy her daughter-in-law's happiness, the tumour had been growing in her brain, slowly, steadily and quietly. Kathryn wondered if it felt like a punishment now.

Grainne rarely got up any more, except to use the bathroom, and then she moved slowly, leaning heavily on Kathryn's or Justin's or Marzena's arm, like the old woman she would never become.

All the fire had left her. When she spoke now, her voice was dull, no life in it. She answered questions and she thanked Kathryn when food that she still barely touched was put in front of her or taken away. She opened her mouth to receive the tablets Justin doled out and she seemed to listen when one of them read to her.

She didn't ask about Kathryn's work or about any of the neighbours. She didn't complain about pain, even to Dr Lynch when he called. He told them she was amazingly stoical.

One evening, they told her about the baby.

'Mother, we have some news for you,' Justin told her.

While he talked, Kathryn watched Grainne's face. And when she heard about the baby, Grainne turned to her daughter-in-law, utterly defeated. 'Congratulations. I hope everything goes well.'

And just like that, Kathryn's rage and triumph dissolved and nothing was left behind but pity.

Number Eight

'Behave yourself – we're getting within eyeshot of my house.' Clara giggled. 'Is there such a word as eyeshot?' She pushed Dan's arm off her shoulders. 'My mother could be looking out the window.'

Dan immediately wrapped the arm around her waist. 'Sorry, I just can't keep my hands off you.' He was feeling wonderful – drunk and happy enough not to care about anything that happened beyond this moment. He pressed Clara tightly to his side, kissed her cheek loudly. 'You're beautiful, d'you know that?'

Clara giggled again. 'Well, I should know it by now – you've been telling me all night.'

They were approaching Miller's Avenue from the alleyway that connected it to the town's main street. Just before they turned into it, Dan stopped, leaned against the park railings and pulled Clara towards him. 'C'mere – let's give the neighbours something to talk about.'

They'd cooked pancakes earlier, flipping them with varying degrees of success, then filled them with their choice from the ingredients that everyone had contributed – diced ham, grated cheese, chocolate spread, honey, sugar, butter, lemon juice, stewed apples.

Afterwards they'd all walked to the nearest pub and Douglas, as good as his word, had bought everyone a drink, and they'd presented him with the blue and green pottery bowl that Judy had collected a fiver from everyone for. They'd all had another drink and then people had started to scatter. By eleven o'clock, only Douglas, Dan and Clara were left.

'So you two are an item then?' Douglas looked pointedly at Dan's hand, which was resting on Clara's thigh.

Clara smiled. 'Since the fifth class.'

'So I'm the one who brought you together? I reckon that qualifies me for a matchmaker's fee.'

Dan grinned. 'How about a drink in lieu?'

Twenty-five minutes later, the three took a taxi from the pub. Dan and Clara dropped Douglas at his flat and went from there to the main street, where they got out and walked up Miller's Lane, which led onto Miller's Avenue.

Dan buried his face in Clara's neck. 'God, you're amazing.' His hands were in her hair. His mouth was against her throat. He was drowning in her scent. He closed his eyes and everything spun gently, so he opened them again. 'Come home with me.'

Clara laughed softly. 'Funny you should mention that.'

Dan put his lips to her ear. 'What d'you mean?'

He bit the lobe gently.

Her hands pushed under his jacket for warmth. She whispered, 'I'm ready.'

'You are?' Dan took her face in his hands and kissed her mouth. 'Wonderful.' He grabbed her hand. 'C'mon, before we freeze to death.'

Miller's Avenue was deserted. A light was on upstairs in number nine. Number seven was in darkness. Dan stumbled slightly against the black railings as they turned in at the gate of number eight.

'Oops.'

'Ssh.'

At the door, he rummaged in his pockets. Was Kieran still up? No sign of life inside, no sound. Not that he cared.

'Hurry up – I'm freezing.' Clara shivered and huddled against his back.

'Here we go.' He pulled out the keys and scrabbled for the lock. He'd just opened the door and stepped back to let Clara in ahead of him when a car drew up outside his gate. Dan turned and watched, swaying slightly, as the engine was cut.

Clara glanced back. 'Who's that?'

The car door opened. Dan's face hardened, his good mood gone, as he recognised the man who stepped out. 'Go on in, I'll follow you in a minute.'

'But who—'

'Just go in, OK? I won't be long.'

When she'd disappeared, Dan pulled the door closed and leaned against it. 'What the hell are you doing here?

Brendan pushed open the gate. 'Dan, I know you don't want—'

'No, I don't. You're not welcome here. Fuck off.' He saw two Brendans drifting in and out of each other. He blinked hard.

'Look, Dan, I haven't come to fight—'

The Brendans stepped towards him. He clenched his fists. 'I said fuck off.'

'It's Ali.' Brendan spoke loudly, over him. 'She's gone into labour.'

Dan looked at them, trying to work out which Brendan was talking. 'She's gone where?'

'She's asking for you.' Brendan put a hand on his arm. 'She sent me to get you. The baby is coming.'

Dan shook his arm away. 'Take your fucking hands off me.'

Brendan dropped it and said, slowly and patiently, 'Look, Ali is in the hospital, Dan – your son is going to be born, and she wants you to be there.'

'My son?' Dan glared at him. 'My son? No way – she's not due for ages.'

'Well, it's happening now, and she's asking for you. Make up your mind. Are you going to come with me or not?'

The baby. It was much too early. Ali wanted him. Dan shook his head, trying to unscramble it.

Brendan rattled his car keys. 'Come on – I can't hang around here. Let's go.'

Dan looked at his uncle with loathing. 'I'm going nowhere with you. I can drive myself.'

'Dan, don't be an idiot.' Brendan's voice was harsh.

'You've obviously had a fair bit to drink. There's no way you can drive, you'll kill yourself.' He turned towards the gate. 'Look, are you coming with me or not? I'm leaving now.'

Dan blinked hard. The Brendans floated together briefly, then wandered away from each other again. He struggled to think. 'Hang on.'

His key was still in the door. He turned it and went inside. Clara was standing in the dark hall. She spoke quietly. 'I heard – you have to go with him. Go on, I'll let myself out when you're gone.'

Dan hugged her quickly. 'Sorry – I'll see you soon.' He shoved his keys into his pocket and walked as steadily as he could down the path to the passenger side of the car that his uncle had already started.

He slid into the seat and slammed the door. He was drunk. His son was being born.

'Fasten your seatbelt.'

'Fuck off.'

His son was being born. He hoped blearily that he'd be sober by then.

Kieran lay in bed, listening to the voices below. He couldn't make out the conversation, but it didn't sound particularly friendly. He wondered if he should go down and intervene, but while he was still debating, he heard a car start up and drive off. Then, straight afterwards, he heard Dan's front door closing quietly and quick, light footsteps going down the path, out of the gate and into number seven next door.

So he'd been right about the pretty blonde girl and Dan.

He turned over and willed sleep to come, but as usual it ignored him. He wondered if he'd ever get a decent eight hours again. Even six would be wonderful. He wouldn't say no to five.

He knew what had to be done, but the thought of it filled him with dread. He closed his eyes.

One Day Later: 25 November

NUMBER SEVEN

Yvonne dropped her bag on the reception desk and rubbed her hands briskly. It had got wintry so quickly, without any real warning. At the weekend she'd been working in the garden, digging out the last of the marigolds that insisted on resurrecting themselves every spring. It had been cool then, certainly, but nothing like this. Today there was a real chill in the air. Today you could definitely smell winter on the way.

Of course, it was nearly the end of November, and since the clocks had gone back a few weeks ago, there was no length in the days any more.

Yvonne pulled the appointments book towards her wearily. She hated the darkness of winter, dreaded the months ahead, full of sleet and ice and biting winds, frozen fingers, raw throats and flu. Give her sunshine and blue skies any day, breakfast out on the patio and long, comfortable evenings watching the sun go down.

But winters would be different from now on. By next winter, she'd be a married woman again, living with her husband in Dublin.

Her husband Greg – when would it stop sounding so strange?

They'd gone shopping for a ring, even though Yvonne had insisted she didn't need one. She couldn't shake the feeling that there was something slightly ridiculous about people their ages picking out an engagement ring.

But Greg had been adamant. 'You may have done it before, but this is my first time and I intend to do it right.'

In the end, they'd compromised with a white gold band inlaid with a scattering of tiny diamonds, that Greg reluctantly agreed could double as Yvonne's wedding ring.

'I'm beginning to think you're having second thoughts.' They were sitting in the jeweller's, waiting for the ring to be polished and boxed.

Yvonne laughed. 'No, I'm just making sure you have enough money left to let me be a kept woman.'

She remembered the ring Brian had given her, a few days after she'd told him she was pregnant, and before they'd found the courage to tell anyone else. They'd been in a park, sitting on a green bench. Without a word, Brian had pulled it out of his pocket and put it into her hand.

She'd looked down at it. 'What's this?' Realising, as she asked, what it was. 'Oh.'

It wasn't what she would have chosen – too ornate, with its tiny raised diamond surrounded with swirls of gold. It must have cost him an arm and a leg.

She looked back at him, at his heartbreaking, hopeful face. 'It's . . . ' She got stuck and started again.

'Is this – are you—'

'Will you marry me?' He tucked his hands under his arms. 'Please say yes.'

Yvonne thought about her parents, her mother who lived in terror of what the neighbours would say, her father who doted on his only daughter, who talked football with Brian whenever he came to tea. And she thought about how Brian loved her and wondered if she'd ever meet anyone who loved her as much. She thought about their baby, growing up with a father it only saw now and again.

And she'd said yes and slipped on the ring, which was too loose, and watched Brian's face light up.

She'd worn the ring, with the matching plain gold band he'd given her on their wedding day, until Clara was ten or eleven. Then one morning, without really thinking about it, she didn't put them on, just left them sitting side by side in the little blue china dish that she dropped them into every evening.

For a while she missed them, felt the absence of their weight on her finger, and then she got used to not wearing them. The night before Clara's twenty-first birthday, she took them out of their china dish, wrapped them in a tissue, slid them into a matchbox and tucked it into a drawer she rarely opened, full of old clothes pegs and mismatched napkin rings and elastic bands that had once held bunches of rhubarb, that she hated to throw out.

She turned the white gold band slowly, watching the minuscule diamonds flashing as they met the light. Greg was coming to Belford almost every weekend now, and apart from a few short visits to his relatives, he spent most of Saturday and Sunday with Yvonne.

But he never stayed the night at number seven. Yvonne felt it wouldn't be right, with Clara under the same roof. 'I know she's an adult now and probably wouldn't bat an eyelid,' she'd told Greg, 'but I'd feel – I don't know – as if I should be setting a good example or something. Does that make any sense at all?'

'Of course it does. It's perfectly understandable.'

They'd already slept together. About two weeks after she'd accepted his proposal, Yvonne had taken a couple of days off work and gone up to Dublin to see a play. They'd stayed the night in his rented apartment.

Greg had been awkward in bed – Yvonne was definitely the more experienced – but she was happy for things to sort themselves out. In time, she was sure, he would relax with her. Great sex wasn't everything in a marriage anyway – certainly not when you were marrying someone who was already an old friend.

They'd decided on a small family ceremony in Belford's oldest church, where the elderly parish priest had known Greg since his seminary days. Clara was going to be bridesmaid and Greg's brother-in-law had agreed to be best man. Yvonne's parents were travelling up from Cork for the occasion, Peggy and Jim would be there, Greg's sister and her family, and hopefully Kathryn and Justin – the baby was due about a month before the wedding.

Clara had made Yvonne swear she wouldn't have

to wear anything frilly or shiny. Yvonne had reassured her. 'You can pick your own outfit – and maybe mine too, you're much better at it.'

Clara was acting differently these days. She'd started humming, for one thing – she'd never been a hummer. She'd sit gazing into the distance, a twitch of a smile on her face, her book forgotten in her lap, humming softly.

Or she'd arrive home from work with a new CD for Yvonne, or a new lipstick – CDs and lipsticks, when she hardly remembered Yvonne's birthday. Last Saturday she'd cleaned the bathroom, had powered through it before Yvonne was up, leaving every tile gleaming. Very strange.

And every few evenings after dinner, she'd drift out, smelling of flowers, eyes shining. 'Don't wait up,' she'd tell Yvonne, and that would be that. Yvonne knew better than to ask where she was going, let alone who she was dressing up for. She'd meet him when Clara was ready for her to meet him.

The clinic door opened, scattering Yvonne's thoughts. An elderly woman was walking towards her, wearing a dark coat and carrying a heavy shopping bag in each hand. She wasn't someone Yvonne had met before.

'Hello. Can I help you?'

The woman glanced quickly around the lobby. 'Hello, yes. I was wondering if Dolores was around, please? I'm sorry to disturb her – I know she's not supposed to have callers.'

She was nervous. She blinked rapidly as she spoke,

her words tumbling over each other. Her greying hair could have done with a wash.

'No problem. I'll phone upstairs and see if she's back from lunch.' Yvonne pointed to the chairs. 'Why don't you sit down?' She lifted the phone. 'Who will I say is looking for her?'

'Her mother.' The woman rested her bags on the floor, her face pinched with worry. 'I know I'm not supposed to disturb her here, but I couldn't get in home, with all this shopping – it's just that I lost my keys, you see, and I didn't know what else to do.'

Dolores had never mentioned her mother, as far as Yvonne could remember. Her mother-in-law, yes, Yvonne had heard about Martin's mother plenty of times, how good she was with the children, how much they loved her, but not a word about Dolores's own mother. How peculiar.

Yvonne held out her hand. 'Well, it's very nice to meet you. I'm Yvonne.'

The woman gave a tiny smile. 'Oh, yes, Dolores has mentioned you. I'm Nuala.' Her hand was very cold.

Yvonne pressed the extension for Dolores's desk phone. 'I know she was going into town for lunch, and I only just got back myself.' She listened to the rhythmic burrs of the phone – one, two, three – and replaced the receiver.

'No, she's not back, but if you take a seat, she won't be long. Here, let me help.' The bags were as heavy as they looked. Yvonne dropped them beside the nearest chair.

Nuala sat, pressing her hands together in her lap.

'Thank you, dear.'

'Do you live nearby?' She couldn't have gone far with those bags.

Nuala looked at her in surprise. 'No, dear, we live in Charleton. I thought Dolores would have mentioned that.'

'Oh – you know, maybe she did. I've a head like a sieve.' She'd said 'we'. Was there another family member, also unmentioned by Dolores?

Maybe they didn't get on. That would explain Nuala's nervousness, reluctant to have to get help from the daughter she never spoke to, maybe.

Yvonne searched for a safer topic of conversation. 'You must be very proud of the children.' Too late, she realised that if Dolores wasn't on good terms with her mother then, more than likely, her three children wouldn't be either.

But Nuala smiled. 'Yes, they've both done well...Dolores really enjoys this job, and her brother Edward is an engineer, you know. She probably told you about him.'

Yvonne stared at her. This conversation was becoming decidedly confusing. 'Actually, I meant your grandchildren.'

Nuala's forehead creased. 'My . . . oh, but Edward has only the one. She's just three now – Sarah.' She smiled again. 'She's lovely, though. Dolores is mad about her.'

Yvonne stared. 'But Dolores's children, Chloë and Fionn and . . .' She struggled to remember the oldest boy's name. Hugh? No, not Hugh.

Nuala was looking equally bewildered. 'Dolores doesn't have any children.' She paused and then said, 'Dolores Mulcahy, I'm talking about?'

'Yes . . .' What on earth was going on? How could Dolores's mother not know about her daughter's children? (Hugo – the name of Dolores's oldest boy leapt into Yvonne's head.) Was it possible she didn't know her grandchildren even existed?

Suddenly Yvonne wondered if Nuala suffered from some form of senility. She didn't sound as if she was losing her reason, but what she was saying made no sense.

'I think there must be some misunderstanding,' she said carefully. 'The Dolores I know is married to Martin and they have three children. They live about ten miles from here, on the way to Charleton.'

Nuala's head was shaking slowly from side to side. 'I just don't understand,' she said. 'I know this is where Dolores works. She told me it's the Miller's Avenue health clinic. She's been here for two and a half years now.'

Yvonne nodded. That part, at least, was right. 'Yes, she started here a few months before I did.'

'But she lives with me in Charleton. And Dolores isn't married, she's never—'

Just then the door to the clinic opened and Dolores Mulcahy walked in. She carried a bag from one of the town's shoe shops.

'God, the traffic on the—'

Then she spotted the woman sitting on a chair opposite Yvonne's desk, and saw the expressions on both their faces, and the sentence died in her mouth.

NUMBER EIGHT

The coffee tasted faintly of disinfectant. On some level, Dan thought that was probably reassuring. He balanced the cardboard cup on the arm of his chair and pressed the heels of his hands to the sides of his head.

There was a tiny but very energetic man with a sledgehammer inside his skull. *Whump, whump.* He could barely keep his eyes open, and every time he blinked it was as though a wire brush was scraping against his eyeballs. His back ached, his throat was raw and his hands hurt where his wife had gripped him. He probably smelled like a brewery that hadn't been scrubbed out in a long time. Now his breath stank too, of disinfectant-flavoured coffee.

It was the best day of his life. He couldn't keep the smile from his face. Waves of euphoria kept crashing over him. He thought there was a fairly good chance that he would die of pure happiness.

His son had been born at three minutes to five on the morning of 25 November, less than two hours ago. He had blue eyes and white eyelashes, a small round head and no hair, and he weighed four pounds twelve ounces. He had ten fingers and ten toes and twenty minuscule nails, and perfect, amazing ears, and he waved his tiny fists and creased his forehead adorably and bawled. For the size of him, his lungs were truly impressive.

They'd let Dan hold him for a second and Dan had cried big foolish hungover happy tears, and fallen utterly in love.

Ali was eating triangles of thick toast. 'Big softie.' Her hair was matted with sweat and her face was misshapen with exhaustion and streaked with her own tears, and she'd left the marks of her nails deep in Dan's palms while their son was being born. But she was happy too.

After the baby had been taken away, Dan sat by Ali's bed until she'd fallen asleep, and then he wiped his face and went to find coffee.

Brendan was sitting in an armchair outside the labour ward. He stood quickly as Dan approached. 'Well?'

He had to know. Dan couldn't not tell him. 'She's asleep. Everything's OK. The baby's fine. He'll be in an incubator for a while.'

Brendan put out a hand. 'Congratulations.'

Dan waited for the feelings of hate and anger to rush into his head, and nothing happened. Here was the man who'd stolen his wife, who'd betrayed his trust, and all Dan could feel was happy. He reached for Brendan's hand and shook it. 'Thanks.'

His baby. His son. Always Dan's son, no matter

what happened in the future. There was nothing anyone could do, no piece of paper, no court order, that could change the fact that, from today, Dan O'Farrell was a father, that he had a son.

He lifted the paper cup and downed the last of the terrible coffee, smiling happily into the cardboard cup.

NUMBER NINE

'Back in a few minutes.' Justin pulled the front door closed behind him as Kathryn climbed the stairs slowly, looking forward to the nap before dinner that had become a daily event in the past couple of weeks. She'd never been one for naps before, never felt the need to recharge during the day. Now she made straight for the bed when she got in from work and slept soundly for an hour or so, until Justin woke her for dinner.

At her last check-up, Dr Lynch had advised plenty of rest. 'Everything looks fine, but I'd rather err on the side of caution, so take it easy whenever you can now. Put your feet up and let that husband of yours pamper you. How's his cooking?'

Kathryn had smiled. 'Improving.'

'And what about work? How are you finding that?'

'Fine. It's more mental than physical, and so far my brain's holding up. I'm a bit tired at the end of the day, but nothing I can't handle.'

'Good.' He wrote in Kathryn's folder. 'All the same, you might consider part-time in a while, if that's an option. In the meantime, just keep going the way you are. Lie down any chance you get, and everything should be OK.'

Sometimes sleep didn't come right away when she lay down. Sometimes she stayed awake, and dreamed.

If nothing went wrong, she and Justin would be parents in a few more months. She imagined him holding a baby in his arms. She pictured them wheeling out a pram, stopping so people could admire their child. She thought about feeding it, imagined it pulling on her nipple. She rested her hands on her stomach. *There you are. Keep safe. Look after yourself.*

And sometimes, if she lay very still, she thought she could feel a tiny flutter. A few more months.

She leaned on the banister as she climbed the stairs, looking forward to the dark bedroom where she could lie quietly and listen to the rain pattering against the window and feel safe as she drifted off.

As she passed Grainne's door, she thought she heard something. She stopped – had she imagined it? She didn't usually look in on Grainne till after her nap, when she was feeling slightly more energetic. She listened intently and heard it again – a muffled groan.

She turned the handle and pushed the door open.

Grainne lay on the floor, a tangle of blankets half pulled off the bed. Her eyes were closed, but as Kathryn rushed over, they fluttered open. One arm was outstretched, her fist curled.

'I can't . . . get up.' Her breathing was very rapid. Her cheeks were flushed. 'I can't . . .'

Kathryn crouched beside her. 'Don't move – I'll get Justin.' She ran back to the landing and called his name as loudly as she could, before she remembered that he'd gone to the garage shop for milk.

She went back into the bedroom and lowered herself onto the floor beside Grainne.

'You'll have to wait. Justin is gone to the shop. He'll be back in a minute. I can't lift you.'

Grainne struggled to get up, scrabbled on the floor, trying to push herself up. Kathryn said, 'Wait, Grainne, please wait – he won't be long. You'll be fine.'

'I can't – I need the toilet.' Grainne kept trying to push herself up, her hands pressed into the carpet. 'I need the toilet . . .'

'Don't worry about that. It doesn't matter – we can clean up. You need to wait for Justin.'

But Grainne was becoming more agitated. 'I can't wait for him, I *must* go to the toilet *now*, I *have* to go now.'

She struggled into an awkward, half-sitting position, and Kathryn reached out to stop her. 'No, please wait—'

Grainne grabbed Kathryn's arms and held on tightly. Her grip was amazingly strong. 'I have to go *now*.'

Kathryn felt the pull of Grainne's hands, felt the weight of Grainne heaving herself upwards, using Kathryn as leverage. 'Please, Grainne, I can't lift you, it's too dangerous for me.'

She struggled to her knees, trying to get further away, trying to ease Grainne's grip on her. 'You need to let go, Grainne, I can't hold you.' The weight of her, the surprising dead weight of her, almost pulling Kathryn to the floor. 'You have to let me go.'

And as she did so, a sharp pain knifed through her abdomen. She gasped and Grainne lost her grip and slid from her arms and thudded back down onto the floor. Kathryn bent double and clutched her abdomen, *no, no*, as the pain shot through her again, *no, don't go*—

Agonising minutes later – five? twenty? – she heard Justin coming back, and she opened her mouth and screamed his name.

One week later: 2 December

NUMBER EIGHT

'Why am I crying?' But she was smiling too.

His voice floated out of the darkness. 'Because you're happy, I hope. Because you were impressed with my performance.'

Clara laughed softly and wiped her eyes. Her head rested on his bare chest, her mouth against his skin, her hair spread across him. 'Well, as you know, I have nothing to compare you with, but I think you did very well.'

Dan played with her hair, lifted it up and twisted it around his hand. 'Thank you. You weren't so bad yourself.'

Her skin was damp. The room smelled of their bodies.

She ran her hand lightly across his stomach. 'I'm sorry about earlier.'

He tapped her arm with a finger. 'Don't be daft. You've nothing to be sorry for.'

'I was afraid.'

'I know. It's OK, honest.' He stroked her upper arm. 'You're not afraid any more?'

She lifted her head, pulled herself up and felt her way to his mouth. She kissed the corner of it. It reminded him of the first time in the car. He remembered the smell of the lemon tarts.

'No. I'm not afraid any more.'

Just as he was about to turn away, torn between relief and frustration, the chipped brown door was opened a few inches.

'Yes?'

Kieran couldn't see who was on the other side: the gap was too small.

'Geraldine?'

A pause, then the gap grew and she stood there. Pink jumper, grey skirt, cream slippers. A blotchy yellow stain low on the jumper.

'It's me, Kieran,' he said, because there was no sign that she recognised him.

'Oh . . . Kieran.' She gave no sign that his arrival was welcome or otherwise. She opened the door wider. 'Sorry. Come in.'

He stepped past her into the hall.

'Excuse the state of . . . I wasn't expecting anyone.'

'Sorry – I should have rung, but . . .'

He hadn't rung. He'd just got into the car and driven there, afraid that if he thought about it at all, if he stopped for a minute to consider what he was doing, it wouldn't happen.

He had little memory of the hall, didn't recognise the faded orange tiles, couldn't have said if the walls had been white the last time he'd been there. There was a smallish painting halfway down, of horses galloping across a beach – had it always hung there?

Geraldine shuffled ahead of him in her slippers and opened a door at the end of the hall. Walking in after her, Kieran smelled the residue of past meals and a staleness that made him glance automatically at the closed window.

The kitchen was small, and slightly more familiar to him. The drop-leaf table, with its yellow Formica top, pushed up against the far wall – yes, that had been there. The narrow cooker – could it possibly be the same one, after so many years? – next to the open shelving that held a jumble of cartons and tins. The chipped white Belfast sink, the uncurtained window above it that looked out onto a small concrete yard, a red-headed brush outside leaning against the breeze-block wall.

A blue cup sat on the table, half full of what looked like very old, very cold tea. Next to it was an opened milk carton. Geraldine indicated one of the two chairs.

'Sit down. Will you have tea?' Without waiting for his answer she took the kettle and held it under the tap.

'No tea for me, thanks.' She'd forgotten he never drank it. 'But have some yourself.'

She turned off the tap and put down the kettle. 'I won't bother so. I'm sick of drinking tea.'

He scanned the shelves and saw beans, cornflakes, creamed rice, a tin of celery soup.

She saw him looking. 'Would you eat soup if I made it?'

'No thanks, I don't want a thing.' He pulled out the chair beside him. 'Sit down. How've you been?'

She shrugged, lowering herself into the chair and pulling the pink jumper down over her hips. 'Not too bad.' She attempted a smile. 'Considering.' She crossed her legs.

'That's good.' He couldn't tell her. He had to tell her. 'Are you working at all now?' Coward.

'I do a couple of days at the recycling centre,' she said. 'Tuesdays and Thursdays, twelve to five.' Her top foot jiggled rapidly, the slipper flopping.

'Right.' He studied his hands, lying on the table. 'I have to tell you something,' he said then. He forced himself to look into her eyes. 'It's about Adam.'

Something passed across her face. Her foot became still. 'Adam?' Kieran became aware of a clock ticking, counting out the seconds of their pauses. 'What about him?'

'Geraldine . . .' How to tell her? 'The night he died . . .' How to tell her?

She watched him, tense as a cat. Her eyes on his mouth.

'I was there.' He could feel his heart pounding inside him. 'I was there when it happened.'

Geraldine stared at him. The clock ticked.

Kieran stumbled on. His palms were damp. 'He was coming out of a pub, and I walked past him and . . . he—'

'You were there?' She barely whispered it.

Kieran leaned forward, reached for her hand, but she snatched it away. 'You were there?' Barely a whisper.

He hardly heard it. 'You were there?'

'He began to follow me, he shouted at me to stop—'

Her mouth was open. She watched him, her hands curling into fists.

'I kept going, I didn't want to talk to him. I was walking along by the river, and he kept following me and shouting for me to stop—'

She said something then, so softly that he missed it. 'What?'

'Did you . . . kill him?' The words pushed jerkily out of her. Her face – the look on her face.

The shock ran through him. 'Jesus, no, Geraldine, of course I didn't.' And terrible as the accusation was, he couldn't blame her. What was she supposed to think?

He rushed on. 'He must have tripped and fallen in – I couldn't see him. I looked in the river but I couldn't see.' Had he looked in? He couldn't be sure now. 'And then the others came . . .'

'You heard him falling in?' The same hardly audible voice, same look of horror on her face.

'Well, I – not really . . . I wasn't sure. I was walking fast, trying to—'

'But you knew he was in the water.' Her voice rose. Her body was rigid, leaning slightly towards him.

'Well, I—'

'Did you try to save him?' The skin was white around her mouth.

'The others came. One of them jumped in—'

'Did you?' Her eyes blazed into him now.

Her hands were fists, her knuckles were white. 'Did you try?'

'No,' he said. 'I didn't. I can't swim. I didn't—'

She sat back then, spoke almost calmly. 'You were there when he fell in. The others were too late, but you were there.'

'I know. I'm sorry.'

She looked at his face. 'You let him die. You did nothing and he died.' So calm. So still.

He bent his head. 'I'm sorry.'

Her fist crashed into the side of his head. The blow, not hard but unexpected, almost knocked him off the chair. She hit him again, anywhere she could – his face, his chest, his side. He put up his hands and she thumped them. She grunted with her efforts, she spat at him, she tried to rake his face with bitten nails.

Kieran struggled to his feet and she followed him to the door, still swinging her fists, hitting him, thumping him. He tried to grab her arms as he backed away from her. They staggered down the hall together in some kind of grotesque embrace. He reached the front door and fumbled for the knob, one hand still trying to fend her off.

As he pulled the door open, she dropped her arms abruptly, slid down the wall and sat on the floor, clutching her bent knees and wailing and moaning and rocking, oblivious to him now.

'Adam . . . Jesus . . . my child . . .'

Kieran walked outside, pulled the door shut after him and leaned against it, breathing hard. Her cries followed him out – 'Oh, God, I can't bear it . . .'

His left ear stung and there was a dull pain on one side of his face. 'Oh Jesus . . .'

After a minute or so he walked down the driveway on shaky legs and got into his car. He slid the key into the ignition and started the engine and drove back the eighty miles to Belford.

Three weeks later: Christmas Day

NUMBER SEVEN

The Christmas morning visit to her in-laws was as challenging as it had always been. No, worse this year, since she'd had the audacity to become engaged to Jim and Peggy's nephew.

Not that any of the other guests would have had the slightest inkling that anything was amiss between the two women. The pair of widowers who'd worked with Jim for more than forty years, the few neighbouring couples who always wandered in, Peggy's old bridge cronies – they'd have seen a smiling hostess, walking through the chattering groups in her navy suit, offering the usual smoked salmon on brown bread, mini vol-au-vents, little cubes of Cheddar sharing cocktail sticks with black grapes.

But Yvonne sensed the coolness, caught a couple of the sharp glances, saw Peggy subtly change direction whenever she approached her one-time daughter-in-law. She got the distinct feeling that the older woman wished her at the bottom of a very deep well.

Thank goodness for Greg, chatting easily with the other guests, one hand draped casually around

Yvonne's waist. Oblivious, as far as she could see, to his aunt's behaviour.

Thank goodness for Jim, pressing a little more Bailey's on Yvonne, asking them about their wedding plans, joking with Greg about carrying his new bride over the threshold.

Thank heavens for Clara, engaging Peggy in conversation, admiring the navy suit, laughing when Peggy asked her if there was any new romance, saying she hadn't time for boyfriends, she was much too busy.

Yvonne looked around the room at the small gathering of people she met once every year. One of the widower's daughters had had a baby in the spring – he was busy handing around photos. A couple were going skiing to Austria the following day. One of the other neighbours was wearing a neck brace, after someone had driven into the back of her car two weeks before. A bridge player called Janice had won a hundred euro on a scratchcard.

All the different lives people led, all the ups and downs. Look at Grainne in number nine, look at poor Kathryn, they'd certainly had their share of misfortune lately.

And look at Dolores Mulcahy.

Not married after all, no loving husband whisking her off to Venice, no perfect children. Constructing her sad, lonely fantasies for years until everything had come slithering down in a few minutes. Yvonne thought back to the ugly scene in the clinic, remembered how Dolores had looked at her mother.

'What are you doing here?'

And Nuala, standing up quickly, speaking in a rush, 'I'm sorry, love, I lost my keys – I couldn't get in at home, I didn't think there was any harm—'

'I told you never to come here – didn't I tell you?'

'But love, I – I didn't know where else to go.'

Dolores swinging towards Yvonne then. 'What did she tell you?' Her face blotchy with irritation, her free hand opening and closing.

'Dolores, I think you need to—'

'What did she tell you?'

And Nuala bursting into tears and stammering, 'Ah Dolores, love, what's going on? Why did you tell this lady you were married? Why did you do—'

Dolores marching over, before Yvonne could react, slapping her mother hard across the face, Nuala letting out a short, high cry as her shaking hand went to her cheek, as she cowered in front of her daughter.

Dolores swinging back to Yvonne, who'd started towards Nuala. 'She shouldn't have *come* here. She had no *right* to come here. I *told* her' – pointing an accusing finger at Yvonne – 'and *you*, always so perfect, with your fancy house and your fancy daughter, and going out to dinner whenever you felt like it. Why shouldn't I make up a few things? What harm was there? Why couldn't I have a good life too, instead of living with my mother, like some pathetic spinster everyone feels sorry for?'

It was tumbling out of her, spewing out. Her face was red with it, she was shaking with it, tears flashing in her eyes, whirling around to Nuala now. 'And *you* – you had to go and ruin everything, didn't you?

You had to come here and *blab* – I *told* you never to come here. Didn't I *say*—'

And then the front door opening and Pawel walking in, and Dr Lynch appearing at the top of the stairs, having heard the commotion, and Nuala collapsing into a chair, sobbing quietly, her face in her hands.

And just like that, the fight went out of Dolores. She slumped against Yvonne's desk, head bent, still clutching her bag of new shoes.

Poor Dolores. She was on extended sick leave now, at home with Nuala after two weeks in the psychiatric wing of a hospital in Galway. Yvonne wondered if she'd ever be back at work.

Hard to believe that they'd never existed – Martin, Chloë, Hugo, Fionn. Yvonne had almost felt that she'd known them, even though she'd never seen them, not even a photo – shouldn't she have realised how odd that was? Such a doting mother not to have at least one family snapshot to wave around the clinic? Yes, she should have wondered about that.

Photos . . . it snagged on something in Yvonne's memory, and then it came to her: Dolores telling her how their camera had fallen into the canal in Venice. Giving Yvonne a bottle of Italian wine.

She'd thought of everything, every little detail – and then her mother had walked into the clinic one day, and it was all over.

A young girl, Hazel, was covering for Dolores at work. She ate a sandwich at her desk or in the staffroom every lunchtime, and Yvonne, feeling slightly guilty, went home for the hour.

'Can I top you up?' Jim appeared, holding a Bailey's bottle.

Yvonne covered the top of her glass. 'No, thanks. I'm on driving duty.' She glanced at her watch. 'Actually, we should get going. My parents will be ringing the guards.'

Thank goodness for her parents, coming to Miller's Avenue for Christmas dinner every year, giving her the perfect reason to leave Jim and Peggy's.

She suddenly wondered where Christmas dinner would be from now on. Where would her parents go if number seven was let to strangers? Could she persuade them to come to Dublin? Would Clara come?

So many changes. She reached out and squeezed Jim's arm. 'I'll miss you when I move.'

'Me too. But we'll still see plenty of you, I hope.'

'Oh, you will.' But even as she said it, Yvonne wondered how true this would be. How often would she come back to Belford, with no house to go to?

She had to admit that the thought of moving to Dublin didn't exactly fill her with delight. The theatre would be great, of course, the restaurants and the shopping – but the traffic jams and the noise and the long distances, when she was used to the compactness of Belford, with nothing more than half an hour's walk away.

And, of course, her friends were all in Belford, and Clara. And her parents, not getting any younger.

But Greg would be in Dublin, and that would make all the difference, wouldn't it?

She caught his eye across the room and mimed

'Time to go'. She looked for Clara and steeled herself to say goodbye to Peggy.

The man in the museum was gone. Dan had taken him away. Dan lived in Clara's head now, and there was no room for anyone else.

Dan had saved Clara. He'd come along and rescued her. She wanted to tell everyone she met how wonderful she felt. How wonderful it was to be in love, and to be loved. For the first time in her life, her naked body didn't make her feel dirty or ashamed. After making love with Dan, after he'd gently entered her, she'd felt pure and cleansed. When she curled up against him afterwards, when she touched his damp skin, when she felt his deep, satisfied breathing, she was filled with gratitude.

He had saved her.

Number Eight

Dan's father placed his knife and fork side by side on his empty plate. 'That was grand, many thanks.'

His wife agreed. 'Really delicious.'

Kieran smiled. 'I'm glad you liked it.'

Dan got up and began to collect plates. 'And I made the trifle, so make sure you say something nice about it too.'

Dan's mother laughed. 'I still can't believe you're learning to cook – never thought I'd see the day.'

'Me neither. But once Kieran moved in, I hadn't any choice.' He brought the plates to the sink. 'I couldn't be shown up in my own house.'

How much had changed since last Christmas, when he and Ali had driven the forty miles to his parents' house and eaten his mother's turkey, followed by a Tesco plum pudding. They'd worn crêpe paper hats and pulled crackers, and his father, after two Irish coffees, had sung 'Phil the Fluter's Ball' and Dan and Ali had gone for a walk with the ancient family collie while his parents dozed in front of the fire.

Oh, and his uncle had been there too. Brendan had

always gone to his sister's house for Christmas.

He'd presented everyone with a lottery scratchcard before dinner, and Dan's mother had won four euro. He'd had them all in stitches doing an Irish jig as Dan's father was singing. He'd joined Dan and Ali on their after-dinner walk.

Dan remembered the three of them talking about Ali's recent promotion to full partner at work, and Brendan's plans to build a conservatory at the side of his house.

The house he shared with Ali now, and with Dan's son Colm.

A fortnight ago, Kieran had asked him what he was doing for Christmas Day.

'I'm going to my parents' house in Seaville. How about you?'

Kieran had shrugged. 'I'll probably lie low – don't normally do much for Christmas.' He glanced at Dan. 'OK if I stay here while you're away?'

And Dan had imagined Kieran sitting alone in the house, eating a perfectly cooked dinner for one, and he'd said, 'Tell you what, why don't I invite my folks here instead, give my mother the day off? I can't remember a year she didn't cook Christmas dinner.' And that was what happened.

His parents arrived at three with their overnight bags, a new briefcase for Dan, a tie for Kieran and a bottle of whiskey. They sat in front of the sitting room fire and drank mulled wine and admired the photos of Colm that Dan had taken in the hospital that morning.

Their new grandson was doing very well, out of the incubator and no longer attached to tubes, already up to six pounds thirteen ounces, and due to go home in another few days.

At five o'clock they moved to the kitchen – warmer than the rarely used dining room – and ate turkey with apricot stuffing and roast parsnips and Brussels sprouts and two kinds of potatoes, and Kieran's butter sauce that went with everything.

As he dropped the plates into the sink, Dan's mobile phone buzzed. He pulled it from his pocket and read 'happy xmas, wish you were here – GND xx'.

GND: girl next door. He tore some flesh from the turkey carcass and put it on one of the plates. 'Back in a sec. Need to feed the cat.'

Avoiding Kieran's glance – Dan hadn't fed Picasso in months – he opened the back door. In the garden he breathed deeply, relishing the sharp early evening air. He texted 'back gate' and emptied the turkey scraps into Picasso's bowl and left the empty plate on the window sill. He walked to the apple trees and waited in the darkness. In less than a minute the neighbouring back door opened and Clara ran down the path and into his arms.

'How's it going?' He spoke into her hair. She felt warm and beautifully familiar. Her breath smelled of wine.

'Fine. Boring, but fine.' She pulled his head down and studded his face with kisses. 'You?'

'Same.' His hands slid over the curve of her buttocks and he pressed her into him. 'Where's a hammock when you need one?'

She laughed and tipped back her head. 'Look, the sky's full of stars.'

Dan ignored the stars and put his lips to the side of her throat, to the hollow place where she loved being kissed.

'Mmm, that's nice.' She pulled his shirt out of his jeans.

He laughed. 'Steady on now.'

'Shut up – I'm freezing.' Her hands burrowed under his shirt and pressed into his bare back, pulling him closer. He raised his head and found her mouth.

After a minute, she eased out of his embrace. 'Better go in. See you tomorrow.' She pressed a finger to his lips – 'Happy Christmas' – and turned away. He stood listening to the crunch of her steps on the gravel, tucking his shirt back into his jeans.

On the patio, Picasso raised his head as Dan approached, then went back to his bowl. Dan took the plate from the window sill and tilted his head. The night was cold and clear, the sky dotted with millions of stars. His breath fogged out in front of him.

He closed his eyes and immediately saw Colm's face, already as familiar to him as his own. He'd been asleep when Dan had visited that morning, mouth slightly open, cheeks gently flushed. Dan had sat beside the tiny cot and watched his son breathing.

Ali had arrived at some stage. She smiled at the fat white rabbit sitting at the bottom of the cot. 'Did you bring that?'

'I did.'

'Wonder how long it'll stay white.'

'Don't care.' Dan stroked Colm's cheek with the back of a finger. 'I'll buy another when it gets dirty.'

Ali laughed. 'And he won't be a bit spoiled.'

It was good, how they were together now. Almost like old friends who'd fought and made up afterwards. It helped that Brendan rarely appeared at the hospital. Dan didn't know whether that was down to Ali or if it came from Brendan himself, giving Colm's parents time to get to know their child without anyone else butting in.

He wondered if Brendan ever worried about Ali meeting her husband regularly at the hospital. They were still man and wife, still tied together by Church and state.

'Happy Christmas,' Ali said when he was walking away from her in the hospital car park. 'Give my love to Picasso.'

She was taking Colm home in a few days. They'd arranged that Dan would come and see him three times a week. Later, when Colm was weaned and able to be apart from his mother, they would try sharing him – one week with Dan, one week with Ali.

They'd review the situation if it wasn't working, or when it was time for him to go to school, whichever came first. They'd deal with the other inevitable hiccups as they came along.

Amazing how easily they'd sorted it out in the end. Wonderful how they'd been able to sit down together in the coffee shop in Charleton and talk things through, neither getting angry, both willing to compromise. Ali had drawn up a draft agreement, Dan had taken it along to David Burton, who'd made a few minor adjustments, and that had been that.

So simple, after all his worry and anger and resentment.

He held up his watch to the light from the kitchen window. Twenty past seven. The evening stretched ahead with his parents and Kieran, the four of them sitting in front of the television, because that was what you did on Christmas Day. Kieran might play the violin later, they'd love that.

Tomorrow night he was meeting Clara. He was picking her up in town and they were driving out to the pub in the country. Still sneaking around, still keeping their secret from everyone.

It was more than eight months since Ali had left him. Maybe it was time for them to come out into the open. He wondered how Yvonne would take it. He wondered what Ali would think.

On second thought, maybe they should wait a bit longer. He opened the door and went back into the house.

NUMBER NINE

'Hi there.'

Kathryn opened her eyes and saw Justin's sister. 'Oh, hi.'

'I know you don't feel hungry, but I've brought up a small bit because you must eat.'

'Thanks.' Kathryn began to pull herself upright. Ann put the tray on the bedside locker and hurried to help her.

All so solicitous, all taking care of her. Ann, Justin, Suzannah. Kathryn's eyes pricked with the tears that were never far away. 'What's happening? I really should come downstairs.'

'No, you shouldn't. You should be taking advantage of having us around and do absolutely nothing. Anyway, there's very little happening. Justin's fallen asleep in front of the fire, Suze is out walking. Mother's watching *Sunset Boulevard* for the umpteenth time.'

Ann had flown in again from Spain, two days after Grainne's fall. She'd brought a box of DVDs with her, mostly old Hollywood black-and-whites, all

Grainne's favourites, which she'd found on the internet.

They'd moved the television from Justin and Kathryn's room into Grainne's, bought a new DVD player and put on *Whatever Happened to Baby Jane?*, *Rebecca*, *Rear Window*, *Guess Who's Coming to Dinner* and the rest, and Grainne had lain in bed and watched them all, and cried silently, and smiled occasionally.

Her fall hadn't done her too much damage, apart from a twisted ankle, which Dr Lynch had bandaged, and a bruised coccyx.

'She's lucky she didn't break anything,' the doctor told Justin. 'The fact is, apart from the tumour, your mother's a tough lady.'

Ironic that Grainne had come out of the episode relatively unscathed.

'Now.' Ann laid the tray across Kathryn's lap. 'Could you pick at it?'

Kathryn looked at the thin slivers of turkey breast, the three Brussels sprouts, the pair of roast potatoes, and her stomach lurched. 'Thanks. I'll do my best.'

'Good,' Ann turned towards the door, 'because you'll get no peppermint tea until that's gone. Enjoy.'

She was wonderful, up and down the stairs all day, tending the two patients. Suze was helping too, bringing Kathryn books from the library, scented candles for her room, bags of tangerines – one of the few foods Kathryn was remotely interested in.

When Suze had arrived three days ago, Ann had

moved out of Miller's Avenue and joined her partner in a nearby B and B. So far, Suze had managed, on her frequent visits to number nine, not to come face to face with Grainne – quite easily, since Grainne hardly ever left her room now. She had no idea that Suze was in Ireland, let alone Belford. Let alone, every so often, in the very next room.

Kathryn poked at the turkey with her fork. She had to keep her strength up. That was what they were telling her. And she was trying her best to eat and to force down the cod liver oil and milk mixture Dr Lynch had recommended she have every day.

'You were very lucky,' he told her after that terrible night. 'You almost lost it. Another few minutes . . .'

Kathryn shuddered to think what might have happened. If Justin hadn't come back when he did, if he hadn't heard her calling from Grainne's room. If Yvonne hadn't been at home when he'd hammered on her door, if nobody had been there to stay with Grainne while he rushed Kathryn to hospital . . .

She remembered every detail of that awful journey, the knifing pain that kept her doubled over, terrified and crying, gripping the edge of the dashboard as Justin broke lights and swerved around corners. She remembered the angry horns of other drivers, the orderlies racing from the Accident and Emergency department, bumping a trolley over the tarmac between them.

But they had been lucky, terribly lucky. The baby was still growing, still holding on. Still healthy.

'I'm giving you a cert for the rest of the pregnancy,'

Dr Lynch told Kathryn. 'We're going to play it very safe from now on. No more work. Stay on your back as much as you can. Get plenty of sleep. Remember what I told you: eat for one, sleep for two.'

Kathryn had promised. 'I'll do whatever it takes.' For the next five months, she was determined to overcome the nausea, to put up with the crying bouts, to cope with the constant pressure on her bladder. What did any of that matter with such a prize at the end?

If it killed her, she'd keep this baby alive.

She speared a piece of turkey, brought it to her mouth and chewed grimly.

Six days later: New Year's Eve

Number Eight

'Here.' Ali peeled the tiny vest over Colm's head and handed it to Dan. 'Throw it in the basket under the sink.'

Dan watched as she laid the baby across her lap, undid his nappy, slid it out from under him and parcelled it deftly together again. 'That goes in the bin.'

So sure of what she was doing, only three days after Colm had come home from hospital. She caught Dan's eye and smiled. 'You catch on quick – the first bath I gave him, I was petrified.'

Naked, Colm seemed terrifyingly vulnerable, flailing his still so tiny arms, kicking his skinny legs as Ali handed him to Dan. 'Hold him under the arms.'

Dan wrapped his hands around Colm's wriggling torso – the tips of his giant fingers just about met – and lowered him slowly into the plastic bath of warm water. Immediately Colm gurgled, and slapped the water with his palms.

'He loves it.' Ali dipped a small blue sponge in the water and squeezed it over the baby's shoulders.

'He'll be an Olympic swimmer.'

'Or a sailor.' Dan picked up the little yellow duck that floated beside Colm. 'Quack quack. Or a fisherman.' He thought. 'No, not a fisherman. Too dangerous.'

Ali squeezed the sponge and ran it over Colm's head, and the strands of dark hair stood on end.

Dan smiled. 'Or a punk rocker.' So impossibly tiny. So unbelievably precious.

Brendan had opened the front door, and had made himself scarce as soon as Ali appeared. The two men were on speaking terms, just about. Dan supposed Brendan usually helped with Colm's bathtime. He still rebelled against the idea of another man having more time with Colm than he himself had, but he could appreciate the advantage of Ali having someone to help out.

And, if he was honest, did it matter that it was Brendan? Wouldn't Dan have resented anyone Ali had chosen over him? The fact that Brendan was his uncle didn't make it any easier – but maybe it didn't make it that much harder either.

He smiled. How mellow he was becoming, now that he was a father. What power his tiny child had over him already.

Ali was watching him. 'You look like the cat that got the cream.'

Dan ran a finger along his son's slippery arm. 'I did – and then she ran off with my uncle.' As soon as the words were out, he regretted them. He looked up at her. 'Just kidding.'

Her eyes sparkled with tears.

Dan put a wet hand on her arm. 'Sorry, Al – I didn't mean anything. That was a stupid thing to say.'

'Doesn't matter.' She blinked quickly, and a tear slipped down her cheek. 'I think I'm still a bit hormonal, don't mind me.' She indicated the towel, hanging on the radiator behind Dan. 'Will you spread that on your lap?'

The moment was gone, and he'd done it all by himself. Dan wrapped the warm towel around Colm, patted him gingerly and tried to think of something harmless to say. 'When do you go back to work?'

'I've another six weeks, and after that I can take parental leave if I want. We'll see how it goes. You need to use talc to make sure he's fully dry. Shake it here, and here, and then rub it in.'

Dan watched, thinking again how capable she was. He couldn't imagine being able to do this on his own. He tried to picture Clara with a wriggly wet baby on her lap. She probably didn't plan on having children for years.

'So, are you going out tonight, ringing in the new year?' Ali pulled a clean vest over Colm's damp head.

Dan shrugged. 'I might meet a few pals, yeah.' He and Clara were driving to a little country hotel, having dinner and staying the night.

Just over ten weeks, since it had all begun. Who would have imagined it? What would Ali say now, if he told her? She'd probably laugh at the thought of Dan and the girl next door. Let's face it, most people would probably laugh at the thought of Dan O'Farrell, no oil painting, one day away from thirty-three, recently separated, even more recently a first-time father, being involved with a luscious twenty-three-year-old.

'Well, enjoy it. I'm hoping to be dead to the world at midnight, if this fellow behaves himself.' Ali lifted Colm, dressed now in a pale green Babygro covered with jumping yellow rabbits. 'Say goodnight to your dad, you monkey.'

Dan kissed the soft cheek, ran his hand over the curve of Colm's skull. 'Can I tuck him in?'

Ali didn't meet his eye. 'Well, he needs a feed. It'll take a while.' And naturally, Dan was no longer entitled to the sight of his wife's naked breasts. That privilege now belonged to Brendan.

'Right.' Dan spread the damp towel over the radiator, tipped the soapy water into the big bath. 'I'll go so.'

'Dan.' He turned, and Ali gave him a quick smile. 'Some other night you can come later, when he's ready for bed.'

'Right.' He was halfway out of the room.

'And, Dan?'

'Yeah?' He didn't turn round.

'Happy New Birthday.'

He felt a brief stab of what might have been pain. 'Thanks. See you.' He walked quickly from the bathroom towards the top of the stairs, praying he wouldn't meet Brendan on the way out.

Driving home, he remembered the other New Year's Eve. They'd gone back to Listowel, eighteen months after their first date there, and booked into a hotel in the square. They'd wrapped up and driven to

Ballybunion, battling gale force winds to walk the beach where they'd first met.

Back in Listowel they'd eaten bowls of creamy seafood chowder in their favourite restaurant and cradled hot whiskeys in a noisy little pub afterwards. A television was switched on for the countdown. Everyone joined hands and sang 'Auld Lang Syne' and Ali had hugged Dan, then put her lips to his ear and whispered, 'Happy New Birthday.'

And later, just over an hour into his twenty-ninth birthday, she'd turned to him in bed and said, 'Marry me.'

He checked his mirror, flicked on his indicator and moved out to overtake a dark van. In less than five hours he'd be thirty-three. And this year he'd be spending his birthday with Clara.

The van driver raised a hand as Dan passed. Dan waved back. *Happy New Year.*

He wondered what it held in store for all of them.

NUMBER SEVEN

Greg held out the little bowl to Yvonne. There was a small pile of grated ginger in it. 'Is this enough?'

'Plenty.' She finished slicing the pork fillet into narrow strips. 'Will you get the cornflour? It's in a plastic tub with cherries on it.' She checked the recipe. 'And sesame oil, in the press above the microwave.' Another pause. 'And coconut milk. It should be there too.'

Like a married couple they were already, Greg beginning to find his way around the kitchen. Until they'd got engaged, anytime he'd come to the house for a meal, there'd never been any question of him helping with the cooking. But it was different now.

She took fish sauce from the fridge. 'I'm so glad you like Thai food – I don't think I could marry you if you didn't.'

Greg laughed. 'Well, in that case, I'm very glad I like it too. What did you say Clara was doing tonight?'

Yvonne mixed the marinade ingredients together and added the pork strips, turning the meat to coat it.

Just out for a meal with a few others, and then on to the nightclub in the Belford Arms afterwards. She's staying at Siofra's – it'll be impossible to get a taxi home.'

'Right.'

'So there's no danger of her walking in on us.'

He laughed. 'That's not why I was asking.'

She threw him a look that she hoped was filled with disbelief. 'Oh, sorry. You were just making polite conversation. I see.'

Their first night together under number seven's roof. She'd ply him with drink and he'd relax, let go a little.

'Clara's seeing someone,' she told him now.

'Really? Has she said something?'

'Oh no – you know what she's like. But I just know there's someone, mother's what do you call it.'

'Intuition.'

'That's it.' Yvonne shook out the tablecloth and settled it on the table. 'There's definitely someone, and she has to be meeting him tonight.' And maybe staying with him too, knowing that Yvonne would never dream of checking up on her.

Greg set out the cutlery and took two wineglasses from the cabinet. 'Are you sure you wouldn't have been happier going out?'

'Quite sure.' Yvonne watched him winding the corkscrew into the bottle of white wine and then levering it up slowly. 'I never enjoyed New Year's Eve in town.' She reached under the worktop and lifted out the wok. 'If you were single you felt left out and pathetic, and if you were attached you felt obliged to be madly in love at midnight.'

Greg laughed. 'Well, I'm sorry to break it to you, but I fully expect you to be madly in love this midnight – I know I will be.'

Yvonne smiled and switched on the hotplate under the wok. 'I'll do my best.' She took the glass he held out and clinked it against his. 'To us – drink up.'

NUMBER NINE

'I didn't even know there was such a thing.' Kathryn watched as Justin eased the cork out of the bottle of non-alcoholic champagne. They were on the sofa in front of the fire in the sitting room. Kathryn was wrapped in the angora shawl that Suze had given her before she and Ann had left for Spain two days before.

'Ah, you can get anything now. If it's not in the shops, it's somewhere on the net.' Justin filled the two flutes and handed one to her. 'Knock yourself out.'

The coffee table held a little bowl of olives, a plate of dry crackers, three peeled tangerines and a tub of pistachio nuts. A fat candle burned, and Bach was on the stereo.

'Let's get these up.' He lifted Kathryn's slippered feet and rested them in his lap.

She ran her hand along his arm. 'Maybe Grainne would like a glass.'

'I looked in just before you came down. She's asleep.'

He must be tired, trying to look after both of them. It had been wonderful to have Ann around, especially since Marzena had gone back to Latvia to spend Christmas and New Year with her family.

'My father phoned today.' Justin scooped pistachios from the tub.

'Did he?' In the nine years she'd been married to his son, Kathryn had met William Taylor just a handful of times. He was good looking – Justin had inherited his long eyelashes and dark hair – and very charming.

And also, Kathryn decided after their third meeting, very insincere.

'He wanted to know how Mother was doing – and I told him about the baby. He says congratulations.'

Kathryn took a tiny sip from her glass and reached for a cracker. She still didn't feel in the least like eating, or drinking anything other than peppermint tea – would she ever be able to face alcohol again? – but she was doggedly working her way through whatever food or liquid appeared in front of her. In the past week, she'd put on three pounds – although Dr Lynch had told her most of that was baby related.

'I'll expect you to have put on about two stone by May,' he told Kathryn at her last check-up. 'Or thereabouts. You're sticking to a healthy diet?'

'Oh, yes,' she said. 'Apart from ice cream and pickles at midnight, and the odd lump of coal.'

'Sounds about right. And you're getting plenty of rest?'

'I am. I'm in bed most of the time, these days.'

'Good, that's fine.' Dr Lynch paused. 'Tell me, on another note – and I'm sorry to have to bring it up –

have you and Justin decided how you're going to cope when Grainne needs round-the-clock care?'

Kathryn looked at him. 'Are you talking about a hospice?' She remembered how adamant Justin had been about keeping Grainne at home. 'I really don't think that's an option.'

The doctor closed Kathryn's file and held it between his fingers. 'There is another way, if you want her to stay at home. There are services provided by the Cancer Society, nurses who'll visit by day, and night nurses too, depending on need. I can contact them if you want.'

Kathryn nodded slowly. 'That sounds good. I'll talk to Justin, see what he thinks.'

'Fine. And when the time comes, we can find out what's available.'

No need to spoil tonight though. They still had time, hadn't they? No need to remind him that his mother would soon be too sick for him to manage. Not tonight.

Kathryn lifted her glass. 'What'll we drink to?'

There was a pause, and then Justin said, 'Happy endings.'

He didn't need reminding.

New Year's Day

NUMBER EIGHT

Clara lifted her watch from the bedside table. 'A quarter past nine. What time do they stop serving breakfast?'

'No idea.' Dan slid his hand along the smooth curve of her back. 'Are you hungry?'

'Starving – I could eat a horse.' Clara turned to face him. 'Happy New Year – and happy birthday. Did you like having a birthday on New Year's Day when you were growing up?'

Dan shrugged. 'Didn't mind. It was better than Christmas Day – that would've been a real bummer.'

Clara smiled, stroking his chest, pulling gently at the dark curly hair. 'Your son could have been born on Christmas Day, couldn't he? How early did you say he was?'

'He was due on the fifth of January. Actually, I was kind of hoping he'd be born on my birthday.'

She ran her nails lightly across his skin. 'It's all a bit weird, isn't it?'

'What is?' But he knew what she meant.

'Well, I mean, you and your wife' – she traced little

circles around his nipples – 'being parents now, and her with someone else.'

'Yeah.' Dan took her hand and held it. 'But so far it's working out OK.' He searched her face. 'How do you feel about it?'

She hadn't said much until now. And he, wary of her reaction, had never brought it up.

Clara considered. 'I'm not sure. I think I'm a bit afraid that you and your wife will never really be able to separate, now that you've a child together.' She lifted her eyes and gazed at him. 'And I'm not sure where that leaves me.'

Dan brought her hand to his lips and kissed it. 'I'm sorry. You're getting a very bad bargain – a half-separated older man with a new baby – while I'm doing a hell of a lot better.' He kissed the tips of her fingers in turn. 'All I can say . . . is that . . . I'm very happy . . . with the current . . . situation.'

Clara gave a small smile. 'OK.' She rolled away from him and slid out of bed. 'Come on – breakfast, before I collapse with hunger.'

Dan looked at her naked body as she walked towards the bathroom. 'Maybe a quick shower first.'

Three weeks later: 22 January

TELEPHONE CONVERSATIONS

Number nine, morning

'Yvonne, it's Kathryn.'

'Everything OK?'

'Well, as OK as it can be right now. Grainne's got a lot weaker in the past couple of days. Justin sat up with her last night – he didn't like to leave her.'

'Oh dear. He can't do that, not when he's got to go to work.'

'He's not working today – I insisted he call in sick. He's asleep now.'

'You'll have to get more help.'

'We're going to. Dr Lynch is contacting the Cancer Society and arranging for nurses to come.'

'So you're keeping her at home.'

'It's what he wants.'

'I know. So what can I do?'

'Well, I was wondering if you could pick up some shopping for me?'

'Of course I will – I'll call round after I finish here and you can give me a list.'

'Thanks, that'd be great.'

Number seven, morning

'Clara? It's me.'

'Hey, you, what's up?'

'Nothing much. Just wondering if you and lover boy would like to come to Matty's tonight.'

'Ah, I don't think so – not just yet.'

'How long are you going to keep him hidden?'

'I'm not keeping him hidden. We're just not ready to tell our families yet, that's all. You know the situation, I've told you. It's all a bit awkward.'

'Right. He's still playing happy families with his wife and child, and you're sneaking around, afraid to be seen with him in public. I could think of better words than "awkward".'

'Siofra, don't be a bitch. It's his son, what do you expect him to do? It's definitely over between him and his . . . wife.'

'OK, if you say so. It's just we never see you any more.'

'Never see me? We had coffee two days ago. We had lunch last week.'

'Ah, you know what I mean. You never come to Matty's. Everyone's asking for you.'

'Are they? That's nice.'

'Barry keeps pestering me, wanting to know if you're seeing someone.'

'Tell him it's none of his bloody business. No, tell him I am seeing someone, and it's going very well. Look, I'll ring you during the week, OK?'

'Right.'

Number seven, afternoon

'Hi, love, it's me.'

'Greg, hi. I was just thinking about you.'

'Were you? Listen, I'm really sorry, but I can't get down this weekend – I've had to schedule extra rehearsals for *Sweeney Todd* on Saturday and Sunday because two of the cast were out with flu till yesterday.'

'Oh, that's too bad. You'll miss Jim's birthday dinner tomorrow night.'

'I know, and believe me, Yvonne, I'd much rather be there than here, but they sorely need the rehearsals. We're opening next Friday and they're far from ready.'

'Well, not to worry – I'm sure you'll lick them into shape. Oh, by the way, Kathryn rang a while ago. Grainne isn't at all well. It sounds like this might be it.'

'That's a bit sudden, isn't it?'

'Well, apparently Dr Lynch told them it could happen quite quickly. I know it sounds horrible, but it might be a relief to everyone. I'm sure they're both worn out, and Kathryn can do without the stress.'

'Mmm . . . well, let me know if anything happens.'

'I will. Take care.'

Number eight, afternoon

'Dan, it's me.'

'What's wrong? Is it Colm?'

'No, nothing's wrong, everything's fine. I just wondered if we could change tomorrow's arrangement.'

'Change? How change?'

'Well, I wondered if I could go to Belford, rather than you coming here.'

'What? Bring Colm to this house?'

'Well, yes. I thought it might save you a trip, that's all.'

'Well, I suppose. Is it not too cold to have him out?'

'I'll wrap him up, don't worry.'

'Right. What time were you thinking of coming?'

'Well, around noon, if that would suit you?'

'Fine, see you then.'

Number seven, late afternoon

'Nuala? It's Yvonne, from the clinic. You met me the day you came in.'

'Oh, yes dear, I remember you.'

'I was just wondering how Dolores is.'

'Well, that's very nice of you, dear. She's not too bad, really, picking herself up now a bit. I'd say it was a rest she needed more than anything. She was in hospital, you know, for a couple of weeks.'

'Yes, I heard that.'

'Dolores wasn't too keen on it, really, but I'm sure it did her good.'

'Yes, I'm sure it did. Is she thinking about coming back to work at all?'

'Oh, no, dear, oh, no, there's no talk of that. She never talks about that at all. I'm not sure that she'd be able, really.'

'I see.'

'To be honest, dear, she doesn't talk much about

anything . . . but she's still on those pills that the doctor gave her – they're bound to have an effect, aren't they?'

'Oh, I'm sure they are. They probably make her feel a bit tired. But they must be doing her good.'

'Oh yes, they have to be helping her, haven't they?'

'Well, tell her I rang, won't you? And give her my best.'

'Thank you, dear. She'll be delighted. It'll give her a real lift to know you're thinking about her.'

Number eight, late afternoon

'Hi. It's me.'

'Hi – what's up?'

'Nothing much – but the trip to Charleton is off tomorrow, I'm afraid.'

'What? I got the day off specially.'

'I know, I'm really sorry. Ali rang just now and asked if she could bring Colm over here instead. I couldn't come up with an excuse fast enough.'

'Oh . . . OK. Obviously Colm comes first.'

'You're upset.'

'Well, of course I'm upset. I was looking forward to a day out with you. But he's your son – naturally he comes first. We'll do it another time.'

'I was thinking—'

'I have to go – there's a customer. Talk to you later.'

'Hang on a sec . . . Clara? . . . Hello?'

Number nine, late evening

'Ann? It's me.'
    'Justin – what is it?'
    'It's Mother. Dr Lynch said you should come.'
    'Oh God.'

One day later: 23 January

NUMBER EIGHT

'She's coming here?' Kieran's spoon of porridge halted, halfway to his mouth. 'What time?'

'She said around noon.' Dan dipped toast into the soft yellow of his boiled egg. 'I just thought' – carelessly, as if it didn't matter – 'you might like to see Colm.'

He'd lit the fire in the sitting room as soon as he was up, and after breakfast he was going to clean the bathroom and run the Hoover around the place. Silly, really, Ali wouldn't even notice – but it would give him something to do while he was waiting. No point in going to work this morning, no point at all, when he knew he wouldn't be able to put his mind to it.

Clara was mad with him. Her phone had been switched off all yesterday evening. He'd call the department store this afternoon when, hopefully, she'd have calmed down.

He knew it wasn't fair to expect her to put up with this weird situation. Maybe it was time now to bring it all out into the open. Maybe if everyone knew about them it would be easier. She could go with him sometimes when he visited Colm, instead of him dropping her in Charleton, which was what they'd been planning to do today, and meeting up with her afterwards.

If she went with him, she'd see that Ali wasn't a threat. Ali was happy with Brendan now, and Dan had Clara.

They'd have tongues wagging for a while, no doubt about that, but wouldn't it blow over? Wouldn't some new bit of gossip come along to take the spotlight off them?

They were planning a weekend away soon, in a small country-house hotel on the coast that a friend of Clara's had stayed in last year. Clara would tell her mother that she was going away with friends. All a bit ridiculous, wasn't it, this cloak-and-dagger stuff?

Yes, they should go public. It was time. He'd tell Ali about Clara today.

He took a bite of his eggy toast. 'So, if you're around . . .'

At the weekends Kieran pottered about, reading or tidying the garden, sometimes going into town for an hour or two and coming home with whatever odds and ends had taken his fancy: a book, a bottle of red lemonade, a bag of strawberry bonbons, a furry mouse for Picasso.

He still went to the bottom of the garden to play his violin, even on the coldest days. 'I don't feel the cold when I'm playing,' he told Dan. 'Sounds daft, but I don't.'

Dan's parents thoroughly approved of Kieran. 'You were very lucky,' his mother said. 'Imagine who you might have ended up with.'

'You could have got someone on drugs,' his father said. 'Or a gambler.'

'Or someone who drank,' said his mother.

'You need to get that washing machine fixed,' his father said.

'Is that a new kettle?' asked his mother.

'How did the toilet seat get cracked?' asked his father.

A drug addict, or a cracked toilet seat. Yes, Dan had been lucky.

'They'll be here for lunch so,' Kieran said now. 'There's some of that carrot and apple soup in the fridge – and you could do scones to go with it.'

'Fair enough.' Wouldn't take Dan ten minutes – he was well used to making scones now. Nothing to it.

Ali arrived at ten past twelve. Dan was upstairs when he heard the rattle of the letterbox – Kieran had broken the brass bell in the past week and they hadn't got round to replacing it. And, of course, Ali wasn't going to use her key.

'Hi.' Her nose was pink with the cold. She wore a blue woolly hat that made her look younger.

Dan took Colm's carrier from her. 'Hi, come in.' It was strange, seeing her standing in the house again. He couldn't decide how it made him feel. 'I have a fire going in the sitting room – it should be warmed up by now.'

Silly to feel he had to treat her like a visitor, when

she'd picked out the blue and cream rug in front of the fireplace, when she'd chosen the curtains and the grey couch.

He saw her looking at the bicycle as she passed it in the hall, but she didn't comment.

Kieran was introduced. He shook hands with Ali, then crouched to peer intently at Colm. 'Hello there. Pleased to make your acquaintance.'

Colm gazed back at him, unblinking.

Ali pulled off her gloves and started to shrug out of her coat, giving Dan a quick smile when their eyes met. Was she nervous? Was she finding this as awkward as he was?

Kieran looked up from the carrier. 'I can't decide which of you he's like.'

'Dan,' Ali said immediately. 'He's the image of him, more and more each day.'

Dan was surprised. 'Is he?' It was the first time she'd mentioned a similarity between Dan and his son. So far, she'd pointed out Dan's father's nose, her mother's chin, her own eyes.

'Oh, yes – everyone comments on it.'

He wondered if 'everyone' included Brendan.

'You want a drink?' he asked her, and when she looked for tea, Kieran went out to make it, saying he needed to check on the lunch.

Ali sank into the couch as the door closed behind him. 'He's nice.'

'He is.'

She rubbed her hands together. 'It's lovely and warm in here. What am I getting for lunch?'

Dan crossed to Colm's carrier and began to unbuckle him. 'Just some soup.' He looked at her over his shoulder. 'And I made scones.'

Ali smiled. 'I still can't get used to the idea of you cooking.'

'I'll have you know I'm pretty good.' He'd wait. He wouldn't mention Clara yet. After lunch, when they were more relaxed, he'd tell her. He lifted Colm out of his carrier and brought him over to the couch and sat beside her.

'Tuck the blanket under him – his feet get cold.'

He smiled. 'Like his dad's.'

She nodded, then leaned forward to look into the fire.

Dan turned his attention to his son. 'Well, young man, what do you think of your other home?'

Colm sucked his thumb.

'That good, eh? Thought you'd like it. Wait till you see upstairs.'

'Dan.' Ali spoke softly, still looking at the fire.

'Yeah?'

She was silent. He stroked Colm's arm, still marvelling at its impossible softness. He should have put some music on. The room was much too quiet.

When the silence stretched, he glanced up. Her face was half hidden from him, firelight flickering on the part he could see. A shiny trail on her cheek.

She was crying.

'What is it? Did I say something wrong?'

She shook her head, fished a tissue out of her pocket and dabbed her face. 'I'm sorry—' But the words only brought more tears. She was crying in earnest now, shaking her head, still trying to speak. 'I didn't want to do it this way.'

'Do what? What are you doing?' Dan was mystified, and increasingly anxious. It must be something big to upset her like this. 'Al, tell me.'

She blew her nose and threw the tissue towards the fire. It landed on the mat. 'I didn't mean to blurt this out the minute I arrived. I was going to wait until—' She stopped and bit her lip, and turned at last to face him properly.

The sight of her tears had always melted him. He couldn't bear to see her so vulnerable.

'Look, whatever it is, you have to tell me.' Dan looked quickly from her to the baby, an awful thought dawning. 'Is there something wrong with Colm? Is something—'

'No, no, nothing's wrong with him, he's fine . . .'

She took a deep breath, her eyes searching his face. Her lashes were spiky. 'But there is something wrong with me.' Fresh tears rolled down her face and she ignored them. She put a hand towards him, then pulled it back.

'What?' A ribbon of fear curled inside him. Was she sick? Had she heard some bad news?

'Dan . . .' her voice was thick, 'Oh God, I've made a horrible mistake.' She spoke quickly, looking straight at him, her hands dashing away the tears. 'Dan, I love you, it's you I love, and I want to come back. Please, please, give me another chance. Let me come back and we can start again.'

As Dan stared at her, stunned, the sitting room door opened and Kieran walked in, carrying a tray.

And immediately afterwards, before another word was spoken, Colm began to wail loudly.

NUMBER SEVEN

She couldn't not have invited Peggy to Jim's birthday dinner. The man was going to be eighty on Tuesday week, and Yvonne and Clara were marking the occasion. They were cooking his favourite pork chops. They were leaving cloves out of the apple sauce, adding lots of black pepper to the mashed turnip, and boiling the potatoes in their skins.

After dinner they were serving the lemon meringue pie his mother used to make, and when they had finished eating they were going to present him with the grey cashmere scarf and matching gloves that had just appeared in the menswear section of the department store where Clara worked.

They couldn't leave Peggy out, however much Yvonne wanted to. So Clara had phoned and invited them both and, much to Yvonne's dismay, Peggy had agreed to come.

And now Greg wasn't even going to be there. He was stuck in Dublin trying to get a bunch of teenagers ready for the stage. On the other hand, it might be for the best if he wasn't there – it might seem to

Peggy like they were rubbing her nose in their engagement.

Yvonne sighed into the saucepan of turnip.

Clara looked over. 'Cheer up – they'll be gone in a couple of hours.'

Yvonne groaned. 'Oh, God – two whole hours. What'll I say to her?'

'You'll ask her how Christmas went, and you'll admire whatever she's wearing, and you'll ply her with sherry. I'll tell her all about my wildly exciting life until she dozes off.'

Yvonne laughed. 'Try to make that happen in the first ten minutes, OK?' She let a good half-minute go by before adding, 'So your life's wildly exciting, is it?'

Clara smiled. She pushed a masher into the pot of cooling apple chunks.

Yvonne decided to take her silence as permission to keep going. 'Somebody nice on the scene?' No harm in asking, now and again. Clara wouldn't tell her unless she wanted to.

'Somebody nice?' Clara glanced at Yvonne, still smiling. 'You mean a nice man, I presume?'

'Just wondering, that's all.' Yvonne emptied the steaming potatoes into a warm bowl. 'Doesn't matter really, none of my business.' *But I'd love to know.*

Clara lifted the masher and began to pick bits of apple from it. 'Well, as it happens, there is someone, and he's very nice.'

Yvonne tried not to look surprised. Clara was actually volunteering information – the sky outside must be full of pigs. 'Oh, that's good.' She opened the oven and put the potatoes on the bottom shelf.

Clara hesitated. Then she said quickly, 'It is good. It's the best thing that's ever happened to me, actually.'

Yvonne closed the door and stood up. 'Sounds serious.' Look at them. Look at Clara, bursting to tell her. Did she ever think she'd see the day?

'It is serious. But . . .' she paused, and after a few seconds she said, 'Look, Mum, it's a bit – complicated at the moment. I'd rather not say too much more about it just yet.'

'No, of course not.' Complicated?

Clara put the masher into the sink. 'Here. You'll need that for the turnips. By the way, what's the news of Grainne?'

'Not good. Justin phoned his sister, she was due in this afternoon. Sounds like this is it.'

Just then the doorbell rang. They both groaned.

'I'll go.' Clara unwound her apron and threw it onto a chair. 'I'll tell them you're in the middle of something delicate.'

Yvonne listened to the exchange of greetings in the hall as she hung both aprons on the hook by the fridge. What did she mean, complicated? What could be complicating things? Yvonne's mind ran quickly through the possibilities. He could be married. He could have a drug problem or some other addiction. He could be much older. He could be living abroad. He could be divorced with children. None of them, except the first two, seemed too serious.

So he was married or he was an addict – and there wasn't a thing Yvonne could do to protect Clara from him, except pray that her daughter would have the sense to finish it before anyone – before Clara – got hurt.

Maybe Yvonne would have been better not knowing. Maybe it was no bad thing that Clara liked to keep her cards close to her chest. Maybe Yvonne could have lived without a brand new worry.

She opened the kitchen door, checked that she was smiling, and steeled herself for two hours of extreme diplomacy.

Number Nine

In an uncharacteristically thoughtful gesture, Grainne didn't die until after her daughter had arrived from Spain and was standing at her mother's bedside, with Grainne's son, his pregnant wife and a nurse from the Cancer Society.

Grainne's ex-husband wasn't there. He was fifty-seven miles away in Limerick, watching a DVD with the woman who had replaced Grainne all those years ago. Perhaps the mother of his first two children – he had three more now – crossed his mind as he sat watching Helen Mirren play a remarkably accurate Queen of England, perhaps not.

In the end, it happened quietly, without fuss. Grainne simply drifted away from whatever halfway place she'd wandered into over the past few days, her chest lifting and falling so slightly, her breath coming and going so gently, you'd have been hard put to notice it. Her eyelids twitching every few seconds, her papery skin blanched of colour. Her cracked lips opening and closing silently, as if she was saying her Act of Contrition.

The nurse, holding her wrist, said gently, 'Ann, Justin . . .' They moved closer, bent to their mother in turn and touched her waxy forehead with their lips. And it was over, and Grainne was dead.

They sat for a while in the bedroom, not speaking. The curtains were half closed, the room dim in the fading wintry light. Kathryn had her hand on Justin's arm, her thumb stroking his inner wrist. Ann sat at the other side of the bed, arms wrapped across her chest, chewing her bottom lip. The nurse stood near the door, her head bowed.

Nobody cried.

Eventually they got up and moved downstairs and the nurse went away, and Justin rang Dr Lynch and his father, and Kathryn rang Yvonne, in the middle of dinner with her in-laws.

In the kitchen Ann made tea, and ham and cheese sandwiches, and then went back upstairs to send an email to Suze from Justin's computer.

As Kathryn, feeling unusually hungry, was biting into a sandwich, she felt a distinct nudge in her abdomen, and a minute later, another.

And she said 'Oh' and put down her sandwich and took Justin's palm and held it against her swelling stomach. When the nudge came again, his face crumpled. He put his head on her shoulder, and finally wept.

She held him and rocked him gently and said, 'Ssh, darling, I know, it's OK. I know. I know.'

Three days later: 26 January

NUMBER SEVEN, NUMBER EIGHT, NUMBER NINE

From the relative obscurity of his position at the outer end of the fourth pew from the top of the church – much to his relief, Justin hadn't insisted that he sit with the rest of the family – William Taylor observed the people who had come to see off his ex-wife.

Across the aisle from him sat a pretty blonde female, he guessed in her early twenties. She wore a turquoise coat that ended just below her hips, a foot or so shorter than the lime green skirt underneath it. One side of her dark blonde hair was held up with a pale green clip that flashed whenever it caught the light from the stained-glass window above her head. William had caught her eye briefly as she sat down, but her gaze had swept past him without interest before she turned to speak to the woman who'd gone ahead of her into the seat.

The mother, he guessed. Similar build, same slightly upturned nose, same high cheekbones. Not unattractive, but of course outshone by the daughter. Wearing a navy coat that was serviceable if not fashionable, and a thick red woolly scarf wrapped a few times around her neck.

They were joined, just before the mass started, by a tall man with receding fair hair, glasses, fiftyish – the husband? – in a well-cut light grey suit under a dark grey overcoat, and the black tie that some people wore to funerals. (William wasn't wearing a black tie – he'd never owned one, thought them far too morbid.) The older woman leaned across in front of her daughter to put a hand on his arm – yes, the husband – and whispered something. He nodded.

Directly in front of William, two men sat. The younger man, thirtyish, had light brown hair in dire need of a good cut, and a worn-looking tweed jacket over faded denim jeans. No black tie there.

His companion, quite a bit older, wore a toffee-coloured coat that was at least two sizes too big for him, if the shoulders were anything to go by, and a blue woollen scarf that had unfortunately been introduced to a washing machine at some stage.

On the seat beside him lay a very strange hat. Considerably worn, retaining little of its original shape, brim frayed and dipping, crown dented in several spots. Impossible to make out the original colour – maybe light brown, but now mottled, a grubby mixture somewhere between grey and tan.

William could only assume that the man was blind, although he hadn't seemed to need assistance getting into the seat, and there was no sign of a white stick. It wasn't as if he needed a hat anyway, with that head of thick white hair, some of it standing on end now.

As the priest walked onto the altar and everyone stood, William turned his attention to the pew second from the top, which was occupied by a very interesting female indeed. Her curly auburn hair was pulled off her face and secured with a bright red ribbon. She wore a long, dark green woollen dress almost to her ankles, under which a pair of very pointed red boots poked out. The upper half of her body was cocooned in a voluminous, and very warm-looking, black and green shawl, which was secured on one shoulder with a chunky silver brooch.

William had been introduced to Suzannah earlier, in Justin and Kathryn's house. 'Suze,' she'd corrected Ann, almost managing to give it two syllables, so richly drawling was her accent. 'Everyone calls me Suze.' She'd fixed him with a pair of dark green eyes and put out her hand towards him. 'So you're Ann's dad.'

And you're Ann's lover, he thought. You're the woman my daughter sleeps with every night. He could see what attracted Ann, what would probably attract quite a number of women – and men too. Suzannah wasn't pretty. Her nose was too small for her face, and her teeth, surprisingly for an American, were slightly crooked, a few shades darker than perfectly white. But her hair, when it wasn't pinned up, tumbled about her shoulders, and she met your gaze head on with those remarkable eyes, and spoke with an assurance that caught your attention and made you listen.

The biggest mistake of William Taylor's life had been marrying Grainne Nesbitt when they were both twenty-seven. She hadn't even been pregnant – Justin hadn't arrived for another four years – but Grainne had been pretty in a fragile kind of a way, and she had made it no secret that she thought he was simply wonderful. He'd been reeling from being thrown over by the girl who had gone on to break his older brother's heart too, and somehow marriage to someone so gratifyingly adoring had seemed like the most sensible course of action.

It took him just under two months to realise his mistake, to understand how disastrous their union had been. Her neediness drove him distracted. Her preoccupation with her health and her tendency to burst into tears if he said the wrong thing irritated him beyond belief. He'd considered his options.

Divorce seemed the obvious way out, but his half-hearted enquiries dampened his enthusiasm for it. Far too much fuss, and an alarming lack of privacy about the whole business. So, characteristically, he decided on the route of least resistance, and took his pleasure where he could find it outside the home.

He was in the middle of his third affair when Grainne, unaware of his extramarital activities, became pregnant with Justin, during one of their increasingly rare episodes of intimacy. He had, in fact, barely got back to work after a lunch hour in his mistress's bed before Grainne phoned the office from her doctor's surgery and told him he was going to be a father.

It had made no difference to his lifestyle, apart from having to leave a dinner date when Grainne phoned him to tell him her waters had broken.

The marriage had stumbled on, with William increasingly absent from home on one pretext or another. Ann was born two years later, leaving Grainne preoccupied with two small children, and William even freer to pursue his outside interests.

When Ann was four, William's business partner had introduced him to his girlfriend, soon to be his fiancée. A week after the engagement was announced, she and William had absconded, leaving an impressive trail of destruction behind them. Five years after that, William had applied for a divorce, having already produced two new children with the woman who, despite being nine years younger, was his match in every other way.

He was pleased at how his first son and daughter had turned out. The fact that both seemed fairly well balanced and content – their current bereavement apart, of course – helped him to feel better about having had practically no hand in their upbringing.

For years after the divorce, William's only contact with Justin and Ann had been through infrequent, stilted letters and birthday cards with five-pound notes, and later ten-pound notes, tucked inside, and horribly formal meetings on neutral ground at Christmas, when everyone sat around politely and tried to find something to say.

But look at them now, each getting on fine, as far as he could see, despite his lousy parenting. He could glimpse, three rows ahead, Kathryn's shoulder touching Justin's. No doubt they were holding hands; those two were very touchy-feely. And what a shame

Suze wasn't brave – or brazen – enough to sit next to Ann and hold her hand; that would have given the good people of Belford plenty to talk about.

News of Kathryn's pregnancy had pleased William. The idea of his first-born son becoming a father was satisfying – if Fate or God or whatever, didn't intervene and ruin everything again. William hadn't seen Kathryn much over the years, but he decided that he approved of his son's choice; you had to admire anyone who'd survived having Grainne as a houseguest for the past two years. He'd love to know how the two women had got on – and Justin, who must have been caught in the line of fire every now and again.

'Let us pray,' the priest announced, and everyone knelt. Out of the corner of his eye, William felt someone looking at him, but to his disappointment, the target of the pretty blonde woman's gaze seemed to be one of the men in front of him. Surely she wouldn't prefer either of those scruffs.

His thoughts returned to the semi-detached house on the other side of Belford that he'd bought more than thirty-nine years ago, which Grainne, as the deserted wife, had been perfectly entitled to stay in, and which, according to the terms of the divorce, was to be considered hers for her lifetime. William had felt it was the least he could do, particularly as his new partner had a thriving business of her own, and a riverside apartment in Limerick.

Still . . . the Belford house should be worth a pretty penny by now.

He wondered how long it would be before the will was read.

It was only about twenty minutes after that, as they were trailing out of the church, Greg walking slightly ahead of her with Clara, that Yvonne stumbled on an uneven tile and reached for the nearest solid object to steady herself. It happened to be the arm of the white-haired man beside her; he had already reached towards her to break her fall.

'Oh, sorry—' She grabbed his sleeve at the precise moment that he clutched at her wrist, and there was a second or two of undignified scrambling before Yvonne got her balance back and lifted her head and met his gaze.

And it was right then, at the door of the church, on their way to bury Grainne Taylor on a bitterly cold January morning, that the most startling thing happened.

Six months later: end of June

DOLORES

She worked in a shop now, a small corner shop that sold newspapers and overpriced groceries. Every day she got dressed and ate the toast her mother made, spread with the thin-cut lemon marmalade they both liked, and at ten to nine she walked to Gilligan's. When she got there she put on her navy overall and changed into her old black shoes and stood behind the counter until lunchtime, doling out Turkish Delight and slices of ham and pints of milk. Mrs Gilligan didn't like Dolores to sit down, she said it gave the wrong impression when someone came in.

Mrs Gilligan didn't like her, full stop. Dolores knew this because Mrs Gilligan often gave her funny looks, and would disappear into the back without saying where she was going or how long she'd be. She always came out the minute there was a rush on, so Dolores knew she was just staying back there so she wouldn't have to talk to her. She probably peeped out every so often to make sure Dolores wasn't sitting down.

At half past twelve Dolores took off her overall and changed back into her good shoes. She walked into town and looked around the shops for half an hour and then went into Murphy's Coffee Corner and got a salad sandwich, no onion, on brown bread with mayonnaise and butter, and a cup of tea. She was back behind the counter at Gilligan's at half past one on the dot.

Her mother cooked dinner every evening. Dolores liked it to be on the table at half six, so she'd have time for a bath after she came home from work. The shop always made her feel dirty, all those people coming in, giving her their money with grubby hands.

But it was better than the clinic, with patients sneezing into her face and coughing with no hankies, complaining if they had to wait more than five minutes, and Yvonne going on every lunchtime about how great her life was. She was well out of all that.

On Sunday afternoons, she and her mother went walking down by the river if the weather was fine. There was a nice round you could do in three-quarters of an hour, which was as much as either of them wanted.

If the weather was bad, they went to a matinée. Dolores's mother liked a nice period drama or something musical, and she preferred English films to American, but Dolores didn't mind what she watched, as long as it wasn't too gory or too sexually explicit.

In the evenings, she and her mother looked at television or read their books if there was nothing on. They never went out at night. It was too dangerous, in this day and age, for two women to be out after dark. And where would they go anyway, except to a noisy, crowded pub or to a snooty restaurant for a meal that they could cook for next to nothing at home?

Dolores slept soundly at night, untroubled by dreams. She didn't believe in dreams. What good was something that never came true, that you hoped and hoped for all your life, and that never arrived? Or that never arrived for you, just for everyone else.

All you got was men looking through you, or past you to the glamorous women. Or men who bought you a drink and pretended to like you and then tried to shove their hands up your dress or under your blouse and called you a bitch, a tease, when you pushed them away. Or once, a man who told you that you weren't in a position to be choosy, that you should take what you got and be glad of it.

Was it any wonder she'd had to make them up, the loving husband who took her away for anniversaries, the children who did her proud, who gave her so much to be happy about? She'd had to make them up because they didn't exist. They'd never exist for her. And where was the harm? Who was she hurting?

But they'd acted like she'd committed a crime, like she wasn't right in the head. Her mother dragging her off to doctors, who'd shoved her into a place that wasn't called a loony bin. Even though it was full of loonies.

Until she'd pretended to be cured, even though she wasn't sick, and they'd let her out and she'd learned to keep her mouth shut and just carry on.

Keep putting one foot in front of the other, that was all you had to do. And eventually you'd get to the end, and it would all be over.

She wondered how long it would take.

DAN

Beside him on the worktop, Colm jiggled in his bouncer and gurgled at Dan.

'What's that?' Dan tipped the can of chopped tomatoes into the saucepan of gently sizzling onions and picked up a wooden spoon. 'Could you repeat that, please? I didn't quite catch it.'

Colm pulled one of his socks off and immediately brought it to his mouth.

Dan reached out with his free hand and grabbed the chubby bare foot. 'Why are you so damn gorgeous?' He waggled the toes and Colm chortled through the sock.

'You want some salt with that?'

'Gah.'

'Gah yourself.' Dan eased the tiny white sock from Colm's hand and quickly replaced it with the yellow rubber teething ring that had fallen between Colm and the bouncer. 'Here, that might taste a bit better.'

Colm eyed the ring and waved it in the air.

Dan added minced beef to the saucepan. 'Now, young man, pay attention. I am making a spaghetti Bolognese.

Repeat after me: spagh-ett-i.'

'Gah.'

'Very good. You catch on quick. You must take after your father.'

He reached up and took the quarter-full bottle of red wine from the open shelf above him. He held it in front of the bouncer.

'Listen up. This is called wine. You will never drink it. Alcohol will never pass your lips. You will take the pledge at your confirmation, and you will keep it forever. Are we clear?'

Colm gurgled and reached a pudgy hand towards the bottle.

Dan regarded him sternly. 'Have you been listening to a word I said?' He pulled out the cork and tipped the wine into the saucepan and turned up the heat to medium high.

'All gone. Now I stir – like this, see?'

They spent their days together, just the two of them. Six months ago, Dan had handed back the keys to his little room at the top of the wooden stairs, and now he worked from home.

Everything was different. His life had utterly changed.

Their daily routine didn't vary much. While Colm slept, Dan worked. When Colm woke, Dan fed him and changed him and talked to him, and kept his playpen stocked with fluffy things and teething rings. When Colm closed his eyes again, Dan managed a little more work. He was getting through about half the jobs he'd done before Colm's arrival, but it bothered him not at all. What did work matter?

Dan adored his son. He sat and watched him sleeping at night, watched the rapid rise and fall of Colm's chest, touched the wisps of damp, dark hair, laid his finger gently against the plump wrist to feel the tiny, precious pulse. He loved the little roll of fat at the back of Colm's neck, the dimples in his knees, the soft curl of his miniature toes. He put his face to Colm's stomach and inhaled him. He nibbled his fingers, kissed the tips of his ears. He rubbed Colm's button nose with his own. He couldn't get enough of him.

He had nightmares about Colm dying and woke sweating, leaping out of bed to check the cot. He imagined someone hurting Colm, and the murderous rage that filled him frightened him. The sound of Colm's laughter, the impossibly sweet gurgle of it, made him weak with happiness.

He cried more, since Colm. He felt more. Every emotion was bigger than it had been before.

'You're so soppy now,' he was told. 'Where's the real man I fell in love with?'

'Still here,' he'd respond, pulling her close. 'Didn't go anywhere.' Starting to open the buttons of her shirt. 'Let me show you what a real man I am.'

They were a proper family, the three of them. And most of the time it felt right. It felt like it was meant. But now and again, usually late at night, he found himself wondering what his life would have been like if he hadn't made the decision he had, if he had chosen differently, six months ago.

And very occasionally, lying quietly in the dark, he allowed himself to imagine the other life he might have had, with her.

He heard the front door open. 'Guess who's home from work,' he said to Colm, and the baby blinked at him and chewed his ring. Dan spooned cream into the saucepan, sprinkled nutmeg and lowered the heat.

The kitchen door opened and Colm's head swivelled towards it. 'Hi.' Ali walked straight to the bouncer. 'How's my favourite little man?' She butted her head gently into Colm's stomach and he gurgled delightedly.

'I'm fine, thanks.' Dan stirred the mixture in the saucepan.

Ali straightened and kissed his cheek. 'That was funny the first three times.' Her hair was shorter, the way he liked it. He hadn't mentioned it, but she'd got it cut soon after she'd come home.

She peered into the saucepan. 'Smells good.'

It wasn't the same as before. It wasn't a bit like it had been before – they'd probably never have that back again. It was different now. They'd both changed.

She was more careful with him. She watched him when she thought he wasn't looking. He was more relaxed with her. He knew, if she left again, that he'd manage. He'd be fine.

They hadn't seen Brendan since Ali had come home. Dan had offered to be there when Ali told him, but she'd refused. Afterwards she didn't talk about it, and Dan didn't ask.

He supposed they'd have to come face to face

eventually – a family funeral, somebody's wedding – and he assumed they'd deal sensibly enough with it when it happened. He didn't dread it. He'd always liked Brendan.

He told Ali about Clara a few weeks after her return. He had no idea how she'd react.

She said nothing for a while. Then, without looking at him, she said, 'Were you getting even with me?'

Dan considered. Was that what Clara had been? Someone to pay Ali back with? Was she his revenge? Was that all she'd meant to him?

He remembered her tipping her head back to look at the stars, the way she played with his fingers when she spoke to him. How giggly she got after wine. The World's Best Dad mug she'd given him when Colm was born. He remembered the scent of her, the softness of her skin. How she'd been planning to go dancing with him, once everyone knew.

Her tears, the way she'd clung to him, that first time.

'No,' he said to Ali. 'It wasn't like that at all.'

Telling Clara had been horrible. He'd put it off as long as he could, not knowing how to do it. He hadn't rung her for almost a week, had avoided her at Grainne's funeral, had felt her looking across the aisle at him in the church. He knew he should contact her, but he couldn't bring himself to tell her.

And then, when he'd finally plucked up the courage to phone, she'd been the one apologising to him. 'I'm sorry – I should have been more understanding.'

He didn't know what she was talking about until he remembered their last phone conversation, when he'd told her they weren't going to Charleton after all. She must have thought he was annoyed about that, the way she'd hung up on him. The way she'd turned off her phone afterwards so he couldn't contact her.

'You've nothing to apologise for,' he told her. 'I wasn't mad at that – it's just that I need to talk to you about something. Can we meet later on?'

And then, sitting beside her in the car, he'd made a complete mess of it. 'Ali wants to come home' – tumbling the words out too quickly, trying to ignore the look of utter shock on her face – 'she's asked me if we can start again.'

She hadn't seen it coming, hadn't had the slightest notion that anything was wrong.

'I have to. We have Colm, I have to . . .'

He'd trailed off, turning away, unable to watch her face crumpling. Knowing he'd done it all wrong because there was no right way.

Clara had burst into tears. She'd cried like a young child, unselfconsciously, letting the tears drip off her chin, making no attempt to wipe them away. 'I don't believe it, you can't do this—'

'I'm sorry—'

'No.' She shook her head violently, hands clamped to her ears. 'No, please, Dan, don't leave me – I can't bear it, please.'

He pulled her hands down and held them tightly between his own. 'Clara, I have to try again – I have to think of my son—'

She cried, she wailed, her face inches from his own, her desperation wide open for him to see. 'No, no – you have to think of *me*, I love you – you love me, you *told* me' – the tears streaming down her face, her nose running – 'I told you everything – I *trusted* you.'

He felt like the worst kind of monster. He wanted her to hit him, to scream at him, to curse him, anything but this desolate moaning. 'I'm sorry – I'm so—'

And then, abruptly, she'd pulled away her hands and fumbled with the car door and had half-fallen out, still crying loudly. She leaned against the car and sobbed, and Dan stayed where he was, hating himself.

Eventually her sobs lessened. She took a deep, shuddering breath and walked away. Dan heard the click of her garden gate, heard her footsteps stumbling up the path. He'd sat in the car until the cold drove him indoors.

He saw her a few times after that, passing the front of his house on her way to work or coming home again. Hurrying up the back garden path, laundry basket in her arms, head bent. Never glancing towards number eight, never tilting her head in the direction of his house.

They'd come face to face just once, on Dan's way back from the garage shop one rainy evening. Clara, walking out of number seven, looked blankly at him as he passed, ignoring his forced smile.

And then, about a week after they broke up, she disappeared.

He met Yvonne a few times. He decided that Clara

mustn't have told her about them because Yvonne didn't look like she wanted to kill him. She cooed over Colm in his buggy and said she was glad things had worked out for Dan and Ali.

She looked younger, and happy. Funny how things had turned out for Yvonne. Who'd have guessed it?

He never asked her about Clara. He didn't feel he had the right.

YVONNE

She lay on a blanket in the back garden with Magoo, and she thought about love.

'You kept me waiting forty-two years,' she told him.

'You kept me waiting fifty-three,' he answered, and that shut her up.

The age difference bothered neither of them. Yvonne told him he looked younger than he was anyway. 'That's without the hat, of course. You look about eighty with it on.'

Their first half-serious argument had been over the hat. Kieran claimed it was part of his personality. 'I've had it for years – I can't just toss it aside.'

'I'm not asking you to toss it aside, I'm asking you to burn it. Or I'll burn it for you, if you can't bring yourself to do it.'

In the end, they'd compromised. Kieran wore the hat anywhere Yvonne wasn't, and she had to be happy with that.

Not that it mattered in the least. Not when she was blissfully, ridiculously happy all the time anyway.

Kieran taught her how to bake focaccia. He kept beating her at Scrabble. He painted her bathroom blue, and he broke the cold tap while he was at it.

She weaned him off blue cheese – 'It's like kissing your grandfather's sock' – and she made him listen to Johnny Cash and she ironed his shirts when he wasn't looking.

He told her about his alcoholism. 'My last drink was fifteen years ago.'

She told him about Brian, about all of that. She touched his face when they made love, and sometimes she cried, because it was too much.

He kissed the soles of her feet and the insides of her elbows and the bottom of her spine. He played Mozart on the violin for her, and Dvořák. He melted bitter chocolate and dipped mandarin orange segments into it and fed them, dripping, to her.

He told her about Geraldine. 'I was thirty-eight, she was a bit over forty.'

'A bit? Didn't you know exactly?' Sitting on his lap, playing with his shirt buttons. Doing them up wrong. 'Was she nearer forty-one or forty-nine?'

He looked sternly at her. 'A lady's age is her own business. Do you want me to tell you about her or not?'

Yvonne slid an arm around his waist and settled herself against his chest, as if she had every right to be there. 'I'm sorry. Carry on.'

He stroked her hair. 'She was a waitress.'

'How cosy – a waitress and a cook.'

'Be quiet.' He paused and then said, in a slightly different tone, 'She had a son, Adam, about fifteen.

He had lots of spots and a ring in his tongue. He'd get up and leave the room if I walked in.'

Yvonne said nothing. His shirt smelled of cigars.

'But in spite of her son I asked her to marry me, and eventually she agreed.'

'Eventually?' Yvonne sat up and looked into his face. 'How many times did you have to ask this silly woman before she said yes?'

He pulled her head back onto his chest. 'Three. One night after the other.'

'And then?'

'And then I went to the church on the appointed day, and I waited for her to show up.'

His pause filled in the missing sentence.

'Oh.'

'Yes. Eventually my best man sent everyone home and took me to a pub.'

Yvonne thought. 'You said your last drink was fifteen years ago.'

'Yes. I'd actually stopped drinking a good while before that, but I figured this was a good enough reason to take it up again. The following day, I swore I'd never touch another drop.'

'And you never did.'

'No.'

They were quiet for a while. Then Yvonne said, closing her eyes, listening to his heart thumping gently at her ear, 'You'd only have to ask me once.'

She heard the smile in his voice. 'I'll bear that in mind.'

'I might be a bit late to the church, though.'

'That's fine. Just so long as I know.'

Another silence, and then he said, 'Adam died.'

'What?' Yvonne lifted her head again. 'The son?'

Kieran nodded. 'He drowned last year. Not too long before I moved to Belford.'

'Oh.' She leaned against him again and waited, feeling the rise and fall of his chest.

'I met him the night he died.'

'Did you?' She stayed where she was, heard the catch in his breath.

'I was coming home from the cinema . . .'

He stopped. She waited.

'I was passing a pub, and he came out.'

Another silence. She picked up his hand and held it between her own.

'He was drunk. I hadn't seen him in a while, but I knew him straightaway. He knew me too. He followed me, shouted at me to stop, that he wanted to talk to me.'

She squeezed his hand.

'I kept going. I didn't want to talk to him, I had nothing to say to him.'

He was quiet for so long that she thought he'd finished. Then he said flatly, 'He fell into the river. I did nothing to help him.'

She realised she'd been holding her breath.

'Two other men came along and tried to save him. I walked away and left them to it.'

She lifted her head. 'You told me you can't swim.'

'I know, but— '

'So you couldn't have saved him. You'd probably have drowned too. What good would that have done anyone?'

He nodded, but she knew the nod was for her, not for him.

'I went back to see Geraldine, just before Christmas. I told her what I just told you. She hit me. She wanted to kill me.'

Yvonne searched for the words, and found nothing.

'I made it worse, I caused her more torment.'

She said, 'Kieran, you weren't to blame. It wasn't your fault.' He held her gaze. She saw the pain in his eyes. 'You can't change the past. We've all done things we'd like to forget.' She kissed his cheek. 'You're a good man.'

They were meant to be together. She'd never been so sure of anything in her life, from the first minute she'd looked at him. And she'd never, ever thought love at first sight could possibly exist – how could you love someone you didn't know? If that wasn't a contradiction in terms, she didn't know what was. And yet . . .

That first minute. Straightening her coat, feeling foolish. 'God, I'm sorry. I don't know what happened there.'

'No problem. Are you OK now?' Letting go of her wrist.

'Fine.' He was familiar. His hair was white, his eyebrows jet black. His eyes were dark. She'd seen him somewhere. 'You're not staying at Dan's, are you?'

'That's right.' He put out a hand, and they touched for the second time. 'Kieran Delaney.'

She'd smelled mints. 'Yvonne, from next door. I've heard you play the violin.' His hand was warm, it enfolded hers.

Just those few words, such harmless words, and she'd known. As he'd crammed his awful hat on his head, as he'd stood back to let her out in front of him, as Greg had half turned to see where she was, she'd known.

She'd sneaked a few looks at the graveside. He stood beside Dan, hands in the pockets of his brown coat. Once he'd glanced in her direction and their eyes collided. Something swerved inside her and she'd looked away quickly, to the coffin waiting by the open grave.

She remembered sitting in the car at the bottom of the garden months before, after that awful dinner with that awful man from the internet, John or Joe or whatever his name was, and hearing the music and just sitting there, listening to it.

And it had been him, standing at the bottom of Dan's garden, not twenty yards from where she was parked. It had been him.

'Maybe we could have coffee sometime,' she had said to him later, uncharacteristically brazen.

They were in Kathryn and Justin's house. The rest of the small crowd who'd come back from the graveyard – Dan, Greg, Kathryn's parents, Justin's father, Ann and Suzannah – were in the front room, eating sandwiches and drinking coffee. Clara had gone straight home from the church with a headache.

Yvonne had slipped out to the kitchen to refill the cafetière, and on the way back, she'd met Kieran coming down the stairs.

She'd said, without thinking, without knowing what was coming, 'Maybe we could have coffee sometime.'

'Yes.' And a very sweet smile had spread across his face. 'I'd like that. How about Thursday?'

But then Clara, in floods of tears the following day. Tumbling into the sitting room, practically collapsing into a startled Yvonne's arms. Sobbing, choking on her tears.

'What is it? What's happened?' Feeling the heave of her daughter's sobs against her. 'Are you hurt? What's wrong, love?'

Clara, face buried in Yvonne's shoulder, shaking her head, unable, for a few minutes, to say a word, finally whispering that someone had just broken up with her. Giving in to tears again, soaking the collar of Yvonne's cardigan.

And holding her, stroking her back, reaching for the tissues on the table beside them, whispering the meaningless words that everyone used when someone needed comforting, Yvonne could only hope that Clara was better off without him.

And some time later, when Yvonne thought she'd gone to sleep, Clara reached for Yvonne's hand and began to speak softly, so softly that Yvonne had to tilt her head towards her, even in the silent sitting room, even with Clara's face just inches from her own.

'Mum.' Fresh tears spilling from Clara's reddened eyes; Yvonne pulling another tissue from the box.

'Mum, I need to tell you something.'

'What is it?' Stroking her back, making circles on it with her palm, like she'd done when Clara was a tiny baby. Please let her not be pregnant.

Clara, turning her face away from Yvonne's shoulder to look into the dying fire. 'Remember when I went on a school tour in fourth class?'

So unexpected. Yvonne had no memory of Clara's fourth class tour. She prickled suddenly with anxiety.

'There was a – there was a man.' Wiping away new tears. Not meeting Yvonne's eyes. 'He – I – he . . . interfered with me.'

Yvonne stiffened, tightening her hold on Clara. Fourth class, Clara was ten. Stay calm. 'What did he do?'

And as Clara spoke, as it all came out, Yvonne had listened, horrified. Appalled to discover that her child had lived with this terrible secret for a dozen years. Horribly ashamed that she, Clara's mother, had never guessed, had put down the change in her daughter's behaviour to puberty. Some mother she'd been.

When Clara finally stopped talking, they were both silent. A lump of coal shifted; a shower of sparks rose briefly.

Yvonne couldn't ask. She had to ask. 'Why didn't you tell me?'

Clara wiped her eyes with the sodden tissue. 'I couldn't. I was afraid. I thought you'd be cross.'

'How could you think that? I'm your mother. How could you—' She couldn't finish it. She squeezed Clara's hand, forced herself to speak calmly.

'Of course I wouldn't have been cross. You're—' She felt her own eyes filling, and blinked. 'If anything ever happened to you . . . it doesn't bear thinking about.'

Clara gave a tiny, tear-stained smile and pulled a tissue from the box and handed it to Yvonne. 'I know.'

And eventually, when they'd said all that there was to say, they'd gone into the kitchen and eaten chocolate spread on toast, and Clara had spent the night in her mother's bed, for the first time in years.

Yvonne had lain awake, listening to Clara's steady breathing, and marvelled that it had taken a broken heart for her daughter to confide in her at last.

She thought about the man who'd violated Clara. She imagined him sitting in an electric chair, and her pulling the switch and watching him die.

No, she'd burn him at the stake – that would take longer.

And then there was Greg.

She'd hated telling Greg about Kieran. She'd felt treacherous. It sounded so lame. 'I don't know what happened. I can't explain it.'

'Do you love him?' Greg's voice was steady. He looked straight at her.

'Yes.' So certain, never as certain of anything, apart from her love for Clara.

Ridiculous. Not three weeks since she and Kieran had spoken for the first time. The day after their fourth meeting – date? – when Kieran had reached across the café table, taken her hand and said, 'What's going on here?' And she'd answered, 'I have no idea,' and both of them had smiled.

'Better that it happened now,' Greg said. 'Thank you for being honest.'

'I'm so sorry. I wish there was something—'

'It's OK,' he said. 'Really. As long as you're happy.' Which, of course, made her feel even worse.

Greg, of all people. One of her staunchest allies. One of her oldest friends.

'I'll be in touch,' he'd said. But he hadn't, no word at all in the last five and a half months, and that saddened her.

She was sad, too, that Jim had stopped coming to dinner. Of course he'd told her it was too tiring for him now, that he wasn't up to driving through Belford any more. He gave no sign that Greg or Peggy had had anything to do with it. She missed him.

Clara had moved out of Miller's Avenue a week after her break-up. She packed two suitcases and three black refuse bags, and Yvonne drove her across town to the little apartment that Siofra had found for them.

'Will you be alright?' Yvonne felt miserable – just when it had seemed she was getting her daughter back.

Clara hugged her. 'Of course I will – eventually.'

'You can always come back if it doesn't work out.' The apartment was poky – Clara's room was about half the size of her one at home.

'I'll be fine.' Clara held Yvonne's hands. 'Thank you. I never tell you thank you.'

Yvonne smiled. 'You don't need to – just doing my job.'

And last week, almost six months after moving out, Clara had come home for her usual Saturday afternoon visit, and had given Yvonne the news she'd been hoping for. 'He's someone I knew before, but we've only just started going out.' She wore a sky blue lacy smock over a yellow top and faded jeans. 'It's early days,' she said. 'Nothing might come of it.'

Yvonne put biscuits on a plate. 'But he's nice.' And not complicated.

'He is.'

She'd lost some weight since she'd moved out, her face was thinner, and in unguarded moments she still looked lonely. But she ate three shortbread biscuits and smiled at Yvonne and said, 'No need to ask how you are.'

Kieran had moved out of Dan's house when Dan had told him Ali was coming back. He'd taken a six-month lease on a studio flat four blocks from Miller's Avenue. He told Yvonne it took him seven minutes to walk to her house and fifteen to walk back to his flat.

They spent at least three nights together every week, mostly in Yvonne's house. On Sundays, they stayed in bed till late afternoon, reading the paper and watching television. Then they came downstairs in pyjamas and cooked dinner and brought it back to bed.

'You've turned me into a floozy.' It wasn't a complaint. She had no complaints, these days.

She stretched out under the sun, pointing her toes, inhaling the grassy scent of her garden. On the blanket beside her, Magoo yawned widely.

'This is the life,' Yvonne told him. 'This is how it should always be.'

He wagged his tail and inched closer to her on his belly. He missed Clara, looked hopeful anytime the kitchen door opened, welcomed her enthusiastically every Saturday.

Kieran had tackled number seven's herbs. He'd replanted the mint in its own separate space, added marjoram and sage and surrounded everything with a low picket fence. He'd pruned the gooseberry bushes at the bottom of the garden and planted a climbing rose next to the shed.

One afternoon Dan had come out to his back garden and seen Kieran over the hedge in Yvonne's. From the kitchen, she'd watched them talking.

'Did you tell him?'

'I did.'

'What did he say?'

He eyed her over his glass of water. 'He says you're a lucky woman.' He ducked, barely missing her slap, spilling water. 'He said, "How did you manage it?"'

She *was* a lucky woman. She was in love, truly in love, for the first time in her life. After forty-two years – forty-three since April – it had been worth the wait.

She heard sounds from the house and smiled at Magoo.

'Here he comes,' she said.

KATHRYN

She added eight tiny white T-shirts to the suitcase and six pairs of leggings in dolly-mixture pinks, yellows and greens, then ten pairs of socks. So far, Emily's luggage was taking up slightly more space in the case than Kathryn's. No more travelling light when you had a baby to pack for.

Emily had arrived two weeks early, in the middle of a sunny May morning. Kathryn had felt vaguely uncomfortable going to bed the night before, had wondered if the twinges she was getting were anything to worry about. Four hours later she'd woken in considerable pain, and nine hours after that, when she was on the point of collapse, Emily had been born.

Healthy, intact, all seven pounds of her. Yelling to be fed in the first five minutes, mouth pulling greedily at Kathryn's nipple as soon as she'd been offered it. Roaring anytime they changed her nappy, waking every two hours demanding attention, grabbing every ounce of energy they possessed, day and night.

Dark blue eyes, delicately pointed nose, permanently open mouth. White blonde hair that curled at the back of her neck. Tiny fists that thumped Kathryn's chest as she sucked noisily, gulping down the milk. Belching loudly – Justin was very proud of her belches – a few minutes later.

Kathryn couldn't remember what it felt like not to be exhausted. Each muscle in her body ached for sleep, her eyes were permanently sore from lack of it. Mealtimes had become an almost-forgotten luxury; food was bolted, usually standing up, when either she or Justin got a chance.

If it wasn't for Marzena coming in twice a week to clean, the house would have been as neglected as the garden, with weeds springing up willy-nilly in Kathryn's once carefully tended beds, and the grass almost long enough to conceal Picasso when he wandered over.

'This baby's a tornado,' Kathryn told Yvonne. 'The house is in shock.'

Yvonne patted Emily's back and the baby immediately produced a large belch. 'Good girl, that's what we like to hear. Now, give your mother a bit of a break so she can talk to her friend.' But Emily began to whimper and squirm in Yvonne's arms.

Kathryn opened her shirt again. 'Here. We'll have no peace till she's full, believe me.' Emily settled to her right nipple and sucked determinedly.

Yvonne smiled. 'You look totally done in, but in a good way.'

Kathryn yawned. 'I am. Totally done in. But in the best possible way.' She stroked the top of Emily's head. 'I had no idea it was possible to love someone so much.'

'I know.'

'Not to care about any of the things you'd cared about before, you know?'

'I do.'

'About keeping the house clean, or getting the washing done, or cooking proper meals. None of it matters.'

'No.'

'I'm so lucky.' Kathryn gazed at her daughter. 'What did I do to deserve her?'

'What do you mean, what did you do? Wasn't she long overdue? You should be asking what kept her.'

Kathryn smiled. 'I suppose so. Isn't it funny that there are two babies next door to each other all of a sudden, after years of just grown-ups in the three houses?'

'You'll be arranging play dates in a couple of years.'

'I wonder if it was the baby who brought them back together.'

'Who knows? I met Dan the other day, and I must say he does look happy.'

Emily came off Kathryn's nipple, still making loud sucking noises. Kathryn propped her against her shoulder and rubbed her back. 'Imagine if they got married.'

'Dan and Ali? They are married.'

'No, I mean Emily and Colm. He is the boy next door, after all.'

Pause. 'And some people just can't resist the boy next door, can they?'

Another pause. 'I love how you still blush when we talk about him.'

'Shut up – I never blush.' Yvonne put the backs of her hands to her cheeks.

Kathryn laughed. 'Tell you what – why don't you have a baby next year and we can open the Miller's Avenue crèche?'

'I'll see what I can do. By the way, did I tell you that Clara has someone new?'

'Has she?' Emily belched again. 'That's good news. You never found out who the last one was, did you?'

'No, and I don't suppose I ever will. Not that it matters now. I hope this one doesn't let her down.'

'Hopefully.' Kathryn laid the half-asleep Emily carefully in the carry cot on the table. 'OK, we should be good for another cup.'

Yvonne plugged in the kettle. 'So . . . how's Justin?'

'Great. Looking forward to the change.'

The sale of Grainne's house had closed a month ago. The surprisingly high sum had been split three ways between William, Justin and Ann. Justin immediately handed in his notice at work and was finishing up in three days' time, just before he, Kathryn and Emily travelled to Spain for a fortnight with Ann and Suze.

And when they got back, he was going to start the online teaching course, and in September Kathryn was going back to work and Marzena would take care of Emily five mornings a week while Justin studied.

In the afternoons, he'd said to Kathryn the other

night, he and Dan could take it in turns to look after both babies.

'We'll be two stay-at-home dads – we need to help each other out. Maybe we could do every second week or something.'

She'd laughed at him, saying they could hardly cope with Emily on her own – how would he manage Colm too? But maybe it wasn't such a bad idea. Maybe he and Dan would work something out.

The idea was appealing. The Miller's Avenue crèche.

In the meantime, they were off to Spain. Ann and Suze would look after Emily, and Kathryn and Justin would sleep. Kathryn hadn't told Ann that there was a fairly strong chance they'd sleep for the entire two weeks, that she would only wake up for long enough to feed Emily.

As she squeezed her sleeveless tops into a corner of the suitcase, she heard a wail from the cot in the next bedroom. She closed the case and opened her shirt.

CLARA

'So what time are you expecting lover-boy?'

'Any minute now.' Clara slipped the wide silver bangle – a moving-out present from her mother – onto her wrist. 'And I wish you wouldn't call him that.'

Sometimes Siofra got on her nerves a bit. Clara knew you had to put up with that when you shared with someone. And, to be fair, Siofra had her good points. She was fanatical about cleaning the bathroom, she made a great lasagne and she never objected to Clara borrowing from her impressive collection of handbags.

'Will you bring him to Matty's after the pictures?' Siofra dipped her brush into the white varnish and stroked it carefully along her nail tips.

Clara considered. 'Maybe.'

No need to keep him hidden. No reason to hide him from anyone. He didn't have a wife or a child – nobody to pull him away from her.

They'd bumped into each other in the health food shop. Clara had been leaning over the cereal bins, scooping muesli into a plastic bag, and he'd said,

'Well, hello, stranger.'

She'd looked up and smiled. 'Hi, how's it going?'

She hadn't seen him since the last night of the cookery classes, when they'd all gone to the pub. Months ago now.

'No complaints. And you? How've you been?'

'Fine. Still cooking anyway.'

He grinned. 'Glad to hear it. How's young Dan?'

The wrench of pain whenever Clara thought of him shot through her again. She shook her head, turned back to the muesli. 'Dunno. I haven't seen him in a while. We split up.' Still hard to say, still needed to be tossed out quickly or it would get stuck.

'Sorry.' He wore a crumpled checked shirt and black jeans. His hair was longer and he needed a shave. 'Me and my big mouth.' He was interestingly scruffy.

Not that Clara was interested.

She knotted the top of her bag. 'It's OK, don't worry about it. Happened quite a while ago.' Then she began to turn away. 'Well, nice to—'

And he said quickly, 'Hey, d'you fancy a coffee?'

She hesitated. No, she wanted to say. No coffee. No anything. But it was only Douglas, who'd made them laugh with his stories of the cruise ships, who'd pretended to be cross when their cakes hadn't risen. And it was only a cup of coffee.

And, whether she liked it or not, life went on.

'OK, that'd be nice.'

She had a latte, and he had a black regular, and he told her about the student in his last group who'd misread the quantities in a recipe and ended up with 'gingerbread you could break rocks on', and the man who'd knocked a cheesecake off the table – 'guess which side it landed on' – and the Vegemite he craved when he wasn't in Australia. 'Listen, you can laugh, but it's an addiction, I swear.'

And she told him about living with Siofra: 'It's a challenge sometimes. I suppose I've been spoiled, having all the home comforts until now,' and about her mother acting as godmother for the first time in her life. 'It's her friend's baby, she cried all through the christening – my mother, I mean, not the baby.'

And afterwards, when Douglas asked if she'd like to go out sometime, Clara gave him her phone number.

That hadn't been in the plan. The plan had been never again. After Dan, after the night he'd sat beside her in the car and stammered that he was sorry, that he hated what he had to do—

She'd made a complete fool of herself. She cringed when she thought of it now. Not understanding him at first, not able to take in what he was saying – and then her dawning horror, and pleading with him, begging him not to leave her, bawling her eyes out. God, she'd really laid it on thick.

'I trusted you. You said you'd look after me—' Gasping it out, her breath coming in painful, sobbing bursts. 'How can you just sit there and – I can't believe – no, no, you *can't*—' Thumping in despair against the dashboard, digging her nails into her palms to make the other pain go away. 'No, no, *please*—'

And she'd still been aching for Dan, still scraped

raw from his rejection, when her mother had told her she wasn't going to marry Greg after all.

'What?' They were sitting in the kitchen, it was Clara's first visit home since she'd moved out. She'd walked past Dan's house, praying that she wouldn't meet him – or worse, his wife – and praying, at the same time, that he'd suddenly appear and beg her to take him back. 'The wedding's off?'

Yvonne didn't seem upset. She didn't look like Clara felt, as if her heart had been ripped out of her, as if Dan had torn her in two.

Yvonne picked up the teapot and refilled their cups. 'Well, it was a mistake really. It would never have worked out – we're better as friends.'

'So . . . it was a mutual decision, then?'

'Hmm . . . not exactly.' Yvonne poured milk into her cup. 'To be honest, it was mine, really. But Greg took it well.' She smiled. 'It's for the best.' Then she put a hand over Clara's and said, 'But how are you?'

And there was a time when Clara would have looked steadily back at her mother and said, 'I'm fine.' But those days were gone. She said, 'I'm heartbroken. But I'm surviving.' Because what else was there to do?

And a few Saturdays later, Yvonne told her the real reason she wasn't marrying Greg. Kieran seemed perfectly pleasant, and the two of them certainly looked happy together.

Kieran had lived in Dan's house while Clara and Dan had been lovers, and now her mother loved Kieran.

There was a kind of horrible symmetry to that – or was it irony? Maybe a bit of both.

Clara wondered if her mother and Kieran would last. Maybe they'd be the lucky ones.

Douglas rang within a week and they arranged to go to the cinema. After the film they went for a drink, and he told her that the Irish girl he'd fallen for, who'd been the reason for him coming to Ireland, hadn't worked out.

'She was too high-maintenance for me,' he said. 'I couldn't keep her in the style she was accustomed to – isn't that the phrase?'

Clare smiled. 'I think so. But I'm afraid most women are pretty high-maintenance – at least, most of the ones I know.

Douglas considered. 'Maybe I need to get a second job, then.'

He wore a moss green T-shirt that matched his eyes and he'd got his hair cut and he'd shaved. And he had lovely teeth. Really he wasn't unattractive.

At the entrance to the apartments, she turned to him. 'Thanks, I enjoyed it.'

'Good.' He looked down into her face. 'Me too.' He was a good eight inches taller than her.

And because he was Douglas, Claire put her hand behind his neck and drew him down and touched his cheek lightly with her lips. 'Goodnight then.'

They'd seen each other three times since, two meals and another visit to the cinema. He still hadn't been invited beyond the doorstep. He still hadn't attempted to kiss her mouth.

But when he did, Clara might be inclined to respond.

The doorbell rang. She took her jacket from the back of the chair. 'Right, see you later.'

Siofra didn't look up. 'Have fun.'

Fun. Yes, that was something to aim for. Clara crossed the room and opened the door and smiled at Douglas.

ACKNOWLEDGEMENTS

Many thanks to Ann Menzies, Liz Skehan and Dan O'Gorman for their help and advice, to Faith O'Grady for her support and encouragement, to Ciara Doorley for knocking me into shape whenever it was needed, and to all at Hachette Books Ireland for everything they've done to get this book on the shelves.

Thanks to my parents Rose and Micheál for their continued faith in me, to my sister Treasa for single-handedly boosting my sales, to my brothers Tomás and Aonghus for turning up and clapping loudly at the launches, and to my other brothers Colm and Ciarán for their long-distance well-wishes — and a special thank you to my Uncle Mike for taking me out to dinner when I made the bestseller list.